Christopher Brookmyre lives near Glasgow with his wife, his son and his St Mirren season ticket.

Visit the author's website at www.brookmyre.co.uk

Praise for *Not the End of the World*

'Brookmyre on auto-rant is a joy' *Daily Telegraph*

'The bastard son of Raymond Chandler, brought up in the Billy Connolly household and educated at the school of Carl Hiaasen' *Maxim*

'Witty, well-organised and vividly peopled' *Sunday Times*

'Hefty doses of humour and action' *The List*

'A crazy, off-the-wall roller-coaster of a book that throws in not only the kitchen sink, but the dresser, the best china and the cook herself' *Irish Times*

'Tremendous fun. Partly it's the black humour and snappy, streetwise style . . . partly the author's ability to make us empathise with almost anyone' *Guardian*

'A hyperintelligent, hip and impassioned apocalyptic romp' *New Scientist*

'Expansive and enjoyable novel . . . The end of the world is no laughing matter, of course, but after reading Brookmyre's treatment of it, you'll at least be able to approach it with a grin' *Scotsman*

not the end
of the world

christopher
brookmyre

ABACUS

First published in Great Britain in 1998
by Little, Brown and Company

This edition published by Abacus in 1999
Reprinted 2000, 2001, 2002 (twice), 2004 (twice), 2006, 2009 (twice)

A CIP catalogue record for this book
is available from the British Library.

ISBN 978-0-349-10928-2

Typeset by Palimpsest Book Production Limited,
Polmont, Stirlingshire
Printed and bound in Great Britain by Clays Ltd, St Ives plc

Papers used by Abacus are natural, renewable and recyclable
products sourced from well-managed forests and certified
in accordance with the rules of the Forest Stewardship Council.

Mixed Sources
Product group from well-managed
forests and other controlled sources
www.fsc.org Cert no. SGS-COC-004081
© 1996 Forest Stewardship Council
FSC

Abacus
An imprint of
Little, Brown Book Group
100 Victoria Embankment
London EC4Y 0DY

An Hachette UK Company
www.hachette.co.uk

www.littlebrown.co.uk

Dedicated to Billy Franks, Billy Connolly and Bill Hicks.
The greatest preachers need no pulpit.

Many thanks: Hilary Hale, Richard Beswick and Caroline
Dawnay for saving me from myself; Pete Symes for kitting out
the bad guys; and Marisa for sanity preservation services.

author's note

Given that there is widespread disagreement regarding the precise running order of Moses' list of lifestyle suggestions, throughout this book the quite reasonable request that 'Thou Shalt Not Kill' is referred to as the Fifth Commandment.

I

the widening gyre

Christianity's such a weird religion.
The image you're brought up with is that
eternal suffering awaits anyone who
questions God's infinite love.

Bill Hicks

prologue

Joey Murphy was a fisherman. He was the captain and proprietor of a small trawler that was the whole world to him, but which he knew to be merely a speck on the endlessness that was the Pacific Ocean.

He believed in God.

He believed in Jesus.

He believed in His death, resurrection and bodily ascension.

He also believed in ghosts, poltergeists, demonic possession, Satanic possession, flying saucers, alien abduction, Roswell, Bigfoot, the Loch Ness monster, the Bermuda Triangle, telepathy, telekinesis, pyrokinesis, spontaneous combustion, levitation, reincarnation, out-of-body consciousness and the rapture.

He believed Elvis was still alive. He believed the FBI killed Marilyn Monroe. He believed the CIA killed Jimi Hendrix. He believed the Apollo moon landings were faked. He believed Oswald acted alone, the Magic Bullet theory being far more divertingly outlandish than any of the conspiracy explanations. And he believed the world was going to end on 31 December 1999.

But, best of all, he knew it didn't actually matter a rat's ass what he believed, because he spent most of his time floating out on the waves, miles and miles from where all this shit was or wasn't going on. Truth was, if you were going to believe something, it was best to believe in stuff that made the world seem a more interesting place. That's what beliefs were for – reality you knew about.

Funny, though, the part of his brain that dealt with what he believed seemed able to keep all his beliefs separate from each other, allowing him to believe simultaneously things that were contradictory or even mutually exclusive. This meant that he could believe in Creationism, which he'd been taught in Bible class when he was a kid, while also believing that dinosaurs had once roamed the earth, which he'd been taught in science class three doors along.

Similarly, the part of his brain that dealt with beliefs seemed somehow separate from the part that generally got on with running the show. That was how it was possible for the former to believe the world had only about ten months left before God pulled the plug, while the latter forked out fourteen large for a refit that would keep the *Mermaid's Kiss* seaworthy for at least the next five years. He guessed it was also what stopped most everyone else who believed the same thing from abandoning their normal lives and setting off on oblivious sprees of spending, stealing, screwing, raping and killing.

But another vital factor that allowed him to believe this and all that other stuff was that he'd never once experienced or confronted anything that put any of it to the test. For all his fascination with the occult and the unexplained, Joey had never so much as heard something go bump in the night or seen a Flying Object that wasn't easily Identified as a civil or military aircraft. Long as that was the case, those two parts of his brain could just happily get along with minding their part of the store.

Problems only arose when something forced the two of them to show up in the same place at the same time, like running into your ex-wife at a mutual friend's funeral. During such uncomfortable and unavoidable face-offs, the casualties were invariably on the beliefs side: in his early years they had accounted for Santa Claus, the Tooth Fairy and the Easter Bunny; in his teens, for fears of self-inflicted myopia; and later in life for the notion that 'no new taxes' meant no new taxes.

The taking-care-of-business part of his brain had never been faced with anything that forced a comparable revision of its rule book and operating manual. That was really what made all that weird stuff so fascinating. With the exception of Reagan winning a second term, there had been a rational explanation for everything he had encountered on a personal basis.

Until today.

The ocean was dead, had been for two days now. That made it pretty to look at, but Joey didn't like it. You could forget

4

where you were when the water was like that, especially with the sun shining. Start imagining you were on a lake or some other more forgiving body of water. You could forget how angry the Pacific got, start to lose your respect for it. And that was usually when the spiteful bastard decided to teach you a lesson.

There had been a request from the Coast Guard. A boat called the *Gazes Also* (dumb name), a science vessel or something, had failed to respond to its regular radio contact on the mainland, and they wanted someone who was in the area to go check it out. Just a transmitter malfunction, he figured, or a power failure – probably some floating laboratory with too many gadgets for the generator to deal with. The ocean had been so calm there was no chance of anything more dramatic having befallen the thing. Still, the *Mermaid's Kiss* wasn't so far from the vessel's last recorded position, and it was always healthy to be in credit with the CG. He gave Rico the co-ordinates and commanded him to change course.

They spotted it less than quarter of a mile from where it had been charted the night before, a solid, unmoving dark shape between the placid blues of the still sea and the cloudless sky.

As they approached Joey hailed the vessel over the radio, just in case they had sorted their radio glitch out and he was about to complete a wasted trip, but there was no response, and a quick scan through his binoculars showed no sign of crew above deck. As the *Mermaid* drew nearer, Joey switched to calling the motionless boat over his loud-hailer system, but this equally failed to provoke any human activity.

The *Mermaid's Kiss* pulled slowly and gently alongside the hull of the *Gazes Also*, close enough for Joey to notice that the oddly named vessel looked to have recently enjoyed a returbishment way more impressive than the paint-job with fries he'd spent so much hard-earned on. Thing looked like it had just got back from a goddamn health farm. Everything about the boat looked neat, clean, fresh and in order.

Except the worrying absence of people.

Joey swallowed.

'I'm goin' aboard,' he told Rico. 'Hold her steady. Pedro, gimme a hand here tying up.'

'Sure thing, skip.'

Joey hopped carefully across the gap between the boats and tossed the *Gazes Also*'s mooring ropes back to Pedro.

'You want me to come with you?' Pedro asked.

Joey was about to decline the offer, but another look at the deserted decks changed his mind. He didn't know what he was expecting to find below but he was pretty sure he didn't want to find it on his own.

Pedro stepped across on to the *Gazes Also*, an iron hook in his right hand. Joey took a step forward, called 'Hello?' again, and began slowly descending the stairs to the galley.

He was bracing himself for every grisly discovery he could imagine, every last B-movie scenario and old salt's late-night tale, but what he found below decks was far more disturbing than any horror he could have anticipated.

He found nothing.

No-one. Dead or alive.

No-one.

They moved tentatively through the boat, fearfully pushing open every door. The cabins looked occupied. There were clothes in the foot-lockers, rumpled sheets on the bunks, Coke cans and candy wrappers in the trash-baskets.

Just no people.

Joey looked at Pedro, who was sighing slowly through pursed lips.

Neither of them said anything. Neither of them had to.

Joey turned back and began heading for the decks again. That was when he noticed. On the way in he had just been looking for people, not paying close attention to his surroundings.

'Jesus,' he said, and stopped dead in the galley.

On the table there were four mugs with cold coffee in them, an empty brandy bottle and some plastic tumblers containing the last shares of its contents. There were dinner plates in the sink, cutlery too, in water that was cloudy with detergent. There was a greasy frying pan and two empty pots on the hob. There was a CD/cassette player on the worktop, the power still on and the LCD readout indicating a disc in the tray. There were butts in the ashtrays, breadcrumbs on the chopping board.

'It's the goddamn *Mary Celeste*,' Pedro said.

Joey said nothing, just walked unsteadily back up the

steps and on to the sun-soaked deck. He looked around himself. Apart from his own boat there was nothing but blue as far as the eye could see, and the *Mermaid's Kiss* itself hadn't encountered another ship in three days. There was no suggestion of anything amiss on the boat, and there was absolutely nowhere anyone could have gone.

The crew of the *Gazes Also* had eaten Sunday dinner and then simply disappeared.

'You okay there, skip?' Pedro enquired.

Still he said nothing.

Then, for the first time in his life, Joey Murphy, whose stomach had survived twenty-eight years of the Pacific and twenty-five of his wife's chilli, leaned over the side of the boat and provided Davy Jones with a generous share of his lunch.

one

'Don't sweat it, Larry, it's a walk in the park.'

Oh, gee, thanks, Larry thought. He was sure it had the potential to be a walk in the park and a precedent for being a walk in the park, but now that Bannon had gone and *said* that, he figured he'd better be on the lookout for gang wars, serial killers, King Kong and Godzilla.

Not that Larry wasn't on the lookout for all of the above anyway, these days, although not for the same reasons as everybody else in this screwed-up town.

'Just as long as I ain't goin' down there to hear any Chamber of Commerce requests to lay off bustin' the delegates for coke on account of the valuable trade they're bringin' into Santa M.'

Bannon laughed, shaking his head. Larry figured if the captain had known him a bit longer he'd have placed a daddy-knows-best hand on his shoulder, too.

'Larry, for the most part, this is the shitcan end of the movie business. European art-faggots, Taiwanese kung-fu merchants and LA independents workin' out of fortieth-floor broom closets in mid-Wilshire. Unless they clean up at the Pacific Vista these two weeks, they can't *afford* any coke. Goin' by the budgets of their movies, you're more likely gonna be bustin' them for solvent abuse. There won't be any trouble, I guarantee it.'

Thanks again.

'The movie market moved down here to the coast from the Beverly Center about seven years back, and there's never been a hint of a problem in all that time.'

Yeah, keep it coming, Larry thought. You've just about got it thoroughly hexed for me now.

'These guys, they come here from all over the US and all around the world,' Bannon explained. 'They show each other their shitty movies, they press flesh, they schmooze, and if they're lucky, they do some deals. Close of business they hit the seafood restaurants, throw ass-kissing parties to impress each other, try and get laid, then it's back to their hotels and up at eight to start over. I did your job the first three years. No trick to it. It's a figurehead deal. In their minds you're kind of the LAPD's corporate representative, someone who'll show his face every so often, smile a lot, and tell them nothing of any substance if they ask questions.

'All the organisers need to hear is that we're maintaining a high profile, so the visitors ain't too scared of bein' mugged, shot, gang-raped or ritually cannibalised to walk around town. That means more uniformed beat officers in the pedestrian areas, plenty of patrol cars on Ocean Boulevard and along the beach, all that shit. Ironic, really. Our purpose is to reassure them that none of their movies will come true – well, not to them at least.'

Bannon sat back on the edge of his desk. 'Think you can handle that, big guy?' he asked.

'Guess so.'

'You don't look so sure. Would you rather be out with Zabriski today, maybe? Let's see . . .' He thumbed through some notes on his desk. 'Railway worker, laid off last Friday, walks into the AmTrak offices on Third at eight thirty this morning and deposits a black polythene sack in the lobby. It's one of these atrium deals, you know, with like three or four floors looking down on to the concourse. Telephones bomb warning eight thirty-five, detonates at eight forty-two. Sack contained a small but significant amount of explosive, probably basic demolition stuff. Not enough to cause any fatalities, but enough to distribute the contents of the sack approximately sixty feet in every direction, including up. Guy was, how'd they put it? a "sanitation engineer". Some of that stuff must have come all the way from Frisco before he syphoned it out the train. Four floors, Larry.'

'I'll just be getting down to the Pacific Vista, Captain. Got someone to talk to about this American Feature Film Market thing.'

'Attaboy.'

It wasn't paranoia, Larry knew. It was plain old insecurity. He'd have been suspicious of being given this AFFM 'liaison' gig anyway, simply because he was still very much the new guy, and it might well be the sort of shit detail everyone else knew to steer clear of. He knew the scene, could see the station house, smell the coffee:

'So who's gonna handle the annual fiasco at the Pacific Vista this year, then? Zabriski? Rankin? Torres? What's that? You already volunteered to escort a Klan rally through Watts? Shit. Oh, wait a minute. The new guy'll have started by then. Let's give it to him.'

Nah. Maybe not. He believed Bannon. It was just that everything new made him nervous these days, like he was a damn rookie again. Loss of confidence, loss of self-esteem. He could imagine the phrases on a report somewhere, sympathetic but scrutinising. 'Let's see if he can get it back together, but we better get a desk job lined up somewhere just in case. Poor bastard. Helluva cop once . . .'

He knew he'd be okay at the Pacific Vista. All Larry's shakes were on the inside. The AFFM guy would look him up and down and see a physically imposing and relaxedly confident police officer, rather than the learner driver Larry felt was behind the wheel. He'd handle everything calmly and professionally, and the market would go off without a hitch. Bannon would be correct. It would be a walk in the park.

He knew what was wrong. He'd lost the reassuring illusion of control. These days he was approaching everything with unaccustomed trepidation; not a fear that anyone was out to get him, but that he wouldn't see danger until it was already upon him. He kept experiencing *déjà vu*, recurring waves of it that would freeze him for a moment, deer in the headlamps. It was unsettling, but at least he could recognise it as a symptom, and from there make the diagnosis:

Fear of the future.

Larry knew *déjà vu* wasn't any mystic or psychic phenomenon, just crossed wires in his head. Signals went from the senses to their regular destination in the brain, except that they took an accidental detour via the memory synapses. What you got through your eyes and ears you thought you were getting from deep inside your mind. It happened to everyone now and again, but to Larry it happened *a lot* when he was under a certain, specific kind of stress: the stress of not knowing what happens next. Not ordinary worries about

10

dreaded or hoped-for possibilities, like before starting a new job or moving to a different city, but the vertiginous, isolated blankness of facing a future you couldn't even speculate upon. A confused helplessness of not even knowing *what* to dread or to hope for, because you just can't envisage what's ahead in any way, good, bad or indifferent.

The part of his mind that normally occupied itself with constructing models of possible futures – next year or even just next week – was left grinding gears, and the *déjà vu* was probably a resultant malfunction.

Sophie had gone for more tests last Thursday. She was the pregnant one, but it was Larry who felt he was going to be sick all the way to the clinic.

Why did he have to feel surprised that everything was fine? Or feel that the doctors were lying to them, maybe until they felt they were strong enough to hear the tragic truth? Why, when he looked at the ultrasound scan, could he not believe he would ever see the child depicted in its hazy image?

Maybe the future was blank because he was scared to let himself hope. He already knew how scared he was to let himself dread.

Larry had worked hard at resisting the 'impending fatherhood' variant of cop psychosis. He had seen it around him on the job and its self-corrosive ugliness provided a vividly appalling warning. Decent cops, guys you thought you knew, underwent a shocking transformation, as the man you used to work with barricaded himself in behind barbed wire, broken glass and howling dogs. It was as if they suddenly saw every crime, every murder or rape or mutilation, as a personal affront, fucking up the perfect world they had planned to bring their new child into. Every lowlife they dealt with on the street was no longer just some scumbag, but a direct potential threat to their delicate offspring. They couldn't see a victim any more without seeing their kid. They got hardened. And then they got brutal.

He had worried he might succumb this time, let the poisonous fears and insecurities transmute within him and secrete themselves as armour and weaponry on the outside. Instead he just felt kind of helpless. As if the future was rushing towards him faster than he had anticipated, and all he could do was watch; watch events develop, even watch himself take a role and play his part. It felt like the old-time raceway down at Disneyland. It might look like you were steering the car, and you could even pretend to yourself that you were, but if you let go of the wheel it would follow the track around anyway.

He and Sophie hadn't been trying for a baby. He didn't think they were even at the stage yet where they could *have* that conversation. Guess it just happened. One or other of those tearful clinches where they just held on to each other in the darkness, pressing their bodies always tighter, where neither of them noticed the moment when holding became caressing, pressing became grinding, and the emotional need for closeness became an animal need for penetration.

So maybe it was partly that he didn't feel ready, but Jesus, when were either of them ever going to be ready? What was ready anyway? Was it when you stopped crying yourself to sleep sitting on the floor in David's room? When you stopped waking up in the night because you saw him dying once more in your dream? When you stopped hearing his voice among the laughter every time you passed a schoolyard?

When you stopped feeling?

Larry had to jump on the brakes as he turned his car into the horseshoe driveway in front of the Pacific Vista. The hotel was split into two seven-storey wings either side of an elongated hexagonal lobby. The first floors of the wings extended inwards to create a wide gallery overlooking the central concourse, but the remaining storeys were glass-walled about ten yards back on either side. This was to accommodate the towering centrepiece, a steeply sloping canopy of glass, rising high above the lobby on four sides to a flattened summit, into which, in an unsurpassed feat of architectural piss-taking, there was sunk a rooftop swimming-pool. The bottom of this was, of course, also glass, allowing the sunlight to continue down through the chlorinated water and dance shimmeringly around the lobby. Up top, the effect was supposed to be of the pool having vast and glistening depth, which was probably true. However, the anticipated further spectacle of bethonged babes floating above the desks, shops, cafés and restaurants had legendarily failed to materialise, as visions of plunging through water, glass and then a hundred feet of nothing at all proved sufficiently discouraging to most guests, however many safety assurances were advertised.

The other architectural oversight was that at certain (i.e. most) times of day, due to the angle of the sun, the whole thing turned into some kind of giant refractor lens, blazing white light out at the front or back like a laser blast. This made the horseshoe avenue a popular hang-out for personal-injury lawyers, as suddenly blinded drivers rear-ended each other, shunted bell-hop carts (and bell-hops) and occasionally ran over guests handing their car keys to the blue-uniformed valets. If you came in on foot, you felt like a bug under a cruel kid's magnifying glass.

Larry had been there once before, investigating a bomb-scare. He'd turned on to Pacific Drive from Santa Monica Boulevard and thought the thing must have gone off, because the bomb-squad truck and two black-and-whites were zig-zagged wildly across the blacktop, which was littered with debris from smashed headlamps and tail-lights. Turned out they had all rushed to the scene in the usual blue-light scramble, then concertinae'd each other when the big beam hit. Damascus Drive, folks called it now.

Larry remembered just in time. He brought the car to an abrupt stop, pulled down the shade-panels and slipped on his sunglasses. Now, through the windshield, he could make out a host of silhouettes against the fierce glow, like the last scene in *Close Encounters*. He edged forward slowly, glancing nervously into the rear-view mirror for advance notice of the architect's next unsuspecting victim. A blue courier truck came rapidly into view, but a paint-scored dent in its fender assured Larry it wasn't the driver's first visit. The truck slowed to a crawl and limped tentatively towards the main entrance behind Larry's four-door.

Larry climbed out and slung his jacket over his shoulder, the concentrated blast of sunlight having briefly turned the inside of his car into a microwave. The hotel had a 'greeter' on duty, standing on the blue carpet in front of the sliding doors, a white-bread blonde in a short skirt and a jacket, her smile almost as fake as her surgically sculpted nose. She was the covert first line of defence, ostensibly welcoming visitors to the premises but actually delaying them a moment while the security desk checked them out via the camera eight feet behind her head. She had an earpiece and a wire-thin mike following the line of her jaw. The say-cheese face and the confidence wavered momentarily as Larry climbed the few steps towards her. The reaction was almost tediously familiar, but some days he still enjoyed the look of helpless discomfiture. This was one of them, and he'd even switched the jacket to his right shoulder so that his holster was visible.

'Giant bald black guy carrying a gun at twelve o'clock. Mayday. Mayday. No information on this. Repeat, no information on this.'

The greeter had clocked the valet accepting Larry's keys, which somehow validated him for Official Greetee status. She took a quick breath and went into action. 'Good afternoon, sir, and welcome to the Pacific Vista hotel. How are you today?'

Larry smiled. Angst-ridden, bereaved, paranoid, nervous, strung out and suffering mild symptoms of *fin-de-siècle* cataclysmic psychosis. Also known as . . .

'Fine.'

'And what is your business at the Pacific Vista today, sir?'

He pulled his badge out of his shirt pocket and pointed it beyond the greeter to the video camera. 'I'm Sergeant Larry Freeman of the LAPD, Santa Monica first precinct. I'm here to see Paul Silver of the American Feature Film Marketing Board.'

Larry watched her eyes stray from him for a second as she listened to a message through her earpiece.

'He'll be right down, Sergeant Freeman.' She smiled, suddenly back on-line. 'Would you like to come inside and take a cold drink while you wait?'

'No thank you,' he said, turning back to face the horseshoe. 'I'd prefer to stay here just for the moment, if that's okay with you guys.'

'Of course, sir. Would you like a cold drink brought out to you here?'

'Why, that would be most civilised.'

A waiter appeared, in an unfeasibly short few moments, carrying a tray bearing a pitcher of fruit punch and a tall glass with ice in it. He poured the drink and handed it to Larry.

'Thank you,' Larry told him, then held up the glass to the security camera. 'Cheers,' he mouthed.

The fruit punch was pink in a way that no fruit had ever

been (not *that* kind of fruit, anyway), and Larry noticed with a grin that it perfectly matched the pink beams that highlighted the hotel's exterior décor. Glass, glass and more glass, with all opaque materials either a soft aqua or this peachy-pink. He figured there must have been a serious paint production surplus in these colours back in about '92, because every new building in the city had sported them since. Sophie's alternative theory was that some real camp guy got elected the city's construction-materials regulator, and you just couldn't get anything else past his Garish-Guard chromatoscope. 'Green? *Green?* By the *ocean*? Are you kidding me? Pleeeease!'

Larry sipped the punch and looked back down the drive, where trucks were being unloaded of chipboard partitions, cable drums and aluminum stanchions by squinting young men in white T-shirts, all bearing the AFFM's logo. Tempers were beginning to get frayed by the frequent incidence of light dazzled collision. After a while they sussed a system of using the boards as sunshields, with the guys carrying the other equipment falling in behind.

More vans were pulling up all the time and stopping suddenly, either in quick reaction to the glare or because they had encountered a stationary object up-front. Their drivers handed boxes, packages and cardboard tubes to T-shirted workers or occasionally to stiffly coiffured women in sharp suits. Clipboards were signed. Receipts were dispatched. Everybody had a laminate. Everybody had a mobile.

Across Pacific Drive there was more scurrying busyness going on, with temporary construction under way on the expansive concrete of the parking lot that used to be the Ocean Breeze Retirement Home, before it became the Ocean Breeze Hotel, before it became the Ocean Breeze whorehouse, before it became the Ocean Breeze insurance fire. Zabriski had worked the case, saying it set a new textbook exemplar in obvious torch-jobs. There was a light scaffold being erected, creating what looked like a platform, even a stage, plus more chipboards, perhaps for concession stands. White sheets were being draped around the wire fence that separated the place from the messy back lots of First Avenue, and horizontal banners were being laid out on the ground in preparation for being hung up someplace. He couldn't make out what they said.

15

More legibly, vertical banners bearing the AFFM legend and this year's dates flapped gently from flagpoles along the horseshoe driveway, as they did from streetlights all around Santa M. This event was a big deal. Larry thought again about Bannon's assurances, weighing them up in the context of the growing ferment around him. He estimated that the trouble factor was indeed low, but the embarrassment and repercussion factors were in the ionosphere, given the high profile any fuck-ups would certainly receive. He figured that if shit met fan – or demolition charge – he should remember to be a politician before he was a cop.

'Sergeant Freeman?'

He turned around to find a short white guy with a real bad perm, big and shaggy yet somehow rigidly neat, like he couldn't decide whether he wanted to be in Motley Crue or the Osmonds. When he smiled, he definitely had Osmonds teeth.

'I'm Paul Silver,' he said, extending a demonstratively confident hand. He was faking it. The little guy was shitting himself, and unusually it was nothing to do with Larry's presence, size or colour.

'Larry Freeman. You the man in charge of this show?'

'Yes sir, that I am. I'm Chief Co-ordinator of Logistical On-site Market Activities for the American Feature Film Market nineteen ninety-nine.' Larry could *hear* the capital letters.

'First time in charge?'

'That too. How did you know?'

'Because you're shitting in your shorts.'

The smile switched off. Pauly clearly feared We were about to have a Problem.

Larry grinned to defuse the situation. 'Don't worry, me too,' he said, gripping the now less certainly offered hand.

'First time, or, er . . .'

'Shitting in my shorts, yeah. But hey, everybody assures me there's never been a problem before.'

The little guy rolled his eyes. 'They keep telling me that too.'

Silver led Larry inside, through the vast lobby with its diamondoid canopy. The orchestral music being pumped through the place was fighting to be heard amid the clamour of hammers, power-screwdrivers, staple-guns, raised voices

16

and the chiming of mobile phones. Stalls and stands were being erected, or finished off with promotional material, posters and cardboard cut-outs advertising company names and movies. Many of the flicks looked like the kind of stuff that always filled the lower shelves at the video store, past the New Releases and All-time Classics: Titles for the Undiscerning Viewer. *Musclebound White Guy with a Big Gun II: Hank Steroid's Revenge. Kickboxing Vigilante with Serious Unresolved Personal Conflicts IV: Showdown in a Burbank Parking Lot.*

The shimmering light of the sun through the rooftop pool painted its own changing shades on every surface. Even the widespread tackiness of the market's paraphernalia couldn't detract from the elegance of the effect. Larry had to hand the architect that one. Still nobody swimming in the damn thing, though.

Larry followed Silver through the doors at the far end, out on to a wide terrace that overlooked the beach and the ocean at the rear (or did that make it the front?) of the hotel. Silver pulled up a chair for him and sat down opposite. A waitress arrived with a pitcher and two glasses. This time the fruit punch was aqua blue. Larry laughed, declining his drink, but took up the little guy's offer of a club sandwich and a Seven-Up.

Silver listened to Larry's assurances about police visibility, more officers on the beat and other half-inspired bullshit with sage nodding. He clearly didn't care. He was too wired about the market itself being a success to have any head-time left for worrying about what was happening to the delegates when they weren't engaged in On-Site Market Participatory Activities.

'Well, I guess it ain't me who should be doing the worrying,' Larry said, popping a stray piece of cooked chicken back between two levels of his impressively towering sandwich. 'Looks like you got a bigger operation running across Santa M than *we* do.'

Silver smiled, but there was an Oh-Christ-don't-remind-me wince in the middle of it. 'Biggest one for years,' he said. 'These events kind of shrank after the video boom of the eighties died off, but with new end-users taking up the slack – satellites, digital delivery, fibre-optics – the worldwide appetite for product is growing year-on-year. AFFM ninety-nine will have more accredited participants than any of its predecessors since the event moved to Santa Monica.'

Larry tucked heartily into his sandwich. He'd correctly anticipated that the right stimulus remark would precipitate little Pauly's prepared PR response, thus buying him time to eat.

'Almost every room in the Pacific Vista will function as an office for one of our participant companies, while all of the cinemas in downtown Santa Monica are screening scheduled programmes of market product, from eight in the morning through to six at night. That's a total of almost fifty screens, showing an average of five feature titles per day. Plus, as a new development this year, two of the hotel's function suites have been designated Video Galleries, with a total of thirty-eight booths where delegates can view tapes of non-premièring product – that's titles already screened at previous markets but with certain rights still available – on widescreen format monitors with digital-quality sound channelled through headphones. We've also installed a product-and-rights database with access terminals on every corridor so that delegates can find out what territories and formats are still available on a particular . . .'

It was a mighty sandwich, but Larry still managed to finish before Silver did. He took a big gulp of Seven-Up and wiped his mouth with a napkin. 'Plus you got all that stuff across the street in the parking lot, too,' he said. 'What's that about? Promotional events? Stunts? Star appearances?'

Silver's brow furrowed and his head shook. It was weird watching all that hair move as one. This guy didn't have a stylist, he had a topiarist.

'Oh, that's nothing to do with us, Sergeant Freeman,' he said. 'It's a real headache, actually. We normally annex that lot exclusively for participants' parking, and this year we've had to rent a place half a mile down the beach and organise a free-and-frequent shuttle-bus service. The lot changed hands recently and the new proprietor said he already had the whole place rented out for the market's dates.'

'So what have they got planned there?'

'We didn't ask. But unless it's the world's first outdoor film market it's unlikely to give us much concern.'

18

'Guess not,' Larry said, thinking he'd better check it out when he was through here.

It was much the same deal as across at the Pacific Vista. Guys in matching T-shirts, chipboard screens, electrical cables, laminates, mobiles. Except these T-shirts said, 'Festival of Light – Santa Monica 1999', and it wasn't just the material that was uniformly white. The focus of the lot's layout was a stage at one end, facing north. Workers were assembling an elevated aluminum structure around it, a construction Larry wasn't too old to recognise as a frame for a lighting rig. There was a big truck backed up to one side of the stage, and through its open rear doors he could make out some black boxes that he figured for a PA system.

Larry walked through the gap in the low fence where cars usually went in and out, ducking under the ticket-activated barrier. He made it half a dozen yards into the lot before two T-shirts made their hasty way from the stage to challenge him.

'Excuse me, sir, but I don't believe you have a personnel pass.'

Neither of them looked more than twenty. It was the smaller one who spoke, shiny straight white teeth probably enjoying their freedom after years behind bars. He didn't look like he'd be getting his hands dirty on any of the heavy lifting work. That – and associated tasks – seemed the remit of his high-school linebacker buddy.

Odd thing to say, even as polite intimidation. Not 'Can I see your personnel pass?' or 'Do you have a personnel pass?', but 'I don't believe you have a personnel pass'. Pretty confident about who does, then. Either there weren't too many of them or there was something about Larry's appearance that made it unlikely he'd be carrying one. What could that be, now?

'It's okay, kids, I got access all areas,' he said, producing his badge.

'I don't understand, has there been some kind of complaint?'

'No, I'm just takin' a look around. Wonderin' what you've got in mind with all this stuff.'

'What do you mean? We've already cleared everything with the police *and* the mayor's office,' the kid said, folding his arms. 'We've got the fire department coming down tomorrow for safety checks, and we've got an official police liaison officer dropping by to—'

The kid was cut off by a hand on his arm. An older man, maybe mid-thirties, had appeared behind them from a partially constructed stall nearby. He was dressed identically to his junior companions – sneakers, jeans, T-shirt, teeth – but his laminate was a loudly important red.

'Who's our guest, Bradley?' he asked, smiling widely at Larry in practised PR mode as he spoke.

'Sergeant Larry Freeman,' Larry said, showing him his ID. 'I'd just like a quick look around.'

'Well, we weren't expecting the police department until tomorrow afternoon, Sergeant, and yours wasn't the name we were given, but long as you're here, why don't I give you the tour? I'm Gary Crane. Festival construction supervisor.'

He put a hand on Larry's back and began walking him away towards the stage. The welcoming committee retreated, shrugging.

'What's the party for?'

'Party? Oh I see. Well, I guess you could call it that. I'm right in assuming you're not involved with the Festival liaison?'

'I'm involved with a different liaison, 'cross the street. Just want to see what the other star attractions are in the neighbourhood this week.'

'Certainly nothing as big and impressive as the AFFM, Sergeant.'

'So what is this . . .' Larry indicated the man's T-shirt, '. . . Festival of Light, Mr Crane?'

'It's a celebration. A youth and family event. We're having music, singing, speakers – hence the stage. There's going to be bleachers that end. We're putting them in that big space behind the sound desk, which will be in that booth there. There'll be cooking, concession stands, face-painting,' he continued, indicating the stalls taking shape around the lot.

Smily Gary was being persistently vague around the point of interest. Larry listened to him describe a few more things his eyes had done a pretty good job of noticing for themselves, then interrupted. 'Yeah, but what are we celebrating?'

Crane stopped, looking Larry pityingly in the eye, as if he couldn't believe he didn't understand, then smiled again. 'The light of Christ. What other light is there?'

He felt relief flow through him like a flushed cistern. Terrifying visions of biker conventions and Klan rallies dispersed from his thoughts, washed away in that glib piety emanating from Crane.

Larry looked back at the lot from the sidewalk on Pacific Drive as he waited for the WALK sign on his way to retrieving his car. One of the horizontal banners that had been laid out face down in the lot was being raised towards supports above the stage; there were similar brackets all around the concourse. The banner, folded lengthways, was being hauled up by some of the T-shirts and secured in place at either end. Then it dropped open to reveal its slogan.

'Festival of Light – Santa Monica '99.'

Larry had a little smile to himself. In an ideal world this would still be the AFFM's parking lot, but Happy Clappies he could live with.

He was about to look away again when he noticed another fold of the banner doubled up behind what already faced out, with T-shirts untying the strings that would let the last section drop down. It unfurled with a slap against the frame.

'American Legion of Decency'.

Uh-oh.

This wasn't a movement or an organisation Larry had specifically heard of, but he suddenly didn't feel quite so comfortable any more.

Something about that last word had always scared the shit out of him.

two

He was committing an act of heresy. This was, in the words of that great Welsh cheeseball, not unusual. What was unusual was that this morning's was a cultural heresy, undertaken innocently through necessity rather than in gleeful protest at the absurdity of the taboo he was supposedly breaking. There were lots of other people breaking it too, quite openly, but their standing in the local social hierarchy meant they had little respect to lose in the eyes of their fellow citizens.

Steff Kennedy was taking a walk along Hollywood Boulevard. It was five thirty on a February morning.

The sky was a lazy blue, like a clear afternoon sky back home in the winter, but without the attendant threat of testicular cryogesis. There was a hint of cool in the breeze, loitering, even trespassing, before the strengthening sun and the heat from cars and bodies chased it out of town. Steff reckoned the air was about as crisp and clear as it probably got around here. Last night it had been an enveloping, acrid haze that you could smell, even taste on your breath, and that you could feel precipitated on the skin of your face. The pavements, the roads, the shop doorways were engulfed by a pervading volatility, like the whole boulevard was a student party in a flat with a low ceiling, entrapping the fumes and vapours of the fast food, the sweat, the piss and, of course, the cars.

They cruised up and down all evening (or at least until Steff crashed out, which was hardly the witching hour), the Latino boys in elevated flatbed pickups with inexplicably swollen wheels; the white girls in Beamie convertibles; and the moneyed unseen in stretch limos and blacked-out windows.

Under neon loneliness, motorcycle emptiness, as another Welsh crooner had put it.

The boulevard was being cruised by a different kind of vehicle at this less fashionable hour of the day. If there was a shopping-trolley dealership nearby, it had cleaned up, because everybody had one. And no wonder: low on gas consumption, four-wheel drive (each independent of its partners), and enough space to store everything the driver owns. In the world.

Only downside was the engines looked fucked. All of them. They trundled by, glancing at Steff with no more interest than as if he was a streetlight or a mailbox. They seemed to be trudging along with the resigned automation of commuters, thinking neither of their journey nor their destination; they just did this, every day. Steff wondered where they were going, where they went when the stores opened and the Japanese teenagers erupted from the Roosevelt in search of a Hollywood that plainly didn't exist any more, if it ever had.

One stopped a few yards ahead of Steff, both hands gripping his trolley, a deluxe model with a brake-bar underneath the handle. He wore a browny-green coat with combat pretensions, perhaps more suited now to purposes of camouflage in an environment of cardboard and shredded polythene. His face was partially obscured by matted dark hair, which draped down as he hung his head, looking towards the floor. His skin was an irregular brown, or maybe even dark ash-grey, and it was only as Steff drew nearer and caught a glimpse of his profile behind a gap in his crusty hair that it became apparent that the man was white. He was pissing from somewhere inside the flapping coat. Just standing there and pissing, the urine splashing down around his feet, directly on to one of the stars that lined both pavements east of La Brea, around Mann's Chinese Theater.

The trolley man unclasped his brake-bar and shuffled on, ignoring Steff's inquisitive presence. Steff looked down at the centre of the puddle. Burt Lancaster. Yeah, he thought. I saw *The Cassandra Crossing* too.

Ah, Hollywood. The glamour.

Steff crouched, his back against a palm tree, and took half a dozen shots of the boulevard as it tapered into the east, those trolley-jockeys with their backs to him looking like they were on a desperate pilgrimage towards and beyond the concrete horizon. He stood up again and stepped away from the tree, looking up at it and clicking off a few frames of its flaccid and ill-coloured foliage. The tree looked like it

23

smoked. You're fooling no-one, he told it. You don't belong here any more. You just hang around, making everyone feel guilty about what's been spoiled. Get your own trolley and get out of here.

He looked at his watch again and swore. He had known this would happen. He'd flown in from Heathrow yesterday: eleven-hour flight, eight-hour time difference. The trick is to stay up as late as you can, so that you crash out at close to the local equivalent of your regular bedtime, even though back home it's already the next morning. The obstacle is your digestive system. He had gone out for a walk around half six, and found the surrounding neighbourhood far too disturbing to explore in his current jet-weary state. Mann's was just opposite the hotel, but the only picture starting around the time he was passing was a Merchant-Ivory number, and he decided this would constitute a foolish and unnecessary element of challenge in his quest to stay awake. He settled for a take-out pizza, a six-pack and an in-house movie. He was asleep in his clothes by seven thirty, and hopelessly awake at four a.m.

Someone called Joe Mooney was picking him up at the Roosevelt, for breakfast and then to take him to collect his hire car. But that was at ten.

He had leaned across the double bed and reached for his bag, remembering even as he thrust his hand inside that the book he was half-way through was now probably some-where above the Atlantic, jammed firmly into seat-pocket 22D, between the lifejacket instructions and the boak-poke. Still, if he fancied a read there was always the Bible, as one had been considerately left in his room (as it explained on the cover) by the Gideons.

The Gideons, whoever they were, had Steff baffled. An organisation dedicating time, money and resources to leaving Bibles in hotel rooms all over the world. What the fuck for, he wondered. Who ever actually sat down and flicked through one at home? Probably the same kind of person who would also carry one around with them anyway. Sure, if one of those people arrived to find they had forgotten their precious tome, they'd be hugely grateful to find one in a drawer by the bed, but what were the odds, pitched against the number of wee brown books they had secreted round the globe?

These guys had seriously miscalculated the demographics, too. The majority of hotel rooms on this planet – outside of stand-up obvious tourist destinations – tended to be used by businessmen travelling to meetings, conferences or whatever, sleeping one to a room. They get there after maybe a ten-hour flight or a long drive in the pouring rain. Steff would put real money on the first thing they said to themselves not being, 'God, I need a prayer. If I don't have a wee prayer to myself soon I'm going to go crazy. Oh, a Bible! Thank Christ! Acts of the Apostles here I come!'

He figured it would be a kinder service to mankind to go round the world *removing* Bibles from hotel rooms and replacing them with wank mags. It seemed a safe bet which one the average businessman would rather find by the bed when he came in alone, tired and stressed out after a long trip or a boring seminar. Just snuggling up against the headboard, all on his own, miles from home, crick in his neck, hasn't seen the wife for four days . . . Only one of the two aforementioned publications would ensure he was fast asleep with a smile on his face ten minutes later, having shouted hallelujah and heartily thanked God for his good fortune.

Steff's tilt at breaking the record for the world's longest bath was thwarted by the hotel's having installed the world's shortest. He had settled for pulling the curtain inside and having a shower instead, but even the duration of that was truncated, partly by the water's intermittent switching between cold and mutilatingly hot, and partly by his having to get on his knees to get his hair below the fixed shower-head.

Kneeling was a problem for Steff. Kind of a psychological thing, one might say.

So, having dried off, got dressed and familiarised himself thoroughly with the hotel's fire regulations, room-service menu, laundry arrangements and international dialling literature, and having flicked through the vacuous TV channels and satisfied himself that the BBC were wrong not to market the test-card as a format overseas, he had opted for the heretical pursuit of taking a (very) early-morning stroll in LA.

His subversiveness was confirmed by the time he had made it as far as the Pantages Egyptian Theater, another archaeological remnant of the fabled lost city of Hollywood. Steff had seen the place in old movies and in documentaries about old movies, once a palatial showcase for the local product, site of legendary premières where the gods of a black-and-white pantheon gathered before crowd and camera. Now it was a second-run cinema, showing last season's hits for two bucks, like an ageing and ruined society beauty turning tricks to pay the rent, wearing the torn and faded dress that wowed 'em three decades ago. From red carpet to sticky carpet.

Steff had clicked off a whole roll in front of the place, and was moving on again when the patrol car pulled alongside. The window slid down and a uniformed white cop in uniform shades looked up at him.

'Excuse me, would you mind stopping there a minute, sir?' he said.

Being stopped didn't surprise Steff. He didn't necessarily cut a suspicious figure, but he did cut a conspicuous one. He was six foot seven, broad-shouldered but not muscular, and had straight blond hair swept away from each side of his face like curtains, running down to between his shoulder blades at the back. What didn't help was that his default expression tended unintentionally to convey anything between bored disrespect and flippant scorn, depending on the observer's particular insecurities. His imposing size had the delicately balanced dual effect of both aggravating those insecurities and diminishing the desire to take the subsequent disgruntlement too far. The real problems arose when the first effect outweighed the second, because that usually meant Steff was facing someone who was a lunatic, armed, or backed up by reinforcements. LA cops scored at least two out of three. For this reason, more than climate, he had listened to a friend's advice about not bringing the long black coat he wore back home, 'because it always looks like you're concealing a shotgun inside it'.

Steff stopped and held out his hands to gesticulate his co-operation.

'Mind telling us where you're going, sir?'

'Eh, nowhere, really. Just taking a wee walk.'

'Along Hollywood Boulevard at this time in the morning?'

'Yeah, I know,' he said, with a please-don't-shoot-me smile. 'I couldn't sleep. Just flew in yesterday and the time difference has kind of messed up my body clock, you know?'

The cop looked confused. The weakness in Steff's tactic was

that he had forgotten how few Americans ever travel beyond the place. Jet-lag empathy was a long-odds gambit. However, his main intention was to give them a taste of his accent and play the no-threat dumb-foreigner card. His information was that the average LA cop's 'you ain't from round here' reflex was an amusedly benevolent one. Long as you were white, anyway.

The cop nodded, his stern expression lightening.

'It's my first time in Los Angeles and I thought I might as well take a look around while the streets are empty, seeing as I was awake,' Steff elaborated, trying to capitalise on the breakthrough.

'You don't sound English. Where you from, Australia?'

Success.

'No.' He laughed, shaking his head. 'Scotland.'

'Hey, I was close,' the cop replied, not, apparently, joking.

'Yeah,' Steff agreed. Right planet, anyway.

'Well, sir, if I was you, I'd get myself a rental car. You'll see a lot more of the city that way.'

And if I was you, I'd lose the shades before Tom of Finland gets his sketchpad out, Steff wanted to say, but wisely settled for 'Picking one up later this very day.' This declared intention of reassuring conformity seemed to do the trick. The cop was putting his patrol car back into gear.

'Well, I hope you enjoy your stay. Thank you for your time, sir.'

Hey, call me Ray, he thought. Ray fucking Bradbury.

Steff had been sitting in the Roosevelt's impressive lobby for a hopeful half-hour before Joe Mooney appeared bang on ten as arranged. He had taken a walk around the overlooking mezzanine level with its Hollywood Golden Age memorabilia, including a photograph of the Pantages in its splendid monochrome prime. Perhaps the most fitting reminder of the area's heritage, however, was in the closer view the mezzanine afforded of the lobby's ornate ceiling, whose wooden cross-beams and elaborate cornice-carvings were betrayed as merely shaped and painted polystyrene. Steff smiled. Fair enough, he thought. This town was selling illusion, and no-one in it was pretending otherwise.

'Stephen Kennedy?' asked a voice beside him. Steff had

been scanning the entrances for his contact, willing him des-perately to show up and relieve the monotony. He was also ravenously hungry, as his body, eight hours ahead of the clock, was largely under the impression that it should have already had at least two meals and be gearing up for a third. Such distractions caused him to start visibly when he heard his name spoken just above his left shoulder, in what was unquestionably a female voice. He looked up to see a petite black woman standing before him, attractive in a 'forget it, you'll just upset yourself' kind of way, and exuding a business-like smiling calm that was probably quake-proof. Her face looked like it had built-in air-conditioning, and she wore a blue trouser suit that an industrial steam-hammer couldn't put a crease in.

'I'm Jo Mooney.'

'What? You're . . .' he flapped. She held out a hand, which he grasped unsurely. 'Pleased to meet you,' he managed, unconvincingly.

'I know, I know,' she breathed, as he rose out of the leather chair. 'You were looking for someone male and white. Good job I was looking for someone gangling and confused, or we might have missed each other completely.'

'*Touché*,' he conceded with a grin, which she returned.

'Come on, let's get to my car.'

Steff was glad to be led towards the valet car park at the rear and not out front to the street, as he feared that the incongruity of his elongated, jet-lagged and generally dazed appearance walking beside Jo Mooney's shampoo-ad prettiness would inspire rescue attempts.

'So are you Josephine, Joanne or what?' he asked, trying to dig himself out of the hole she had dropped him into.

'Joely. And, in answer to your next question, one of my great-grandmothers was Irish. It's a real messy story. There's an orphanage involved somewhere too. The details are pretty sensitive around my extended family. I learned not to ask.'

'I wasn't going to,' Steff insisted innocently.

'Well, why not? In case I told you Mooney was the name of the family that owned my ancestors in the Old South?'

He was hugely relieved to spot the sparkle in Jo's eye that betrayed a hidden smile. She knew she had been rumbled and burst out laughing.

'You know, I'm going to come round and take the piss out of you when *you're* jet-lagged,' he told her.

Jo laughed again and handed a ticket to the valet.

'So did you get a cab out here from the airport?' she asked, pulling her red Pontiac out on to Sunset Boulevard. Steff noted with disappointment that she was indicating left at the junction with La Brea. He didn't know what imagined wonders he was hoping to see on Sunset, but the wide-eyed teenager inside him fancied it anyway.

'Not so much a cab, more a kind of minibus affair, driven by a manic Korean and his co-pilot. I think we spent longer going round the terminals circuit than getting up to the hotel. Or maybe it just seemed longer, what with my whole life flashing before me every time we pulled in or out of a lane. It was like Cowdenbeath Racewall on a Saturday night.'

'What's that?'

'It's back home in Scotland. Kind of like your Indy 500, but much bigger. Huge scale, hundreds of thousands of fans. Frightening money in the corporate sponsorship.' Steff smiled to himself as he expanded the outrageous fib. It was revenge for earlier. Like she didn't just *love* turning up and telling people she was the Joe Mooney they were expecting.

'The minibus thing did more laps of the track, though,' he continued. 'I think the driver was going round until he had picked up enough passengers.'

'No. He was just building up to escape velocity before he could slingshot out of the circuit. You're lucky he was good. Come off at the wrong angle and I could have been picking you up in Tijuana.'

The car swung into a busy car park outside a twenty-four-hour diner on La Cienega, just south of Melrose. Jo led him inside, where Steff was delighted by the rows of booths along each window and the long dining bar punctuated by fixed stools. It was the diner of teenage dreams and Phil Spector records. There were even uniformed cops on two of the stools, having coffee cups refilled by cheerfully harassed middle-aged waitresses with big hair. Many of the clientele looked rotund enough to have their own gravitational pulls, which told Steff that croissants were probably not on the breakfast menu; not without steak, eggs, hash browns, muffins and a side order of raw lard. Steff looked again at the Michelin

29

people around him, then back at the dainty Jo, and calculated that the choice of venue was courteously for his benefit.

'You are an understanding and deeply caring person,' he told her, looking up from the bounteous plate the waitress had placed in front of him.

'Don't mention it,' she said, digging a fork into her unaccompanied slice of melon. 'I've chaperoned a few Brits in my time. They're always pretty hungry first morning. Bet you were wandering around before dawn, too.'

Steff laughed and put up his hand, unable to elaborate for the mouthful of Tabasco-laced steak he was ravaging.

'So you must be flavour of the month with *Cinema Scope* for them to fly you way out here,' she stated.

'They didn't,' Steff said, swallowing a gulp of apple juice. 'I'm paying for this myself. I've got a deal with *Scope* for pictures from the AFFM, but I'm hoping to flog stuff to a few other magazines back home later. Depends how many B-list celebs and players I'm lucky enough to run into. I've got a newspaper interested in a kind of photo-travelogue of LA too. If the trip pays for itself, at least, I'll be happy. I wanted to see the place anyway.'

'You slow down to look at car wrecks too?'

Steff grinned. 'Anyway, what about you?' he asked. 'I guess you must *not* be flavour of the month at *Cinema Scope* if you've been sent to babysit this shambles sitting here. Or did you just draw the short straw?'

Jo smiled, tilting her head to one side. 'I'm doing the piece,' she said. 'I'm going to be your guide through the labyrinth down in Santa Monica anyway, so I figured I might as well volunteer. Give us a chance to make sure we're approaching this thing from the same angles.'

'So what's *your* angle?'

'Revenge,' she said, a conspiratorial glint in her eyes. 'I was LA bureau chief on *Picture Press International* – you know it?'

Steff shook his head minutely, so as not to interfere with the business of scooping more scrambled egg into his mouth.

'It's a movie trade paper, based out of London. Most of their material is domestic and European, but the bulk of the ad revenue comes from out here, from independent companies, not the studios. Studios all have European operations and they deal direct. Bottom line is that I had to kiss-ass to all these piss-ant C-movie assholes to keep 'em sweet so they'd keep placing ads come AFFM or Cannes, when they're hawking their wares to the rest of the business. But now I'm with *Scope*,' she said, eyes flashing, 'I'm gonna get 'em back while they're all in one place, at their most puffed-up and self-important.'

'What does *Scope* think about that?'

'They're cool. I mean, *Scope*'s British too, but it's a big-league consumer title so they aren't worried about upsetting Chuck Fuck from Schmuckfilm. Obviously we gotta tread lightly round Miramax and New Line, but they aren't the story.'

'Who is?'

'Like I said, Chuck Fuck and company. Lowlifes with artistic pretensions, making soft porn and karate movies for late-night cable slots in Taiwan, except they want you to treat them like Ingmar goddamn Bergman. That's why you're here, I guess.'

Steff looked up from his breakfast, attempting to convey puzzlement somewhere amid the gluttony.

'When I told Dave Geraghty in London what I had in mind, he said he'd try and get you instead of a local freelance. He said your pictures were, how'd he put it?, "emotionally honest".'

'Well, I don't get much work from *Hello!* if that's what he meant. I don't like affectation. That doesn't mean I try and make everyone look like they just got up in the morning – that would be a form of affectation too. I like to try and get behind the screens folk put up, get an image of the person they are when they think no-one's looking. Far easier said than done, right enough. Soon as you point a camera at somebody, they perform. Some do it more subtly than others, but they all play a part.'

'Dave made your pictures sound like, I don't know, psychological X-rays.'

'Nah. Nothing quite so wanky and sophisticated. But you can usually tell what I think of the subject without much in the way of in-depth analysis.'

Steff got back to his plate, oddly relieved to have headed off the discussion.

Many of his pictures *were* psychological X-rays. Fortunately, most people didn't recognise who of.

31

three

'You're telling me you knew all about this and you didn't think it might be of value for *me* to hear it?'

Bannon sipped from a styrofoam coffee cup, steam rising in substanceless wisps from above his mouth like he was an asthmatic dragon. His brow furrowed in confused consternation, which tipped Larry off that he might just be overreacting again.

'It's a bunch of folks in a parking lot, for Christ's sake,' Bannon argued. 'I wasn't withholding it, Larry, I just didn't figure anyone would give a shit. What's the problem?'

That was a good question. Larry was aware that his hyper-cautiousness lately had been pushing the needle pretty close to the edge of the rationality meter, but it wasn't simply the proximity of this outdoor event to the AFFM that had him concerned.

'Who are these people, boss? I'd just like to know that much. Who *are* or what *is* the American Legion of Decency?'

'The hell should I know? But if they live up to their name you shouldn't have any trouble out of them, should you?'

'Well shouldn't someone have checked this sort of shit out before we let them set up camp in front of the Pacific Vista Hotel?'

Bannon rolled his eyes. 'I'll be straight with you, Larry. I don't know who these people are, and it wouldn't make a difference if I did. Permission – and I mean permission with gold trimmings – came down from the mayor's office on this thing, with instruction to the police department to adopt a Yes-I-can policy, 'stead of looking for potential problems. All I know is it's some kind of Christian rally deal, and there's a lot of Christian votes in Santa M. Work it out. Inside your fortune cookie with this particular meal, it just says "Deal with it", okay?'

'Okay sir.'

It was more a statement of resignation than committed intention.

'And for Christ's sake lighten up about it. I know you ain't been down here long, but I also know that in your time on the job you've survived gang warfare, the mob, earthquakes and mass riots. Suddenly you're antsy about a parking lot full of Bible-bunnies. Jeez. Everybody in this town's so goddamn edgy these days, it's like fuckin' New York.'

Larry couldn't help but laugh, watching the chief get steamed. It was like looking into a mirror, seeing him chase his tail and snap at himself. Thank God he still found the sight of it ridiculous.

'Understood sir,' he said, and turned to grip the handle on Bannon's office door.

'Know what you need, Freeman?' Bannon asked, putting down his cup and leaning across his inflammably cluttered desk.

'No sir.'

'You need somethin' real to be worryin' about. My guess is the Bible-bunnies wouldn't get allocated too much brain-time if you had more meat to chew on. My fault, partly, I guess. Been ridin' you light until you got used to the place, just lettin' you get to know all the main faces and places down here at the beach.'

'Believe me, sir, I *was* happy to pass on the AmTrak thing.'

'Yeah, well, let's see what else we got.' Bannon looked down at his desk. It was impossible to determine what he was focusing on, how many layers down into the paperwork strata his gaze was penetrating. 'Woah!' he said, eyes widening, face grimacing. 'You'll be glad that one's already allocated. Movie time. "Honey I shot the kids because I was piped high as the ozone layer and I thought they were trying to eat me." Yuk. Rankin's treat, that one.'

He picked at the growing nest in front of him, tossing some faxes towards the coffee-spattered bin behind him where he'd no doubt be angrily searching for them half an hour later.

'Oh yeah, here it is,' he said, holding up a hand-scrawled note. 'Movie time again. "One of our submarines is missing."'

'What?'

'No shit. Coast Guard called. Some kind of scientific research boat, based out of Santa M. Found abandoned and drifting in

33

the middle of the Pacific Ocean. Entire crew MPD. Coroner's office needs an official police once-over for the fatal-accident report.'

'I don't know anything about boats, sir.'

'Don't sweat it, neither does the coroner. You haven't "liaised" with the Coast Guard yet, have you?'

'No sir.'

'Well now's the ideal opportunity to introduce yourself, don't you think? Take a spin down there this morning, see what the deal is. And don't make any gags about their shorts, they don't like it.'

Once again, Bannon was right. The whole town was wired. It wasn't like paranoia, which was what you got in New York, a constant state of heightened alertness like mainlining caffeine, whereby the moment you closed the front door behind you and hit the street everybody had to be treated as a hostile threat until they could prove otherwise. An outgoing personality and a trusting nature would be filed as contributory negligence on an NYPD homicide sheet. It was like a sustained vibrato note in the symphony of a city: high, discordant, always audible but sometimes dampened in the ear by its very familiarity; and the pitch was determined by how many people were crammed into the city's limited space. In New York or Chicago, for instance, it was a piercing note indeed.

LA was different. The conurbation spread so far and wide that the note was low and bassy, but occasionally it built up, gradually, powerfully, irreversibly, like a wave. You felt it grow around you, noticed it in people's attitudes, noticed it in yourself, even the off-duty self that wasn't purposefully taking the city's temperature every day. Maybe in the route you took to the ball game, cutting out a neighbourhood you'd have driven through six months ago. Maybe in how long you'd drive around looking for a parking space that would cut down the distance you'd have to make on foot. Maybe in how many times you looked at the clock waiting for your spouse to come home. And these waves didn't recede naturally: first they had to break, which was the scariest part. That, in itself, added to the tension. People knew something had to give, and they were wound so tight

34

these days because they couldn't envisage what it might be.

A wave had been building up through the late Eighties and into the early Nineties. It broke over the Rodney King beating trial, but if that hadn't happened it would have broken on something else; the later the more violent. The next wave was broken early in its rise by the quake two years later. It wasn't just a few buildings that got levelled – an event like that gave everybody a big enough scare for them to forget all the other shit they usually got so worked up about, at least for a while. But eventually the wave started to grow again. The OJ trial proved something of a curve-ball. It kept everybody distracted for the best part of a year, and the outcome denied the South Central powder keg its spark, but that courtroom had used race and prejudice to twist justice in a way that was even more ugly than in Simi Valley in '92. Meantime, the wave kept on growing.

Larry called it 1999 Syndrome. It was a new and potent strain of a very old disease, called Things Are Getting Worse.

He figured that once upon a time a bunch of Australopithecines were sitting around a fire, discussing in guttural grunts how the neighbourhood wasn't what it used to be, how the paths weren't so safe no more, and how it all must be heading for some dreadful culmination. Such a shame, too, because they all remembered the days when you could leave the cave without rolling a big rock in front of it.

LA used to be such a great town, he had been told. Such a great, great town, but not no more. Larry remained confused about the historical dates and duration of the Angelino Golden Age, as he had never heard two corroboratingly consistent opinions on when exactly it ended, what caused the Fall, or what the signs of decay had been. Funny thing was, he'd lived here his whole life and had apparently missed it; missed that crime-free, drug-free, opulent epoch, living instead through decades consistently peopled by rich and poor, good and bad, healthy and sick. The years passed, the crimes changed, the motives changed, the diseases changed, but there were always crimes, always motives, always diseases.

So many times he'd heard that story, that story of the lost LA, sunk for ever like Atlantis, its splendour and achievement never to be repeated. Guys in the station house, guys in the bar, folks round the table in a restaurant.

'Sure, there was always crime,' they'd concede, 'but *these* days, well . . . They're coming into our neighbourhoods, stealing our cars from in front of our houses. Our own streets ain't safe. Never used to be like that.'

Then they wouldn't know where to look for a minute, embarrassed, hoping Larry would 'understand' what they meant; then angry if he was going to make a deal out of it.

What they meant: niggers and spics used to steal from each other, shoot each other, rape each other, what the hell did we care? They stuck to their neighbourhoods, we stuck to ours. But these days they're crossing the invisible line, all the balls in the world, stealing from *us*, shooting *us*, raping *us*. Never used to be like that.

Things Are Getting Worse.

And the big fear, the big question, was where was it all leading? Where would it end? All the time that wave kept growing, so how would it break this time?

Now the calendar had flipped over into year 1999, providing the dash of Tabasco that really spiced up the recipe. As if folks in LA weren't spaced-out enough, now we had a biblical overtone running through everything, and Larry had seen enough corpses in his time to know the equation: psychotic + Bible = disaster. There were the national legends if you wanted extreme examples – Ted Bundy, Jeffrey Dahmer, John Wayne Gacy – but every cop who'd worked murder or rape cases knew there was no publication more destabilising to an already fragile mind. Maybe it was the mysticism and superstition; maybe it was the notion of something greater ultimately being in control, that abdication-of-responsibility deal; maybe it was the images of supreme power. Who knew? But it fucked them up every time. Dangerous software, a former colleague had called it. A lot of machines simply weren't equipped to run it.

There was always someone on TV calling for shows to be banned or movies to be banned or skin flicks to be banned, all on the grounds that they provoked violence and decay in society. If they asked around a few homicide cops who'd worked serials, it wouldn't be Schwarzenegger pictures they wanted out of circulation. Larry wasn't the only one who wished St John the Divine had taken that vacation somewhere less vulcanological than Patmos, and had stayed off the opiates while he was at it. He figured a lot of dead women had wished as much too, once upon a time.

Nagging fear of cataclysm was part of the way of life in California. You didn't think about it much – or rather you *tried* not to think about it much – but inside you knew the possibilities. That little voice of concern was always yabbering away at the back; just that you couldn't always hear him while you had so many other things to get wound up about. It worked like a personal stress gauge: if you found yourself worrying about The Big One, the rest of your life had to be running pretty smooth.

But with that voice always yabbering away inside people's heads, Larry feared that people didn't just grow used to the *possibility* of cataclysm; maybe they grew used to the whole idea. So when 1999 came along, they thought they had something to be genuinely afraid of.

'"Things fall apart,"' as Sophie put it, quoting that Irish poet she liked. '"The centre cannot hold." All that stuff. "The falcon cannot hear the falconer."'

The shit is hitting the fan.

This is an APB. All units in the Bethlehem area: be on the lookout for a rough beast with a slouching gait.

1999 Syndrome took plain old Things Are Getting Worse and changed it into Things Are Getting Worse Because The End Is Nigh. Crime used to be seen as instances of anti-social behaviour, sins against society. But now there was this resigned attitude at large that it was indicative of a greater, inexorable process of decay. Each crime now had to Mean Something, each new atrocity held up as the next marker on our descent into uncharted depths of stygia.

And *everything* was a fuckin' omen.

Everything.

War breaking out in some far-flung country was an omen. Peace in a different country was an omen too. Flood was an omen. Drought was an omen. Mass murder was an omen. Mass suicide was an omen. Births were omens. Deaths were omens. Oppression, emancipation, invasion, liberation: *all fuckin' omens*. In short, stuff that had been going on regularly down the years and centuries was now, suddenly, in 1999, darkly and profoundly portentous.

Bullshit.

The vicious circle of self-fulfilling prophecy was turning like a wash-tub on spin. You whipped people into a frenzy by telling them the end of the world was nigh, then you pointed at the frenzied folks and said, 'Look, everyone's gone crazy, the end of the world must be nigh.'

Sophie's poem, the Irish guy. She'd read that to him one night when they were talking about all this, few weeks back after the news ran with Luther St John and his prophecy or prediction or whatever. They'd talked about this millennial panic crap lots of times, in fact. Jesus, these days who didn't? Poem was written way back at the other end of this century, she told him, after our last collective bout of cataclysmic heeby-jeebies. This stuff, this end-of-the-world-as-we-know-it stuff, had all happened before. It was normal. It was natural, even. Individually, you get nervous about anything new: new job, new house, new city, new date. With a new century, everybody gets nervous about the same thing at the same time. It infected the cultural consciousness, Sophie said. *Zeitgeist* was the German word for it. Happened to an extent after WW2. The whole country, maybe the whole world, has occasion to think 'Where do we go from here? What happens now?', and a lot of folks get scared because they don't know, can't see, can't imagine.

Larry, of all people, knew how that felt.

But 1999 wasn't just the end of any century, it was the end of the *twentieth* century. Not only was that the end of a whole millennium, but it was also the end of a century that had a conceit of itself like none before it. No previous century could possibly have had such a confidence in its own modernity, with a widespread tendency to view all the previous ages of man as steps on the road towards this apotheosis. Us citizens of C-Twenty thought we were the cat's pyjamas, basically.

Science had never advanced at such a furious pace, far less had that pace ever accelerated at such a breathless rate, and no civilisation had ever become so intoxicated by the capabilities of its technology. Certainly every era must have taken pride in its achievements and liked to measure its progress against the culture and learning of its hundred-year predecessors, but surely none had indulged such a sense of climax.

Hence the omen-peddlers.

This was the It century. Time of the biggest, smallest, fastest, slowest, longest, shortest. The conceit of zenith meant that the twentieth century had failed to inherit from its forebears the words 'so far'. Whatever we achieved, these days, instantly became the defining superlative, which was where the doomsayers came in.

We had put men on the moon. That was, of course, a fuckin' omen, as it was some sort of ultimate in travel and exploration. If we had put men on Mars, then that would have been the ultimate in travel and exploration too. If we had only put men in orbit, guess what?

Then there were the twentieth century's unprecedented acts of evil, most notably the attempted systematic extermination of an entire race of human beings. Our number must surely be up because, as we approached the end of the millennium, man had never been so base, so without conscience, so inhuman (whatever that meant).

Except that he had.

Larry had read all about it, a previous holocaust, near the other end of this same millennium: the Albigensian Crusade. The *successful* systematic extermination of an entire race of human beings, in this case the Cathars in France. By command of the Church, around a million men, women and children were slaughtered because they were preaching and practising a different version of Christianity, the spread of which had been a threat to the Holy Roman Empire. A long way short of six million, numerically, but given the contemporary population of Europe, proportionally an even greater genocide than we had managed in the supposedly superlative twentieth century.

Seemed we had forgotten the word 'since' as well.

This self-satisfied century was coming to an end: this time of extremes and ultimates, of unrivalled progress and unparalleled decay, when man had ascended to heights beyond the planet and plumbed depths below mere sin. This age with its arrogant delusions of culmination.

And the problem with such delusions was that they were incompatible with the concept of succession. So, effectively, the world was supposed to end just because some folks couldn't imagine what might come next.

39

Which was pathetic.

Larry knew, because he had been there. He and Sophie. Both been there. Thinking there couldn't be a tomorrow after this.

A hospital. A gurney. Tubes, lines, fluids, bags, machines. A numb car-ride under streetlights. An empty house. A bedroom. A glass of water. Darkness. There couldn't be a tomorrow after this.

But there was.

The Coast Guard's office was south along Pacific Drive, a crisply white building that couldn't have been open more than a few months. From the road it looked like a one-storey deal, but a lower floor extended beneath it on the ocean side, descending to the purpose-built marina that harboured the CG launches. There were dozens of marinas all along the coast, at Venice, Malibu, Long Beach, but even without the signposts Larry would have known that this was the place because it was the only one that didn't have a fish restaurant on it. He had come past the old Coast Guard premises on the way. It was being reconcreted and turned into another private marina, with a hotel under construction at the back. Larry figured the realty deal must have paid for a large slice of the set-up before him. The location wasn't as picturesque as its predecessor, but on the other hand, the new offices didn't look like a canning factory.

He got out of his car and began walking towards the automatic doors. A girl in long blue shorts and a white T-shirt was squatting down in front of the soda machine that stood on a platform walkway running around the building on the right-hand side. She stood up again, Coke can in hand, and fed more quarters into the slot, then turned around. She wore a blue baseball cap with the Coast Guard's badge on the front, and had a blonde ponytail sticking out neatly through the gap above the adjustment strap.

'What'll it be?' she called, smiling, as he approached.

'Huh?' said Larry, unsure what she was referring to or even whether she was referring it to him.

She laughed. 'To drink.'

'Oh right. Coke's fine. 'Less you got Mountain Dew.'

'Sure have.'

She hit the panel and retrieved the can, tossing it to him as he drew near. 'Larry Freeman, right?'

Larry ceased reaching for his ID. 'How'd you guess?'

'I know an unmarked police car when I see one. Nobody under sixty would be driving that thing through choice. Not a new one, anyway.'

Larry looked back at the frumpy lime four-door. She had a point.

'I'm Janie Rodriguez.' She held out a hand, which Larry gripped firmly. He noticed the wedding band on her other one, which explained why the least Hispanic-looking woman on the coast had a name like that. She looked mid-twenties, barely five feet but all of it bursting with energy. Must be the sunshine and the ocean. Larry figured there was a film crew shooting a Wrigley's commercial round the corner wondering where she had disappeared to. 'Been expecting you,' she continued. 'You're here about the *Mary Celeste*. Let me show you.'

Janie led him along the walkway a few yards and around the corner to the front, stopping where the platform looked down on the boats in the marina. They both rested their elbows on the rail and leaned forward. Larry opened his can and took a long drink, a light sea breeze playing on his face, sun glinting up off the water and drawing squiggly patterns on the underside of the walkway's wooden canopy. Janie had one foot on the base of the railing, and Larry realised she was looking at him.

'What are you smiling about, Officer?' she asked.

'Just thinking,' he said. 'This beats working for a living.'

'Well, 'fraid we gotta do that too. That's the boat in question down there.'

'You mean the big one that don't say "Coast Guard" on the sides?'

'That's correct, Officer. Scientific research vessel the *Gazes Also*, out of the Californian Oceanographic Research Institute right here in Santa Monica.'

'What's that all about?'

'From what I gather they were conducting a study of the sub-oceanic topography. Undersea landscapes, in layman's terms. There's mountain ranges bigger than the Himalayas down there, and trenches deeper than the Grand Canyon.'

'The *Gazes Also*, huh? Cute name for that sort of work.'

Janie squinted against the sun and turned to look at Larry, who had moved further along the walkway.

'I hadn't thought about it,' she said. 'We come across so many dumb names for boats, you stop wondering what they're referring to. Most of the time it's probably someone's wife. Or their dog. What's cute about this one?'

'It's Nietzsche,' Larry told her, turning away again to stare at the vessel, the name etched on the bows and the life-savers. '"When you gaze into an abyss, the abyss gazes also into you".'

'Jesus, they got cops quoting Nietzsche now?' Janie said with a wry smile, nudging up the peak of her cap with her Coke can. 'What, you gotta answer on philosophy for the sergeant's exam these days?'

'No, I read it on my cereal box this morning. It's a thought for the day deal. If I'd had Cheerios instead of corn flakes I'd never have known – Cheerios are still running their Gems of Kierkegaard series.'

'Of course.'

Larry thought the boat looked somehow humbled tied up in dock. Manacled here, where it didn't belong, balefully lifeless, humiliated by its captivity.

Janie finished her soda and arced it practisedly into a trashcan nearby.

'Okay, here's the scene,' she said. 'The *Gazes Also* failed to respond to radio contact from CalORI last Monday morning.'

'The research institute?'

'That's right. So they reported it to us. It's no blue-light thing. Happens now and again – maybe a power problem or damage to transmission equipment. So first of all we tried a relay off vessels in the area of its last reported co-ordinates. Still incommunicado. Then we got in touch with a trawler that was pretty close by and requested from the captain that he make a detour and check it out. He radioed back Monday evening sounding real spooked. The boat's there, all right, it's drifted a little, but he's found it. First he tries to radio again, but still no reply. When he gets close enough he calls over his loud-hailer. Still *nada*. Eventually his boat ties up alongside and he boards.'

'And nobody's home?'

'Yeah, but that ain't what spooked him. Come on, I'll show you.'

Janie led Larry down a gangway to the boardwalk that skirted the water. She traded greetings with two guys tying up a launch as they walked past. They wore the same get-up, even the baseball caps. Larry understood what Bannon meant about the shorts. One of those guys really should have been told he didn't have the knees for joining the Coast Guard.

There were official tapes across the rails either side of the gangplank that led on to the *Gazes Also*. Janie ducked under, catching her cap on the yellow plastic strips as she did so. She pulled her ponytail free of the hat and gripped it by the skip. Larry stepped wide-legged over the tapes and climbed aboard. She beckoned him to follow her down some steps into the cabins below deck. He folded up his sunglasses into his shirt pocket and descended.

'This is pretty much as was,' she said, indicating the galley. 'The trawler captain swears he touched nothing and I believe him. These guys can get very superstitious and I think he wanted off this boat as fast as his legs would carry him.'

Larry looked around him. The stale smell and the sound of flies had made his stomach go rigid as he came down those stairs, a reflex conditioned by years of forced entries into locked buildings where the occupants were in no condition for greeting visitors, and frequently in no condition for open-casket funerals either. But there were no such unfortunates here. The stale smell came from the sink, where dinner plates and cutlery lay submerged under a murky fluid that looked eight parts water to one part food detritus and one part resultant scum. There was a ring of the greeny-brown matter a couple of inches above the fluid, evidencing days of gradual evaporation. Dead flies floated amid the surface flotsam, reminding Larry of birds caught in an oil slick. The live flies were concentrated around the small, compact dinner table, flanked by an upholstered bench against the wall and lightweight chairs opposite. On the table there were coffee mugs and plastic tumblers on top of place mats around a brandy bottle and a basket of brittle-looking lumps of bread, dotted liberally with flies and mould. Two of the tumblers and one of the coffee mugs lay upturned, their contents having dried on the wooden surface to leave contour lines, like hills on a map. The other three still had at least an inch of coffee in each.

'We flew a guy out on the seaplane to pilot this thing back. It was more than three hundred miles out. Just got back last night.' Janie picked up some photographs from on top of the microwave oven on a worktop by the sink, handing them to Larry. 'He took these before moving the boat anywhere.'

Larry flicked through them. The pictures showed scenes of the galley, mostly identical except that all the cups and mugs were upright, there was no spillage on the table and the water-level in the sink was higher.

'It was in case things got choppy on the way home. He wanted to capture the full impact of the scene as upon discovery. As you can see, the trip home was pretty smooth. The spook-factor hasn't depleted much.'

'Jesus,' Larry breathed.

Janie pointed above the microwave to a shelf supporting a ghetto-blaster.

'CD player was still switched on too, with a disc in it. The Sex Pistols, for what it's worth. You just imagine being that trawler guy. I mean, *you*'re seeing this here in the Coast Guard marina. He found all this shit floating in the middle of the Pacific.'

'No thank you.'

Janie frowned. Larry could tell that seeing the scene one more time wasn't helping her make any more sense of it.

'Civilised little Sunday dinner at sea,' she said. 'Coffee, conversation, music and a *digestif* of brandy. Then they vanish before the coffee's even cold. Just disappear without trace.'

Terrific, Larry thought. A latter-day *Mary Celeste*. An abandoned boat in the middle of the ocean. Disappearing scientists. No doubt another fucking omen.

'Nothing disappears without trace,' he stated. 'If you vanish in a puff of smoke, you're still gonna leave a carbon stain on the ceiling. So, you got any theories what happened here, or do you figure the aliens just beamed 'em all up to go meet Elvis?'

Janie arched her brow. 'Well, if the aliens took them, they would have needed room in their flying saucer for a submarine, because that's missing too.'

Larry's eyes widened involuntarily. He thought Bannon had just thrown it in as a figure of speech.

'A submarine?'

'Yes indeed. CalORI told us about it when we said we were sending someone out to pilot the boat home. I mean, keep your pants on, it wasn't Polaris. Still, a real smart craft, from what I'm told. The *Stella Maris*, it was called. It could go pretty deep, depending on how long the crew could face in decom afterwards. Look, do you mind if we get back on deck? Two more minutes and this smell's gonna make me puke.'

'Yeah, sure,' Larry said. 'I'll follow you up in a minute. Just gonna take a little look-see. I'll hold on to these pictures, if you don't mind.'

'They're yours,' said Janie, with a dismissive wave, her hand then moving up to cover her mouth and nose as she began a hasty retreat.

Larry explored the remainder of the boat. The sleeping cabins were along a narrow corridor from the galley, with stairs to a sub-level at the near end. He had a brief glance into each one. Clothes and books cluttered the beds and the tight floorspace. They were uniformly messy, but ramshackle messy rather than ransacked messy. He thought of the post-burglary look Sophie could effect in their spacious bedroom and imagined it concentrated. These guys were anal by comparison.

The sub-level housed a shower cubicle on one side, and occupying the majority of the area under the galley was what had to be the boat's nerve centre. Radar screens – wait a minute, that would be sonar, right? – computers, and all sorts of science-lab shit. There were worktops on all sides supporting glass tubes of stratified sand, charts, printouts, lumps of rock, jars of what looked like mud, and, like guess-who-doesn't-belong, a carton of UHT milk.

'So, apart from a submarine, anything else missing?' he asked, emerging back on to the rear deck where Janie was leaning against a side-rail.

'Can't be sure. We don't have an inventory; need to wait until someone from CalORI can take a look around, which won't be pleasant for whoever it is. They were all real close, it seems. Big happy family. But it doesn't *look* like anything's missing. Life-savers are all in place, so no man-overboard scenarios. Sub-aqua equipment accounted for – four sets of tanks and wetsuits.'

'So all that seems to be gone is one submarine and four people.'

Janie nodded.

'Now, I know I'm a landlubber and all,' Larry said, 'but doesn't it sound a lot like . . .'

She nodded again. 'This whole *Mary Celeste* scenario's had everybody here freaked out since the trawler captain called it in, but having had time to reflect, and if you'll forgive the fish reference, I think the abandoned dinner scene could be a red herring. I checked the ship's log. The last entry says they were taking the sub on a dive, to the slopes of something or other, some undersea location they must have been checking out. The entry isn't timed, just dated. According to the entries before it, they spent that Sunday doing running repairs, maintenance, odd jobs, ready to get serious again on Monday. Seems possible to me they stuck the plates in the sink, went to bed then got up and made an early start, figuring clean-up duty could wait. That could be *morning* coffee in those mugs, remember.'

'But the U-boat springs a leak, taking everybody right down the "slopes of whatever" and into the sweet by-and-by?' Larry offered.

'Works for me. There are variations on the theme. As you can imagine, it's been a popular discussion topic round here.'

'Keep talkin'. Long as aliens ain't involved.'

'Okay. First is the "sounds like a great idea after six beers and some brandy" theory. They're drunk and someone suggests taking the *Stella Maris* for a midnight spin.'

'Don't buy it,' he said. 'These guys were pros, not teenagers out on Dad's fishin' boat.'

'Experience can breed complacency and misplaced confidence, Sergeant. I've seen it before. But anyway, it wasn't my theory.'

'Well forget it. Can you see the coroner's office telling *that* to the bereaved families? I can't. So what other spins did you guys come up with when you "workshopped" this thing?'

Janie looked like she wanted to take offence, but she couldn't help smiling. She rolled her eyes. 'All right, well, there's the "all a big hoax" theory. It's some sort of stunt. They took off in the sub, rendezvoused with another boat and are lying low while the world gets interested.'

Larry just grinned, shaking his head. 'Next.'

'Just one more. The nineteen ninety-nine theory.'

He closed his eyes and took a deep breath. Whatever it was, he knew he wasn't going to like it.

'Suicide pact,' she said. 'End-of-the-century psychosis combined with cabin fever after weeks on this little boat, plus maybe a bit of depressurisation trauma. They grow real close and real crazy. A last supper, then . . .'

Larry glared.

'I mean, it's not my theory, I'm just . . .'

'Let's pretend we didn't have this conversation,' he said in a low, bassy near-whisper.

She held up her hands. 'You got it.'

'We'll just stick with the basics. You figure they took off in the sub – let's stay with that and not dream up any crazy reasons *why* they took off in the sub, other than they were doing their jobs. You know where the boat was found, so you know where the sub would have set off from. Any chance we can recover this thing?'

Janie laughed drily. 'Boat was somewhere around Fieberling Guyot. That's a kind of sub-oceanic mountain.'

'So?'

'So the sea-bed, the foot of that mountain, is about fifteen thousand feet down. If the *Stella Maris* lost power or hit a turbidity current, Jesus.' She grimaced, looking away. 'It would implode on the way down. Crushed like a beer can.'

'What's a turbidity current?'

'It's kind of like an underwater landslide.'

'Okay. Okay. But effectively, you're saying if we take out the spook factor for a moment, we're looking at a bunch of folks who didn't do the washing-up one night, then went out in the morning and had a real bad day on the job.'

'In short, yeah.'

'Well let's go with that first and see how far the facts carry it. I'll need to speak to someone from this CalORI place. First one over there to dry their eyes, get them to gimme a call.'

'Sure thing.'

'Meantime, I'd appreciate it if we could keep a tight lid on this thing regards the media. If they ask, all we got here is a tragic accident at sea, okay? I don't want them knowing anything about coffee cups and dinner plates. I've already heard the half-assed theories your buddies produced. I don't want to find out what the tabloids' imaginations can dream up using the same material. The families will have enough to deal with without reading any *X-Files* crap about their lost loved ones.'

four

Maria thought the e-mail would set her off crying again. That was one of the countless symptoms of her grief – you never knew what trivial or unlikely thing was going to trigger another painfully cherished memory, bring back a part of what was lost for just long enough to remind you of what you were missing. Strangely, it was never the obvious ones, like the sight of their empty desks or the growing piles of unopened letters. Maybe that was because you knew to put up your guard at those times, so it was the sucker punches that got you, the ones you didn't see coming.

Like this e-mail. Soon as she saw who it was from, some part of her that hadn't kept up with current affairs was telling her to look over her shoulder in case Coop or Taylor saw, as it would only give them more ammunition for their dumb jokes.

What she wouldn't give now to be hit with both barrels.

The message was from Jerry Blake in the Lebanon, following up on something that had seemed the most exciting thing in the world to her this time last week. It seemed death liked to come along every so often and remind you how little value or purpose anything really had as long as it was ultimately in charge. That the message was to do with archaeology – dead people, dead civilisations – seemed to underline that in red pen.

Maria's interest in the Minoan empire was very much an extra-curricular pursuit, hence the jibes from Coop and Taylor when she was indulging it on 'company time', but it was an understandable fascination for a seismologist. The Minoans' native Crete had been ground-zero during the most destructive seismological disaster known to man, and in studying it she had become intrigued by the ancient civilisation. Unfortunately, research and evidence were thin on the ground, partly due to the effects of the aforementioned disaster, and partly due to the Minoans having been 'rediscovered' by archaeology only at the beginning of the century. Further obscuring this lost culture was the fact that the only surviving documents were written in two as-yet indecipherable script forms, known as Linear A and Linear B. The latter had been identified as a very primitive form of Greek, but the former, although having contributed words to Linear B, seemed to be a different language altogether. So although the archaeologists possessed artefacts that gave clues as to the make-up of the Minoan civilisation, they were without any first-hand depictions of what life in it was like.

Until Jerry Blake excavated a site just outside Beirut last year, discovered when developers were clearing the ruins of a bombed-out apartment block. A number of scrolls were sealed inside an earthenware jar, written in an early form of Hebrew that instantly dated them from around 1500 BC. The anticipated biblo-archaeological feeding frenzy failed to ensue after the first cursory translations of text fragments revealed them to be first-person accounts of events not in the Holy Land, but in 'Kaftor', the contemporary name for Crete.

In the smaller field of Minoan archaeology, however, the find was nothing short of explosive. Questions – and arguments – had already arisen over whether the scrolls might themselves be a translation of original Minoan documents, or whether their author had command of both languages. This issue had important ramifications for the authenticity of what the texts depicted and, Jerry predicted, would be the bloody battleground for many archaeological bust-ups. It was inevitable that the scrolls would largely contradict certain established theories about Minoan life, so the scholars who adhered to those theories would have to defend their academic reputations by discrediting the reliability of the new accounts.

Which was where Maria came in.

Contrary to Coop's relentless innuendo, Maria had never met Jerry Blake – their relationship was purely electronic, her Internet research forays having led to regular correspondence with him on the subject of the Minoans. This had made her one of the first to know about the Beirut find, and initially Jerry had promised to keep her updated about whatever secrets the scrolls yielded, as and when the translations were sufficiently coherent. However, when those translations revealed that the texts included what purported to be a first-hand description of the destruction of Thera and its cataclysmic aftermath, her involvement became rather less passive. Jerry recruited her to assess the veracity of the scrolls' account from a seismological point of view, because if that part sounded like bullshit then it would cast serious doubts over the credibility of the rest.

From all she'd seen so far, Maria was satisfied that if whoever penned these scrolls *wasn't* around when Thera went bang, then he sure as hell knew a man who was. All that he described, even the most fantastic-sounding phenomena, was seismologically and vulcanologically authentic. Events that even Jerry had assumed to be 'the narrator laying it on pretty thick' were not only scientifically explicable, but highly unlikely to have been inspired by anything other than direct witness. From the preceding years of earthquakes and lesser eruptions to the insanity of Thera's last hours, this chronicler was talking about things he simply wouldn't have *known* to make up.

The eruptions had begun long before dawn, heralded as ever by the night's tremors, spewing forth pumice upon the waters and blackness into the air, confounding we who thought there could not be so much ash in the world as had already smothered the life from our lands on Kaftor. Those fleeing in boats from Tira's shores found their eyes and skin begin to burn, as if their bodies had been flayed and vinegar poured upon the wounds. Their throats and noses became choked with this searing vapour, which ate through flesh and smelt of death and decay.

Upon the stricken island, the mountain's heat had crazed the very winds of the air. Men and beasts, even trees, were lifted bodily from the earth, drawn into the rage of debris and flame that filled the skies, there to be torn apart as by a thousand spears in flight.

Then the sea itself began to boil.

The waters in the bay convulsed in frenzy, rising as if to escape the earth, falling back in fearsome swoops, like carrion fowl in fiercest dispute. The waves had no purpose or direction, only the wildest agitation. Those boats in the bay were smashed like tinder by this violence. The stout beams of hulls that

51

had traversed all the seas of the world were shattered like baked clay.

Neither were all the vessels spared that had reached the open sea. Though there was no wind for their sails, they began to speed back towards land, all together, faster than ever they had ridden the waves before. It was as though time had turned upon itself as the boats' journeys were reversed, unknown forces drawing them irresistibly into the bubbling cauldron where they met their end, disappearing beneath the waters as though swallowed whole.

From the mouth of the mountain, a vast pillar of steam violated the skies, punching through the heavens and beyond in a white, unbroken shaft, reaching in the blink of an eye higher than all the mountains of the world piled one atop the next.

Then in one moment, one single moment, Tira, our neighbour, our sister, was torn from the earth.

Obliterated.

Even on a hillside in Kaftor I was thrown to the ground as the air was shaken by the greatest sound any man had ever heard. There was a dark shape on the horizon, expanding into the sky and in all directions about itself, a great cloud with fire flashing through it like the jagged barbs of lightning, and all the while the sound continued to boom and rumble, as though the air was crashing upon us in waves. An island. A country. Lands and farms on its back, towns and villages. Ports, woodlands, fields. All turned to flame and dust and stone in one terrible instant.

Maria had thrilled as she read each of the passages, sent to her at tantalisingly random intervals as Jerry's translation team made their unsteady progress. This narrator, whoever he had been, was describing a devastating caldera eruption, which fitted exactly the theories that had been hypothesised about Thera's destruction. More than that, the description actually divulged something further about the nature of the eruption than extant knowledge had been able to suggest. It indicated that the final explosion had been caused by the collapse of a giant magma chamber, as had happened at Krakatoa. The 'boiling of the sea' and the spontaneous retreat of the boats would have been created by billions of tons of seawater flooding into the chamber. Then, when that enormous body of water met an equally enormous supply of molten magma and turned instantly to steam, there suddenly wouldn't have been room for it all.

Hence, bang. Or more accurately, the biggest bang ever seen or heard on the planet.

But that – unprecedentedly destructive as it was – had been only the start. The real action would have got going about forty minutes later, when the largest seismic waves in history, or indeed prehistory, encountered the first thing in their path: Kaftor.

The last message she'd got from Jerry had been about two weeks ago to say that he was almost ready to send her 'the money shot', as he called it, mocking her ravenous impatience to see the passages depicting the flood. Ever since then she'd been scanning her e-mail for his name each morning before being disappointed and having to get on with what she was actually paid for.

Now, finally, it was here, and it didn't seem to matter. She sat staring at the blue and white envelope icon through tear-welling eyes, lacking the will even to move the mouse and open it. She didn't want to know what it contained. She'd far rather have two thirty-year-old adolescents standing behind her making dumb jokes about it instead.

Jesus.

It hurt. It hurt so much.

Maria knew there were some at CalORI who hadn't accepted it yet, who were holding out for a happy ending. Dreaming up crazy scenarios, torturing themselves with a desperate hope that had no greater foundation than the fact that no bodies had been found. She appreciated the tempting succour it offered, but appreciated also that that way madness lay. Like signing up to join the mothers of the disappeared.

Sandra Biscane's death last year had forced her to understand that terrible things do happen, that your worst fears do get realised, and the big question marks still hanging over that dreadful episode had made her that bit more ready to accept further tragedy. But she wasn't going to let her imagination run paranoid until all the facts were out in the open, any more than she was going to torment herself chasing the mirages of merest possibility.

53

Whatever had happened to them, it happened three hundred miles out in the world's biggest ocean. There would *be* no bodies. Only an endless absence.

No more Mitch, no more Cody, no more Coop, no more Taylor. No more all-night work-ins with longnecks and pizza. No more lunch-time two-on-two in the parking lot. No more discussions, no more arguments, no more falling-outs, no more making ups. No more dumb jokes.

Ironically, there had been a sense of impending doom in the air for a while before it happened, although *this* was hardly the outcome everyone had been afraid of. Nonetheless, there had been a pervasive feeling of time running out. That wasn't hindsight putting a spin on it, and it wasn't some stupid 1999 thing either. There had been a precariousness about the St John business from day one, and it had intensified in recent weeks. Maria hadn't been involved in the project herself, being four months into her own team's current study when it began, but it was CalORI's biggest undertaking in years, so it had infected the mood of the whole place.

Time running out. Or, more accurately, money running out. They were all just waiting for the financial plug to be pulled on the whole deal, and every day it didn't happen was a bonus.

Backing for ocean geological research tended to come from three main sources: oil companies, oil companies, and occasionally, if you were real lucky, oil companies. Coop and Cody had found stuff twelve layers down in sediment cores that dated more recently than the last known government cash, and with a vision as wide as Gingrich's (about two molecules; three tops) looking out from the public purse, that was unlikely to change. The government wouldn't spend two bits on any kind of research that didn't have a projected military or industrial application. It was as though they had decided we already know all the avenues the human race might ever need to go down; no time for the frivolities of the road less travelled-by. Jesus, girl, you might discover somethin' we can't monopolise, process, package and sell. And if we can't blow folks up with it, what in the hell are we s'posed to do with it?

As Mitch had put it, the money men don't window-shop. They know what they're in the research market to buy. They go to the petroleum geologists to buy 'where's the oil'.

Seismologists like him and Maria they approach looking for 'how can we stop this' or 'give us some notice'. Which was why he had spent so much time in Honolulu with the *tsunami* early-warning project.

The sort of 'pure research' exploration the *Gazes Also* was undertaking – and with those kind of resources – lay in the realms of what they called DBS. It was a cynical in-joke that had two definitions but one meaning: forget it.

Dream Benefactor Scenario.

Don't Be Stupid.

Except that it had happened. It happened to CalORI, right out of the proverbial blue. Admittedly, Luther St John was nobody's dream anything, except maybe cell-mate for Hannibal Lecter, but what the hell, his face wasn't on the banknotes. Mitch was the only one of them to have met the man, and his reluctance to discuss 'what he's really like' was palpable enough for everyone to quit asking.

They had all seen him on TV down the years, although obviously not on his own network: sentience tended to interfere with reception of the Christian Family Channel, perhaps the CFC most guilty of fucking up the atmosphere. He had kept a comparatively low mainstream-media profile in recent years, only sticking his head above the public parapet again in the past eighteen months or so, but everyone still remembered with great fondness his hugely entertaining Presidential bid in '92. Back in the Eighties he was so much the detested totem of religious ultra-conservatism that if he hadn't existed already, liberal students like Maria would have had to invent him. He functioned as a kind of anti-catechism: if you weren't sure where you stood on something, you just had to find out Luther's opinion and take a large step to the left. In latter years, though, he had been mainly a figure of fun, a laughable anachronism. As if rendered harmless by his humiliation, his opinions and pronouncements were now, to most, a source of amusement where they had once seemed an ugly threat. To most, but not to everyone.

Maria had read the *Vanity Fair* article last summer, tracking what its author, Gilda Landsmann (whose journalistic scrutiny had dogged St John for years), perceived to be a calculatedly strategic re-ascent towards the limelight. Landsmann said that when St John looked at you, as one outside his 'Communion

55

of the Saved', you could physically feel his revulsion, like a leper before a king.

Mitch disagreed. Revulsion was a kind of contempt, and contempt ran hot in the blood. When St John looked at you, it was with cold pity.

'He doesn't look at you like he hates you,' Mitch had told her. 'He looks at you like you're already dead.'

The fear that his patronage was too good to be true didn't survive the *Gazes Also*'s blank-cheque refit, far less St John's gift of the submarine *Stella Maris*, but it didn't quite die either. Instead it transubstantiated into the fear that it was too good to last, and each month, each *week*, brought in new rumours on the breeze.

As St John was a far from hands-on kind of sponsor, Mitch often seemed like the only link the institute had with him. This, of course, wasn't true. CalORI's accountants were in rigidly regular contact with St John's organisation, and the scientists' remoteness from the institute's bean counters – on a number of levels – was the wasteland where the winds of rumour whipped up. But Mitch – and only Mitch – was the guy who presented St John with the fruits of their labours and of his cash. St John wasn't exactly looking over their shoulders, but he took more than a passing interest in their work. His funding wasn't just some tax side-wind and it certainly wasn't a PR exercise. He genuinely wanted to know what was going on, enough to send a private jet to fly Mitch to and from Arizona to make his presentations.

Presentation being the keyword. Maria had watched Mitch work hours and days perfecting computer models of his findings, 3-D rotatable graphics of the sub-oceanic landscape, with animated demonstrations of the seismic and geological stages in that landscape's evolution: the fractures, trenches, plains, seamounts and guyots. He also knew how to pander to his audience, putting special emphasis on samples or developments that could be dated to coincide with biblical periods and events. This involved playing somewhat fast and loose with the error margins of several different dating systems, but Mitch figured if it kept his wallet open to hand the guy a test-tube of compressed shell fragments and tell him their former owners bought it around the same time as Solomon, why burst everybody's bubble?

Then St John's prophecy went top of the news.

They heard about it over the radio. Mitch's team were back on-shore at CalORI at the time. Under any other circumstances they'd have found it as hilarious as everyone else, but when the two-minute news item ended, no-one was laughing. They all saw the same ghastly eventuality.

There was no scientific basis in anything the *GA* had discovered, anything Mitch had presented, to support what St John was predicting. Fortunately, their research hadn't been cited, yet, but they all knew that if it was, or if the source of their funding was made public, they would be put bang on the spot and asked for their expert opinions. Which would come down to a straight choice between sacrificing all professionalism, dignity and future credibility on the altar of their paymaster, or declaring unequivocally to the nation that their benefactor was talking out of his ass.

Mitch had got on the phone straight away and demanded a meeting with St John, who was surprisingly happy to accommodate him. Mitch's insistence had alarmed the rest of his team, as they were still wondering what oil could be poured on this troubled water, but Mitch reasoned that they could not afford to sit around. Far better that he explain to St John what position they would be put in and what response they would have to give, than for the media to squeeze them for an answer first, and St John to hear them rubbish him over the airwaves with no prior warning.

Far better, true, but effectively just the difference between committing financial suicide and *politely* committing financial suicide.

The jet was dispatched that same afternoon, to convene a meeting that might have reassured everyone at CalORI if it hadn't clearly disturbed the hell out of Mitch.

'Don't worry,' St John had told him, in the back of his white stretch Caddy. 'I've no intention of putting you or your colleagues in an uncomfortable situation.' Mitch said St John spoke to you like he was reading from a prepared statement. There might be an opportunity for questions later, but definitely not until he had finished. Drink your water, sit comfortable and listen up. Press packs will be available on your way out.

'Let me assure you that I have not made and will not make

57

reference to your work or your organisation. Let me also assure you that my funding of the Institute remains an entirely confidential matter. I would not expect you to support my, ah, theories, from your strictly scientific perspective, but I can guarantee that no-one will approach you for such an opinion in direct connection with myself and my statements. If, by coincidence, you are questioned solely in your capacity as a seismologist – and I mean *a* seismologist, not *the* seismologist connected to the research I have supported – all I *would* ask is that you might do me the courtesy of making your excuses and being too busy to comment.'

Mitch knew his team could live with that. The odds were very long on himself or anyone else at CalORI ever having to cross that particular bridge. The networks and the news agencies already had their seismological rentaquote vacancies filled, especially in the Southland, where tremor discussion was practically a full-time job.

But there was one thing he had to know.

St John knew that what he was theorising was not supported by the *GA*'s findings, so if he wasn't planning to make reference to the team's research . . .

'Mr Kramer,' he told him, 'you are correct in saying that your *findings* do not support my theory, but I believe that your research does. Now, I'm not going to present your research to anybody, *anybody*. Don't you worry about that. The difference between you and me is that I'm not trying to prove a scientific point. This isn't about science, Mr Kramer, this is about faith. If I could present a catalogue of evidence that scientifically proved the threat of what I've predicted, people would believe it, but they'd believe it because they could explain it all away, account for it within their rules, their *indifferent* values. They could weigh up the probabilities, decide whether to ship out, make plans, contingencies. It'd be their rational response to a rationally evaluated possibility. But I'm not saying this is going to happen because *science* has told me so. So even if your findings did support what I'm saying, it would be you and not me who would be taking it to the networks.

'You look at this research with your scientific mind, seeing how it fits your scientific models and your scientific laws, and within that framework, sure, there's nothing to substantiate what I have foretold. We both look at these rocks, these mountains and plains beneath the ocean, and you see the work of nature, Mr Kramer. The physicality, the facts, the equations, the history, the development. You understand that, you and your people, you understand those things well, to a sophistication far beyond what an ordinary man could comprehend. That's your gift. But I see the work of God, and that's mine.'

Then he had looked Mitch in the eye and said: 'We're two men from different fields approaching the same body of research, the same raw materials. I would not pretend to intrude upon your area of expertise, Mr Kramer. Do not presume to intrude upon mine.'

Maria had been called in to authenticate the content of the scrolls' later passages, but if anyone doubted the accuracy of the texts that preceded them, she reckoned Jerry should just wheel out Luther St John as exhibit A.

The big myth about the Minoans was that they were like some kind of prehistoric flower-power people, beating their swords into jewellery, lounging around pastoral idylls and generally being beautiful. There was a bit of that going on, sure, but when you're at the heart of the world's biggest trading empire, expanded and defended by the world's most powerful fleet, you can spend your leisure time how you like. The Minoans built their empire on two foundations: unrivalled cultural advancement and unmatched maritime prowess. Baubles and trinkets, yeah, and if you fucked with them, they sealed your fate. They loved colour and spectacle, but they were obsessed with blood. They took time and pleasure in their costume but they dressed to kill. Art and savagery, aesthetics and violence. Were they contradictory or symbiotic?

Often have I wondered, watching the rhytons being filled in sacrifice from a quaking beast's throat, would we do the same were it a cold, clear water that issued forth, and not this liquid jewel, this decorative prize? For in Kaftor, colour delights us, and while we may honour gods, we worship beauty. It is in the finery of our metals, the attentive hours with hammer and flame, the patient hewing of stone, the deft dance of weaving, that our true devotion, our true religion, is to be found. And

in its dark reflection is the wish to paint in gushing streams
of a precious red.

Finery and brutality. Beauty and blood. Certainly there
was a tension between the two, and according to the scrolls
it lay at the centre of a great turmoil during those final,
earthquake-haunted days. There were those who saw their
compatriots as effete and decadent, spending too much time
making new shiny playthings and looking in the mirror when
they could be out kicking new, undiscovered asses with their
warships. Kind of like a bronze-age Republican Party.

Poteidan is angry, Damanthys tells us, and by coincidence
Poteidan is angry about the self-same things of which Damanthys
disapproves. What, then, can save us? Surely only to live our lives
as Damanthys would prescribe . . .
Plus ça change.

Maria almost jumped out of her chair when she felt a hand on
her shoulder, her reaction giving Chico an equally big fright.
'Shit, sorry Maria,' he said, putting a hand on his chest.
'Guess you were pretty far away.'
Maria looked at the monitor. It still showed the envelope
icon, unopened. She didn't know how long she'd been staring
blankly at the computer screen. The screen-saver was set to
kick in after half an hour, so it was less than that, but she
suspected not by much.
'Wish I was, Chico. But I'm here, so what's up?'
The lab technician sat down on the worktop a few feet from
her computer.
'Got a phone call. From the Coast Guard. They want . . . I
mean, they said it can wait until somebody's . . . They want
someone to take a look around the *Gazes*, see if anything's –
I dunno – not as it should be. Maybe help figure out what
happened.'
She nodded.
'I mean, I'd go, but I don't know the boat so good and I'm
not sure that I'd be able to . . .'
'It's okay, Chico. I'll do it.'
'They said just as soon as somebody feels up to it, you
know? You don't have to . . .'

'I'll go this afternoon,' she said, telling herself more than him. 'I'm not gonna be much use around here anyway.'

'You sure you're gonna be all right?'

She nodded again, trying to give him a smile.

'Can I get you anything?' he asked. 'A Coke maybe?'

'Got any morphine?'

'Not today.'

'Coke'll be fine. Thanks, Chico.'

Maria sighed and sat back in her seat, running both hands through her hair for the hundredth time. Keep this up and she was going to look like something out of a metal video. She took hold of the mouse and shut down the database program. She wasn't going to get any work done today, why pretend?

Chico came back and handed her a cold can from the machine. She opened it, took a sip and double-clicked on the envelope.

five

'Save the world,' it said.

Or rather, he thought it said. It was only as Steff neared the corner that he could see the remainder of the banner, which ran perpendicular to the first part along the high fence.

There hadn't been a parking space to be found in Santa Monica. This had come as little surprise as there hadn't been a hotel room to be found either. It had soon reached the stage where Steff felt embarrassed asking at the desks, like it wasn't enough that he was a big, weird-looking guy from *way* out of town with a funny accent, he had to advertise his ignorance by the gaucherie of asking for a room in Santa Monica *this* week. He wondered if the hotel management courses in Californian colleges actually tested candidates on that 'of course not, you fucking idiot' look they all gave you.

'This is going to sound like a daft question,' he had said at the last place, 'with the AFFM going on this week and everything, but would you happen to have any free rooms?'

The girl at that particular reception desk had been more courteous than the others. Perhaps making an open declaration of being an arse meant they didn't feel so obliged to point it out to you.

'I'm sorry, sir,' she said with an apologetic smile. 'And most years it wouldn't be such a dumb question. The AFFM doesn't usually fill us up, but with this Festival of Light thing happening at the same time, we're just bursting at the seams.'

'Festival of Light? What's that?'

'I don't know, myself. I just heard a lot of the guests say that's why they're in town.'

He had called Jo Mooney for advice, and she suggested he backtrack to West Hollywood, which was only a half-hour along Santa Monica Boulevard depending on traffic, and, she assured him, 'a lot more fun'. She had recommended he try the Armada, near the junction with La Cienega. It was a huge pink affair, vaguely suggestive of an aircraft hangar. He had walked into the antiseptically tasteful lobby in the late afternoon, when the place appeared to be deserted, and booked a room. By the time he had unpacked, showered and shaved, darkness had fallen with a speed he'd really need to get used to. Back home, dusk could be a process of slow hours and changing colours. Here, it was like someone just reached up and switched off the sun.

It was when he wandered downstairs to check out the hotel bar that he realised the guest register probably included zero females and one heterosexual (Kennedy, S.).

Jo Mooney, he decided, had less than twenty-four hours to live.

He had driven in from West Hollywood, his route taking him past the Beverly Hills signs and that avenue of palm trees so familiar from TV, depicted always as a gateway to mythical splendour. Unfortunately there was fuck-all at the end of it, just more grey tarmac, glass towers and shopping malls. He had felt a wee tingle upon catching sight of that building from *Die Hard*, right enough. It was south of the road he was on, and it had just peeked into view for a moment as he drove through a crossroads. He thought he should go and check it out close up at some point, then decided that would spoil it. Better for it to have winked at him as he passed, like a girl in the street who might have nothing to say to him if he actually stopped to talk.

After an hour of circling Santa Monica's town centre, he had finally spotted a neon parking sign with the *Spaces* part lit up underneath. It turned out to be a shopping mall, and it was going to cost him about eight dollars to leave the hire car there all day unless he was 'validated', which he took to be a euphemism for 'spent enough money'. This didn't work out quite so badly as he feared, as it provided a fine excuse to have a quorate five dollars' worth of hamburgers for breakfast.

Then he had walked down towards the ocean, unmolested by the constabulary this time, Santa Monica apparently not having outlawed Shanks's Pony as a form of transport. Up in Hollywood, the words pedestrian and pederast didn't just sound alike: they invited comparable disdain.

The big banner was clearly a gimmick. You saw it from a

distance, 'Save the world', then the punchline was delivered when you reached the corner: 'from our sins'. Boom boom.

He had heard the music from about a block back, the sound of a crowd and the smells of outdoor catering carrying through the air. A lot like a summer fairground down the local public park, except without the three feet of mud and the twelve-year-olds smoking menthols and demanding money with menaces. The architectural acid trip that was the Pacific Vista sat across the road, about two hundred yards away, looking from Steff's angle like a big engagement ring: a giant glinting jewel flanked by opaque bands on either side. Draped banners with understated colour schemes and a tidy logo announced that the 1999 AFFM was taking place there.

Opposite, markedly less understated banners announced that the 1999 Festival of Light was taking place there. They announced also the presence of something called the American Legion of Decency, and advertised that a Mission of Purity was being undertaken, as well as, of course, urging onlookers to 'save the world from our sins'.

He figured the banners' authors were (just a mite presumptuously) including the entire global population in the ranks of the implied sinners, rather than just those attending the Festival of Light. The possibility of any such ironic interpretation of 'our' was unlikely to have occurred to them; or if it had, they were probably confident that it wouldn't occur to their target audience.

Steff checked his watch. He had a loose arrangement to meet up with Jo 'around lunch-time' – a less specific time frame it was almost impossible to define. He was supposed to give her a call on her mobile when he got inside the Pacific Vista, and they'd take it from there. It was half eleven. He grinned to himself and popped open a new tub of film. Time enough to find Jesus.

He paid five dollars at the gate, trying not to think about what ideologically distasteful project he might be indirectly funding, and had a date stamped on the back of his hand, allowing him to 'just walk right in and out, many times as you like, all day'. He resisted asking the Colgate advert who had taken his money whether it counted towards the validation of any future parking tickets, and 'just walked right in'.

It was worse than the Barras. He estimated there were close

to three thousand people thronging the place, an area about the size of the pitch at Fir Park. There was no doubt room for more, but the sense of constant motion as the crowd moved around the stalls and platforms gave the impression of a greater host. The comparison with Glasgow's famous market ended with the teeming bustle of the place. For a start, by some meteorological phenomenon, it was always raining when you went to the Barras, and the resultant smell of two thousand damp jackets in a confined space was just one of the olfactory delights the experience offered. The clientele were a little different, too. The Festival of Light was like a Californian shininess convention. It was easy to believe he was the only person in the enclosure who had ever farted.

The omnipresent Barras paranoia of having your pocket picked was unlikely to set in either: Steff felt pretty confident of being the poorest person present. All around him were shiny adults dragging along shiny kids, miraculously born of these shiny parents who simply looked far too wholesome ever to have shagged. More disturbingly, there were shiny teens and shiny adolescents in attendance of their own free will, in blatant defiance of the aeons of evolution that dictated they should be out getting pissed on sweet cider, or locked in their bedrooms wanking themselves to death.

Once he started moving around the place, he was able to glean some idea of the format. The crowd, seemingly amorphous upon first impression, was in fact divided up into groups around each stall or platform, with a rectangular hub of food and drink stands in the centre of the concourse. On closer inspection, he saw that some of the canopied stalls were actually entrances to tents, inside which a selection of meetings and activities was taking place, from biblical puppet shows to your basic, bog-standard sermonising. At the far end there was a wide stage, raised about seven feet, upon which stood a small choir singing excruciatingly hoaky countrified hymns to the accompaniment of a woman strumming a steel guitar, which Steff thought should be confiscated with the instruction that she'd get it back when she had learned what such a fine instrument should really be used for. Behind the choir, the world's cleanest-looking roadie was assembling a drum kit.

Steff felt a blow to the ribs and looked down to see a

face-painted child reel away dazed, now moving with less rabid enthusiasm towards the candy floss stall, or 'Manna on a Stick', as it was advertised.

'So-rreee,' said Mrs Stepford, giving Steff a big, empty smile and hugging another child, whose face had been painted red with a white cross in the middle. Steff looked down at his grey T-shirt. Stepford Junior had imprinted half the stars and stripes on it.

'We'll get Tommy back to do the other half – save you buyin' a flag,' said Dad.

Steff felt deeply privileged to have been present when this, the world's funniest remark, was made. One day he would be able to tell his grandchildren, and they theirs. It was surely only the distractions of such dreamy thoughts that prevented him from collapsing in uncontrolled laughter just like Mr and Mrs S. He settled instead for clicking off a few shots while their faces were really contorted. It was silly and childish, he knew, but then so was the Festival of Light.

'God bless you,' they said, moving off, still laughing, in the direction of Manna on a Stick and the adjacent Bibleburgers on a Good Book Bun.

'Amen,' Steff said, grinning. This was fun.

'Let me tell *you* about the information superhighway,' said a voice. He turned around to see that it had come from one of the stalls, where an adolescent male in a 'True Love Waits' T-shirt was standing on a platform beside a cardboard fake computer. Steff moved a little nearer, to the back of the small gathering, around which the skinny blonde True Love the speaker was presumably Waiting for was handing out accompanying leaflets.

'Imagine it. All the information in the world, at your finger-tips,' he said. 'Everything you need to know, everything you *could* ever need to know for living on this planet, at your immediate disposal. Sounds like the privilege of an advanced age, doesn't it? Wrong! We've had it for nearly two *thousand* years. All the wisdom, all the knowledge, all the understanding you could possibly want, all readily accessible, right here.' He held up, with cringeworthy inevitability, a copy of a well-known religious publication. Five letters. Starts with a B.

'Forget the Net,' he shouted triumphantly. 'Surf the Bible!'

Steff lowered his head and retreated. He felt a mixture of embarrassment on the poor bloke's behalf and vague guilt at deriving vicarious amusement from watching him. There but for the grace of – well, you know. He wandered off and joined the queue at a refreshment stall. 'Sin-free sodas,' the sign advertised. 'No sugar, no caffeine and no alcohol – because you've got enough spirit *within*.'

'Jesus . . .' he said in involuntary response, drawing an interrogatory look from the woman behind the counter, '. . . eh, would be so proud if He could see us all here today,' he added, hoping his cover wasn't irretrievably blown.

'Jesus *can* see us. Jesus *is* here,' she told him. Her face had brightened a little but Steff still wasn't sure if what she said was an assurance or a rebuke. He bought a caffeine-free Diet Coke and ambled over to a shaded bench to drink it. What he had really fancied was a can of Irn-Bru. He knew you couldn't get it in the States, but reckoned even if you could they wouldn't be flogging it here. It was a soft drink that had built its reputation on consoling Glaswegians the morning after their crimes of fleshly indulgence, most satisfy-ingly consumed in bed with a stinking headache while better citizens were out at church. Jesus would have liked Irn-Bru, Steff reckoned. It was an unjudgemental friend to sinners, helping and comforting them as they strove to overcome the wrongs of their recent past and return to society.

'It's a cool scene, huh?' suggested a voice, inviting his agreement. Two kids – definitely an item – in True Love Waits T-shirts had sat themselves down opposite. They both looked about seventeen, bright-eyed, attractive and energetic, all of which was a hell of a waste, given the slogan. Steff hoped the guy who had spoken was just naturally outgoing; otherwise that meant he had been looking vacant enough to pass for one of them.

'Yeah,' he said, smiling back.

'Where you here from?' asked the girl, taking time out from going cross-eyed as she tried to focus on the hairs she was blowing upwards away from her brow.

'I was just passing by. Thought I'd check out what was going on.'

'You impressed?'

'I'm flabbergasted.' Which was no less than the truth.

'You're from out of town, right?' she said. 'You got a weird accent. Where is that?'

'The People's Republic of Motherwell. It's just south of Scandinavia.'

'Oh, cool. We're from Wichita Falls, here for the whole week. We won the trip watching CFC. Gordy's mom pledged a thousand dollars, which got us into the quiz, then Gordy's Bible knowledge did the rest.'

Gordy chucked her bashfully on the shoulder. 'With a little help from someone too modest to say,' he laughed.

'A whole week?' Steff asked, trying to prevent his tone from adding, 'Are you out of your fucking minds?'

'Oh sure, it's a great programme they got, ain't it, Sally?' Gordy said, pulling a glossy brochure from his canvas satchel. 'Look, there's different events here every day. Different speakers in all the booths, new activities, and all kinds of attractions on the big stage. Plus there's stuff at night around town, too.'

'Yeah,' added Sally. 'Like, the Believers are doing a show in Santa Monica tomorrow night. And there's the Stand Up for Christ comedy bill at the Open Mike Club on day four.'

'Things are only getting started,' Gordy assured him. 'Today is just sort of a welcome event. The real action'll get going after that. We got campaigning workshops, protest co-ordination seminars . . . The Festival of Light is kind of like a launch party for the Mission of Purity. The Legion of Decency is ready to get serious.'

'About what?' Steff asked, growing slightly concerned. Anyone or anything so much in approval of Purity and Decency was unlikely to be much in approval of him. He kept having images of a six-foot seven-inch stake surrounded by kindling.

'You don't know?' Gordy asked incredulously. 'Oh, but then I guess you don't get CFC where you come from.'

'Afraid not,' Steff said, trying to sound profoundly regretful. It wasn't strictly true, he thought. There was a CFC back home, and it was watched every week, mainly by Catholics. There was an RFC too, watched by Protestants. And it was true to say that both of them were never off the fucking TV. But as explaining the relationship between religious sectarianism and the Celtic and Rangers football clubs of Glasgow was not something he wanted to get into with Gordy, he left it at that. 'Tell me all about it, maybe I can sign up,' he prompted.

'Oh, you gotta, man, you gotta,' Gordy enthused. 'It's nineteen ninety-nine, you know, the signs are all around. The omens are everywhere. We're on our last warning. The Lord's getting ready to call time-out on us, and we've gotta prove we can clean up our act before it's too late. But it's like, the nearer we get to the end of this century, the more sin and godlessness there is, and the less people seem to worry about it. So much homosexuality, prostitution, abortion, promiscuity, atheism. The human race can't go breaking God's rules so flagrantly and not expect to be punished.'

It was Steff's guess that this spiel wasn't entirely Gordy's own words, more likely something he'd heard on this CFC shite. He looked a bright enough kid, but terms like 'flagrantly' probably didn't pop up in too many of his normal conversations.

'That's what the Mission of Purity is all about,' he continued. 'For evil to triumph, good men must do nothing, right? So it's not enough for people like us' – Steff was flattered by Gordy's inclusive hand gesture – 'just to obey the rules. We've gotta do what we can to stop the sinning. We've gotta protest, we've gotta campaign. We've gotta educate people because they've forgotten what's right and what's wrong.'

'And the worst of it is how many sins are *legal* and therefore condoned in this country,' Sally added. 'Abortion is legal, sodomy's legal in some states, atheism's legal, pornography's legal. What must God think of America now when He sees that?'

'We've got to remind people about God's rules before we've outraged Him so much that He destroys us all,' explained Gordy. 'And it's not like He hasn't warned us that He's upset. Look at AIDS – how big a hint do you need? But people still didn't listen, so now He's getting ready to talk a little louder.'

'How d'you mean?'

'There's just so much weird stuff going on, man. Strange phenomena. Unexplained occurrences. Folks try and tell you it's aliens or it's government conspiracies, stupid stuff like that, but they're just fooling themselves.'

'Yeah,' Steff agreed. 'It's amazing how gullible some people can be.'

'Darn right. It's God getting ready to rock'n'roll, I'm telling you. They laughed at the Reverend St John in this city when he warned them, but he had seen the signs, and they won't be laughing when the tidal wave hits. Then after that, we gotta spread the Word against the clock, because if this world doesn't start some serious repenting . . . it's over, man.'

Steff was confused. 'Hang on, were you talking metaphorically when you mentioned a tidal . . .'

But neither Gordy nor Sally was listening any more. There had been a loud, crackling sound from the stacked PA speakers either side of the main stage, and Sally had looked up first then gripped Gordy's shoulder to draw his attention.

'Oh-my-God-oh-my-God! I don't be*lieve it*!' she screamed, suddenly standing up on the bench.

'You gotta be kidding me! You gotta be kidding me!' Gordy yelled. Then the two of them grabbed each other, laughing and shrieking, punching the air and clapping.

'Yeeeeaaaaah!'

'All right!'

The air filled with cheering, like Jesus had scored the winner in the last minute of the Moral Cup Final against the Godless Gay Abortionist Prostitute Pornographers XI.

Steff twisted around on the bench and looked back over his shoulder at the stage. All around the Festival, people were pouring from tents and stalls to congregate in front of the main platform, where four shaggy-headed youths had ambled up mock-bashfully behind a white-suited, middle-aged man who was holding the microphone stand, beckoning the crowd's attention. Gordy and Sally had clocked the scene ahead of the announcement now being made, and were clearly initiants into whatever rite was about to be executed.

'. . . *very* special surprise for you all today,' the man in the white suit was saying. 'They're playing in town this week as part of the Festival of Light's programme of evening events, but they've come down here RIGHT NOW just to see how it's all going, and – what d'you say, guys? – maybe play a coupla tunes?'

The shaggy heads nodded and shrugged, in a hopelessly choreographed-looking display of nonchalance. The crowd roared approval, few as loud as Steff's soft-drinking buddies. Many of them were making a Cross sign with their forefingers, holding their arms in the air. It was like a well-brought-up cousin of that daft carry-on with the forefinger and the pinkie that metalheads did.

'Ladies and gentlemen, I know these young men need no introduction, but I'm gonna do it anyway 'cause it's such an honour to have them here. They're currently top of the charts on K-ROS Christian Radio, and tomorrow night's show will be going out as a special on the Christian Music Channel – so if you couldn't get a ticket, set your VCRs for that one. Here they are, America's number one Christian band: THE BELIEVERS!'

Steff stood up and faced the stage. This he just had to see, with plane-crash fascination. He suspected the on-going history of rock'n'roll was about to witness a particularly unbecoming development.

The Believers looked to Steff like what you might get if you put the Ramones into a big washing machine for maybe half a dozen cycles, then tumbled them dry and ironed them. They had managed to affect a jeans'n'leather look that you could confidently take home to meet your granny; and they looked like they would smell of fabric conditioner up close. Rock bands, as a rule, shouldn't really smell of fabric conditioner. Fags, blow, whisky, spew, engine oil maybe. Not Lenor. Steff understood: they wanted to look *baaad*, but they were fundamentalist Christians, so there was kind of a conflict-of-interest problem. In short, they represented a Disney illustrator's idea of a rock group.

'Okay, how y'all doin' out there Santa Monica?' barked the lead shaggy, plugging in his guitar lead with one hand and gripping the mike stand with the other. He growled out his words in a rapid, throaty staccato. The crowd roared.

'All-right-everybody-here-I-wanna-hear-you-say-praise-the-Lord.'

'Praise the Lord,' the crowd screamed.

'One-more-time-wanna-hear-you-say-praise-the-Lord.'

'Praise the Lord.'

'One-more-time.'

'Praise the Lord.'

'One-more-time.'

'Praise the Lord.'

'One-more-time.'

71

'Praise the Lord.'

'All-a-right-a-one-two-three-four-one-two-three-hup!'

Then they started playing.

Oh dear. Oh dear oh dear oh dear.

Since its beginnings it had been said in America that rock'n'roll was the music of Satan. Steff always thought that was fair enough, given that for centuries longer it had been said back home in Scotland that 'the de'il has aw the best tunes'. the Believers obviously could not be playing the music of Satan, and although the beat, chord structures and arrangements matched the standard criteria, it would be folly to describe what they were doing as rock'n'roll.

From what Steff could make out, their opening number was supposed to be a bitterly sarcastic protest song about the teaching of evolution theory in American high schools. It was only when Shaggies two through four joined in for the chorus that the lyrics became intelligible.

> 'Me I ain't no MONKEY MAN!
> 'Cause God made me just AS I AM!
> Diiiiivine, deeeesign,
> Me I ain't no MONKEY MAN!'

Listening closely to the machine-gun vocals, he was able to interpret from the ensuing verses that Charles Darwin was currently being made to pay a heavy price for his heresy in a location a lot hotter than the Galapagos Islands; and that he would inevitably be joined by those foolish enough to 'fail the dinosaur test'. This last, he guessed, must be in reference to the fundamentalists' explanation for hundred-million-year-old bones being found on a planet they claimed to have existed for no more than twelve thousand years; viz, that God had placed them there as a test of faith.

Then they launched into an attemptedly thrashy affair called 'Exit Only', an instruction to homosexual males as to the exclusive function of the anus. Steff felt he ought to defer to superior knowledge on this one: if anybody was an expert on arseholes, it had to be the singer up on that stage.

Gordy and Sally clearly had the album. They were singing along to each track, saving special enthusiasm for air-punching bridges or favourite lyrics, such as 'Forty jalapeños and an X-Lax bar/Soon teach 'em what their ass is for: EXIT ONLY! EXIT ONLY! EXIT ONLY! Na-na-na-na-na, EXIT ONLY . . .' and so on. Steff took the couple's picture as they danced and sang, a delightful image of young, smiling, innocent faces, happily and energetically chanting words of ignorant bigotry and blind hatred.

Next up was the inevitable power ballad, in which the Believers betrayed their formative listening years to have been coloured less by speed metal than by Speedwagon. It was, Steff gleaned from Sally, the title track of their new double-CD, 'True Love Waits', a plodding power-chord symphony about two dreamy teens resisting the temptations of pre-marital sex and reaping the rewards on wedding night with the shag of the century. This was definitely a new low: a rock band exhorting their fans *not* to get into each other's pants.

In a gleefully morbid way, Steff was now starting to enjoy it. There was an element of suspense about seeing just how bad it could get. He would have to get a tape of these guys to take home: stick this stuff on the stereo after a few spliffs and everyone in the room would be pissing themselves for hours.

Unfortunately, his pleasure was cut short when he realised that a bleeping noise nearby was actually the mobile phone Jo had loaned him.

'Hello?'

'Steff. Where the hell are you? What's that noise? Are you in a bar?'

'Eh, no. In fact I may be in the spot furthest from a bar on this planet, morally speaking.'

'Huh?'

'I'm across the road. I'm attending the Festival of Light. We're all rockin' out to the Believers.'

'Are you serious? What the hell are you doing there?'

'I'm having fun.' Steff caught Sally's smile as she overheard. He smiled back, holding her eye as he spoke to Jo. 'No, honestly. You should check this place out.' More smiles and a cross sign. 'I've not seen so many stupid people in one place since I covered a Celtic–Rangers match last year.'

No more smiles. Sally looked like Steff had shat on the table.

'Still, you can have too much of a good thing,' he decided,

still smiling as Sally looked away and prodded Gordy's shoulder to get his attention. 'Where are you?'

'Waves Café. It's in the atrium. First floor. That's ground floor to you.'

Sally was filling in Gordy on developments. He didn't look pleased.

'See you in five,' Steff said, hanging up.

'Can't say we appreciate your attitude.' Gordy scowled.

'Then forgive me.'

Gordy didn't get it.

Steff feared his retinas had been fried by the blaze of refracted sunlight that dazzled him as he approached the Pacific Vista's main entrance. By the time he made it to the shade of the awnings over the front door, his pupils had contracted like an arsehole in a prison shower, and he was able to make out no more than an outline of the person examining his laminated press pass before gesturing him inside. Visibility improved in the spectacular lobby, but the wobbly shapes the light picked out around the place didn't particularly assist his foot–eye co-ordination. Further impeding his progress was the compulsion to look upwards rather than at where he was going. He had never seen interior light like it, the massive prism crowned by a transparent pool of water. It wasn't long before he started bumping into people, which in the fundamentalist Angelino code of personal-space etiquette seemed a mortal sin. The bumpees looked at him with the sort of disgust he'd previously thought reserved for those caught buggering small furry animals on the back lot of a children's TV show. He said sorry, but suspected that didn't cover it.

The Waves Café was on the far right, its interior disappearing under the gallery level, with a terrace area at the front, roped off from the sprawling lobby and the terrace of the snack bar next door by arcing gold cords. Jo was sitting at a table by the wall, facing two young men in big trousers, both no doubt duped into this sartorial ruse by a recognised designer name somewhere on the inside waistband; or chestband might be nearer the mark. He could see a small tape recorder next to the bottles of this month's *de rigueur* mineral-water brand, and a notepad in Jo's lap. She sat nearest the wall with her elbow resting on stone and her hand behind her head, nodding occasionally as one of the trouser brothers spoke. Without taking her eyes off her subject, she rippled her fingers in the air behind her head, letting Steff know she had seen him.

He had been stretching his imagination since last night to dream up some form of revenge upon her for the Armada, but resolved on reflection that simply not mentioning it whatsoever might be the cutest tactic. He climbed over the cord and took a seat at the next table, placing his camera down gently on the metal surface.

Both of the trouser brothers turned to look at the new arrival, and were visibly outraged that the hotel's security had been sufficiently lax to allow this affront into their vicinity. He might have had an accreditation, but he simply did not look the part. His jeans fitted him, for starters. A waitress breezed by, and Steff ordered a bottle of Dos Equis (the nearest thing he could get to McEwan's Export; it was dark and rough) in a near-whisper, diligently earwigging the conversation on his right.

'And was there British subsidy money for this?' Jo was asking.

One of the brothers laughed dismissively. 'You must be joking,' he said, in that polished but regionally rootless RP accent. 'Compared to the rest of Europe there's so little in the way of public cash for film-making in the UK, and despite my first film's reception, the coffers remained tightly closed when I came calling.'

'But you received funding from UK public sources for your first film.'

'Yes, *The Lace Parasol* did receive financial assistance from the National Lottery,' he replied.

'And you say it was well received.'

'Indeed,' he insisted, pointing at Jo with his mineral-water bottle. 'It was invited to seven festivals across Europe, including Deauville. And the critics were most impressed.'

'Yes,' cut in his companion in the sort of French accent that provoked invasions. 'The *Guardian*, the *Telegraph*, the *Observer* – all these newspapers acclaimed it.'

Christ, Steff thought. Trevor Trouser and Pierre Pantalon.

'So how'd it do at the box office?'

The trouser brothers looked a little sheepish.

'Well, we did not tie up deals for theatrical distribution in many territories,' admitted Pierre. 'Although rights are still available.'

'But it ran for three weeks at the Ecran in London,' Trevor added. 'That's good going. The rest of the UK . . . well, it's a dead loss. Total Philistines, but then what can you expect? *The Lace Parasol*'s champagne taste was hardly going to appeal to an audience reared on popcorn.'

'So, the funding bodies were reluctant to back you again for *Hampstead Reflections*,' Jo prompted. 'That must have been very frustrating for you.'

'Pfff!' sighed Pierre.

'Unbelievable,' Trevor muttered. 'This funding . . . It's supposed to subsidise *art*. The box-office return should be irrelevant. It is the artistic achievement that matters. If anything, public subsidy should be used to support films that crude market forces would not tolerate. Otherwise, how can British cinema contribute to British culture?'

'Well,' said Jo, 'some might argue – and I'm just playing devil's advocate here – that public money should be spent on subsidising films that the public actually wants to see.'

'And I would counter,' Trevor stated, 'that only by subsidising films like *The Lace Parasol* is there any chance of educating the public about cinema, teaching them to appreciate it as an art-form, not a latterday music hall.'

'*Oui*,' said Pierre. 'But at the same time, who can know what the British public will want to see? They may not have responded to *The Lace Parasol*, but ironically, *Hampstead Reflections*, made without British money, has attracted big offers for video rights in the UK.'

'Really?'

'Yes,' Trevor confirmed. 'We've got two very large deals on the table, and not from small-time art-house labels either. Major distributors. And that is because the public *can* be made to appreciate art as well as car chases and explosions. '

Steff could take no more. Jo was being, well, if not misled, not entirely informed.

'These UK video offers,' he interrupted, drawing looks of mixed incredulity and sheer horror from the TBs, 'they wouldn't have anything to do with Annabel Greer getting her kit off in the film at all, would they?'

'What?' squawked Trevor. 'Who is this person?' he demanded of Jo. 'Do you know him?'

'Steff Kennedy,' Steff said, leaning over and offering a hand to shake. No-one took it. 'I'm a photographer. Mind if I snap you guys for *Cinema Scope*?'

'Yes we do,' Trevor said, getting up. 'I'm sorry, Ms Mooney, this interview is over.'

And off they stormed.

Jo had her elbows on the table, and her head, which was resting in her hands, shook convulsively. Looked like big sobs.

'Whoops. Guess I hit a wee bit of a nerve,' Steff said, by way of apology. Jo seemed both a likeable and formidable character; he wasn't sure whether his remorse was motivated by regret at upsetting her or fear of consequences. She'd set him up with that gay hotel for nothing – what might she do to him if she was really fucked off?

Jo looked up. There were tears in her eyes, but not of distress. She tried to speak then buried her head in her hands once more. This time peals of uncontrollable laughter escaped from her mouth. Steff breathed again.

Eventually she recovered sufficiently to ask who Annabel Greer was.

'She's a nubile British soap starlet. Had half the country's teens and adolescents crying themselves – and other things – to sleep at night. But she left the series to have a crack at becoming a "proper" actress. First gig was this wanky film.'

'So how do you know she's got a nude scene?'

'Because those two arseholes leaked it to the tabloids to generate interest in their shitey movie. Only reason anybody's going to want to see it. If they hadn't shot the crow like that you could have asked whether it's getting a theatrical release anywhere. Short answer, no. Or whether it's got a video deal anywhere else in the world. Again, no. The only reason it's got video offers is because the market for *Hampstead Reflections* consists entirely of *Manor Park* fans who want to see wee Annabel's tits.'

'Did you recognise the two of them?' Jo asked.

'No. I just realised who they were when they mentioned the titles. The Brit's the director, right?'

'Oliver Harris, with Jean-Jacques Mercaud, the producer.'

Steff shrugged his shoulders. 'Sorry I blew your interview.

I just had to say something. I've got a low pretentiousness threshold.'

'Well you'd better beef it up some if you're gonna hang out here. I'll cut you some slack on this one because that was funny, but I'd appreciate it if you kept to the camera from here on in.'

'I'll do my best.'

'You better.' Jo smiled. 'Those won't be the only assholes round here trying to sell tits'n'ass and pretending it's something profound. Just wait till Maddy Witherson breezes in for her promotional appearances.'

'Who she?'

'Whoah, you ain't from round here, are ya boy? Well, I guess the story didn't really travel. In short, she's sorta this year's Divine Brown. Porno actress who's moving into more respectable roles – although that's debatable. It's my theory the porn flicks had more honest integrity than the trash she'll be doing now. You know, "erotic thrillers". Like that.' Jo pointed to a poster adorning a partition screen in the lobby, one similar to dozens on shameless display around the concourse. *Preying Mantis II: Love Kills*, it said, below a hazy silhouette of a naked female holding a knife above the man she was straddling. 'Four or five soft-lit, soft-core sex scenes strewn around a low-rent serial-killer plot,' Jo explained. 'Sells mainly to cable channels. It's jerk-off material for travelling businessmen in hotel rooms who want to watch a dirty movie but don't want to *admit* they're watching a dirty movie.'

'So why's this Maddy Whatsit in the limelight?' Steff asked. 'Who'd she screw?'

'Maddy Witherson. It's not who she screwed, it's who she's related to. Her father's *Senator* Witherson, Republican, ultra-conservative, fundamentalist Christian, usual profile.'

'Golly gosh.'

'Like I said, big story. Little else on the news here *that* month, let me tell you. Of course the biggest irony is that the son-of-a-bitch's poll ratings have gone *up*. Seems a lot of parents out there understand how it feels to have a kid go off the rails despite your best efforts – at least, that's the spin. What can I say? We're a very screwed-up nation.'

'And young Maddy's in town for the AFFM?'

'Photocall right here at the Pacific Vista, Mr Kennedy. That accreditation badge'll get you close as you like. Course, that's if you're not too busy with your religious friends across the street. What were you doing there, boy?'

'Seeking to be tutored in the ways of righteousness,' he said with a grin. 'But I think I'm beyond redemption.'

'So what are they up to?'

'Well, allowing for cultural misinterpretation on my part, it looks like they're all revving up for some kind of moral crusade. Those are quite popular back home in Blighty, usually when a government is in the advanced stages of ideological bankruptcy and needs to blame somebody else. So do you know what this American Legion of Decency is?'

Jo shrugged. 'Not really. Far as I've heard it's just another vehicle for Luther St John to preach about the errors of our ways. I know he's the one bankrolling the little party out front there.'

Steff took a slug of his beer. 'Once again, forgive my foreigner's ignorance. Who is this Luther St John bloke anyway?'

'TV evangelist. One of the biggest. Owns the Christian Family Channel, among other things. Used to be more of a mainstream public figure once upon a time, but he's pretty much been preaching to his own converted on CFC since running for President in 'ninety-two.'

'That's *him*?' Steff said, surprised. 'The Texan guy?'

'No, you're thinking of Ross Perot. St John ran too. The foreign media didn't pick up on him much, except maybe for kicker stories. His campaign was a never-ending source of screw-ups and embarrassments. If Perot was a distraction, St John was the comic relief. The worst thing that happened to him was the early summer polls indicating he might be making ground. I think he stopped listening to his image-makers and started calling it like he saw it, convinced America was ready to hear it straight.'

'And America wasn't?'

'America freaked. Let's just say the word "miscegenation" had not previously entered the political lexicon of a presidential campaign. Before that, the Republicans had been trying to sweet-talk him into giving in and backing Bush, bringing his supporters with him, but when the real Luther St John stood up, they couldn't get away fast enough. The analysts figure it swung the election.'

79

'He divided the conservative vote?'

'No, I don't think many people were ever *actually* gonna stand in a booth and vote for him. But he didn't reflect well on the Right in general, and they really *couldn't* get away fast enough. They were tarred. Theory is that a lot of folks who'd been planning to stay home on election day thought, "Shit, what if," then went out and voted Clinton.'

Steff laughed. 'I suppose the Democrats might say God moves in mysterious ways.'

'Yeah, well. Looks like Luther's spent time enough licking his wounds. He seems to have regained his appetite for publicity – although given his last stunt, I'm surprised he's gathering his flock here at the beach. Guess the big wave ain't due yet.'

Steff put down his bottle and sat forward. 'Yeah, I was going to ask you. What is this about a wave? One of the Holy Credulous mentioned it, but I thought he was speaking metaphorically.'

Jo sneered. 'No. CFC viewers ain't intellectually equipped to deal with metaphors. He meant what he said. St John was on TV a few weeks back predicting that a tidal wave is gonna hit LA, presumably to wash away its various iniquities. I didn't follow the story real close, you can probably appreciate. Prophets of doom are getting as regular as commercial breaks these days, so even if they're billionaire evangelists, that's my cue to channel-surf. Still, it was hard not to hear about that one. These guys ain't usually quite so specific about the shape our destruction's gonna take – and they don't normally give a time-frame, either, 'cause that sets a sell-by date for their credibility.'

'St John predicted a *time*?' Steff asked, laughing.

'Sure. Not exactly a calendar date, but he said it would happen "early in nineteen ninety-nine". By the most liberal interpretation, that gives him until about June before he starts to look even more stupid than he did in 'ninety-two. Maybe he grew inured to ridicule, doesn't care no more. I mean, this is California he's talking about, for Christ's sake. I could understand what he was up to if he predicted a big quake. Odds are a lot better for being able to stand up and say, "I told you so." But a tidal wave? It's kinda sad, really. We shouldn't be laughing at these people.'

Steff had another mouthful of darkish beer and a thought occurred to him in a rare moment of sensitivity. 'Are you religious yourself, Jo?'

She shrugged, which said it all, really. Religion was not about shrugs.

Jo looked up at him and smiled. 'I'm a Clippers fan,' she said.

Which he took to mean 'don't ask'.

'What about you?'

'I don't even watch basketball.'

Which meant 'you don't want to know'.

And Christ, he thought, you *really* don't.

How could he begin to explain to her just what religion had meant to him throughout his twenty-eight years? What an enlightening and enriching impact Christianity had made upon the native life and broader culture of the West of Scotland? It was such a thing of wonder that he could not understand it himself, so how could a native of California possibly comprehend the spiritual mysteries of Glaswegian sectarianism?

Jo was able to make a sports reference to divert the conversation away from religion. Where Steff came from, the two were linked inextricably. He was a Motherwell supporter. As he came from Motherwell, this should not have been remarkable. But it was. Like the Hamilton dwellers who supported Hamilton, the Airdrieonians who followed Airdrie, or the Paisley punters who watched St Mirren, people from Motherwell who followed the home town's team were dubious subversives displaying a perverse interest in football, rather than the important matter at hand, i.e. bigotry.

Where Steff came from, football was about religion and religion was about football. Kaffliks supported Celtic. Proddies supported Rangers. And they hated each other with heart, soul, flute and drum. Naturally, the clubs concerned occasionally professed their revulsion for this, but down the decades they had both well understood that it kept the turnstiles clicking during the times when the teams weren't delivering anything to get excited about on the park. Rangers and Celtic weren't known collectively as 'the Old Firm' for nothing.

Outsiders would ask whether the sectarianism was there first and attached itself to the football, or was it that the

81

football created a focus and a stimulant for the sectarianism? The truth was that it was entirely symbiotic, the two blending into one another until they were barely distinct. The Catholics considered turning up at Parkhead on a Saturday as much a part of their religious identity as turning up at chapel on a Sunday, and there were as many Rangers jerseys worn on Orange Walks as there were sashes and bowler hats.

Nobody on either side would understand or even believe that you didn't actually give a fuck – allegiance was assumed and presumed on your behalf, because of your 'background'. Religion wasn't considered a matter of beliefs, but a matter of ethnicity. Therefore Steff, an atheist who had not been inside a church in more than ten years, would nonetheless always be a Catholic, because he'd been 'born one'. Thousands of Scots who barely knew the first thing about these 'traditions' (as they were euphemistically known) would be surprised and appalled to discover the complex prescription of stances and opinions they were firmly believed to hold by these bampots, according to which side of the fence they were thought to lie.

It wasn't as heavy as in Ulster, of course. They didn't actually go around blowing each other up. It was more like a hobby than a vocation, and their interest in events in Northern Ireland was as vicarious a thrill as watching their teams play football. It wasn't political. They weren't freedom fighters or loyalists. Just wankers. Sad wee wankers who'd never had an independent thought in their narrow wee lives, and who needed to associate themselves with a greater 'cause' to compensate for the desolate nothing that was their existence.

But then, Steff thought, remembering the Festival of Light, where would any religion be without a steady supply of those?

six

'Beginning our descent now, sir. We've received clearance from Brook Airfield and I'm told the chopper is fuelled and ready.'

Luther pulled up the screens over two of the windows on his left-hand side, sipped a glass of chilled water and watched the endless sprawl of Los Angeles scroll along below the Lear. It was a cloudless, clear day, and a brief rainstorm the previous night had flushed the air of the smog that built up in the vast conurbation because there was nowhere for the wind to blow it away to. The sight pleased him. It was a sign of how strong he felt that even the sight of Los Angeles pleased him. Sin-ridden as it was, it was still America. Still God's country. Still *his* country.

He could look at anywhere in America, these days, and it would bring hope to his heart, now that he knew it could be saved. Now that he knew God wanted it to be saved. More than hope, pride. The pride and love Jesus described in the father whose prodigal son had returned to his bosom. True, America hadn't returned to God's bosom yet, but he knew it would, soon, and could already sense what that would feel like when at last it happened. The depths of Luther's past despair and the reaches of his anger would be more than matched in the boundless joy of reconciliation.

It was an unusual thrill, a kind of ante-euphoria, an anticipation of emotions still to be felt. And the best of them would be loving America again. Not fearing for its future, not despairing of its follies, not resenting it for its infidelities.

God had always loved America. God had never feared or despaired or resented – that was the difference between Him and those of mortal flesh. Luther knew now that he had been weak to succumb to such faithless and selfish indulgences. However, God *had* been angered, so surely understood what trials Luther had endured to give rise to his despair.

There had been dark times, dark, dark times, like that father must have felt when hearing of his son's remorseless profligacy. Times when he could not look at his country and feel any love, only fury and, at best, pity. And the worst of it was that he knew this was down to his own failure. In 1992 when he ran for President, he had failed himself, failed America and, saddest of all, failed God.

He had been naïve and, he would confess, vain back then. The growth of his empire, his fortune and his influence throughout the 1980s had been awesome, and he had been seduced by his own success into believing that he could achieve anything as it was surely God's will. That was his vanity. His naïveté was in playing politicians at their own game, because he was always going to take a beating. He wasn't just inexperienced and tactically unskilled – he didn't even know the rules, far less the way those sons-of-bitches changed them as they went along.

He thought he could play it his way: tell America God's word and God's will, uncompromised by so-called modernisation and the we-know-best presumption that was political correctness. That's what he had been selling all his life, so his success proved that America wanted to buy it. And that success had been built merely on his own radio and TV channels: once his hat was in the presidential ring, he'd get to spread the word over the mainstream networks, reaching out to millions of people who had never heard his message before.

Naïve, vain and not a little stupid. For one thing he had failed to anticipate how much harder it was going to be to convey the point and image he intended when he didn't actually own and control the TV station he was appearing on.

The media ate him alive.

He was used to being under the spotlight. What he wasn't ready for was the microscope. They picked up and magnified the tiniest little things, blowing them up into grotesqueries, as though the viewer was Gulliver in Brobdingnag. It was like being in school again, where the other kids were always on the lookout for any little transgression of the social codes among their classmates. Wearing odd socks one day. Having the wrong colour lunchbox, something weird on your sandwiches, not cussing, not knowing cool slang.

His opponents were used to the microscope and knew that surviving it wasn't about what you did, but what you didn't. They knew what not to do, wear, eat, drink, smoke, touch, visit or meet under it that could ever be blown up for the repulsion of the voter. And most importantly, they knew what not to say. They knew how every last word could be twisted, stretched, decontextualised, recontextualised and wilfully misread, so they stuck tightly to a guaranteed foolproof script of opinions, policies and statements, and otherwise talked without saying anything.

Luther spoke his mind, spoke his beliefs, told it like it was. He was a lamb to the slaughter. Microscope? A dime-store magnifying glass would have been enough.

They got hold of a statement he made about the Bible forbidding miscegenation. Luther wasn't a racist: he had nothing against black people, nothing at all. He wasn't saying they were inferior, nothing like it. He was only pointing out that in the Bible, it says clearly that the races should not be mongrelised, and he was firmly of the belief that we shouldn't be picking and choosing what parts of God's Word it suited us to believe at any given time. We have to follow the rules as He has dictated, and if one of them seems strange or even wrong to us, we must have faith that its purpose will reveal itself in time, not abandon it because we think we know better than God Himself.

When the media were done he was looking like some Southern Good Ol' Boy with a Klan costume and a noose in the back of his rusty pick-up. It was just one little issue, hardly the cornerstone message of his campaign, but once the microscope got to work it might as well have been. Practically everything else he said faded into the background behind it.

But even without that indiscretion, his political credibility was being rent and torn from every side as he quickly learned how ill-equipped he was for this kind of fight. When he'd stepped into the arena he'd thought it was for a gladiatorial contest – he should have known that was never the Christian's role at the Circus Maximus. And the lions weren't even his opponents, but the pundits: commentators, columnists, comedians, 'satirists', chat-show hosts, basically any smart-ass with a microphone or a by-line. That's who was really out to destroy him. His opponents, he understood in retrospect, recognised he was out of his depth and therefore didn't worry about him. But these guys, well, they were out for blood, and they had their motives too. These were the real godless: the so-called intellectuals and so-called artistic community. The fornicators, homosexuals, perverts, atheists. He'd always been their enemy and they didn't spare the boot once he was down on the floor.

Amid such a frenzy of assault, the knock-out blow still came out of nowhere.

He hadn't exactly taken any journalists into his confidence – he wasn't *that* naïve – but he had been obliged to let some of them get a lot closer than usual when he was 'on the campaign trail'. It was a political necessity dictated by the Oscar Wilde logic regarding the only thing worse than being talked about. Gilda Landsmann was one of those working his campaign 'beat', he guessed for some doubtless unflattering candidate profile or election diary. He feared nothing worse: there were no Jimmy Swaggart-style skeletons rattling in Luther St John's closet.

Then Landsmann approached him one day and presented an early draft of the story she was giving to *Vanity Fair*. Sure enough, it unearthed no secret that he was keeping from the world. Only a secret that the world had been keeping from him.

'I first met Mary St John in 1942,' Roberts says on the porch of her Fredericksburg home, where she offers me a pitcher of ice-tea and hands me a photograph of herself and her wartime college room-mate. Mary St John smiles self-consciously from the frame, as if embarrassed but too shy to refuse the photographer. 'She was a nice girl, but real quiet. She came from a pretty well-to-do family, real strict about religious matters, and I think Mary had always been on a pretty short leash. I think once she got used to being outside the family nest she started to open up a little, started acting a lot more like a regular girl instead of the little mouse who first turned up on my doorstep.

'She was – I think the word I'd use is "giddy" about the whole idea of "boys", probably because that sort of thing was never discussed in her home-life, and she'd gone to an all-girl school. Fascination with the great unknown, you know? The problem was her ideas about romance were better suited to Austen, Jane, than Austin, Texas.'

Roberts gives a regretful, almost apologetic smile, and looks out towards the corral where her two mares, Pliny and Ovid, are being groomed by her eldest grandson, Mark. She shakes her head and winces, then reaches for her glass. For a moment I fear she is going to cry.

'I met my husband, Tom, at a dance hall. He was on leave – he and some buddies – before being shipped out to the European theater. You know what's coming, don't you? I had broken curfew to go along with my older sister and her friends. Us college girls weren't supposed to be out unchaperoned, you know? Mary knew I was going to see him at another dance on his last night before he had to report for duty, and she threatened to put a spoke in it if I didn't take her along. I admit it, I was a lot more interested in dancing with Tom than keeping an eye on Mary. She started dancing with this guy, and Tom vouched for him, so I guess I put her out of mind.

'When I met up with her later she was distraught, sitting on a bench, crying. I asked her what had happened, but she wouldn't tell me. All she said was, "Norma, I've done a terrible thing."

'I sat up with her in her room when we got back. I couldn't ask her whether she had been raped because I wasn't sure Mary would know what "raped" was. But what she told me didn't sound like it. Not by 1944 definitions, anyway.

'Tom's friend and she had kept on dancing together. She said he was a nice guy: charming, polite, chivalrous enough to set Mary's heart racing. He was probably also, like everyone else of his age and circumstances, horny as an old goat. He got her to come out and walk around the block "for some air". Mary said there were couples necking in every doorway; she probably passed me and Tom without knowing it. She must have been like a kid outside a candystore, seeing all that canoodling right before her eyes. So when he kissed her it was dream-come-true time.

'She started crying again when I asked her what happened next. It took some coaxing, let me tell you, but she eventually poured out the whole thing. "He started touching me," she said. I pointed to my own chest and she nodded. I asked whether she didn't ask him to stop, and her answer told me everything I needed to know. "I didn't want him to stop," she said.'

Ignorance, curiosity, hormones and a liberal dash of unaccustomed alcohol: what family-planning specialists would later refer to as 'the prom cocktail'. Mary St John was neither the first nor the last young woman to discover how potent it was.

'Mary was just ridden with guilt,' Roberts continues. 'And it's pretty significant that her greatest concern at this point was what God would think of her, and not what every other girl who'd "gone too far" was worrying themselves sick about. Well, Mary was sick soon enough – every morning. When she finally got up the courage to tell her folks – I came with her – it was ugly in the extreme. I don't care to repeat or even to remember what exactly was said, but I did feel that I'd fallen through a hole in time and come out in the Seventeenth Century. In Salem.

'They didn't abandon her, I'd have to give them that, but she was definitely disowned. They supported her financially but she had to give up her studies. They wanted her out of Austin, away from them and anyone who knew the family. She moved to Bleachfield, Arizona, where her brother, Nathan, was a preacher. I helped her move but she kind of cut me off after that. She had come up with a story for herself so that she wasn't some shamed "woman with a past" moving to town, and I think she wanted to sever ties with anyone who knew the truth.

'I learned that she was calling herself Mary Baker and wearing a wedding band, telling folks her little boy's daddy had been killed in action a few weeks after they got married. It wasn't a story that was likely to raise much suspicion – there were several like it in every town at the end of the war. And in Mary's case it was true, apart from the being married part. Tom's buddy got blown up by a land mine his third week in Italy.'

She had sat across the table from him and watched him read it, then had the nerve to ask what his reaction was and whether he'd known this before. His reaction was to throw her out of the office and call his lawyers, seeking an injunction that would prevent publication.

His lawyers came back with bad news. Landsmann had corroborative quotes from a retired obstetrician and from some cousin Luther had never met. She also had a photocopy of the appropriate entry in the Wightford County register of births. The story ran a couple of weeks later, further embellished and rounded off with a final up-yours.

I got a telephone call from Norma-Ann Roberts on the 28th of last month, September. I had never met her or even heard her name before. She sought me out, she said, because she'd read my articles on the Donna West rape trial last year, and thought I came across like someone she could trust. The question I had to ask though, and the question people will all be wondering right now, is why did she wait all these years to tell her story?

'I always knew who Luther St John was,' Roberts says. 'Mary might have shut me out but I didn't forget about her, and I kept an ear open for news. I was at her funeral, such as it was. I know she was a disappointment to her family and all, but I wouldn't have buried a dog that way. Anyway, when Luther started to get all big and famous, I didn't care much for his message but I didn't pay much attention to it either. I was happy enough to leave all I knew in the past, out of respect to Mary's memory. I'd always felt sorry for Luther too, I mean, his own mother murdered in front of him at that age. But recently, with this election campaign . . .'

Roberts grimaces, like there's too much lemon in her tea.

'Making that phone call to you was the hardest thing I ever did,' she says. 'But believe me I had to do it. I'd switch on my TV each night, and there'd be Luther, campaigning against sex education in our schools, or pontificating about unwed mothers and the evils of sex "outwith the sanctity of marriage". And this man wanted to be *President*. I couldn't keep it secret any more. I just thought it was time for him – and all the fools who listen to him – to know the truth.'

Luther was laid very low indeed. His political aspirations were a no-questions write-off and he found himself with a job on his hands salvaging his credibility in the eyes of the CFC flock, many of whom might be having second thoughts about following someone who had become a national joke.

But, like after any storm, through God-given strength he picked himself off the floor and got to work on repairing the damage. He poured balm on the wounds of his disappointed flock by regaling them with tales of the Christians down through the centuries who had been ridiculed and persecuted for their beliefs. These people, he reminded them, were easy to spot in the history books: they all had the word 'Saint' before their name.

He knew better than to contest Landsmann and Roberts's assertions, but felt fewer misgivings about challenging the latter's account of how his mother fell pregnant. Luther charged that she had, in fact, been raped, and that Roberts was protecting the late culprit's identity because he had been her husband's comrade-in-arms. Roberts claimed that she had never known the man's name, and that her husband had taken his knowledge to the grave. She conceded that this man had certainly taken advantage of Mary St John and that his conduct might be defined in today's terms as date-rape, but couldn't resist adding that 'Mary would have been a lot less vulnerable if she'd had a fraction of the sex education Luther St John wants to deny to American schoolchildren'.

Luther depicted his mother as a victim of the carnal lust in this anonymous soldier, fuelled by society's obsession with sex; an obsession that was getting worse and worse: 'It's no wonder men become like rutting animals when all around they see depictions of fornication as normal, acceptable and desirable, as well as prurient images of women in states of undress and arousal. It was bad enough in the Forties, when my poor mother was fallen upon . . .'

Mary St John's tale was also an ace to play in abortion

debates, when the old chestnut about pregnant rape victims came up. With God's help she had accepted her baby as a blessing that had emerged from a dark episode, showing her the way to the light . . .

Luther focused his attention on what the financial analysts would call his core interests, having burned his fingers on an ill-advised expansion attempt. He stuck to what he knew, what he was good at, and found that the Lord had not deserted him. Within a few years CFC was stronger than ever, his losses at the highly expensive crap-shoot of politics long since recovered. But having steadied the ship and set it on a prosperous course, he was restless. He had more subscribers than ever, he was making more money than ever, but what did any of that matter when he was still a lone voice crying in the wilderness? When neither followers nor finances could any better assist him in stemming the tide of immorality that was gradually engulfing America?

The Lord said, 'What does it profit a man to gain the whole world but lose his soul?' Luther had begun to fear that, for all his achievements, his life would still be a failure if he couldn't turn that tide, if he couldn't make America once more embrace the Word of God.

The future was like a long tunnel, moving steadily towards a light in the far distance. Sometimes the tunnel's path dipped and the light grew dimmer, like after the '92 débâcle. In recent years, it had been climbing again, but slowly, and though the light was in sight, he feared he hadn't enough years of walking left in him to reach it.

And just when he thought time was starting to run out, God sent him a man named Daniel Corby.

Steff was leaning over the gallery rail to get an elevated perspective on the clutter and bustle in the lobby below. He was directly above the main doors that led out towards the horseshoe drive, a wide-angle lens swallowing up the tapering hub of the Pacific Vista, a note in the back of his mind telling him to get back here tomorrow with a fish-eye. He was probably the first to notice the helicopter, as the shadow it cast over the rooftop pool ruined the light for the shot he was setting up.

He was up there through self-banishment. He and Jo had

gone to the 'office' of Moonstar Films, which turned out, like most other AFFM offices, to be a bedroom with the beds upturned against one wall, a few portable desks, a PC and some cardboard stands bearing promotional material for the duff-looking videos the company was hawking. Jo was interviewing Charles 'Chip' Ryker, Moonstar's chief executive officer, while Steff tried not to get in the way as he snapped the man and his minion, a ferocious adolescent energy-ball called Tia. Tia answered phones, sent faxes, offered and dispensed refreshments and compiled glossy info packs in a near-noiseless flurry as Jo chatted to her boss. Steff kept checking that there was still just the one of her.

'With intellectual properties such as these,' Chip was saying, 'we have to maximise the resource throughput while rendering the rights package more pro-actively saleable to our upscale end-user groundbase.'

Pretty early on Jo shot him a warning glare, having seen Steff's eyes begin to bulge. He tried. God knows he tried. He was doing all right through another five minutes of 'critical mass', 'out-sourcing' and 'hyper-aggressive acquisition strategies in nascent digital micro-niche tertiary consumption media'. And he thought he was going to make it through the whole interview as Chip wound down from 'brushstroking his corporate futurescape' and moved into misty-eyed reflections on the gentler side of the business, remembering 'that this is an art-form as well as an industry'. In fact, Steff was feeling pretty composed as Chip talked about 'painting with light these active, living, moving visions of ourselves' and 'communicating in a medium that shines directly through the windows of the soul'.

Then Jo asked what was premièring on his market slate.

'*Slayground III: Finishing School Bloodbath*, *Venusian Biker Chicks IV: Space Harleys*, and the first in a new horror franchise, *The Dentist*. Great effects. This guy's got like drills and probes and shit instead of fingers. Got two sequels in pre-production.'

Steff reckoned he had made it out of the bedroom slow enough for it not to look like he was about to be sick, but as he had not excused his exit, it must have looked suspicious nonetheless. Jo and Chip were still talking as Tia came out into the corridor and found him doubled up, tears streaming down his cheeks.

'Gee, are you all right?' she asked.

Steff had looked up long enough to nod, then his eyes screwed up again as the next wave of laughter seized him. He stumbled away, leaving Tia to her bafflement.

Steff didn't know it was a helicopter until after it had passed overhead, when it began its descent and the noise became loudly audible from the front of the hotel. He could see through the sloping glass walls that it was coming down to land on the horseshoe drive outside. He could also see that this was neither expected nor appreciated by the staff and delegates standing out there. Two cars bumped into each other as they swerved to clear a space for the inexorably descending machine, while bell-hops and porters dragged trolleys clear and waved people away from the wind-whipped area. Delegates were pouring out of their stands and 'offices' into the gallery and lobby, massing near the doors to get a view of whatever was going on.

Steff felt a hand on his arm and saw Jo push in beside him to look down through the glass at the scene outside.

'What the hell's this about?' he asked, prolifically photographing the mêlée.

'Publicity stunt, I guess – probably not the last this week, neither. Hotel security's gonna chew their ass, whoever they are. This kind of thing needs all sorts of clearance. It's never supposed to be a surprise.'

The helicopter touched down and was soon ringed by hotel staff and undeterred AFFM participants, shielding their eyes from the dust and draught kicked up by the rotor blades. A door opened and a bear in a sharp suit climbed out. From upstairs, Steff could make out the earpiece and coiled wire running down the back of his collar. Bodyguard.

The bear turned around and faced the door, then reached up a hand and helped the next passenger climb out. It was a neat little man, maybe mid-fifties, in a pair of jeans and a crisp white short-sleeved shirt. He got down on to the tarmac, ran a hand through his silver hair and looked back at the second bear climbing out behind him.

'Well, speak of the asshole,' Jo muttered.

The trio stepped back on to the grass island in the drive's centre and the helicopter began to rise up once more.

'Who is it?'

'America's inverse answer to King Canute. Luther St John himself.'

'That wee guy? That's him? What's he doing here?'

'I suspect those gentlemen are asking the same question.'

A delegation of hotel security personnel were attempting to remonstrate with the new arrivals, but were being steadfastly ignored. St John walked down the drive away from the hotel, bear on either side, saying nothing, but smiling and waving to the onlookers as he progressed. As he reached the pedestrian crossing, two cars that had been sitting by the pavement suddenly turned on their flashing hazard lights and slewed themselves across the road, causing approaching traffic to halt. The same thing was happening on the other carriageway too.

St John and his minders marched triumphantly across without missing a step, and headed for the Festival of Light, where a hysterical crowd was forming a cheering human avenue before the entrance. St John and party disappeared from view and the avenue was sucked back inside the Festival ground like a miraculously cured rectal prolapse.

Back at the Pacific Vista, bewilderment and outrage were tying for number-one emotion, as the assembled crowd began to realise that what had just taken place was, in effect, an elaborate practical version of 'the finger'.

'There's nothing like making an entrance at your own party,' Jo said. 'I guess he's dropping in to rally the faithful.'

'Well I'm not guessing,' Steff told her, changing lens and sticking the dismounted one in his shoulder-bag. 'I'm going to find out.'

'What? They'll never let you near the place.'

'You're forgetting,' he said, holding up his hand and showing off the ink-stamp on the back of it. 'I'm a true believer.'

Luther St John was nothing Steff had expected and a great deal more than he had feared. This was probably down to his sum knowledge of fundamentalist Christian TV evangelists coming via the filtration processes of film and television, fiction and reportage. The fictions created expectations of appearance; the reportage (certainly when it was British) tended to accentuate the ridiculous in the message. Those crazy Yanks and their wacky TV preachers. What a laugh.

This wasn't funny.

Steff had an image in his head of a rotund and orotund shitkicker-made-good in a white suit and a white hat, ranting in a cadence that was part Southern cracker and part parade-ground sergeant, ruddy of cheek and hammy of gesture. St John, in fact, was slim and short, relaxed of manner, walking the stage calmly in his casual attire, a boyish youthfulness behind the lines on his face that owed nothing to makeup or surgery. He looked, as they said back home, like his mammy had knitted him. So neat and compact, and yet that short-sleeves-and-jeans look stopping him comfortably short of Niles Crane anal. Like Ben Folds dressed for Sunday lunch.

He was attractive in an antiseptically asexual way. Women might want to mother him or invite him round for tea and scones, but there was an air of unworldly purity about him that would surely make them feel sinful were they to harbour any more physical feelings. The men, clearly, wouldn't find him a threat. Steff figured, therefore, that he must pitch himself as a prophet rather than a leader. American males didn't follow wimps, unless they were under the impression God was telling them to.

He spoke in soft, measured tones, deeper than his build suggested, with a lilt in his voice that was hypnotically easy on the ear. The accent seemed neutral – somewhere in middle America – but with the occasional Southern inflection surfacing sparingly to add just enough colour. It was a voice you could imagine reading Mark Twain on audiobooks, and breaking all sales records with it. A voice that sounded as if it could lull monsters to sleep, talk down suicides from the ledge, a voice that could sell its words to any listener, sand to the Arabs, coals to Newcastle, rosaries to Rangers fans. Which was the scary part, because the words it was selling today . . .

Steff sighed.

Words like these built concentration camps.

'Friends,' St John said, taking the microphone from its stand and gesturing for the applause to cease, a look of strain on his face conveying his understanding of how difficult an act of self-control he was asking of them. 'Thank you for being here. Thank you for making the trip. Thank you for the commitment, thank you for the belief. Thank you for the faith.

Now, I don't know how many of you-all brought life-rafts on your station-wagon roofracks, but . . .'

All around Steff people were guffawing at this last remark. It reminded him of the corpses-in-waiting you saw on telly at Conservative Party conferences, chuckling vacantly at some fanny-merchant's dismal, scripted one-liner. St John's crowd were more animated, and Steff felt he had solved the mystery of where they got the studio audiences for *Cybill*. Jesus, laugh at this pish . . .

'No, no,' St John continued, smiling, 'don't worry. We're safe here a little longer yet. But more seriously, time *is* running out. The countdown *has* begun. And though we may not know the day nor the hour, we *will* be ready when the Master calls.

'Unfortunately,' he said, his tone lowering ominously, 'that won't be enough. Not by a long stretch. And I know that seems harsh. I know that seems unfair. You want to say to me, "I *am* ready. I *am* pure. Why am I condemned by the sins of another?" Well, the answer is right there at the start, my friends, all the way back in the Book of Genesis. And that answer is, "Because I *am* my brother's keeper." Jesus taught us to hate the sin but love the sinner, so how can we be Christians if we abandon them to their fate? The difficult truth is, we can't be. And that is why God will punish us *all*. Because we have failed Him, all of us have failed Him. The sinners have failed Him by their deeds, but we will have failed Him by not acting to prevent those deeds.

'God wants us to love, wants us to care. Love thy neighbour as thyself, He taught us. And when He visits His wrath and we ask Him, "Why, Lord, why, when we followed Your Word?", He will say, "How were you following My Word when you spurned your neighbours by abandoning them to their sins?" Our neighbours are our responsibility. The whole world is our responsibility. And if our neighbours sin, then *that* is our responsibility.'

St John walked over to the mike stand, placed the microphone back in its holder, and leaned upon the aluminium tripod for a quiet few seconds, looking down, as though gathering his thoughts. Great pose, Steff thought, taking a couple of shots while the crowd waited in eerie near-silence.

He was more like a good stand-up comic than a preacher. He had timing. He had presence. And he had that voice.

He lifted the mike again, walking forward, head down, the crowd breathlessly quiet in anticipation.

'It's time to rock'n'roll,' he breathed. The audience erupted in cheers, applause and other euphoric histrionics. The word 'woo', whatever it meant, seemed the preferred form of expression.

'It's *time*,' he said louder, over the subsiding shouts, 'to be our brother's keeper. To *save* our brother from his sin – even if that means having to re-educate our brother about what sin is, because he may have forgotten. And who can really blame him, in this country of ours? This country that was once so great, once held all God's promise, but now spurns Him. This country that God intended to be our land of milk and honey, but which has been turned instead into Sodom and Gomorrah. Who can blame our brother, when he walks in a land turned upside down, where the word of God has become polluted and distorted beyond recognition, until it is used to excuse the very permissiveness it expressly forbade? Where the Bible is quoted to support the toleration of that which the Lord condemns. A land where they tell us we will be *safer* from evil-doers if we let them take away our guns. A land where our beloved, sacred freedom has been bent and twisted by poisonous serpents, so that men can burn our flag and deny the very existence of God *with the blessing of the law*.'

St John's face distorted as he put on a whiny fake voice. '"It's a free country," they say, "so that includes my right to burn the flag and say there ain't no God." Well I say to them, "It was GOD who made you free – it would be *polite* . . . to start showing a little gratitude."'

Another hysterical roar. Steff looked at the faces around him. Seductive seemed a singularly inappropriate word in the context of Luther St John, but whatever he was doing to them, they were buying it with everything they could give.

'This is a free country,' he resumed, 'but you are *never* free to sin. That's what we've got to remind our brother of. The law may allow you to fornicate like a mangy dog, it may allow you to sodomise, it may allow you to blaspheme, it may allow you to peddle pornography, and it may allow you to murder a child in the womb . . . but GOD DOES *NOT*! No wonder our brother is led astray when we have become so arrogant as to supersede God's laws with ones we've dreamed up for our own convenience. God's laws weren't made for convenience; they were made for our good and His glory. And it's up to all of us to remind our brother of that.

'Now I know many of you have been trying to do that for a long time, maybe even all your lives. You have suffered ridicule and contempt as you stood up for the truth, as you stood outside the abortion clinics, as you picketed AIDS funerals, as you stood at the gates of your kids' schools in defiance of the filth they told you was "sex education" and the blasphemy they told you was "natural history". You have been trying to save your brother from his sins with all the efforts you can muster. So you must be looking up at me on this stage today and asking what more I think you can give if this has not been enough. Well, my brothers, my sisters, my friends, I understand that frustration, and I also understand the cause of that frustration.

'You've been shouting God's word to your brother, but he cannot hear it above the deafening clamour of evil that issues from our TV sets, from our radios and from our movie screens. You have tried to tell your brother that blasphemy is wrong, but he hears it and sees it unchecked, uncondemned, across the airwaves and on the silver screen. You have told him a man cannot lie down with another man, but he sees sodomites on his television, depicted as figures accepted in society, their *sin* accepted in society. You have tried to tell him about the virtues of chastity, of fidelity, of the sacred state of matrimony as the only sanctification for sexual intercourse, and yet he sees all around him pornography, images of sexuality and the condoning of free fornication. From the filth of "adult" movies, to TV shows aimed at our *children*, sex is promoted as a personal plaything.

'Never before in the history of our world has evil had such a voice, and it is no coincidence that never before has there been so much sin, so much depravity, and so much godlessness. God couldn't possibly expect you to compete with such a cacophony, could he?'

St John stood still, looked down at the floor, building up expectations. He turned his head skywards a fraction, and smiled. 'Well, friends,' he said quietly, the crowd stilling

98

their breathing lest they miss his soft words (the old Bill Shankly trick), 'maybe He did expect that and maybe He didn't. But He now knows it couldn't be done, and remember that although life is a test, God wants you to succeed. That's why He has decided to give us a hand in getting the world's attention. He's going to clear His throat pretty loud so that everybody turns off that racket and listens to His words.

'I know, because I have seen His work beneath the ocean. I have seen detailed research – photographs, charts, plans – that the scientists who scoff at us cannot understand. They have refused to recognise His work etched in the earth in the past, so how could they have the vision to recognise His hand now? But I recognised it, and what I saw was awesome to behold. He is preparing to strike, preparing a mighty wave to demonstrate His wrath, to literally wash away the sinners.

'And sagely He has chosen as His target the Twentieth Century's combined Sodom and Gomorrah. For here, in Los Angeles, is the source of the river of filth that pollutes His word and poisons His people. From this city emanate the anti-Gospels of atheism, of immorality, of *anarchy*. The pornography that turns people into rapists, the images of violence that turn them into murderers, the lies that tell us it's *okay* to rut like an animal, it's *okay* to sodomise, it's *okay* to murder your baby – it's all produced here in so-called Tinseltown. Well,' he said, shaking his head and walking to the very front of the stage, 'not for long it's not.'

Steff swallowed. The crowd were screaming approval and jumping up and down like it was the World Cup Final. He thought fleetingly of *Lord of the Flies*, and wondered whether he'd better start joining in if he didn't want to be dragged down to the beach for a terminal kicking.

'Now I'm sure some of you have been wondering, under the circumstances, why I decided to stage this little get-together here on the coast. Well, that's nothing to do with the tidal wave, but *everything* to do with its target.'

St John pointed towards the Pacific Vista. Everyone turned to look at it then winced as the setting sun gave them a sharp poke in the eye via the glass canopy.

'Over there at the AFFM you'll find no better – or rather no worse – collection of filth and filth-peddlers. American Feature Film Market? I call it the UnAmerican Festering

Filth Market. So I thought there could be no more appropriate setting to launch our Mission of Purity than right in front of that den of pornographers, atheists and sodomites, that Pandora's box of evil and sin. Where each year they get together to plan the dissemination of their corrupting trash throughout the whole world, and where this year – nineteen ninety-nine, the end of the century, the end of the millennium – as predicted in the Book of Revelation, the Whore of Babylon will flaunt herself, a portent of the destruction to come.'

Heads nodded gravely around Steff. He didn't have a scoob what the man was talking about. That's what you got for not watching CFC. That and a fully functioning brain.

St John pointed at the hotel again. This time, the crowd's eyes stayed on him, their pupils still recovering from the last assault. 'People like them are the reason your voices haven't been heard. People like them are the reason sin proliferates. People like them are the reason our lawmakers have forgotten God. And people like them are the reason God is angry.'

It was getting worryingly Nurembergesque.

'Them,' he continued, with a sharp stab of the finger. 'Those in that building, those in the film studios, those at the TV networks. But their time is running out, and our time is coming. Our. Time. Is. Coming. Our mission, our responsibility to our neighbour – if we truly want to be our brother's keeper – is to make *our* voices heard and theirs silenced.

'We *will* save the world from sin – and the battle starts *right* here, *right* now!'

St John punched the air, clasping the mike to the stand with his left hand. The cheers were deafening, the adulation awe-inspiring. He leaned forward and shook the hands that were thrust up towards him, waving and punching the air again as he manoeuvred along the front of the stage, bouncers straining to hold back the hysterical devotees.

From behind Steff came an incongruously deflated sigh.

'Ah, shit, I really wish he hadn't said that,' rumbled a deep tired tone. Steff looked back. There was a big bald guy standing just behind him with his arms folded. He and Steff both stood out in the crowd for their height and demonstrable lack of euphoria, but this bloke had the further conspicuousness of being the only black person in the place.

'Said what?' Steff asked, catching his eye.

'All of it.'

seven

The Whore of Babylon ran a hand through her hair and sighed, switching the TV set off with the remote and heading for the fridge. She grabbed an enticingly condensation-cloaked bottle of beer from beside a clingfilm-wrapped remnant of yesterday's pizza and flipped off the cap against the wall-mounted opener with an unfailingly satisfying wrist-action. She walked over to the stereo and stuck on some Indigo Girls, turning the volume up an indulgent couple of notches.

Then the Whore of Babylon pulled the cord tighter on her silk dressing gown, opened the slide door and took a seat on her balcony to watch the sunset. She sipped at her cold beer and looked at the evening sky's play of colours, a palette Mother Nature had never intended, certainly, but a pleasing one nonetheless. She was trying to immerse herself in the moment, trying to relax, drink her drink, look at the view. Trying to tell herself she wasn't going to get pissed off, that what St John said hadn't got to her.

But she was, and it had. She just needed to listen to the music to know that. She always put on the Indigos when she was furious about something she'd seen on TV or read in the newspaper, as though Emily Saliers and Amy Ray could respond on her behalf, strike out in a riposte that expressed her feelings more powerfully than she could herself. Or maybe it just renewed her strength for the fight to hear their voices ring out in anger, joy or sorrow, and know that she was less alone.

The fucking TV. Why did they give the asshole airtime? He had his own goddamn network – if anyone was stupid enough to want to hear him, they knew where to look. But these days the son-of-a-bitch was all over the six o'clock news, having apparently rediscovered his taste for nationwide ridicule. And no matter whether he spoke for ten minutes or for two hours, and no matter what else he talked about, they always picked out any soundbite that mentioned her – and found time to reiterate once more for anyone recently returned from Mars who the Whore of Babylon was: 'Republican Senator Bob Witherson's daughter Madeleine, who shocked the world when it was discovered that she was in fact notorious porn actress Katy Koxx, star of *Babylon Blue* and several other XXX-rated movies.'

Notorious porn actress. That always made her smile. Among porn actresses she was hardly notorious, indeed before the big revelation, barely known, and well down the cast list of anything she'd worked on. But in tabloid media-speak, all porn actresses were notorious porn actresses; well, at least the ones who had somehow made it into the wider public eye.

The media at large had latched on to her because of who her father was, and had been too busy salivating over the news-value godsend of this hyper-conservative religious moralist having a daughter so disgrace him to dwell much on what the irony told them about cause and effect. They weren't very big on analysis in journalism, these days. Hand-wringing usually stood in as a poor replacement.

She liked to think Luther St John had latched on to her because she had been outspoken in defence of herself and in criticism of the hypocritical bullshit the likes of he and her father made a living peddling. But in truth she knew it was more to do with her serendipitously having been in a skin flick with the word 'Babylon' in the title, allowing the manipulative little prick to squeeze maximum biblical portent out of a very tenuous association.

And he *would not* let it go. It had been the same old schtick for months, banging on about catastrophic prophecies being fulfilled because the Whore of Babylon had been made manifest here in 1999, omitting to observe that she had only been made manifest through him attaching that soubriquet to her. He tended also to skirt around the inconvenient fact that she no longer actively fitted even *his* definition of whore, as she had bailed out of the business right after the big story broke. The 'former whore of Babylon' didn't quite have the same ring. Not even 'notorious former whore of Babylon' would send chills down many fundamentalists' spines.

Madeleine would admit to waking up in a fairly misanthropic mood now and again, but she didn't really feel much like a fount of ultimate evil, not even on Monday mornings. It would be laughable if it wasn't so cynically calculated. Never mind dictators, torturers, war criminals or realtors, Maddy Witherson was the true baddest of the bad just because she had balled a few guys, none of whom complained. But Luther knew what he was doing. He had made her a figurehead, not just for the pornography industry but for everything people hated about any kind of movies, TV shows, books, whatever.

Talking to Tony, her agent, usually helped give her a sense of perspective about the whole thing. Tony was pissed off because St John was considered too much of a fringe figure for them to get maximum mileage out of his declamations. The news would quote Luther because wackos were good copy, but he wasn't taken seriously enough to really put stars on Madeleine's infamy-rating. 'If we could get someone in DC to back up some of this biblical shit,' he'd say, longingly, 'maybe Ed Meese or Pat Buchanan . . .'

Not that she was short of outraged barbs from big-name Washington rentaquotes, but they did tend to stick to 'decency' issues rather than apocalyptic visions. In politics, it never hurt anyone's career to join a moral lynch-mob, especially when sexuality was involved.

She had been curious at first to see how her father would react to St John's onslaughts, whether he'd quietly use his influence to ask his political bedfellow to lay off a bit, less for the sake of his daughter than because it was heaping more embarrassment on him. But not a bit of it. He'd played the wounded parent for a little while, giving her a repentance ultimatum. When she didn't deliver, it was open season. The Christian Right could cut loose on little Maddy much as they liked. Look what that ungrateful bitch had done to her poor daddy, and after all he'd done for her.

Yeah. All he'd done for her. More than anyone would ever know.

Madeleine adjusted her chair and sat with her head back, gulping down more beer. As she placed the bottle on the floor she noticed that the cord had come loose again and her gown had fallen open. She looked down at the dark shadow of her pubic hair and the slight mounds of her breasts, and wondered, not for the first time, what exposing them to a video camera had to do with a Jewish philosopher preaching tolerance in Roman-occupied Palestine.

She had been over it in her head a million times; the signal absurdity was not a comfort before, so it certainly wasn't going to offer solace now. Couldn't these fucking primitives find something else to get stirred up about? Thousands of years into the development of human civilisation and America, supposedly the most advanced country on Earth, was still putting fertility rites at the centre of its social morality.

Because that was all it was: pagan fertility rites. The superstitious ascribing of inflated spiritual significance to the sexual act. Mystifying it, cloaking it in ritual, and, most importantly, attempting to control it. Telling you when you could and couldn't do it. Telling you how you were allowed to do it. Telling you who you were allowed to do it with. Telling you why you should or shouldn't be doing it.

The bottom line of all of which was, of course, reproduction – the divine miracle of childbirth.

You don't do it because it's fun; the pleasure is an unfortunate side-effect that we'd eradicate if we could (and with female circumcision we're halfway there). You do it to expand the tribe, for the greater glory of its God. Your sexuality *is* your reproductive potential; any abuse of it is a blasphemy against your God, incurring His wrath and that of the tribe.

So doing it yourself is selfish and arrogant. Doing it with someone of the same sex is a grotesque and bestial insult to His honour. And doing it in front of a camera for other people's voyeuristic pleasure will, apparently, bring about the end of the world.

It was said that the dumber an idea was, the more likely its proponent to come forward brandishing a flag and a Bible. This was because the normal political currencies of reason and logic could offer no support. Men like St John – men like her father – had plied both totems with such vigour that the currencies of reason and logic had become devalued. You might be able to quote facts to back up your position, but they could counter with The Truth.

Stark and utterly self-evident realities seemed to have their relevance sapped from them by a constant bombardment of pseudo-theological horseshit. Perhaps it was the fundamentalists' ultimate revenge on the detested Darwin: they were actually *reversing* evolution. The next step in man's development would be to shed his cognitive abilities, because he no longer needed them. Heck, all that thinking just made things too darn complicated. Besides, we already know all the answers.

She remembered her father engaging in a TV debate, advocating parents' rights to exempt their kids from sex education at school. It had been pointed out that in Europe, the countries with the lowest teenage pregnancy and abortion rates were also those with the frankest sex education, and where that education began earliest. The average age of first sexual activity in those countries was also several years older than in the USA.

'Do you want our children's innocence ruined at five?' he'd countered. The age five had come from nowhere; it hadn't been mentioned by his opponent, it was just helpfully emotive.

'Do you want our kids hearing about oral sex and sodomy on *Sesame Street*?' Again, this was no answer, but then he wasn't talking to his opponent, he was talking to 'America'. And America was dumb enough to listen.

'The choice here tonight is between the Condom and the Cross. Which do you want *your* children to learn about?'

Nobody asked why they couldn't learn about both – the sex educationists weren't seeking a parental opt-out for religious lessons. But implied and imagined threats were the politician's stock-in-trade.

However, Madeleine thought, if there had to be such a choice, America might want to ask itself which would better equip its children to deal with the most powerful instinct in the human condition. One that would explain the physical and emotional changes, the longings, the desires, the fears and insecurities; or one that would simply tell you not to ask, not to think about it if you're a good little girl or boy, you'll know what to do when the time comes, and you'll know the time has come because you'll be in your wedding gown. One that would tell you what you were dealing with and assure you that it was normal and healthy (as well as complex, dangerous, baffling and frustrating); or one that would tell you it was dirty, alien, foreign and forbidden, vulgar and base, bestial and depraved.

One that would give you control of your sexuality; or one that would leave it vulnerable to the control of others.

One that could make it control you.

That was why this moral code of abstinence and ignorance was utterly irresponsible. Sexuality was like a constant flow from an endlessly productive source. It could not be stopped, could not be suppressed, only regulated. If you tried to block it off, it would build up and build up until eventually it either found a way out or smashed a way out. Then it would come out in places it shouldn't, or come out with violent force. When it did, pity help you if you were in its path. Especially if you were a woman or a child.

'The choice here tonight is between the Condom and the Cross.'

Well gee Dad, let's ask about the relationship in this country between sexual violence and Christian family background, huh? Let's talk about the correlation between rape rates and religious fundamentalism. Hey, guess what? The more Bible-thumpers there are in any area of the United States, the higher the incidence of violence against women. What a far-out coincidence!

'Do you want our children's innocence ruined at five?'

First, why don't you tell me what innocence means, Dad? Because in your mouth it's always been interchangeable with ignorance. Shit, they even sound alike.

So what was this 'innocence' that would be so damaged by knowing what your genitals were for? What disturbing realisation about the true nature of life were we deferring in children to whom we had already described the torture, mutilation and slow, agonising death of a human being by crucifixion; that we could tell them about driving nails through a man's feet and wrists in a merciless act of violence, but we couldn't tell them about the act of love and affection that preceded all of their existences.

What kind of unspeakable ordeal would childhood become if kids missed out on all the foreboding, confusion, embarrassment and guilt associated with body parts everybody had but nobody talked about?

Boy, Madeleine was sure glad *she* had been spared it. Who knew? If what was between her legs hadn't been shrouded in so much shame and mystery, she might have thought no-one else should be touching it! Just think what she might have missed out on if she'd thought she had the right to say no when Daddy started coming into her room at night. Thank God her innocence had been protected. Jesus, if it hadn't been for Christian morality's triumph over the obscenity of sex education, she might have been in her teens before she even knew what sperm tasted like!

The phone rang out somewhere behind her, inside the apartment, but she wasn't in the mood for talking, so she let the answering machine deal with it and stayed put on the balcony. Her brief outgoing message passed in a mumble, followed by the loud bleep, and then she heard a familiar and cheerful voice sound out over the speaker.

'Hey Maddy, Zip Spigelman here, your fellow filth-peddler.' Madeleine smiled. Zip was the producer of the movie she was about to make her legit début in, and with such a talent for putting people at ease, she was sure he'd one day be working on far more prestigious projects. Herself she was less certain about.

'I caught a little of the news, saw the Reverend's still working hard to keep your profile high. I don't know what Tony Pia's paying that guy, but he sure delivers. Anyway, I was just callin' to say Tanya's got a dress for you. It's one of the costumes you'll be wearing in the movie and we thought it'd be cool if you wore it at the press conference on Wednesday. If you can maybe drop by her place tomorrow, she can make sure it fits okay and make with the needle if it don't.

'Oh yeah, and the other thing is Tobe Delgado's gonna come along to the press conference too. We figured it would take some of the heat off you, and having the director there might remind some folks that we are actually making a movie. So, three filth merchants together. Look forward to it. See ya.'

Madeleine walked into the room and played back the message again as she raided the fridge for another beer. She glanced across to the open bedroom doorway, through which she could see the script lying on her bedside table.

Movie scripts. Costumes. Producers. Press conferences. It made her head spin, although in a pleasant way, like a healthy beer buzz. She smiled to herself as it occurred to her that Luther St John wouldn't be the only person in this world cursing her name to the skies. Every out-of-work struggling actress in LA would be throwing darts at her picture for the way this opportunity had fallen into her lap. She thought of her own disdain down the years for the endless succession of talentless teeny-boppers – suckers of Satan's cock, someone had once described them – shot to fame by a pretty face and slick marketing while hard-working singers and musicians waited years for a break that usually never came.

She hadn't harboured ambitions to be an actress or a movie star. It had all been Tony's doing. Even when she was working in the adult business she never saw legit acting on any list of possible futures; indeed, at that time she hadn't been thinking much about the future at all, at least no further than the inevitable discovery of her true identity.

When that particular storm broke, she realised that while she had always anticipated it, she could never have been ready for it. There were so many lights downstairs outside the building that night she remembered thinking flights into LAX were going to start landing on the boulevard. She felt scared, besieged and thoroughly alone. She didn't know who else she could turn to so she'd called Marco, who had always looked out for her since getting her started in the business. He had directed four of the features she appeared in, and she only did the other two upon his recommendation of the director and producer involved.

Marco wasn't much more equipped to deal with what was developing than she was, but his brother Tony was a different story. Tony was an agent representing several of the biggest names in the adult industry, as well as a few actresses who had moved on to parts in the mainstream B- and C-movie business. He was, by his brother's description, precisely the kind of slippery sleazeball you wanted on your side in a situation like this. To him, controversy wasn't a problem; it was the material he worked with, putty in his hands.

The first thing Tony did was get her out of the deal she'd signed to make her next hard-core feature. Aside from the unmanageable circus it would undoubtedly become, she wanted no part in it because her porn movie alter ego Katy Koxx had disappeared the minute the truth got out. It was the real Madeleine Witherson who would be in that picture, and the real Madeleine Witherson could not strip off and

109

fuck somebody in front of a camera crew. The producer was whining about reneging on a contract, asking Tony whether the name Kim Basinger meant anything to his client, but Tony pointed out that this was a skin flick they were talking about, and that meant his client had to consent to having sex: if she did not consent, no contract and certainly no court could make her. He also added that six million bucks was a cheap ticket out of a film as crappy as *Boxing Helena*.

Madeleine had enlisted Tony on Marco's recommendation purely because she needed help to survive the media onslaught. But Tony saw it as an opportunity rather than an ordeal. The notion that discovery would be a platform to greater things rather than the end of something good had never crossed her mind.

Not that it was going to be easy, but when the wolves came for Madeleine she was prepared, and she had a long-fanged lupine of her own in tow. Instead of being wiped out by the wave of media attention, Tony helped her surf it. Opinion polarised between those who painted her a villain or a victim; she refused to be brow-beaten by the former or seduced by the sympathy of the latter. It almost broke Tony's heart that she turned down appearances on the more lucrative *Oprah* and *Geraldo* in favour of *Larry King Live* and *Sixty Minutes*, but he stood by what she was trying to do, which was prevent the media making her its property. The pundits quickly learned that if they were going to make free with their opinions on Madeleine Witherson, they'd better be ready to go head-to-head, because she always demanded her right to reply, and for a while ratings dictated that she got it.

Soon enough, though, in accordance with Warhol's Law of Temporal Physics, her news value began to decline, but not before Tony had harnessed her notoriety to secure a three-picture acting deal with Line Arts, beginning with a starring role in *Angel's Claws*. That was the upside. The downside was that her exposure to blowhards like St John would continue, but then loudmouthed religious assholes were nothing new in Madeleine's world. It was a trade-off she could live with.

Fame – or she guessed that should be infamy – had granted her access to certain circles lately: certain company, certain parties, certain dates (for what *that* was worth). But, truth be told, she felt like a tourist: it was interesting to visit but she couldn't see herself living there, and she wasn't comfortable enjoying the trappings of celebrity without feeling like she'd earned it. (A militant part of herself might tell her she darn well had earned it, but that would be to deny the real reasons she'd got involved in the adult business.) She was looking forward to shooting the movie, nervous in case she really stank, but excited by the opportunity of getting inside her character. Granted, her part was hardly Ophelia, but she did have a few good lines amidst the slashing and vamping. Mainly, though, she was keen on the prospect of working, of getting on with something constructive, artistic merit notwithstanding.

She'd spent a long time sticking herself back together, and more convalescing. It was time for Madeleine Witherson to start getting on with her *life*.

Funnily enough, while Madeleine Witherson was thinking about getting on with her life, across town in Glendale Daniel Corby was thinking about ensuring she wouldn't have much life left to be getting on with.

This was because Daniel Corby was a Christian. And, obviously, because he was pro-Life.

Mr Irony didn't pay Daniel too many visits.

He scrolled his cursor down the screen, watching the names flash past in two columns until he reached hers. Daniel observed with satisfaction that her status had been reclassified as C (for confirmed), having graduated since yesterday from a week of TBC (to be confirmed) and from a fortnight before that of NRY (no response yet). Then he scrolled back up again past the Moonstar logo and clicked to move on to the schedule information on a different page. Nothing had changed. The charter, the harbouring, the catering, the timetables, nothing.

A few more double-clicks and he was heading over to the charter company to check on arrangements their end. The little hourglass icon sat stubbornly in front of him as he sipped his root-beer through a straw. The Net was slow tonight. Too many jerks playing stupid games and sending dirty pictures around the world. Savages. The most advanced communications technology known to man and they were using it to exchange grainy beaver shots or blow each other up in VR combat. He looked up from the screen while he waited, catching his reflection in another monitor, which had been switched off. After all these years some part of himself was still expecting to see his old face each time he looked in a mirror, and was therefore disappointed in what was actually there. The scarring and disfigurement didn't hurt any more, but he still felt it tingle sometimes, especially when he got mad, thinking about sluts like Witherson and anyone else who chose to scorn God's Word.

The hourglass changed to a key turning in a lock as his 'skeleton key' patch got to work accessing the charter firm's files. It took about a second and a half. Their security wasn't hot, but then, who would have any incentive to hack them? Apart from him, of course, and if he wanted in, he'd get in no matter what. Computers were Daniel Corby's thing. They were his vehicle, his weapon, his agent, his world. But they were not his life.

God was his life.

He looked at the packages on the table in front of him, wrapped innocuously in Cellophane. They took up hardly any space, and seemed insignificant compared to the plethora of state-of-the-art electronic hardware that surrounded them here in the basement. But those little packages were going to carry God's Word louder and further than all the CPUs in the world.

Daniel had always believed he could serve God through computers. However, those striving to serve Him were a precious few compared to those using computers and every other medium to spread filth, corruption, sin and evil. So ultimately he had learned that he could better serve God through computers *and* plastic explosives.

He had done what he could to fight the good fight down the years, at college and beyond. Uploading viruses on to pornographic websites, spamming pro-abortion newsgroups, and, of course, he had been part of Life Guard California. Life Guard was an anti-abortion group, which had grown out of a regular Internet forum, meeting up IRL and carrying out real action instead of just sitting around talking about it. They'd all had enough of stupid gestures like picketing clinics and pleading with women to turn around and save their babies. It never worked. The kind of woman who could even

112

contemplate slaughtering her own flesh and blood clearly had no morality to appeal to. Life Guard knew you had to talk to these bitches in a language they'd understand.

They hacked abortion clinics' client lists and got the addresses of women who were due to have baby-murders carried out, then they would send them Cellophane baggies full of blood and little plastic limbs through the post, along with flyers telling them they'd be held accountable one day for the slaughter when America woke up to itself. One day there was going to be the abortion equivalent of the Nuremberg trials, the leaflets warned.

They would also find out where these women lived, then put up posters on neighbourhood streetlights and around the entrances to their places of work. The posters carried the name and photograph of the woman concerned, stating first that she was pregnant and second the date she was intending to kill her baby.

Unfortunately one of the clinics mounted a sting operation, feeding the cops the names of the women on their list, and several of Daniel's partners were arrested pasting up flyers outside an office in Van Nuys. And what a joke: when the media found out about it, it was Life Guard who were called sick. How insane was that? They weren't the ones who were murdering innocent children. The whole country was screwed up. Not only did it permit this holocaust to continue, but it punished anyone who lifted a hand to try to stop it.

In the end the members who had been caught weren't prosecuted, but the experience and the publicity were enough to puncture their commitment to the cause, and the group soon began to disintegrate. Daniel was disgusted. Who could be so spineless as to put their public image above their principles? Especially when what America needed was more people prepared to stand up and tell it like it is, not hide behind all that political-correctness bullshit. People like Pat Buchanan. People like Rush Limbaugh.

People like Luther St John.

But this had been before he met the great man, when he was just a face on TV and a voice on the radio, not a guiding light whose destiny was bound up with his own. Maybe if their paths had crossed back then, he reflected, he'd never have had the accident. But then, wasn't it the lessons of the accident that provided the insights they had shared that momentous night? Would they have found so much to say to each other without it?

Daniel had been rash and impetuous back in those days. He had just felt so boilingly angry, so frustrated by what had happened to Life Guard that he seemed compelled to do something, to strike out. And though he now understood that it had been a mistake, a grave, grave mistake, he also knew that bombing the abortion clinic had taught him two very important things.

The first was that God's will could not be achieved through random acts of wanton violence.

The second was the necessity of synchronising your timer device with the watch you are wearing rather than the clock on your garage wall.

eight

'No,' he said, into the pillow. 'I ain't goin'. I resign. I ain't gettin' up. I ain't even openin' my eyes.'

Sophie kissed the back of his neck and ran a finger slowly down his spine. 'Come on, Sarge. You gotta get up. You gotta protect and serve the people of Los Angeles.'

'No,' he mumbled, goosebumps and small hairs on his back rising in response to Sophie's touch. 'I decided. I don't even *like* the people of Los Angeles.'

'Well you still have to protect our mortgage payments and serve the man holding the note at the bank. Come on, Larry.' She kissed his neck again. 'I'm the one should be wanting to stay in bed today. I'm supposed to be teaching *Titus Andronicus* to thirty wired teenagers. Just what you'd want to calm them down – the Jacobean equivalent of *Natural Born Killers*.'

'I thought you said you were gonna do *Othello* this semester.'

'Yeah, well, that was before Janet Richardson gave it to her senior class at Truman High.'

Larry turned his face around out of the pillow. 'Ain't that the school they had the race riot?'

'You got it.'

'Shit. Of course, if you ask me, the real tragedy in *Othello* is that he didn't have OJ's dream team to get him off later.'

Sophie punched him in the back playfully, digging her knuckles in until he giggled. 'Wise-ass,' she said, giving his buttocks a squeeze.

'Well, this morning I'd trade your teenagers wound up on Shakespeare – *Othello* or not – for my Christians wound up on Luther St John. Moral righteousness can be worse than PCP. You just don't know *what* these assholes might get up to if they think they're doin' it for God.'

'So the Reverend SJ was whipping up a storm last night,

huh?' she asked, in between nibbles at the back of his ear. 'He talk about the M word again?'

'Which one? Miscegenation or Mongrelisation?'

'Same difference. Did he?'

'Nope. This was a high-profile deal. The networks were doin' news coverage, and he wouldn't want that to be the only thing they were talkin' about. But I'm sure it's on the agenda some time this week.'

'So you reckon it's still a sin?'

'These guys only revise the sin list to *add*, honey, never subtract.'

Sophie took his hand and placed it on her belly, swelling from the growth within. 'Well I guess we're pretty much condemned,' she whispered.

'I sure hope so,' Larry replied softly. 'Because if heaven's full of those motherfuckers, I *want* my ticket to hell.'

Sophie giggled, burying her face between his shoulder blades and holding his hand tight against her stomach.

'Shit, well I guess I better get up.' Larry yawned.

'Honey,' she said, moving her other hand around his body until it rested on his thigh. 'Will you be mad if I make a confession?'

He laughed. 'How do I know until you've made it?'

Sophie drew her left hand up slowly until it cupped his balls through his shorts, at the same time pulling his fingers down away from her stomach and inside the elastic of her panties.

'I set your alarm an hour early last night,' she whispered. 'It's only just gone seven.'

Endorphins, hormones and adrenalin were still coursing through Larry's body for much of the morning, providing a rejuvenating retreat that went a long way towards maintaining his composure while all around him the world had turned into a hyperactives' kindergarten where some clown had given all the kiddies Gatorade. He could withdraw for a few moments now and again, step outside his thoughts and just *be* inside his body, feeling the tingle of his skin, the buzz through his muscles, the languid ache in his cock. He wished he could hand some of this stuff round, try and calm everyone the fuck down for long enough to forget whatever they were all so worked up about. He'd thought about St John's speech, how when you broke it all down there didn't seem any greater evil in the Legion of Decency's world than consenting adults getting laid. It struck him that if they'd all worry less about other people getting it on and concentrated on doing it themselves a bit more often, then none of this shit would be necessary. No legions, no banners, no missions.

'What you doin', baby?'

'I'm makin' a banner. Got a moral crusade to go on.'

'Shit, you got energy to spare? Put the paintbrush down and come back to bed. Relax. Just get laid and you don't have to hate nobody.'

'Ooh, baby, hurts so good. Banners? *What* was I thinkin' about . . . ?'

If only.

He knew he was 'gonna have to get down to the PV right away, they're all having a collective canary' well before Bannon told him to; before he'd even left for the station house. There were uptight movie-biz suits in close proximity with religious fundamentalists, and St John had shaken the jar. That was why he hadn't wanted to get up.

'A walk in the park, sir, huh?' he couldn't resist reminding Bannon.

'Hey listen, Freeman,' Bannon replied, after rolling his eyes. 'Don't be wishin' it to get worse just so you can say, "I told you so." Right now it's a storm in a teacup, okay? I want you to calm everybody down, make out it's no big deal, all right? Show these guys you ain't worried, and if you ain't worried, they shouldn't be neither.'

'Oh, sure thing sir, I'll get right on it. What do you want me to use, cannabis? We got some of that down in Evidence you could let me have, maybe?'

'No, Larry, I want you to use your natural calming influence.'

'Do I make you feel calm, sir?' he asked with a grin.

'Oh sure. Every time I see your ass walk *out* that door. So get the fuck down to that hotel and I'll just be calmness personified.'

Paul Silver was not calmness personified. Not that Larry was expecting him to be, having had to flash his badge at the clamouring protesters blocking Damascus Drive before they would move aside to let him take his car up to the hotel entrance. He recognised the slogans on some of the placards from St John's Epistle to the Caucasians yesterday, and given that most of them were printed rather than painted, he figured neither the speech nor the protest were improvised.

'UnAmerican Festering Filth Market' was the favourite, rendered in the same style as the AFFM's logo. 'Save the world from celluloid sin' was also popular.

'Shouldn't you guys be across the road with the rest of your Festival of Light buddies?' he asked a group of them, as he tucked away his badge again.

'The Light is all around,' one guy replied.

'Well, you got that right,' he'd muttered, shielding his eyes as the protesters vacated the space between his windshield and the infamous PV glare.

'So aren't you going to do anything about them?' Silver asked. They were in the hotel manager's office, Larry sitting in a chair watching Silver pace back and forth. It looked like his hair was on gimbals, so little did it seem to move as he walked the carpet. Larry kept expecting it to stay still each time Silver turned about-face, his head and body pivoting underneath it.

'Right now, no sir, I'm not. They aren't breaking any laws. They've got a democratic right to protest and they are staying outside the boundaries of the hotel grounds, so they ain't trespassing.'

'But they're intimidating the delegates. Can't you cite them for threatening behaviour or something?'

Larry laughed a little. 'No,' he said, smiling. Bannon knew Larry better than he had given him credit for. He was naturally reacting to Silver's agitation by relaxing and giving off the impression that there was nothing to worry about. He had been so long in the company of his worries, he'd forgotten how adept he was at riding the storms of other people's. He began to recognise the two-handed dialogue: freaked civilian going hyper, laid-back cop amused at the former, and with a galvanised feeling he began to recognise the latter as the old Larry Freeman, finally showing up for duty again after extended compassionate leave. In fact, he suspected that while everybody had been giving him time and space, the therapy he'd really needed was some quality chaos.

'Think about it, Mr Silver,' he told him. 'These people are all pumped up with moral indignation. If I bust any of them, they can add state oppression to the mix, and you'll have twice as many out front tomorrow. In my judgement, the worst thing you can do right now is react. It's basic schoolyard psychology.'

'You're saying we should pretend like it isn't happening? We've been identified as the source of all evil known to humanity and you're saying we should just ignore it?'

'You've been identified as the source of all evil known to humanity by a guy who's gone on national television to say that this whole city's about to be wiped out by a tidal wave. I'm saying don't dignify him with a response. As soon as you do that, then you are, in the world's eyes, taking him seriously. Nobody else is, why be the first?'

Silver ran a hand through his rigid hair. That's gotta hurt, Larry thought.

'Well maybe you should ask Tom Wilcox of CineCorp whether he's taking it seriously, Sergeant Freeman. Because he had red paint thrown over him as he came in the side-path entrance first thing this morning, by protesters shouting about violence in the movies. Protesters who, I suspect, had tipped off the news crew that managed to film the whole thing for Channel Five's breakfast bulletin.'

'Really? I was too busy to catch the news this morning.' He smiled to himself, just a little, couldn't help it. 'Hotel security get these guys?'

'No, there was a crowd. Hard to see who actually threw the paint. But I've also been told by Alice Kilgour of VentraFilm that they had slogans daubed on the walls of their offices in Burbank last night.'

Larry nodded, trying to look sincerely concerned. 'This Mr Wilcox, is he okay? Does he want to file a complaint?'

'I don't know. I imagine so. I've been so inundated with calls over this whole Luther St John thing that I haven't had time to talk to him yet. I think the hotel manager went to see him earlier, sort him out with a shower and a loaner suit.'

'Well, give him a call,' Larry suggested. 'If he wants action, I'll see him right away. I'll get straight to it. Otherwise . . . schoolyard psychology, Mr Silver.'

'Okay, okay,' he said, flipping open his electronic organiser and looking up the number of the CineCorp stand.

The door opened and a flush-faced woman in a tan suit walked in, holding a glinting Coke can to her forehead and sighing loudly. She put down the can and smiled, approaching Larry with an outstretched hand. She was tall, early forties, jet black hair streaked minutely with isolated strands of grey. She looked formidable but attractively approachable with it.

'You must be Sergeant Freeman,' she said. 'I'm Conchita Nunez, manager of the hotel.' She glanced aside at Silver, but he had turned his back as he muttered quietly into the telephone.

'Tough morning so far, Ms Nunez?' Larry enquired.

She rolled her eyes and took a gulp from her can, still smiling. 'Diverting,' she said. There was a radiance about her features which suggested to Larry that this morning's events weren't entirely her idea of a bad time. 'Can I get you a drink, Sergeant?'

'No thanks. You look more in need of refreshment.'

'I'm all hot and bothered. Running around the place, telling people not to panic, but that's part of the job.'

'Hey, that's my job too. Maybe between us we can convince Mr Silver here of the same thing.'

'Huh!' she said with a toss of the head. Not convinced. Larry smiled.

Silver finished his call.

'Well?'

'Tom Wilcox doesn't want to file a complaint.'

'So he sees the wisdom in keeping a low profile?'

'No, not exactly.' Silver now looked more baffled than perplexed. 'He says CineCorp have closed deals for just about everything on their slate in the last two hours, for the US and three European territories. He's apparently got them lining up along the corridor looking for tapes to view, and it's going to be standing room only at their première screening in the AMC multiplex this afternoon. Turns out the buyers are just dying to see what sort of explosive material provoked this morning's little incident. He says he's telling the trade press it was "a gift from God".'

Larry laughed, looking across to Nunez, who waved her hands as if to say she wanted nothing to do with it.

'You see, Mr Silver?' Larry said. 'I know you're shook up because you could do without this whole St John thing, especially your first year in charge, but it's here now, the genie's already out of the bottle, so just ride it. Things are gonna be a little crazier than you anticipated this week, but remember that it isn't a problem until it's a problem. Now, what I recommend you do is get out there and walk the floor, talk to the buyers and sellers, make out you think it's all a great joke. They know your job is to worry about this shit, so if they look at you and you ain't worried, they ain't worried.'

Silver sighed loudly. 'Okay,' he said, nodding, 'okay. And I guess that should work for me too. I look at you, you aren't worried, so I shouldn't worry.'

'That's right.'

'But when I go down there, I'll be faking it.'

'That's right.'

'But they won't know that.'

'That's right.'

'So how do I know you're not faking it?'

'You don't,' Larry said with a smile, getting up and heading for the door.

He had just emerged into the bustle of the lobby when he heard a voice calling his name.

'Sergeant Freeman, Sergeant Freeman.'

He turned around to see the manager's assistant running towards him from the stairwell that led up to the offices he had recently vacated. From the pallor of her skin and the fear in her eyes he could guess it wasn't that he'd left his keys behind.

'What is it?'

'Not here,' she said breathlessly, taking hold of his arm. 'Come back upstairs, quickly.'

She hurriedly keyed in the access code on the door leading to the stairwell, then ushered him inside and closed it again.

'Upstairs to Miss Nunez' office, quickly,' she urged, in a semi-whisper. 'There's a man on the telephone saying there's a bomb in the building. Said he's going to level the place so that the "filth market" can't take place.'

'So what's the rush?' Larry said. She thought he was joking. 'If I miss him, I'll catch the next guy later on.'

121

'What next guy?' she gasped, dismay flashing in her eyes as she trotted up the stairs, but Larry wasn't saying.

When he strode back into the office, Silver was standing on the carpet chewing his knuckles while Nunez sat at her desk talking into the telephone. Silver tried to give him a chastising now-will-you-take-me-seriously glare, but Larry's grin unnerved him too much.

'Yes, of course,' Nunez was saying into the mouthpiece, looking up at Larry with worried eyes. 'We are treating your threat with all seriousness, sir.'

Larry leaned across the desk and hit the silence button on the phone.

'Tell him he's got to talk to me. It's procedure – you can't evacuate without it. Do it.'

She nodded nervously. He released his finger.

'No I didn't cut you off, sir,' she said. 'No, I wouldn't mess you around. But I can't evacuate the building right now. I have a member of the police department here and I need his clearance first. It's his call. I'm going to put him on.'

'Very good,' Larry mouthed as she handed him the phone.

'Hello sir. My name is Sergeant Larry Freeman of the LAPD. I understand you are warning us of an explosive device here in the Pacific Vista hotel.'

'That's right,' said a male voice. Larry pressed a button to put the incoming signal through the speakerphone. 'A bomb. A big one. I'm warning you, I'd get everybody out of there right now if I was you.'

'Yes sir, safety is our first priority. And I'm assuming you wish to avoid human casualties, otherwise you wouldn't be giving this warning, which is why I need to ask you a few questions about the device. I don't suppose you'd be prepared to tell us whereabouts in the hotel it's planted?'

'You're darn right.'

'I figured. Well, that's your prerogative, sir. But I do need to know a little about it so that we can estimate what kind of distance we need to evacuate around the building. How big is the device?'

'Big.'

'Like what, twenty pounds?'

'Bigger. Try forty.'

Nunez closed her eyes. Silver looked like he was about to run to the bathroom.

'And what kind of explosive is it?'

'C4.'

'Jesus, sir, you're playing for keeps, aren't you?'

'Darn right. And don't take the Lord's name in vain.'

'My apologies. Just one more question sir, and this is extremely important: we really *have* to know this. I'm assuming the device is on a remote trigger. Are you using a bilateral transept detonator or just the old faithful MUB linear?'

'What? The second one. MUB linear.'

'Uh-oh,' Larry said to Nunez in a stage whisper, partially covering the mouthpiece so that the caller could still just hear him. 'He's using an MUB linear.' He took his hand away again. 'All right sir. I understand exactly how seriously we have to take you. I'm going to initiate a KMA drill right away.'

'What's that?'

'Kiss My Ass,' he said, and put the phone down.

Silver's eyes bulged in horror. The more phlegmatic Nunez just stared at Larry in anticipation.

'Are you nuts?' Silver asked.

'There's no bomb.'

'You don't know that. How can you be sure?'

'Do you know what MUB stands for?' Larry asked him.

'Made Up Bullshit?' suggested Nunez, with a raise of her right eyebrow.

'Exactly. Just like bilateral transept detonator. Bombers first need to know how to build a bomb, Mr Silver. This guy didn't. He just wanted to disrupt the party. Bombers also don't wait around answering questions on the telephone, in case the cops are tracing their call.' He turned to Nunez. 'I'm afraid you're probably gonna be getting more of these calls over the next few days. I'll organise for a trace on this line so that we can maybe bust a few of them as a deterrent. The guys running the trace will also be there to talk to the callers, and they'll soon let you know if there's anything genuinely worth worrying about.'

'Thank you Sergeant,' she said warmly.

'Don't sweat it. And Mr Silver?'

'Yes Sergeant?'

'Relax.'

*   *   *

Larry got back to the station house around two thirty, carrying a late lunch of coffee and half a sub, which in retrospect wasn't entirely appropriate, but then he wasn't to know. There had been a folder for him at the front desk, and he carried that in his left hand, coffee in the right and sandwich bag in his mouth as he shouldered open the door to the office he shared with Zabriski. There was a Latin-featured woman at Zabriski's desk, looking up expectantly as he barged in.

'Ee ight ith oo,' Larry said through gritted teeth, kicking the door closed and dropping the bag on to a pile of newspapers on his desk. He found a space for the coffee then turned around to face the visitor, just as Zabriski came in the door with a similarly steaming polystyrene cup, which he handed to the woman.

'Larry, this is Maria Arazon of the Californian Oceanowhat-chamacallit. I forget, I'm sorry. I said she could wait here for you. I gotta go. I'm trying to keep the press off of the exploding shitbag thing at AmTrak. Last thing we want is copycats on a stunt like that. Miss Arazon, this is Sergeant Larry Freeman.'

She put down her coffee and stood up, extending a hand as Zabriski retreated. She was young, late twenties, early thirties at the most. Her wide hazel eyes were bloodshot and dark-ringed, her hair as tousled as her T-shirt. Either she hadn't slept or she'd slept in what she wore.

'Good afternoon, Ms? Miss?'

'Doctor, professionally. But Miss,' she said, holding up a bare ring-finger. 'As of about two years.'

She looked unsure of herself and distrusting of everything around her, lost as to where she fitted in. Larry recognised it. The victims, the bereaved, they would often tell you something personal straight off that they'd otherwise never dream of mentioning to someone they'd only just met. He wasn't sure why: maybe their defences were so shot they didn't bother putting up the usual screens; maybe they needed to talk to someone like they were a friend, not just part of the state's clearing-up machine, not just another aspect of this horrible process.

'Dr Arazon. I won't say I'm pleased to meet you because I'm sure we'd both rather not be having this conversation.'

'You got that right,' she said quietly, traces of a Mexican accent in her few words.

Larry wheeled his chair over to the other side of Zabriski's desk and sat down facing her, but a few feet to one side so that it didn't seem too confrontational.

'So what can I do for you?'

'I spent yesterday afternoon at the Coast Guard Marina,' she said. 'It was requested that someone from CalORI take a look over . . . things.'

'That's right. Thank you very much for doing that. I appreciate how difficult it must have been. And did you find there was anything unaccounted for?'

'Yes, Sergeant.' She took a sip from her coffee and nodded to herself. 'What remains unaccounted for is what happened to my friends. I've seen the boat and I've read the preliminary draft of your report, and to be perfectly frank I don't buy it.'

Larry paused, breathing in for a second. Don't bite back, you'll learn nothing. 'Let me just get my file on it,' he said, and got up to retrieve it from his own desk. 'Okay.' He sat back down and uncapped a Biro. 'So what exactly don't you buy?'

'The part where four trained professionals got into a submarine one morning and never came back.' There was a fiery challenge in her tired eyes; Larry recognised that too. Deny the bad thing is true, argue for how it can't be true, and maybe in the end it'll turn out it wasn't true. Except it never does.

'Okay,' he said again, nodding. 'But Dr Arazon, I have to ask you this: given that the four trained professionals we're talking about were your friends, is it that you don't buy the story because you don't believe it happened that way, or because it hurts to think that it did?'

She looked away from him impatiently, swallowing. She'd probably thought she was all cried out before she came in here, but having to do this was unwrapping the bandages again.

'I don't buy it principally because it doesn't make any sense.'

'Well I can appreciate that it doesn't make—'

'You're not hearing me, Sergeant. I'm not in here to blub and say, "Boo-hoo, my friends are dead it's so unfair, why why why?" I'm saying it doesn't make sense because all four crew would never go off in the sub at once. At least one person stays top-side during every dive. It's basic safety procedure.'

Larry nodded, looking away for a second from the relentless

insistence of her eyes. 'All right, I hear you now,' he said. 'And I understand what you're telling me. Now, let me ask you not to take this wrong, and to try and see it from my position for a second. What you're telling me is that it would be *unsafe* for all four crew members to take off in this sub at once. So as we're left sitting here with no crew and no sub, from an investigative point of view, the information you've just given me would tend to support rather than contradict my conclusions.'

Her eyes flashed again, but Larry resumed before she could respond. 'I know how hurtful, even how insulting this sounds to you, to suggest that your colleagues would do something negligent like this, but we've got to accept the *possibility* that that's what happened.'

She had a bitter smile on her face. Larry suspected he wasn't the first person who had failed to satisfy her need for a better explanation.

'I thought you'd say that,' she told him. 'That's why I've waited to mention the log book.'

'What about the log book?'

'Ship's log, written by Mitchell Kramer. Last entry untimed, undated. Just said they were taking the *SM* to the Slopes Of Stronghyli.'

'Yeah, I remember now. What are you saying?'

'There's no such location. Stronghyli's the geological name for a place in Europe that doesn't exist any more. The biggest undersea feature near where the sub went missing is Fieberling Guyot.'

'So why would he write the slopes of whatever?'

'Not the slopes of whatever, Sergeant. The Slopes Of Stronghyli. With a capital O on the word "Of". I've seen the entry.'

'I don't get it.'

'Think of the initials.'

He did.

Oh shit.

'Get it now?'

Larry nodded, then exhaled slowly. Experience had taught him not to let such surprises intoxicate the detective in him.

'Okay Doctor,' he said. 'This all sounds pretty weird and mysterious, I'll grant you, but let's try and keep our feet on the ground for a minute, huh? If the boat was in some kind of trouble, some kind of danger, why not put a call out on the radio? Why not shoot a flare? Why make your cry for help in a coded message? An SOS is supposed to be a scream, not a whisper.'

'Depends on whether someone has their hand over your mouth at the time.'

'That's true enough,' he conceded. 'But if you're suggesting someone else was on board, well . . . You've seen the place yourself. We don't have any evidence of a struggle having taken place, no breakages, no signs of blood. And the other thing we don't have is a motive. Why would anyone wish your colleagues harm, and better yet, why would they go all the way out to the middle of the ocean to *do* them harm?'

'No witnesses, for one thing,' she snapped. 'I don't know, Sergeant, I thought motives and explanations were your department. I've only got questions, and I was hoping you'd be interested enough to look for more answers than are in your report.'

'Oh, I'm interested,' Larry assured her. 'After what you've told me I'm gonna request a forensic sweep of the boat, see if anyone else *was* on board. I'm not here to brush this aside with the first plausible theory that comes along. But I can only take it as far as the evidence will let me, and so far there ain't much of that. Unless there's somethin' else you're holdin' out on.'

She looked back at him just a little too quickly. There it was, he thought. He could see there was something she wanted to tell him, but by the same instinct he suspected she wouldn't. Not yet, leastways.

She got up from her chair.

'I've got to get back, Sergeant,' she said, making for the door.

'Thanks for coming in, Dr Arazon. I'll let you know if we find anything.'

'Sure.' She opened the door, then paused with her fingers around the handle. 'Sergeant, if you really are interested, two words: Sandra Biscane. C-A-N-E.'

'Who's that?'

'You're the cop. Look it up.'

Sandra Biscane. The name meant nothing to him, nor did he

think it was supposed to. Maria Arazon was trying to draw him into something, playing her cards one at a time, and he'd bet that whatever this one turned out to be, it wouldn't be the last. She had the fatigue and fragility of the bereaved, but she wasn't simply looking for answers to console her for her loss. That lady knew something, but she wasn't going to give it up until she figured he'd earned it.

Larry took a seat at the computer terminal, placed his coffee next to the keyboard in front of the sign that expressly forbade doing so, and logged on to the database. Arazon hadn't given him any pointers or any parameters, so he'd just have to feed in the name alone – no categories, no geographical locations, no connections – and sit back. Maybe even go for a walk. He settled on finishing his coffee and watching the little egg-timer icon empty out then up-end itself over and over in the centre of the monitor.

The boat had been troubling him since his visit to the marina. At first he'd put it down to being spooked by the weirdness of it all, but even if Arazon hadn't come along, he still wasn't certain he'd have remained satisfied with his report as it stood. This Slopes Of Stronghyli thing didn't have to mean everything Arazon might imagine it could mean, but he'd be surprised if it meant nothing at all. All down the years they taught you that when you hear hooves, you should look for horses, not zebras, but that didn't mean that it never turned out to be a herd of the black-and-white critters once in a while. Despite Rodriguez opining that even experienced sailors can screw up, there was still something left unsaid about this one. Especially now he knew that it was not the done thing for all four of them to go down in the sub at the same time.

He arced his cup into the trash basket just as the screen flashed back into life.

'Biscane, Sandra NOT FOUND,' it read. 'NEAREST MATCH? YES/NO.'

'Shit,' Larry muttered. He hit Y.

The computer offered him a 'Biscane, A' and a 'Biscane, Monica'. He hit the key to look up the former. The screen went blank then scrolled out its information.

'Biscane, Alexandra.' That's my girl, Larry thought. 'Homicide. San Bernadino. Reported: 7.7.98. Case file opened: 7:7:98. OPEN/PREVIOUS SCREEN.'

He typed O.

'No access to file. File classified by Federal Bureau of Investigation. PREVIOUS SCREEN/MAIN MENU.'

He stared stubbornly at the screen as if it might be intimidated into changing its mind.

Homicide. Classified. FBI.

SOS.

'What ain't you tellin' me, Dr Arazon?'

The restroom's triptych of mirrors confirmed Maria's suspicions: she looked like shit. She didn't want to think about what impression her crash-victim appearance must have made on the cop, but at least she felt sure of the impact her words had had. She splashed water on her face, like that was going to make a difference, and sighed at the wasted image gazing back at her. Too bad junkie chic went out. The most constructive thing she could do right now, she figured, was shut down her terminal and go home.

She hadn't been sleeping too well since the disappearance, but last night she'd barely got under at all. She had prepared herself for what she might feel when she saw the boat again: the feelings, the memories, the torments of a fevered imagination. Her greatest fears had been about what a thudding impact the experience would have on her delicate grieving process. She thought she was only dealing with loss. The logbook told her otherwise.

Walking around the *Gazes Also* hadn't quite been the ordeal she'd imagined. The Coast Guard had removed the dirty plates and cups from the galley for purposes of hygiene, so the *Mary Celeste* effect everyone had been talking about failed to register. The very orderliness that contributed to other people's bafflement meant there was nothing to jar Maria's sense of familiarity. She felt no auras of lost companions, no 'atmosphere' of imprinted human emotion. There was far more of that to be found at CalORI, probably because that was where she was more used to spending time with the four of them. It was, basically, an empty boat.

The log, however, changed everything.

It wasn't just the initials, or the fact that the place specified could not have been their intended destination. There was more than that, she was sure. If Mitch had reason to leave a coded SOS, he could have made up any name – Sands Of Somewhere, Slopes Of Someplace else – but he said Stronghyli, which was like underlining the message several times. Admittedly, if this meant what she thought it meant, he might not have had the time or presence to be thinking too much about wider connotations, but he'd still have been aware of what that name referred to. Stronghyli was the geological name for pre-eruption Thera. It was also CalORI slang for a situation that was about to go disastrously wrong.

The nauseous feeling in her gut that the phrase unleashed was not a reflex, more the lowering of a barrier, allowing an in-rush of fear and anger that had been backed up since last summer when Sandra was murdered.

Maria had grown used to not thinking about it, knowing that the lack of answers only tugged at her wounds, and that unsolved homicides were not exactly a rarity here in the Southland. The fact that the FBI were all over the thing had heightened the mystery, but she soon garnered the impression it was the murderer they had a special interest in, not the victim. Even amid the current climate of hysterical paranoia, it hadn't occurred to her to draw any link between Sandra's death and whatever had happened on the *Gazes Also*. Then she had read those three little words.

She could tell Freeman understood what they entailed. He was bound to resist accepting it straight away, but he would accept it soon enough.

Someone else had been on that boat.

Larry was fixing to clock off and head for home when his phone rang. He thought about ignoring it, as strictly speaking, he should have been out of there ten minutes ago, indeed would have been but for a long call from Conchita Nunez. She wasn't requiring any form of assistance, just to unburden herself to someone of similar mind and thus avoid letting rip with a less-than-diplomatic outburst at the next act of stupidity she was faced with. There had been two more bomb calls since he left, but the trace hadn't been up in time to get a location on them. Nunez had transferred the first guy to Tommy Andrews, who had been allocated bomb-hoaxer duty, but she recognised the second as the same loser from that morning, and took the call herself. The poor dumb shit thought he had been caught out by giving the wrong answer to Larry's trigger question, and had confidently asserted straight off that he was using a bilateral transept detonator, which Larry had made up too.

Further inconvenience had come in the form of a second paint-throwing incident, but this time hotel security had managed to catch the two culprits as they ran away. A brief interrogation revealed that they were both in the employ of ReelCo and that they had been under orders to splatter their executive superiors, who had been enviously observing the activity around CineCorp's market office all morning.

This little revelation led in turn to the forcible dispersal down on the beach of a group of demonstrators, who had for the previous hour been waving placards and chanting in denunciation of certain 'sinful' titles on the ProTel slate.

Larry looked at the clock. Market business was closed for the day, and the unhappy-clappies would have packed up too. He figured it was safe to answer.

'Hello, Sergeant Larry Freeman here.'

'Good evening, Sergeant, this is Agent Peter Steel of the Federal Bureau of Investigation.'

They always said that. Like you might be unfamiliar with the abbreviation, or like FBI could stand for more than one thing.

'Good evening yourself. What can I do for you, Agent Steel?'

'Sergeant Freeman, I understand you were attempting to access the computerised case files on Alexandra Biscane this afternoon. Is that correct?'

'Shit, what you guys got, a hidden camera in this station?'

'No sir, there's a crossover trace on that file. If anyone looks it up, I get a message on my computer telling me who and where, so that I can do what I'm doing now, which is asking you why you're interested in Professor Biscane.'

'Oh, it's *Professor* Biscane,' Larry said. 'Well at least I'm finding out something. Tell you what, why don't you tell me why it's classified and then I'll tell you why I'm interested?'

'I'm afraid I can't do that, Sergeant.'

'Well in that case—'

'Not that way around, anyway,' Steel interrupted. 'I'm sorry about sounding like an asshole G-man, but I need to know why you're interested first, and depending on your reason, I might be able to open up a little.'

Larry sighed. A self-aware asshole G-man was a major step in the species' evolution. It was therefore in his interest to assist the new breed's survival.

'I'm investigating the disappearances – probably safe to say deaths but we got no bodies and probably won't never have, neither – of four scientists from a research vessel in the Pacific.'

'Who were they? What did they do?'

Larry reached for a folder on the desk in front of him, cradling the phone between his shoulder and his chin as he flipped through the leaves inside.

'Let's see,' he said, 'Mitchell Kramer, seismologist, Cody Williams, geologist, Grady Cooper, also a geologist, and Taylor Svenson, also a seismologist. All from the Californian Oceanographic Research Institute, or CalORI for short. Boat was called the *Gazes Also*, and they vanished off it last week along with a miniature submarine.'

'They vanished off it? You mean the ship didn't go down or anything?'

'No. The ship was a genuine latterday *Mary Celeste*. Found drifting, dinner plates in the sink, coffee cups and post-prandial brandies still on the table. Only thing out of place was a conspicuous lack of personnel and the absence of their submersible vehicle, the *Stella Maris*. So far I've been working on the explanation that all the missing components fit together. Crew get in submarine, submarine takes its remit too far. However . . .'

'What were they working on out there?'

'Research, whatever that means. Taking samples, charting stuff. I don't know. But they weren't looking for oil, if that's what you're wondering about.'

'And why were you looking up Biscane?'

'Someone from CalORI mentioned her name. Someone who wasn't convinced of my theory that these guys had an accident. I don't know the connection, because right now I know nothing about Sandra Biscane. So you gonna throw something back my way, or do I just run along now?'

Steel breathed in slowly on the other end of the line. 'Alexandra – Sandra – Biscane was a professor at UCLA, specialising in ocean seismology. She was murdered in her home last summer, apparently having disturbed a burglar.'

'But you didn't buy that.'

'No, we didn't. We took over the investigation from Homicide in San Bernadino pretty much from the start.'

'Why?'

'This is classified information, Sergeant, so it goes no further than either end of this phone line, okay?'

'You got it.'

'Does the name Southland Militia mean anything to you?'

Larry swallowed. He hadn't heard of this particular pustule but he was familiar with the disease. Groups of extreme-right, paranoid, white-supremacist, Christian fundamentalist brain-donors with a gun obsession and the arsenal to feed it. Yet another cauldron of unstable hatred that had been simmering away throughout the Nineties and threatening to boil over the nearer we got to year zero.

'That's like the Michigan Militia, right?' he said, trying not to enunciate the concern and revulsion he was feeling. 'They go running around the woods with assault weapons at the weekend, training for when they have to fend off an invasion by the UN. That it?'

'Right. But these guys are from southern California – LA, Orange County, San Diego – and they go running around the desert rather than the woods. And yeah, they're training for something, but we're concerned it might be something a little more soon and a little less imaginary than an invasion by the UN. The FBI's been monitoring all the militias pretty closely since Waco, obviously not closely enough, given Oklahoma City. Our intelligence suggests the Southland Militia are gearing up for a major outing. They're stockpiling weapons, recruiting new bodies. Trouble is, we have no idea what's on the agenda.

'To cut to the chase, we've had several members of the Militia's high-rank inner circle under surveillance, and last July our agents witnessed one of them enter Biscane's condo the evening of the murder.'

'So you figure he did it. And this is the part where you tell me you didn't bust him, right?'

Steel paused. 'That is correct. Our agents didn't know why the guy was there, so they just watched him leave and followed him as per instructions. Physical evidence was negligible. He left no prints – we guessed surgical gloves. He killed Professor Biscane with a single stab-wound to the chest using one of her own kitchen knives. Left it sticking in her – plausible interrupted-burglary spur-of-the-moment scenario. To complete the effect he opened a few drawers, emptied her pocketbook of cash and even unplugged the VCR and left it on the kitchen floor like he was making off with it when she woke up and found him.'

'But you had witnesses – Federal officers, in fact. So why didn't you bust him?'

'We still intend to, don't worry. But we held back because we didn't know what he – and by extension the Southland Militia – wanted with Biscane, far less why they wanted her dead. It was the first real lead we had on what they might be up to.'

'And if you pulled him straight in you figured they'd circle the wagons.'

'Exactly. We wanted them to think they'd gotten away with it.'

'So why *did* they kill her?'

There was a long pause.

'We still don't know,' Steel admitted. 'That's why there's a crossover trace on the file – to alert me to anything new connected to her death or to her personally. Which brings us back to you and your missing scientists. You said you were given Biscane's name by someone who didn't think they'd had an accident. Who was that?'

'Dr Maria Arazon.'

'I remember the name. Another seismologist. Friend of Biscane. Guess it's understandable she thinks foul play. What do *you* think, Sergeant?'

'I'm thinking nothing I'd like to be quoted on yet, Agent Steel. Not until I've seen the forensics report. I've seen the boat, though. There's plenty weird about it but nothing suspicious. Except that the – I'd guess you'd call him the captain – wrote what Arazon believes to be a coded SOS message in the log's final entry. It said they were all taking their submarine to a place called the Slopes Of Stronghyli, which doesn't exist any more, apparently.'

'Slopes Of Stronghyli. SOS. Why would he write that?'

'Beats the shit out of me. Arazon thinks it was the only way to signal something was wrong, presumably under duress, but I figure there's gotta be a few explanations further up the plausibility table than that.'

'Sure,' Steel agreed. 'Sure. But do you think it's possible, I don't know, maybe they saw something they weren't supposed to? They're way out in the Pacific – a drug exchange, gun-running?'

'All of these things are possible, Agent Steel. But a man could go crazy counting up all the things that are *possible*. Here's as much as I know for sure. I've got four scientists missing presumed dead, and an understandably emotional colleague of theirs gives me the name of a fifth scientist, who it turns out is dead too. But as right now the only connection is that your victim and two of my MPDs were seismologists – and as the emotional colleague who connected them is a seismologist too – I'll wait till I know more before I go reading too much into it.'

He got CalORI through Information and convinced the lab technician still on duty to surrender Arazon's home number.

'Sergeant Freeman, what can I do for you?' she asked, trying too hard to sound surprised that he was calling.

'Well, you can start by telling me whether you knew I'd end up with the FBI on my tail when I looked up that name you gave me, Doctor.'

'Was it Agent Steel?'

'How did you know that?'

'He came to interview me after Sandra's murder. It didn't take much intuition to work out she wasn't just a random victim if the FBI were involved.'

'And because she wasn't a random victim, later on, when some more associates of yours disappear, you think that ain't a random event either?'

'In the space of six months? It's a bit of a coincidence.'

'This whole world's just full of coincidences, Dr Arazon, believe me, and they'll lead you a crazy dance if you let them. Tell me this: can you connect the victims of these two incidents through anything more than a shared academic field?'

She sighed irritably. 'No, Sergeant, right now I can't.'

135

'Me neither. So to graduate from coincidence to conspiracy, we'd need at least one more link.'

'Well you won't find one if you're not prepared to look.'

'Oh, I'll be looking, Dr Arazon, and I'll be looking hard. But you gotta understand this: I do needles in haystacks, I don't do wild-goose chases. So anyway, why did Peter Steel come see *you* back then?'

He heard her swallow, sigh, try to still her frustrations.

'I was a friend and one-time academic colleague,' she told him. 'Steel was looking to build up some background on Sandra, what her work was about, who her contacts were.'

'Trying to figure out possible reasons why she was killed.'

'I guess so. What'd he tell you?'

'Everything and nothing, which is consistent with the FBI. Just when you think they're getting expansive, that's usually the sign that they're keeping the good shit back. He says they still don't know why she was murdered. I believe him on that. He was scrubbing in the dirt for leads. That's why he chased me.'

'Hmm,' said Arazon, wryly unconvinced. 'He tell you about her computer?'

'No, what about it?'

'Sandra's sister Beth was what you'd call executor of her estate. She passed Sandra's books, papers, folders – and her Apple Mac – on to her department colleagues at UCLA for them to salvage what they could of her work. But when they hooked up the machine, the hard disk had been cleaned out.'

'Erased?' asked Larry.

'Not exactly. The system software was still installed, and there were a few basic applications on board, but whatever else had been on there was gone. Plus she had a SyQuest drive in the apartment but no SyQuest cartridges, suggesting they'd been removed – possibly by her killer.'

'So what should have been on this Mac?'

'Plenty. She did *everything* on her computer. Sandra and I went through college together, and we shared a lot of interests, but that was where we seriously diverged. I mean, I use computers, in fact I couldn't exist without them, but I didn't share her enthusiasm for how you actually program the things. I like to come along when the technical part's done, just press the right buttons and get the results. Sandra liked to take the programs apart like they were the engine on her car. Whenever she started talking about it, I'd just be lost. Stuff was way over my head.

'Obviously I didn't follow the number-crunching side, but I do remember her big hobby-horse was constructing 3-D seismological models, you know, for trying to project what would happen along *this* faultline if *that* crustal plate moved in such-and-such a direction. Hardly explosive material, I know. So there must have been other stuff on her files that somebody was either interested in or worried about.'

'Certainly sounds like it,' Larry observed. 'But now it's gone and so's she. When did you last speak to her?'

'Around May of last year, on the telephone. She was taking a sabbatical for the spring semester to work on a personal project.'

'And apart from computers, what was Professor Biscane's particular area of interest?'

'Tidal waves.'

From: Jerry Blake
Date: 3 March 1999 01:21
To: marazon@calori.com
Cc:
Subject: The Money Shot!

Hey Maria!
Had you teased and on tenterhooks with all this foreplay, huh? Well, now I'm finally delivering the juicy bit — as far as a seismologist like you is concerned. Finally, a first-hand (oh really? — we'll let the journals argue about that) account of the big one. Sorry this has taken so long after me whetting your appetite. Rather predictably, it's been politics that's slowed things down. We've got workable translations of the whole lot now, but with different people handling different aspects of each fragment, you inevitably generate a degree of territorial cliqueyness. I haven't even seen all the texts myself yet, and there's one small fragment that Helen Schwarz and Bruno Calvi have been sufficiently cagey about for no-one else to have had a look.

Mind you, I should count my blessings — this project has been the essence of harmony and haste compared to the Dead Sea Scrolls fiasco. The only thing anyone really learned from those was that if you make a find that might shed light on biblical history, don't hand it over to Catholic academics! Almost forty years on and the truth of those things is still buried as deep as if Qumran had never been found.

Jerry
blakej@past.participle.com

Extract: (site GY / scroll G / fragments 4,5 inc.)

> We struggled to the shelter of an outcrop, our arms about one another as we climbed, and drank from a gourd to clear our mouths and throats of the acrid blackness. The winds seemed to clear the air of ash and then cast it forth again in alternate gusts, but as all of it issued from the north some relief was to be found behind barriers of rock.
>
> As the air stilled itself awhile, I chose that moment to stand atop the rocks and look back down the hillside, upon the sea, upon the harbours, upon Knossos, from which we had fled.
>
> I stared long at the familiar shape of the Daidalaion, and when I gazed back at the sea I saw the impossible: the waters were withdrawing. In the port, boats were left helplessly on their sides, stranded on banks of drying sand like gasping fish

as the sea retreated from the land. Beyond the bay the remains of lost vessels were exposed, nestled amid great plains of rocks and reeds, the sea-bed's secret terrain revealed for the first time. It did not look so different from the hillside I viewed it from.

Then from the north there came a sound of thunder, growing, deepening, approaching, and when I looked there I saw the waters climb and swell. There was a wave, a single impulse the width of the entire horizon, travelling forth at a thousand times the speed of the swiftest ship.

And as it drew nearer it piled higher. It rose and rose as it sped towards the land, a wall of water higher than our mightiest cliffs and wider than all Kaftor, still growing as it charged.

The wave was at least a hundred times the height of the tallest man when it devoured the last shallows of our retreated sea, and from the mountain I could see what bulk of water rampaged behind its livid face.

Just as the waters had retreated to uncover the lands beneath the sea, now they retaliated, claiming Kaftor's coasts and beyond in covetous recompense. The wave engulfed all in its path, swallowing Knossos in an instant, and plunged on inland, its height diminishing but its momentum and its endless volume still driving it relentlessly forward.

I watched as the waters uncovered poor Knossos, sacked by a force greater than a thousand armies. Only that which was hewn of stone remained even as testament to the destruction. I looked tearfully upon the Daidalaion, our temple, still standing in proud defiance, and thought of Asturis my beloved sister, of noble Ankham, and of all who had surely perished.

But to my growing alarm the waters did not end their retreat at the harbour. Again they drew back from the coast, beyond the shoals and sandbanks. Again a sound like thunder hailed from the north.

Again a single wave spanned the horizon.

nine

Strictly speaking, you couldn't call it love at first sight, as Steff had seen Madeleine Witherson on television before meeting her face to face. But then maybe TV didn't count, and maybe in-the-flesh was the only true, 'fishell first sight. Steff sincerely hoped so. His reminiscences might not seem quite so soft-focus and dreamy if he had to admit that his first glimpse of the woman with whom he'd become besotted was of her being shagged doggy-style by some bloke with a catastrophic Michael Bolton mane while she simultaneously blew a second hairspray ad at the other end.

At least, that's what he'd assumed was going on: the hotel's in-house pay-per-view adult movies had suffered the vigorous attentions of a censor's scissors to render them soft-core, and this had lent the film a certain New Wave ambiguity. Steff estimated that if the male duo's barber had shown half as much enthusiasm, they'd both look like Ed Harris. In fact, he thought it was a pity the coiffeur's and censor's roles hadn't been reversed: all right, you'd lose the Greek-god look, but at least there'd be some honest humping on view.

Steff was baffled as to whose sensibilities the PPV company were attempting to protect. Maybe they'd had letters from irate businessmen, saying that they had paid their money and pressed the button in good faith, expecting wanking material that observed certain standards of taste and respectability, then were horrified to be presented with programming that was no more than pornography. He thought of what Jo said about businessmen in hotel rooms wanting to watch dirty movies without thinking they're the kind of guy who watches dirty movies in hotel rooms.

Steff was less troubled by such duality: he was inclined to fire off a sharp note because he didn't normally like his filth quite as clean.

Actually, that was a lie. Steff was troubled by plenty of

duality over his decision to press the SpanVision button and watch *Babylon Blue*. For a start he was carrying the standard confused-lefty baggage about 'the exploitation of wimmin' as well as concern as to whether he should be putting in an advance order for a big raincoat. And topping it all off was a generous helping of the sexual turmoil that comes free with every Catholic upbringing. Nonetheless, he justified watching the movie on the time-served rationale that, as it featured Maddy Witherson, it counted as research. But the main factor influencing his decision was that he had woken up at five again, and there was, in the immortal words of the Sex Pistols, fuck-all else to do.

He'd been in hotel rooms with pay-per-view systems before: for more than the price of any cinema ticket you could watch a slightly out-of-focus, shakily pan-and-scanned four-month-old movie. Still, it was amazing what a bargain this could seem like at twenty past five in the morning. Unfortunately the Armada's PPV selections were all in the 'adult' category, with *Babylon Blue* the only heterosexual option on offer, and that was probably only for the curiosity value surrounding the star being a senator's daughter. As it turned out, Steff might as well have plumped for one of the gay features, as the 'softening' of *Babylon Blue* had meant the majority of the footage was of hairy male arses bobbing up and down, wobbling male buttocks having been deemed less likely to shock and corrupt the viewer than the sheer horror of labia.

From what was left of the flick, Steff could deduce that Maddy Witherson was not exactly a megastar of the famous West Coast porn scene. He was able to recognise which of the girls she was because it was her face that adorned the card atop the TV set, advertising details of the available features, but on-screen she was listed well down the opening credits, and not by her own name, either. Her alias, or *nom de shag*, was Katy Koxx, as was also explained on the glossy card, and it didn't grace the screen until Lotte Luv, Felia Cumming and Randy Steed had been flashed up in larger lettering. The discovery of Katy Koxx's true identity, and more significantly her father's identity, had evidently happened after *Babylon Blue* hit the shelves down at the local Whacking Emporium.

Each time a new female appeared in the movie, Steff checked to see if it was her by looking up again at the small thumbnail of Maddy's face on the card, sixth in a row that also included *Boystown IV*, *Pump Action VII* and, rather entertainingly, a feature entitled *Postman Pat's Backdoor Deliveries*. The film had run for more than half an hour before she appeared, and when she undressed Steff decided that the card would be more helpful if it informed you not that Maddy Witherson was '(a.k.a. Katy Koxx)' but '(the one with her own tits)'. Few of her co-stars looked entirely biodegradable.

She was small and skinny, with blonde strands curling half-way down her back in a hairstyle that looked suspiciously too big for her head. At one point she straddled one of the Bolton Brothers, facing the camera, the screen framing her from head to navel. She was moving up and down, eyes closed, accompanied by moaning noises that just *had* to be dubbed. No woman really made noises like that. Farm animals didn't even make noises like that. She seemed, like all the girls in the feature, to be doing an impression of what men thought a woman should look like while having sex; movement, gestures, facial expression. Hollywood-style dramatic humping. Then for a second, Steff noticed, she giggled. Just a tiny laugh and a smile, a bashful bite of the lip, before the 'serious shagging face' came back on. That was when Steff understood that even though she was having sex on-camera, she was still playing a part.

It was the only remotely titillating bit in the whole movie.

Steff saw her in the flesh later the same day, but he had to wait longer still for a sighting of the real Madeleine Witherson.

There was a press conference and photo-call scheduled to promote *Angel's Claws*, the pish-looking 'erotic thriller' *la* Witherson was making her feature film début in. It wasn't due to start shooting until April, but its producer, Line Arts, was giving it big licks to boost the pre-sales while its star was still news. The photo-call was to happen beside the main swimming pool, down on the Beachview terrace, with the Q&A set up around a table nearby. Jo wasn't going, and she told Steff he had no real need to either. Jo had set up a proper one-on-one with Witherson, who had agreed to it because *Scope* was a British mag and she quite fancied giving her viewpoint to a readership who wouldn't have quite so much prior information – or misinformation. It had helped also that Jo knew her agent, Tony Pia, whom she described as 'a sleazy bastard in a hazardously appealing kind of way'.

She further informed Steff that Pia was treading on egg-shells around the AFFM after the uproar he had caused two years previously, when a stalker was apprehended for plaguing an actress client of his. The problem was that Pia had in fact hired the stalker in an attempt to increase his client's media profile, on the grounds that it was the latest *de rigueur* accessory for a Hollywood star, and 'far cheaper than a Humvee', as he told Jo. The whole stunt had the actress's blessing, and it had been working out, too, until one of the PV's security staff made his own bid for stardom and collared the guy.

Jo told Steff the press conference wasn't really worth bothering with, as it had been made clear that Witherson was there only to answer questions about *Angel's Claws*, and anyone enquiring about other matters would be asked to leave. The photo-shoot was to be a strictly staged affair, an opportunity for the trades to get a glamour pic to fill a space in their market dailies. There'd also be photographers from the agencies, consumer film mags and a few of the less pretentious newspapers, getting some fresh stock-shots of Maddy Witherson before the world forgot her name again.

Steff was, like Jo, going to get her to himself later, but he decided to check out the circus anyway. He thought it might be illustrative to include some shots of her doing the star-holding-court thing, but mainly he was just impatiently intrigued. It was like a reverse of the normal male curiosity. Having watched Madeleine Witherson naked and having sex earlier on, he was dying to see what she looked like fully clothed and just going about her day.

The party had already started when Steff breezed down to the terrace at the edge of the hotel's private beach. The hacks sat in a semi-circle of chairs facing a wide table, sipping mineral water laid on by Line Arts, taking the odd note and holding up their pens for the chance to ask the next question. Maddy Witherson sat behind the table flanked by two men, a clutter of tape recorders surrounding the microphones in front of them. The men were, according to place-cards, Zip Spigelman and Tobe Delgado, respectively the producer and director of *Angel's Claws*. Witherson had no place-card; Steff didn't know whether this was an oversight or a compliment to her supposed celebrity.

The big blonde curls, almost certainly a wig, were gone. The new Madeleine Witherson had short, straight black hair in what, in his limited knowledge of such terminology, Steff could only think to describe as a Cleopatra cut. She wore a lightweight black dress that was presumably supposed to be vampish and thus suggestive of her role in the film, black gloves up to the elbows surely serving no other purpose at that time of the morning. Her heavy makeup was consistent with the vamp look, and served more to obscure than enhance her features; a plastered-on face, as they said back home. But then she wouldn't be wearing her own face: she was still acting. Saying the right things in the right enthusiastic-but-relaxed tone, smiling all the time, talking about the story, the script, the director, playing the actress at the press conference.

Steff took up position ten yards or so back from the encircled hacks and clicked off some shots of the whole assembly. To his right he could see the photographers setting up by the Beachview pool, around which the film's cardboard promotional displays had been erected. He zoomed in on the main attraction, and was momentarily surprised to see that she was effectively zooming in on him, her gesticulative, including-everybody delivery suspended for a second as she stared with consternation at the giant blond geek with the camera. The hacks didn't notice, as she hadn't skipped a word. Steff, aware that his presence could be distracting at the best of times, decided to cut the girl some slack and sit down, pulling up a chair in the backmost row of the semi-circle.

He glanced around at the reporters. Most of them looked bored; after all, it was just another market puff conference for a straight-to-video B-movie. But a few others wore a uniformly ironic sneer, in which assorted forms of contempt were writ large: Maddy Witherson was merely the latest recipient of random, lightning-strike fame that would otherwise never have been conferred upon such a nonentity. Tomorrow's oh-so-fucking-hilarious columns were taking shape behind smug faces. Arch glances were exchanged, a silently conspiratorial hackpack version of the schoolboy snigger. The nature of her previous career was playing a big part in wrinkling their noses, Steff guessed, as they smirked at the thought of her perceived indignities, or made the snobbish but common assumption that having worked in dirty movies meant she had to be thick. Eventually, one of them remembered what he was being paid for and asked a question.

'How do you envisage that your role in *Angel's Claws* will differ from your previous acting experiences?' he said, loading as much innuendo into his tone as was possible without hiring Eric Idle to pop up and add, 'Know what I mean? Eh? Eh? Nod's as good as a wink to a bliiiind bat, eh?'

Witherson reached for a gulp of mineral water, the producer looking to her for a signal that she'd like to skip the question. Steff caught the tiny shake of her other hand that told Spigelman she was cool.

'Well,' she said, putting the glass down and smiling again, 'I guess first of all there'll probably be fewer come-shots, and it's my understanding from the script that I won't have to fuck anybody. Is that what you were getting at?'

Stick *that* up your arse and light it, Steff thought, delighted. The hack turned pale, then tried to look unruffled and continued his question, but it was too late. The tables had been turned and the schoolboys dismissed.

He ambled around to the photo-call later, again keeping his distance and observing from the side, like a lion checking out the herd for the infirm. He had the haircut for it. It was also pretty obvious which of the assembled photographers a predator would go for. There was one poor bastard in there who looked like he had spilt a napalm-bomber pilot's pint then paid for the cosmetic surgery with the last of his pocket change. It was short odds the guy didn't do a lot of portrait work: having a melted head can be very distracting for the subject. The boy looked like he really ought to be covering air crashes and car pile-ups, although the difficulty there might be fighting off the paramedics mistaking him for one of the casualties.

Steff backed up a little and took some pictures of the picture-takers taking pictures of Witherson. Who watches the watchmen? Juvenal asked. Me, Steff answered. The girl posed amid the cut-outs to the whining accompaniment of film-winders and shutter clicks. She threw a few sultry shapes for a while, then her two press conference buddies came along for a three-shot that no one would use, because who the hell was interested what *they* looked like? Steff remembered the first time he had seen Witherson between two men and felt vaguely embarrassed.

He hooked up again with Jo at a quiet table on the far side of the terrace, looking out on the Pacific while the cut-outs and tables were disassembled and removed. By the time Steff's drink arrived, there was no trace left of the earlier activity, and within ten more minutes there were people putting up a different promo display in the same spot.

'I want you on your best behaviour, Shorty,' she warned. 'No smartass one-liners and no hysterics. We got this interview because Witherson thinks this is the one time she's going to get spoken to like an intelligent human being.'

'She is an intelligent human being. I watched the conference, remember. I wouldn't try taking the piss out of her – she'd eat me alive, pardon the phrase. I won't say anything, honest.'

'That won't do either. I do want you to ask her some questions. She's doing this because we're not an American publication, but first thing she's gonna find is her interviewer's from LA. Your accent should put her at ease a little, if she can understand a damn word you say. Plus, everybody over here knows – or thinks they know – all there is to know about Madeleine Witherson. British readers know dick about her, *pardon the phrase*. So if there's something I'm not covering, feel free to ask, long as it's not "What's it like to fuck eight guys at once?", or something equally sensitive.'

'I think I'm getting a very bad press here,' he complained, grinning. 'You're a cold and cynical hack, Jo Mooney, with no capacity to see the love and goodness in people. In fact, I think I'll tell this Witherson lassie she should stay away.'

'Too late. Here she comes.'

Steff was about to ask where, when he realised he had been looking through her as she walked towards their table. He had subconsciously been looking out for the black dress she'd worn earlier, which he would admit was stupid, but even if he hadn't he guessed he'd still have been surprised. This wasn't the porn star, public-scandal figure or aspiring actress. *This* was Maddy Witherson. And this was the moment Steff Kennedy began to experience the sort of feelings only previously inspired by Tommy Coyne and Paul Lambert.

She wore light-blue Levi's and a plain white T-shirt, dozens of thin bangles chinking on each wrist. Her hair sat untidily in a mop of wet black strands, still damp from the shower. But it was her face that threw Steff most, divested of all the warpaint, glowing from recent bathing, and much younger. Behind the microphone, behind the cut-outs, behind the makeup, she had been like a picture in a magazine, attractive in a strictly aesthetic manner, but a cold remove from reality. The woman in the black dress answering journalists' questions didn't exist any more than the vamp in *Angel's Claws* existed. The face he was looking at now was not attractive in that classical way; indeed some might say it was plain. But in it Steff saw stories, secrets, fears and a natural beauty his camera had taught him was all too rare.

'You're Jo Mooney, right?' she said, as Jo stood up and offered her hand.

'This is Steff Kennedy,' Jo said. Steff stood up and tried not to tower too much.

'Oh my God, it's you,' Witherson gasped, taking his hand in a waft of shampoo and body spray.

'You know him?' Jo enquired.

'I was hovering about at the press conference,' he explained to Jo. 'Sorry if I freaked you out, Ms Witherson,' he added.

'Not at all. You were just kinda hard to miss. Call me Maddy.'

Jo offered to get her a mineral water. She asked for a beer, Dos, same as Steff was drinking. Jo got the chat going, Maddy's answers getting longer with every few mouthfuls.

Steff watched her as she spoke, glad that he had the 'working out your best angle' excuse to fall back on in explaining why he couldn't take his eyes off her. Something about her was really getting to him, more so every time he caught her glance, but he had no idea what it was. The natural beauty bollocks didn't cover it at all; that was just the sort of thing you told yourself to explain the unexplainable, that which you couldn't render in language. Not without making a total arse of yourself, anyway.

She reached for her beer and the bangles slipped down her arm when she tipped the bottle to her lips. As they slid back they revealed that her wrists were scored by several scars, criss-crossing the soft-looking skin. Steff looked back at her face, where he found the feared confirmation that she knew what he had seen. He felt more shamefully voyeuristic than if she knew he had been watching *Babylon Blue* that morning.

Jo either hadn't noticed or had been more discreet in spotting the scars. Witherson looked down at the table for a second and swallowed her beer. Steff had seen her capably ride out the press conference earlier on, but just then she seemed a little jolted. This was a lot more intimate, right enough, and the person in front of him looked a lot more fragile than the persona who had paraded for the hacks.

She hit her stride again soon enough, quickly becoming expansive in Jo's easy company, enlivened by the prospect of getting her story across to an audience who hadn't heard the prosecution speak first. She spoke with an appealing mixture of passion and humour, like she had a lot she needed to get off her chest but wasn't taking their interest for granted. She didn't talk much about her time in the porn business; she wasn't being evasive, it just didn't stand a chance against the more pressing issues of what had happened since.

'The weirdest thing was that suddenly everybody felt qualified to pass judgement – or at least diagnosis – on what I had done or what was somehow wrong with me,' she told them. 'As they say, opinions are like assholes: everybody has one and they're usually full of shit. For instance, it was said I had only done this to hurt my father. Did it never strike these people that there were simpler ways to embarrass him, if that was what I was trying to do? Or did they forget that I used an assumed name, told no one who I really was, and that it wasn't me who broke the big secret to the world? Why did this have to be about my dad? This was about me.

'And they always talk about it like it was an affliction, or something that "happened" to me. It's like if you break ranks from society's code of sexual behaviour, there must be something wrong with you, like mental illness. Like you couldn't possibly make *that* decision if you were in proper command of your faculties. That used to be the attitude towards homosexuality. Still is in a lot of places.'

She rolled the bottle between her hands, shaking her head with an ironic grin.

'Some of the feminists have been more vicious than the moralists. I was ready for the stuff about being some kind of traitor to my gender. I never bought that one, and it's pretty sexist if you think about it. You can't make these things without guys. Why does no-one talk about *their* bodies being exploited? It's always the woman's fault – so what's new there? But worse are the ones who want to save me, like I'm a victim. Like my sexuality has been somehow damaged or violated or, I don't know, enslaved. Like I can't be in control of my sexuality if that's what I'm doing with it. Let me tell you, doing that was . . .' She paused. Steff saw the same look in her eyes as when he had noticed her wrists: afraid of what someone might have seen, but knowing she had no way of hiding it if someone wanted to look.

'Making porn was *about* being in control of my sexuality,' she said, quieter, then reached for the bottle again and finished it off.

Steff wanted to spare her any silence that might follow and weighed in with a question. 'Did you have any security concerns about coming here after what thon eejit across the road said the other day?'

'Excuse me?' Her eyes squinted in concentration as though looking into the sun. 'Who did you say? Jonny Jit?'

Steff laughed.

'Sorry. I meant that eloquent gentleman with all the laundered-looking friends, calling you the Whore of Babylon and generally laying the blame for the decline of Western civilisation at your door.'

'Is Western civilisation declining? I didn't catch *Sixty Minutes*.' She smiled and shook her head. 'No, it's old news, really. The Reverend Luth's been calling me that for months on CFC. He just brought it up again because, conveniently for him, he knew I'd be attending the market.'

'So why'd he call you that in the first place?'

'I was in a feature called *Babylon Blue*, and as I was effectively having sex for a living, that made me a whore. Again, very convenient for biblical rhetoric.'

'No, I meant, why *you* specifically,' Steff stressed. 'I mean, you weren't . . . I, eh, heard, the top-line star of that film. Why wasn't one of the other actresses singled out?'

'Why isn't one of the other actresses sitting here right now? Because their daddies aren't in the Senate. The film wasn't remarkable or notorious, it was just one more skin flick that nobody would have heard of, or admit to having heard of,

149

until the big scoop. Porn actresses would normally be too far beneath Luther's contempt for him to talk about any of them individually, but in the public eye, I wasn't *born* a porn actress, unlike those other poor unfortunates. St John got pissed off because he and my dad were sort of allies in the great crusade for all-American family values, and some of the embarrassment rubbed off. But what really jerked his chain was that I didn't sit back and take my scolding. Somebody shoved a microphone in my face, I gave my own moral viewpoint, which shared little with the Reverend's. That meant I graduated from being a wretched sinner to a full-scale force of evil.

'You, eh, *heard* right, by the way,' she added, looking Steff sharply in the eye. He felt like he had his dick out. 'I *was* way down the cast on *Babylon Blue*. I was way down the cast on everything. I did get second billing on the last flick I made before the news broke, but I guess it's hard to get a suitable pulpit soundbite out of a title like *Clam Lappers IV*.'

More beers arrived. Steff was planning to repair his image by taking confident charge of the bill, but he caught a glimpse as it hit the table and backed off sharpish. Jo was on exes.

'You're top billing now,' Jo observed. 'Above-the-line credit on *Angel's Claws*. That's not bad going for a feature début.'

'Would be if it was the *movie* people were interested in, but I think we all know why I got the part and why *Angel's Claws* isn't just blending into the market slates along with all the other straight-to-video trash.'

'But surely you must be pretty excited about, you know, just *being* in a movie, aside from what it might lead to?'

Maddy smiled, sipping from the bottle. The bangles were revealing her scars again, but she was either no longer concerned or wanted them to think she was no longer concerned.

'I am excited. I'm riding this thing for all it's got, believe me. It'll be fun, it'll be different, it's money in the bank, and it is a great opportunity. I'm not putting it down. Zip and Tobe have been great, they really have. But I guess it's a little easy-come-easy-go. If I had striven all my days for this I'd be freaked out with worries, hopes, you know? But I didn't get into adult movies because I wanted to be a "proper" actress, and Christ help anyone who does. This has fallen into my lap and I'm gonna take full advantage, but I've no delusions about it. Susan Sarandon can sleep easy.'

'So are you worried about not having acted properly before?' Jo asked.

'I'm not sure quite what constitutes proper acting, but I don't think it's *Angel's Claws*, you know? A film like this, if I can stand up and say my lines with a modicum of expression, the direction, the photography, the costumes and the lighting will all make me look at least competent. But they won't make me an actress.'

She had a long gulp of beer and shrugged. 'This'll be the last lead role I ever get. I was 'ninety-eight's news, my fifteen minutes are almost up. Next picture I'll probably be the cop's girlfriend, the one who gets murdered to piss him off before the showdown. Picture after that I'll get murdered in the first reel. But like I said, I'm gonna ride it as far as it'll take me. I've no illusions I'm gonna be a superstar, but I'd like to think I could learn enough as I go, and one day be a half-way-decent character actress. Maybe in ten years getting little roles just because the director knows I'll do a good job, long after everybody's forgotten why I got my first break.'

'These sound like very modest dreams,' Jo said.

'Yeah, but I don't know whether I suck yet. If I do a Sofia Coppola out there, the thought of being a small-time character actress might seem pretty far-fetched.'

'You sure you want me to quote you on the Sofia Coppola thing?' Jo asked.

'Sure, go ahead. It's not like Francis has me in mind for something and I'm gonna blow it.'

Jo's mobile interrupted the conversation. She pressed Receive and spoke quietly for a couple of moments, then stood up and made her excuses.

'I'll just walk over there and take this call,' she said. 'Back in a few minutes.'

Steff was left sitting diagonally opposite Maddy, trying to appear nonchalant but ready to settle for anything north of lurking. He knew Maddy could have looked away, struck a pose, even just smiled to place an 'intermission' sign up while Jo was away, but she didn't. She did smile, but it was a nervous smile, an 'all right, I admit it, I don't quite know what I'm doing here, am I coming across okay?' smile.

'You're a much better actress than you make out,' he found himself saying, perhaps injudiciously. He'd been searching for something to prevent a silence, and voiced his thoughts directly without the usual vetting he employed on those rare occasions when he really did care what the other person thought of him.

'What do you mean?' she asked, a mite defensively.

No way out but forward, Steff thought.

'Well, you gave a very convincing performance earlier on at the press conference.'

'Performance?'

'As the actress, the star. Glamorous, composed, graceful, behaving like it was all second nature. That was acting, wasn't it? That wasn't you "just being yourself".'

She said nothing, simply met his eye, leaving the ball in his court.

'I mean, everything about you was different, and I'm not just talking about dresses and hairstyles. You talked differently, you even walked differently. Obviously I've never met you before, but I'd guess – at least I'd like to think – that how you look right now, how you *are* right now, is more like the real you.'

'So how do you know I'm not acting now?' she asked. She wasn't being coy. It was a challenge; she wanted to know. 'That I'm not playing the no-makeup, casual clothes, honest-to-goodness unpretentious me because I think it would come across better for this kind of interview?'

'I don't,' Steff admitted. 'But nobody's that good an actress. All roles involve masks. All roles require make-up. You're not wearing any. You could have worn long sleeves too, but you didn't. I'm sorry, I shouldn't have said that.'

She rubbed at her left wrist, an automatic response, as though Steff's words had made it itch.

'Don't apologise. It's been a while since someone didn't *tactfully* ignore it to avoid embarrassment – usually theirs.' She waved a hand. 'You're right. This isn't an act, or at least as little of an act as in any conversation. You and me aren't even playing interviewer and interviewee any more, are we?'

'Doesn't feel like it.'

It certainly didn't. Nobody had smiled for a while, for a start, politely or otherwise.

'Unless this is how you get your subjects to open themselves up before you shoot them, to get to the heart of their characters.'

'Believe me,' Steff said, 'I'm not that sophisticated. But this *is* how I'd like to shoot you. No makeup, no dressy gear, no hair-stylist waiting in the wings.'

'So you don't see me as glamorous? Don't worry, I can take it.'

Steff shrugged. 'I didn't say that. I know you can *do* glamorous, I just think it isn't you . . .' He swallowed. Normally the photographer could say this and it didn't matter. Today it mattered to him. Would it matter to her? '. . . at your prettiest.'

'Thank you,' Maddy said, as though it was the weirdest thing in the world. 'Really, thank you.'

'You sound like that was the first time anyone ever paid you a compliment.'

'Well, it was the first one in a long while that actually meant something.'

Steff saw Jo walking back towards them. He wished he could teleport her to Paisley. Her timing was mince.

Jo sat down again and whatever had been going on between them – real or optimistically imagined – evaporated. What was worse was that the females' easy rapport resumed instantly, not only making him feel isolated and excluded, but eating excruciatingly into his appointed shoot time.

Jo finally finished up and took off, at last leaving Steff and Maddy alone together once more, but just as he was about to suggest a location Maddy overheard someone at a nearby table tell his companion the time, and sat up straight, eyes wide with shock.

'Oh shit. I've got to be somewhere in like four seconds. I totally lost track. Oh God, I'm so sorry, but I'm gonna have to run out on you.'

Steff's heart relocated to a snug part of his colon as he watched her prepare to disappear from in front of him. No fair. Referee.

'I'm so sorry,' she repeated, sounding harassed. 'And we're supposed to be doing this picture thing, too, God, I'm so sorry . . .'

'Could we maybe rearrange the shoot for later in the week?'

he asked, sounding professionally calm and pragmatic, disguising the mixture of dire pessimism and full-on huff that his tone would have otherwise conveyed.

'You can do that? I thought you must be on a tight . . . Well if it's okay by you, yeah, just whenever you can . . .' She closed her eyes, apparently attempting to defluster herself. Steff found it adorable, but he didn't know if it was the gesture or the fact that it meant she was still really up for the shoot.

'How's tomorrow?'

'Fine.' He nodded, hoping he didn't sound too surprised and ecstatic. 'It won't take long, really. What time? Where else are you meant to be, because I can meet you wherever?'

'Well, I'm supposed to be on a boat all day, drinking champagne, eating lobster and generally schmoozing. I'm on the invite list for the Moonstar hospitality cruise.'

'So when will you be back?'

'I won't be going.'

'Why not?'

'I got a better offer.'

Daniel Corby had never been so close to evil before.

In the flesh, living and breathing, mere feet away. So near he could have reached out and touched her. The Whore of Babylon, walking, talking, posing, preening, clad shamelessly in black, painted like the mega-slut she was. And all around her the idiots, the fools, taking her picture, practically bowing before her, treating her like goldarn royalty.

His anger and hatred were tempered by the thrilling sense of power he felt, standing undetected among the sinners. It had taken billions of dollars to make the Stealth bomber invisible. All he'd needed was a laminated press pass. Looking at the Whore through the lens of his camera, it might as well have been through the scope of a rifle. So much smaller than he'd imagined, so much more vulnerable, it was easy to feel that he had her in his grasp as she stood there, like all the others oblivious to the true meaning of his presence: no dumb paparazzo, but the instrument of God's will.

She'd flashed a smile at him, his own face hidden behind his camera, the empty film spindles whining as he pressed the shoot button.

That's right, he thought. Smile, you bitch. Smile and flaunt yourself like you've always done, proud, vain, shameless and arrogant. But soon enough you'll be humble before the Lord, and you'll be begging on your knees for His forgiveness.

He'd made his way from the swimming pool to the lifts with his camera still dangling around his neck, the aluminum flight case gripped tightly in his right hand, its weight a constant reminder of the importance of his mission. He stood a few yards from the doors, pretending to fuss over his camera as the people nearby got into a lift and its former occupants dispersed. Then he waited for an empty car to arrive and stepped in.

Once inside, he pressed the rooftop terrace button and pulled the hood of his sweatshirt over his head. The lift began to climb and his heart-rate seemed to plot the same trajectory until it was past the residential floors, where there was a chance of it stopping for some idiot who'd pressed up instead of down, or worse, fancied checking out the view from the roof.

The car continued up unmolested, announcing its arrival with a loud 'ding'. The lifts didn't go all the way to the roof, due to the stupid design of the building, so there was a last flight of stairs to reach the terrace where the famously under-used swimming pool was located. Daniel walked out, head bowed, eyes lowered. The surveillance camera would be on his back, but he should be out of sight once he'd ducked under the stairwell.

He reached into his pocket and retrieved a screwdriver, then proceeded to remove the access panel in the wall in front of him. Behind it was the rooftop swimming-pool's regulation controls: valves, pipes and filters, plus gauges for monitoring temperature, chlorine levels and pH. Below all that was a storage space piled with plastic gallon jars full of blue-tinted chemicals, plus spare or used filters that looked like they fitted into some of the pipes.

Daniel flipped open the locks on the flight-case and gently pulled up the lid. He keyed the authorisation code into the number-pad, ex of a pocket calculator, and watched the blue light change to orange. He looked at the neat wiring, the snugly fitted circuitry, and felt such a pride in his construction that he was almost sorry to have to leave it there. He had sure come a long way from that abortion clinic in Pocoima, when his first-time incompetence at bomb-construction had saved his life. His estimate of required quantity had been based on watching movies, in which they tended to use C4 rather than controlled-demolition shaped-charge explosive.

He had downloaded his amateur anarchy information from the Net back then, and through other cyberspace contacts procured himself a fake driver's licence. He bought a tenth-hand wreck in Tijuana and drove it to Nevada to buy the demolition explosives under the name on the phoney ID. Then, having constructed his bomb, he drove the wreck into the parking lot of the abortion clinic and walked away.

When he made it to the Greyhound depot to buy his ticket back to Glendale, he discovered he had lost his wallet, and realised there was a chance it had fallen out of his jacket when he last picked it up off the passenger seat. It contained all his cash, credit cards *and* the forged licence. He knew that in all probability it would be destroyed in the blast, but what if it wasn't? What if it was blown out of the windows, or the leather proved a lot more flame-resistant than withstanding the department store demonstrator's lighted-match test? He had checked his watch and estimated he would still have time to get back there, retrieve it – or at least establish that it wasn't in the car – and get away again.

According to his wristwatch, he still had three minutes' grace after he picked up the wallet from the foot well and quietly closed the door. The watch in the trunk disagreed.

God spared his life, but sorely chastised him for his folly. Daniel had sought to punish, and that was neither his role nor his right. That was the prerogative only of the Lord, a fact the Lord underlined rather stiffly, at the cost of three fingers, four toes, half his face and an awful lot of skin. Such isolated punishments were futile anyway. If you killed one abortionist doctor, for instance, they'd have his or her job filled by another child-murderer before the end of the week.

Daniel closed the lid again and placed the case gently into a space between two of the gallon jars. Then he replaced the access panel and returned, head down, to the lift, which took him back to the ground floor where he walked once more among the sinners. He made his way through the lobby towards the exit, the booths and stalls either side of him advertising their lewd wares, the whole sordid circus surely a far worse infestation even than Jesus himself had railed against in the Temple. It was inevitable that some of the casualties would deserve their fate more than others, but like Lot had found, he knew there would not be enough of them to justify staying the hand of justice. Everyone inside that hotel was guilty, because everyone who was allowing the UnAmerican Festering Filth Market to proceed was complicit in the evil it disseminated. Everyone. From the organisers to the participants, to the hotel staff, to the journalists reporting it and the photographers recording it.

This was not an act of terrorism. He was not rattling a sabre or publicising a cause, advertising a potential future threat or demanding shallow political gains for a ransom of human lives. Again, God's disapproval of such behaviour was writ large down the left-hand side of his body.

He tried not to look at any of the faces that surrounded him, faces of people; he thought only of their sin and the greater cause for which he was fighting. He felt a momentary sickness as he passed through the bustling human throng, thinking of the device upstairs, and it danced fleetingly into his head to go back and retrieve it. But he had known that such moments, such temptations, would come. He knew he had to be strong, that God *needed* him to be strong. And he knew that when it came to the Fifth Commandment, sometimes there was a difference between honouring it and hiding behind it.

St John had taught him that.

ten

The icon blinked in changing colours on the screen in front of him. Pale pink, dark red, pale pink, dark red, against the blue all around. He could zoom in and zoom out, overlay the longitude/latitude grid at whatever calibration he desired. He could scroll the image to display the distance travelled and the route ahead. He could hit a key to pull up a box showing the exact current co-ordinates, triangulated by satellite. He could feed in average velocities and windspeeds and receive a figure for Projected Remaining Journey Time, and with the click of a mouse change that to plain old ETA.

He could monitor the ship's progress to whatever decimal place from these thousands of miles away, the view on his computer monitor like that from the eye of a digitised seagull. But what he could not do was affect it.

Blink. Blink. Blink.

God's will, like time, set in motion. You can't speed it up, you can't slow it down, you can't alter its course. You can only wait.

Blink. Blink. Blink.

This was the hardest kind of patience. There had always been waiting, always been limbos, the necessary relegation of the ultimate goal in his mind for months at a time while pieces moved themselves gradually into place. Patience came easily then, welcome time to shape the project's evolution. Time for consideration, time for contemplation, time for anticipation. But this now was a purgatorial impotence, after the decisions had been made and the process initiated. This was when control passed from his hands.

Blink. Blink. Blink.

This was the vigil of the countdown.

From one of the pull-down menus he could display the date and time the ship had set sail, but was that really when the countdown had started?

No. It was in progress before that, before the engines were started, before the cargo was loaded on board. So what moment had set it in motion, what word or deed had been the irreversible instigator? Perhaps it had been when he handed over the money, that second of knowing, overt purchase, that second when he went from desire to ownership, intention to means. He didn't lay hands on the merchandise himself, but when he had let go of the briefcase in that lousy Kiev hotel room, there was no question that it now belonged to him.

Or perhaps that was just another blink of an icon. A flashing church, or jet, or briefcase, or statue, like this flashing ship. Maybe the clock started when the computer program confirmed that the idea was feasible. Or earlier still, when he commissioned the software. Maybe it was before even that, in the moment he told another soul what he wanted to do, enlisting Liskey as the first conspirator. Because in speaking he had committed the first action, when thought became word, and word could not be unsaid.

Back in the 1980s, with so many millions of dollars piling up in his personal fortune, it had pricked Luther's conscience that he should donate some of the cash to a charitable cause. This kind of went against the ideological grain prevalent in America during that avaricious decade, but it would have been simply unChristian not to. And there seemed no cause more deserving than those brave souls who were fighting to free poor Nicaragua from the tyrannous shackles of the Sandinistas.

It was such donations that led Luther to be introduced to Art Liskey in a hotel suite in Phoenix after a $1000-a-plate fundraising dinner. Liskey was a mercenary whose expertise had been leased to the Contras through the generosity of Luther and other like minded donors, and he was back on US soil to explain just what their money was buying.

He and Liskey had a memorable meeting of the minds, discovering a common viewpoint arrived at from such different experiences, and had stayed in touch down the years, albeit infrequently. Latterly Liskey had given up roaming foreign fields and taken the freedom fight back home, founding the Southland Militia with some former comrades-in-arms.

Luther had thereafter striven to keep his links with Liskey quiet, as conspicuous amity with the militias was an invitation to the FBI to start sniffing around you and yours. Liskey understood that. America, he said, treated the true defenders of freedom like hunting birds: they were happy to unleash them when needs dictated, but at other times they must remain hooded. He accepted with good grace that Luther couldn't be seen consorting with him. He accepted a lot of covert funding from him too, which probably made accepting the former a lot easier. Luther had been generous in all dealings with Liskey ever since that first night in Phoenix, it having struck him how useful it might be to have a man like that owing him favours.

Later it proved to have been a prescient investment.

Blink. Blink. Blink.

But what an egotistical fool I am, he thought. Looking for some act, some trigger he had pulled, button he had pressed, like it had ever been his decision or even his option to instigate this. He had not set this in motion.

God had.

He was merely God's instrument, and it was a vain conceit to pretend his contribution was anything greater. Luther himself was a flashing icon on God's computer, moving, progressing, overseen, programmed, controlled.

The countdown had started before the vision came to him, before he knew what part he would play. It had already been under way back in '92 when the country he loved so betrayed him; now it soothed the hurt to know that it was part of God's plan, and that He asks only the most faithful to bear the heaviest crosses.

Blink. Blink. Blink.

No. It had begun decades before any of this, when God took pity on the poor wretch who had been Bobby Baker.

He had been in a dark place, alone, scared and in pain. Terrible things had happened, terrible. He did not know where he was, did not know even whether he was dead or alive. He could see nothing, he could hear nothing, and he could remember nothing. Perhaps the Catholics had been right and this was the place of Purgatory.

Then he saw a light, somewhere above him. It was a strange light, in that it did not illuminate anything around him or around itself. It just existed in its own brightness.

The light of God.

He heard voices too, though he could not remember what they said. He was aware that they were talking about him, though. Somewhere above him.

He awoke in a bright room, light all around him. The walls were painted crisp white and morning sunshine poured through the large windows. He was in a bed, and his uncle Nathan was sitting on a chair beside him, a tearful smile on his gentle face. He blinked, his eyes adjusting to the warm brightness, and looked around him. Both his forearms were in casts, and he felt as if he was wearing a balaclava. He reached a weighted arm up tentatively towards his face, but Uncle Nathan took his hand and placed it back down on the sheets.

'Lie still, Bobby,' he said softly. 'Lie still. God's brought you back to us. God's gonna heal you, too, but you'll have to give Him time.'

Blink. Blink. Blink.

Nathan had sat by his bed at the hospital, waiting for him to wake up, and he stayed there after that, when Bobby would need his uncle most. When he had the strength to hear it Nathan told him the tragic news: his mother was dead, killed saving Bobby from the intruder who had come close to putting him in his grave at the age of thirteen.

In time the police visited Bobby, to ask him what he could remember of that night. Bobby started crying, but Nathan held his hand and told him to draw on the Lord's strength. He never saw the man's face, he told them through his tears. He had come in the night, in the darkness. He had woken up and been aware of someone in his room. He'd said 'Mom?' and that was when the man attacked him. He remembered being hit in the face with something hard, and remembered trying to curl up in a ball, but the blows wouldn't stop. He thought he remembered seeing his mom come in, in her nightdress. Or did he only hear her voice, her screams?

But he couldn't remember anything else, and it hurt when he tried.

In fact, not only couldn't he remember anything else about that night, but he couldn't remember anything else about his mom. He remembered their house, and the town and the church and the school, but he couldn't remember her face, or her voice, or anything she'd said to him.

'It'll come back,' the doctors told him and Nathan. 'It'll all come back in time. The memory can be a funny thing. Sometimes it just shuts things off until it's decided you're ready to have them again.'

When he went home from the hospital, it was to live with Nathan, at his church on the other side of town. He was enrolled in a different school, under his uncle's surname, and would begin studies there after the summer, which gave him a few months to recover from his physical and mental traumas. To complete this fresh start, Nathan suggested he begin calling himself by his first name, as it sounded more grown-up. Thus, L Robert 'Bobby' Baker became Luther R St John.

The doctors were right. As that long summer wore on, the memories of his mother started coming back, but only slowly, and only in pieces. They didn't come back by themselves, either. It always took some kind of spark. Sometimes a smell, a taste, sometimes a conversation with Nathan. Sometimes a drive through a certain part of town. Some of the memories he talked to Nathan about. Others he found he didn't feel like sharing. And others still seemed to remain out of reach, as if, the doctors said, he wasn't ready for them.

His mom loved him, he remembered that. When he was very little she fed him and she dressed him, played with him, sang to him as she ironed their clothes or cooked, told him Bible stories as she put him to bed each night, and twice a week she bathed him. She made sure the water was not too hot and not too cold, then she would undress him to his underpants and place him in the tub. She was always real careful when washing him not to get suds in his eyes because that stung and made him cry. Then she'd give him the soap and he'd rub inside his underwear, front and back, only touching with the bar, never his fingers. Afterwards, she would lift him out and rub him down with big, soft, white towels, then she'd wrap one around his chest while he took off his wet underpants and put on a dry pair.

She taught him how to go bathroom, when he was a big boy, too big for diapers. She helped him climb up on to the wooden seat, and fastened his modesty bib around his neck before he took his pants down. This was a leather strap with a buckle, attached to a stiff piece of Bakelite, which jutted out all around his collar and saved him from catching a glimpse of what was going on below.

She brought it with her in her bag when they went out to town, and took him with her into a cubicle in the ladies' restrooms when he needed to go. There were parts of the body that belonged to God, she explained, and it was forbidden by God to look at them. Nakedness itself was a sin, and had been since Adam and Eve were expelled from Paradise. It was a sin to expose those parts and a sin to look at them. It was a greater sin to touch them, except to wipe or clean them. A greater sin still was to look at someone else's.

Bobby was worried. Wouldn't God be angry, then, that he had to expose those parts when he sat down to pee or do number two? But his mom reassured him that God saw him through his own eyes, and if he did not see his own nakedness, neither would God. His modesty bib was a shield from sin.

When the time came for him to go to school, his mom told him that not all the other kids' mommies loved them enough to teach them all of God's true ways. He would have to go to the boys' restrooms, she warned him, where there were filthy trenches to pee in – standing up! But there would also be cubicles: he was to use those for peeing as well as number two, and he was to take his modesty bib with him in his satchel.

Bobby thought it sounded disgusting. Peeing standing up, like dogs or cats, when God had made man greater than the animals. He resolved never to use the school restrooms – he would just hold it in until his mom took him home at the end of each day. But on his first morning, his bladder betrayed him after two hours, and with a sick dread he walked into the boys' toilets. There was indeed a long trench, but to his slight relief it wasn't the wooden, leaking, farmyard thing he had pictured. It had smooth white walls running around it, and cascades of water at regular intervals washing into the groove at the bottom. Two bigger boys stood with their backs to him, laughing and looking across at one another. He could see arcs of liquid over their shoulders, fanning out where it hit the white surface. He realised with horror

163

that it was their number ones, jetting into the air like garden hoses.

'Beat ya again, Tommy,' one was saying.

'Did not.'

'Did too. Mine was right up where it says "vitreous china".'

'Mine was higher than that. Mine was hitting "Shanks Barrhead".'

'Was not.'

Bobby looked around him. There were two cubicles, like his mom had said, but one was boarded up with an 'out of order' sign hanging off it, and the other was engaged. He had never held off going for so long before, and the pain in his gut was growing. One of the boys turned around and walked to the engaged cubicle, banging loudly on the door with his hand.

'Didn't you make yet, Kosinski?'

'Get lost,' came the reply. 'I got the squits.'

'Oh not again. What's your mom feedin' you?'

The older boy glanced down at Bobby. 'Hope you ain't in no hurry, little guy. Kosinski's dug in for the winter, ain't ya?' He banged on the door once more.

The two older boys left. Bobby gripped his satchel and felt tears begin to form. He had no choice. He walked forward and unzipped his fly, letting his privates fall out by pulling at his shorts, not once touching skin on skin, and peed, eyes shut tight. And in that moment of glorious relief, it occurred to him that if his eyes were closed, then he wasn't seeing his nakedness, and neither was God.

He told this excitedly to his mom when she got him home and asked him what his first day in school had taught him. She took hold of his hand tightly, and spanked him on the bare legs again and again until they were bright red, his screaming reverberating around the kitchen. He was sent to bed right away with no dinner, and lay sobbing in his room for hours until his mom came upstairs later with a glass of soda and a cookie for him. He had been a bad boy, she told him, and needed to be punished, but God also forgives. Bobby hadn't been mean, just stupid. What if another boy had come up to this trough and started peeing alongside? He could have seen Bobby's private parts, couldn't he?, and that was a sin for both of them.

164

He promised Mom and God always to wait for a cubicle, and always to use his bib.

Luther performed much better at his new school, living with Nathan. He was a little quieter than most kids, but he didn't stand out so much as before, and nobody knew anything about his past that he hadn't told them himself. He'd always liked learning things, liked to hear the teacher tell him stories, of far away lands and of America's past. But his other memories of school were far less pleasant.

He didn't much like the other kids, and they didn't like him. They weren't the same as him. Many of them were scruffy, wearing clothes that didn't fit, and keeping the same ones on every day of the week. They talked differently, too, not at all like his mom had taught him. They used slang words, they cursed, they swore and they blasphemed. Mom had warned him that he would hear bad words at school, instructing him to ignore them and never, never to repeat them.

Bobby asked how he would know which words these were. His mom said he would know when he heard them, and for the most part she was right. But now and again he'd say something and she'd erupt that way she did, her face boiling into redness and her eyes going as wide as her head, before a hard spanking and no dinner. Like the time he told her about overhearing some big boys say they wanted to see Miss Hathaway's pussy. He knew he wasn't allowed to call horses 'nags', or a cow a 'steer'; he hadn't realised 'pussy' was such a bad word, but he knew now always to call a cat a cat.

The other kids were mean to him. They teased him about the way he spoke, just because he pronounced all his words and letters properly. Johnny Finnegan was the worst. One day he and his friends got hold of Bobby, and two of them held him while Johnny slapped him across the face and punched him in the stomach.

'You think you're better'n us, don'tcha, Mr Hoity Toity? Think you're better'n us 'cause ya talk all fancy, an' ya never use no cusswords. Well, I wanna hear ya use a fuckin' cussword now. I wanna hear ya holler "fuck", an' I'm gonna hit ya till ya say it.'

Bobby said nothing. Johnny punched him some more, hitting him between the legs where no-one was supposed to touch. It was the sorest pain Bobby had ever felt; he knew it was extra sore because those parts belonged to God, and God was reminding him of the pain he'd suffer for ever if he sinned. Johnny got angrier and angrier, hitting Bobby more and more.

'Holler fuck,' he screamed. 'Holler fuck, ya little prick.'

But Bobby wouldn't. He could take the beating, because it was nothing compared to what God could give out, and even less compared to what God would give out to Johnny and all the other kids.

It was Johnny Finnegan who noticed that Bobby always went to a cubicle in the restroom, never the 'urinal', as they called the trench. He'd bang on the door and shout things, filthy things.

'You ain't never done shittin', are ya, Baker? Can't you ever just take a piss without takin' a dump too? Or maybe it's 'cause you ain't got no dick, you gotta sit down. Baker's really a girl. Ain't ya, Roberta?'

Then one time Johnny and his friend climbed up the walls of his cubicle and peered over, seeing him sitting there with his pants at his knees and his modesty bib around his neck. They asked him what it was, and he told them. That just made them laugh even harder.

The teacher, Miss Graham, was alerted by the shouting from the restrooms, and came in to see what was going on. There were about thirty boys crammed in there, chanting and yelling, gathered around the open cubicle where Bobby sat, crying, under threat from Johnny Finnegan not to remove his bib or pull up his pants.

Miss Graham took Bobby's mom into her class when she arrived to pick him up. He saw them talk through the window as he sat on a swing in the yard outside. When they got home, his mom told him he didn't have to use the bib in school any more, though he had still to wear it in the house. Wouldn't God be angry? he asked. God would forgive him, she said, for Jesus had known what it was like to be persecuted, what it was like to be made fun of for trying to do what was right. He suggested his uncle Nathan could teach him to box, so that he could fight back and beat up on the kids who made fun of him. That way he could still use his bib and give God His glory. But his mom said he was giving God His glory by suffering with quiet dignity; and besides, he didn't need to beat up on the other kids – God would beat up on them for all time after they left this earth. They were sinners, she explained, and all sinners would be punished for eternity, while the pure and faithful received their reward.

The bullying didn't bother him so much after that. Nothing the other kids said could hurt him, because he knew they were all worthless, all condemned.

Uncle Nathan didn't mind him using slang words now and then, as long as he could prove he also knew the correct English for whatever he was talking about. He learned to tailor his language according to whom he was talking to: perfect grammar pleased teachers, but it won less respect in the schoolyard, so he dropped the right consonants here and there to sound more like his classmates. He was pleasantly surprised to learn that slang could be a rich and inventive vocabulary on its own, rather than the sublingual resort of the inarticulate he had been taught it was. He still never swore or blasphemed, but this was less conspicuous as his language altered and his confidence grew; he could express the extremes of emotion with a blend of wit and imagination that disguised the absence of a swearword.

The pleasantest surprise at his new school, though, was PT. He really loved it, and made up with sheer effort what he lacked in skill or experience. He was class champ at running the mile, his light frame demanding less effort to maintain pace over distance than his bulkier classmates. He turned out to be a pretty good pitcher, too, and while his batting wasn't great, his speed still allowed him to steal home often enough. He hadn't been allowed to do PT before. He suffered slightly from asthma, and his mom got a doctor she knew to certify him unfit for gym class each semester. But his breathing only got bad a couple of times a year, so he knew that the real reason was so that he wouldn't have to take a shower with the other boys, as he'd either have to go naked or get picked on for not taking his shorts off.

At his new school he was able to change and shower with the other boys, having been assured by Nathan that it wasn't a sin. It was a sin to look at girls who had no clothes on, he explained, because that was lust, and that was why boys and girls had separate change rooms. It was a sin for a girl to look at a boy naked, just the same way, but boys could be naked in front of boys, because they didn't lust after each other. And if they did, then they were already in enough trouble with God that nakedness was the least of their sins!

It made him feel easier that he could talk to Nathan about this kind of stuff. In fact, he could talk to his uncle Nathan about anything, and figured that was what made him a good preacher. He always listened, he always understood, and if you needed it he had a lesson for you.

Luther felt able to start telling him more of his memories, partly because it helped to relate them to someone else, and partly because Nathan was so close to him and his mom that it didn't feel like he was betraying any kind of secret trust.

He told him of the problems he'd had with his body when he lived with his mom, especially when his body started changing. He'd been curious now and again about what the parts that belonged to God looked like. He had gathered some information from the schoolyard, enough to know that girls and boys were different down there. He knew also that grown-up women had round chests where men's were flat, and that on women, those parts also belonged to God. He was tempted to sneak a look sometimes, to leave off his bib when his mom was outside in the garden, or to leave his eyes open when he peed at the urinal, but his will was strong, and the curiosity was fleeting. Besides, these were the parts smelly things came from, and that aspect reduced the desire to investigate them.

But when he got a little older, he became aware that his body was changing. His skin started to feel greasy, and his hair felt like it needed to be washed nearly every night, not just on Sundays before worship. Due to the frequency of his bathing, his mom allowed him to start doing so on his own, but she would still come in from time to time to check up on him. Hairs began to appear under his arms, and although he still never touched with his fingers, he could tell from the rubbing of the soap that there was hair growing around the parts that belonged to God too. He was aware also that they were getting bigger, and the temptation to look at them seemed to grow in proportion.

His pee-spout sometimes grew on its own, very quickly,

becoming longer, fatter and very stiff, and he often needed to adjust his underwear to make room for it. It could happen at any time, but he started to notice that it happened a lot if he was looking at pretty girls in class, or pictures of pretty ladies in magazines. Soon enough he noticed that it worked the other way around too: when it happened and he was on his own, it made him think about pretty girls and pretty ladies.

The problem was, it started to happen more and more. It used to be just now and again, but by the time he was thirteen, it seemed that his pee-spout was stiff almost as much as it was soft. He wondered if the proportions kept changing until, when you were an adult, it was permanently stretched and hard. It happened all the time, when he wasn't looking at girls or even thinking about girls (although he'd have to admit that was kind of seldom). But the worst of it was that it kept happening in class, and he was terrified someone would see. It was easy to hide it from his mom at home, because he always wore jeans and they held their shape pretty well, but his school trousers were made of softer cloth, and the lump it made was really obvious.

One morning he had Mrs Harriwell's English class first thing, which was the time of day it seemed to occur the most. She called on him to hand out the new textbook, and as he got up to approach the desk he saw Gloria Reese drop her pencil-sharpener into the trash basket and bend down to retrieve it. His eyes seemed to ignore everything his mind told them, and fixed upon her chest where a button was loose on her blouse. He could see two small, white mounds of flesh enclosed by white lace, like those things his mom hung up on the washing line, and his pee-spout sprang up in an instant.

He picked up as many books as he could carry and held the bottom of the pile in front of his middle, hiding the bump. He walked slowly, handing them round, praying to God to make it recede before he got to the bottom of the stack. Unfortunately, the pressure of his pee-spout against the books seemed to make it worse, ruining all his efforts to think about Job and his boils and sores. The books ran out as he got to Andy Mulligan and Jake Delaney.

'Woah,' Andy said, 'that's a big candy bar you got in your pocket, Bobby.'

'Hey look!' Jake barked. 'Baker's got a woody! Baker's got a woody!'

All the boys round about started shouting and joining in, but what was worse was he was sure the girls were staring too. He wanted to run back to his desk or cover his middle with his hands, but he felt paralysed, standing there with this bump showing and the class chanting at him.

'Baker's got a woody! Baker's got a woody!'

He felt a burning shame, a vulnerability as if he was in fact naked in the midst of the whole English class. Then the shame turned into anger, anger into rage, rage into fury, and with a scream he lunged at Andy. Andy's chair tipped backwards and Bobby fell down on top of him, punching, clawing and biting at him. Then he got hold of Andy's ears and started banging his head off the floor.

Mrs Harriwell had to get Mr Steiner from the class next door to help break it up. Bobby, Andy and Jake were sent to the principal's office, and remained seated outside there while their parents were called in and informed of what had happened.

Bobby's mom drove him home in silence. She didn't look at him the whole way, either, just kept her eyes straight ahead. When they got to the house she opened the back door and he walked in ahead of her, into the kitchen. He was caught on the side of the head with a blow that knocked him to the ground, then his mom started kicking at him as he lay there, reeling.

'Filthy boy! Filthy, sinful boy!' she shrieked. 'No better than the animals, no better than the animals.' She walked to the cupboard and took hold of the belt she kept in there. Bobby got slapped or spanked if he broke a plate or forgot one of his chores; the belt was for when he had sinned, a thick leather strap with three thongs at one end and no buckle at the other, just a rounded edge with a hole for hanging it up. It said 'Lochgelly' on it. Bobby didn't know what the word meant, apart from pain.

Usually she'd hit him on the BT or the legs with it. Sometimes she'd make him hold out his hands and hit them in turn. That day she just lashed out at his body as he lay on the floor, licking it across his back, his face, his thighs; whatever he presented as he squirmed and cried.

'Base, filthy goat!' she yelled, striking out with every word.

170

'Disgusting, vulgar creature! Forsaking God, forsaking me, filling your mind with lust and your soul with sin. How could you do this to me? Have me sit there in that office in front of those people, and be told you had . . . a *bulge*!'

'I'm sorry, Mom,' he sobbed. 'It just happened.'

That made her fall upon him again with renewed frenzy. 'It didn't just happen. It couldn't just happen. Thou shalt not covet thy neighbour's wife. That means thou shalt not lust, Bobby Baker, and you've *filled* your mind with lust. Sinful boy! Wicked boy!'

Mom kept him off school until after the next weekend, by which time most of the welts were starting to go down again. But still he had bulges, and no amount of effort, no amount of concentrating on the Bible could either stop them or reduce the regularity. If his mom noticed, he got belted. Not as much as after the fight in class, but depending on her mood it could still be pretty bad. She kept him off school a few more times, and made him wear long-sleeve shirts in the hot weather to hide the marks.

Nathan got very sad when Luther told him this. He got this weakened, strained look on his face and his eyes went red, like he might cry.

'I was bad, wasn't I, Uncle Nathan?'

Nathan shook his head. 'No, Luther, no.'

It wasn't a sin to get a bulge, Nathan told him, or an 'erection' as it was properly called. It was sinful to think the dirty thoughts that could cause erections, but if one just happened, then that was nobody's fault.

'So was my mom wrong . . . to, you know, to, to . . . hit . . .?'

'I'm sorry about what your mom did, Luther. I guess I should have been around more. Your mom meant to teach you right. Your mom was a good woman. It's just . . . she had it hard. What happened to her, it made her confused. Angry about things.'

'You mean my dad getting killed before I was born?'

'Your dad? Yes. Yes. That's right. Your dad. She had a lot to cope with, mentally. I should have come around more.'

Luther started to do better and better in his classes. The teachers began to make comments about what a bright boy he was turning out to be, and they complimented him on his enthusiasm for his studies. His greatest enthusiasm, however, was for the Bible. When he was younger, he'd liked the big adventure stories best; the Bible had seemed a compendium of wonder – giants, floods, plagues, wars, miracles. David slaying Goliath, the parting of the Red Sea, Noah's ark, Solomon planning to cut that baby in half, the walls of Jericho falling down. Uncle Nathan had once given him a book about the Greek myths for his birthday. These were also full of incredible tales: heroes, monsters, warriors, kings and battles, but they didn't seem as exciting because he knew they were just made up.

Uncle Nathan told him the world had been full of crazy legends and weird religions before Christianity came along, but people now knew all those old stories were just remnants of extinct cultures, civilisations not yet mature enough to comprehend the true nature of God's universe. 'Folks back then would just make stuff up to explain the things they couldn't understand. The Greeks, for instance, believed the Earth was a goddess and that her husband was the sky! But our knowledge is thousands of years advanced from theirs, so we know that God created the Earth, the sky and indeed all the rest of the universe.'

There were other parts of the Bible that had interested him less when he was younger; parts with no real story, just 'teachings' that he had given up on as matters for the adults. But as his education advanced, he found that these were now the verses that most fascinated him. It was as though he had discovered a whole new Bible to explore. He began to appreciate the sheer wisdom of the words before him, how they applied to the world now as then, realising that the Bible set down the rules of life a great deal more specifically and elaborately than in the Ten Commandments.

With growing anger he began noticing the many ways the world was straying from God's path, how people were conveniently reinterpreting or even ignoring the clear designs the Almighty had presented to mankind.

When his homework was done each night, Luther would study Uncle Nathan's countless books of biblical scholarship, and often the two of them would sit up late discussing the meaning, divine intention and consequences of certain scriptures. These discussions soon began forming the basis for Nathan's Sunday sermons, and it wasn't much longer before Nathan was delivering homilies that Luther had penned alone.

Luther was always top of Bible class, by a stretch too, and this despite his tendency to get engaged in rollicking arguments with Mr Woodburn. The first of these had erupted over the teacher's assertion that the story of Adam and Eve should be interpreted metaphorically, which he had backed up with the off-colour remark that 'you only have to take a trip to Alabama to see the disadvantages of too many people being descended from the same relatives'. Luther had drawn upon a wealth of reference in his refutation, gleaned from those nights in Nathan's study, quoting philosophers, scholars and poets, Aquinas through Milton, in a rousing demolition of Mr Woodburn's arguments, which the class thoroughly enjoyed. Mr Woodburn generously admitted defeat by saying he must 'defer to your superior knowledge, Luther', but he always found new ground to battle on the next week.

Luther, for his part, enjoyed new levels of respect from his classmates, who had seldom witnessed such courage in a pupil gainsaying a teacher's opinion, far less the oratory to come off best. Kids who usually skipped Bible class started to come along in the hope of seeing another duel, and they were seldom disappointed.

'The boys say I've got Mr Woodburn outgunned,' he proudly told his uncle, but Nathan said he suspected the teacher was 'playing devil's advocate, and doing a real smart job into the bargain'. Luther thought of the renewed interest and improved attendance in Bible class, and understood what his uncle was saying. He also understood that there was a great opportunity before him, too.

He introduced Nathan to the idea of a youth service on a Sunday, earlier in the morning before the main one at eleven. At this, Luther suggested, the scriptures and sermons could be targeted at kids and teenagers, who had different interests, different worries and needed different wisdom from their parents and grandparents. Luther also figured they'd be happier to attend then because a lot of them thought it a drag to go to church with the whole family.

Nathan decided to try it for a month, and to Luther's delight insisted that he not only write the homily, but deliver it too. Nathan had taken a leaf out of Mr Woodburn's book, realising what or rather who was the box-office attraction. Just about every kid who went to Nathan's church came along to the youth service, but the real success was that kids whose families went to other churches started coming too. There were even a few Catholic kids, although their parents insisted they attend their own mass on a Sunday also. What worries these parents might have had about their kids attending another church were muted by the pleasant surprise of their youngsters suddenly taking an interest in their religion at all.

'When you talk about God, and the Bible and stuff,' one classmate said to him, 'it ain't like when the ministers talk about it, or the teachers or my parents. They make it sound all ancient history and far away. You make it sound like we're all still part of it. Like we can get a piece of the action.'

Luther liked that. It summed up what he was trying to say. Christianity shouldn't be about remembrance and observation, as though most of the story had been told and we all simply had to sit tight until our own individual grand finales. It was about making the next chapter happen here and now. Fighting the same battles in the name of God as the Israelites once had, and recognising the armies of the enemy where they manifested themselves. Once they were Philistines and Romans; today they might be Communists and atheists, but the fight remained the same.

However, around this time something happened to knock Luther painfully out of his stride. It didn't seem like much at the time, but somehow it unlocked the door in his mind behind which his darkest memory had lain confined. He woke up one morning to find his underwear damp, and found a sticky, bleach-smelling fluid inside. He didn't know what it was, or how it had got there.

And then in one awful moment he realised that he did know both those things. The words, the feelings, the images came rushing in upon him like a flood. The doctors said his memories would be released when he was ready for them, but he knew he'd never have been ready to remember this. He tried to shut it out of his mind, but it was all around him, and when he closed his eyes it was inside his head, staring back out.

He lay in his bed and cried, cried and cried, bawling uncontrollably like he was a baby again. The noise brought Nathan into his room, white with concern, asking whatever was the matter. He couldn't tell him and yet he had to tell him, didn't want to tell him and yet couldn't contain this, not on his own. Not for ever. Not even for a day.

He sniffed back his tears as Nathan sat on the bed, rubbing a hand through his hair.

He had to sit at the side of the hall or the field and watch while the other boys did PT, he told his uncle. He didn't get along with them much, but that was still when he felt loneliest, not being able to join in, listening to their laughter, hearing their shouts of encouragement and congratulation. But the worst part was having to wait in the change rooms with them before and after.

They played games while they waited for coach. They used to play 'run the gauntlet', whereby everyone got given a number while Jake turned his back. Then Jake would pick one at random, and that kid had to run through the change room while the others lined the benches and punched and kicked him as he went past.

One day Jake and Andy and Jimmy O'Rourke started playing a different game, called a 'come race'. Bobby always sat with a book to stare at while his classmates got changed, as he knew it was an even worse sin to look at the parts that belonged to God on other people than on yourself. There were plenty of times he accidentally caught a glimpse of someone's BT, and he'd always say extra prayers for forgiveness in bed that night. But despite the beltings, the fascination with his pee-spout continued. He'd feel a nervous thrill if he heard what his mom called 'dirty talk', or when he saw the girls doing PT in their tight T-shirts and short skirts that let you see their underwear when they jumped up.

He felt that same thrill when Jake, Andy and Jimmy started playing their game, aware that they had all exposed their pee-spouts. (They called them 'cocks' and 'dicks' and 'pricks' but he knew it was a sin even to think these words, let alone say them, and he tried to keep them from slipping into his head.)

Everyone else was looking at whatever the three of them were up to. Bobby desperately wanted to look too, but he knew he had to resist. Then he noticed Johnny Finnegan staring at him. He knew that look: it was the look Johnny had when he was about to make a big deal of whatever Bobby was doing or specifically *not* doing. This time he was specifically not looking at the game.

So it was a reflex, really. He didn't mean to look, he just did it without thinking, in response to the threat of Johnny making another excuse to pick on him.

The three of them were sitting in a line on the bench with their pee-spouts exposed, standing and stiff. Each had a hand around it, rubbing up and down, while staring at pictures on the floor. They were black and white pictures Andy's dad had brought back from the war, from France, and though he was a few yards away, Bobby could make out that they were of women, and he guessed they must have no clothes on. Once Bobby began to look, he couldn't take his eyes from the scene. His stomach felt like it was turning cartwheels, and his own pee-spout was rock-hard. He felt a driving urge to get closer, to see the pictures of the naked women; in that moment he wanted to see those pictures more than he wanted anything else in the world.

Suddenly Andy began to grunt, and Bobby looked at him in time to notice white stuff shooting out of his pee-spout.

'Winner!' he shouted.

Bobby could think of little else for the rest of that day, but it was not what he had seen that most occupied his thoughts, as much as what he had not.

Those pictures.

There had been a thrill about seeing the other boys' pee-spouts, but he had realised in those few moments that his curiosity about women's bodies was even greater. The thought that there were women who would take their clothes off and allow themselves to be photographed might normally have appalled him, but that day it seemed the most exciting idea in the world. The blood rushed around his system all the faster, its noise in his head, and the voices that reminded him of what God considered sinful seemed drowned out by it.

When he got home, Bobby went to his room and unpacked his schoolbag, getting his homework books out. As he reached for his history textbook, he felt some loose sheets of paper on top and pulled them out first. He looked at his hand, and with a racing pulse saw that he was holding Andy's dad's pictures. Then he remembered that Andy and Jake had been called out of class that afternoon because the principal heard they were smoking cigarettes behind the school kitchen. They must have sneaked the pictures into his bag after PT and been planning to 'discover' them on him, but they'd been kept out of class until home-time.

Mom called him downstairs for dinner, and he stuffed them back inside the bag before going to the kitchen.

The nervous thrill returned, except a dozen times as strong. The pictures were in his bag, in his bedroom. He could look at them. He could see what he so burningly wanted to see. And he knew he *would* look at them, too. He could hear the other voice, the one that told him God forbade it, and he knew inside, quite definitely, that he was going to ignore it. Somewhere else he knew he'd feel guilty later, knew he'd regret it, knew he'd be punished, but he also knew nothing was going to stop him. It was as if he was possessed. He wasn't just going to look at the pictures, either. He knew he was finally going to look at himself too, and to touch himself, the way Andy and Jake and Johnny had done.

He did the dishes and cleaned up the kitchen, before getting on with his homework. Then he waited, as the seconds ticked slowly by, for his mom to go to bed. He heard her click her light out, and almost immediately his pee-spout hardened as he knew his fulfilment was imminent. He waited as long as he could in his bed for when he thought she must be asleep. Eventually he could wait no more, and took the pictures from the bag, sticking them under his pillow. With an ever-quickening heart he pulled his underpants away from his pee-spout and stared at it as it bobbed free in front of him. He cupped the balls beneath, lifting them up and examining them, then moved his hand to the pulsing thing between his legs and began stroking it the way he had seen that day.

He pulled the pictures out on top of the blankets where he could see them better.

His mom burst through the door as the white stuff shot out.

Bobby remembered her grabbing hold of his old replica Winchester by the bed, with its heavy metal barrel and sturdy wooden shoulder-stock. The first blow bust his nose as he grabbed at the pictures to hide them. The next one came down somewhere on the back of his head. He fell to the floor from his bed and covered his head with his arms. His mom smashed the gun into his ribs, lifting it above her head and swinging it down with all her strength, shrieking and yelling at him as she did so.

And she wouldn't stop.

The weighty hardwood stock bore into him again and again, into his arms and hands, his ribs, his back. He remembered his vision going swimmy, and somewhere inside the knowledge that he had to get away, he had to stop the blows.

His mom raised the rifle above her head with both hands once more, and that was when he summoned up whatever strength he had left to spring up and run for the door. She moved into his path and he barrelled into her, the pair of them bashing against the open door and rolling into the hallway. He remembered her rolling over him at the top of the stairs and then she wasn't there any more. When he looked down the staircase, he saw her lying at the bottom. Her nightdress was pulled up to her waist and she wasn't moving.

'I killed her, Nathan,' Luther told him, almost in a whisper. 'There was no intruder that night, Uncle. It was me. I killed my mom. I murdered her.'

Then Nathan held him and started crying too.

'I'm sorry, Luther,' he said. 'I'm so sorry.'

'I killed her. I should be in jail. And I'll go to hell.'

'You won't go to hell, Luther,' Nathan whispered. 'You didn't mean it. It was an accident.'

'But I will. I still killed her. And maybe deep down I did mean it. I killed my mom. It's the worst sin. The Fifth Commandment.'

Nathan took both of Luther's hands, holding them tight, and looked deep into his eyes.

'You won't go to hell, Luther. Listen to me. You're right – the Fifth Commandment is the worst one to break. But sometimes . . . sometimes . . .'

He swallowed, then squeezed Luther's hands again.

'You were protecting yourself, son. Your mom was a good woman, Luther, a good, good woman. Things were hard on her. She didn't mean to hurt you – she loved you, loved you more than anything. But she did hurt you. She lost control of herself. She needed help and, God forgive me, I wasn't there for either of you. She lost control and . . . and she would have killed you. And then look where we'd be. You'd be dead, and she'd be a murderer, condemned to burn for ever, and she didn't deserve that. You saved her from that, Luther. You saved your mom's eternal soul.'

'But now I'm a murderer.'

'No you're not, son. You did what was right. God sees that. Sometimes the rules ain't so straightforward, and this was one of those times. You saved your mom from what she would have done, what she would have become. And more than that, you saved your own life, and what a life that's going to be. You've a gift, Luther, a real gift. A gift for teaching God's word. You're already more of a preacher than I'll ever be and you're still a boy. You've the gifts to spread God's word further and save more souls than any preacher this land has known. But if you hadn't done what you did, then you'd never have got the chance to use those gifts, and those souls would never be saved.

'The Lord said Thou Shalt Not Kill. But sometimes it ain't that simple. Sometimes there's more at stake than the life that would be taken.'

Blink. Blink. Blink.

Soon after that, Nathan asked Luther to address the congregation in place of himself at the regular eleven o'clock service, and this was to become a regular feature, second Sunday of every month. Nathan noticed and approved of how much care Luther took about his appearance before these guest sermons – his hair, his clothes and such – and one day he gave Luther the money to buy a really good new suit.

'You're starting to look more like a businessman than a preacher,' he remarked when he saw Luther's dapper purchase.

'Preaching *is* a business, Uncle,' he replied. 'It's God's business, and God's businessmen should look as smart as any other.'

Nathan had looked the same to Luther as long as he could remember: kind of old, but in an energetic and approachably eccentric way. He'd always worn the same sort of shirts and pants, always had that thick shock of white hair flowing backwards over his head and down to his neck. He looked like a frontier preacher, mellowed by years but still able to crank up the furnace when he felt the occasion demanded it. But Luther knew that all Nathan's frontiers had been crossed a while back, and suspected Nathan knew it too. His uncle knew a different challenge was looming on the frontiers of a changing America, and it would take a man of the new generation to meet it.

Which was why Luther had no difficulty recruiting Nathan's influence to borrow Pete Arthur's radio transmitter in the winter of '61.

There had been storms for weeks, winds and rains with a ferocity few could remember in that part of the state, and a lot of the people – especially the older folks – who lived out of town were finding it tough to get into Bleachfield for worship on a Sunday. Luther knew that Pete Arthur, who ran the hardware store, had been a radio operator during the war and still owned a transmitter (although reports differed as to whether it was a damaged one he'd been allowed to hold on to and had subsequently repaired, or whether the US Marines just didn't realise they were one radio short the day after Pete Arthur was demobbed). Luther suggested to Uncle Nathan that they could broadcast a Sunday message for folks who couldn't make it to church: all they'd need to do was tune their Marconis and listen in.

Nathan made one phone call, and the very next day Pete drove over with his transmitter wrapped in tarpaulin in the back of his Dodge. Pete helped them set up the equipment in Nathan's study, and relayed it to a signal booster he had rigged on the church steeple.

Nathan phoned the folks who'd been having difficulty reaching Bleachfield in the bad weather, but Luther went a little further. He passed out flyers at school and got store-keepers to place them in their windows, so that word got round to everybody about the impending broadcasts.

Luther selected an appropriate gospel reading and wrote a homily for Nathan about the need to spread God's Word far and wide with the new tools of communication He had given mankind. But when the Sunday evening came, Nathan froze. They were both sitting in the study after dinner, the Bible

180

and the homily on the table in front of the microphone, the minutes ticking down until their announced broadcast time.

'I can't do it,' Nathan said, shaking his head, his hands trembling.

'Of course you can, Uncle,' Luther told him. 'You've been preaching God's Word to the people of this town for years, every Sunday. Just close your eyes and pretend you're in your pulpit downstairs, and they're all assembled before you, with Miss Kent finishing off the hymn on the organ.'

'Okay,' he said, closing his eyes and nodding. 'Okay.'

'It's your voice they need to hear, Uncle.'

Nathan took a deep breath and began introducing the broadcast, nervous and unsure, his voice lacking all of its familiar character and authority. His delivery improved a little when he started reading aloud from the Bible, God's power no doubt flowing into him through His divine words, but he still didn't sound himself. He concluded his reading and reached for the sermon Luther had written, his hand shaking as he grasped the sheets of paper. Then he thrust them into Luther's lap and leaned back towards the microphone.

'I would now like to welcome my nephew Luther St John, a fine young man you all know very well, to continue our first radio service with some thoughts he has written especially for the occasion.'

He looked imploringly at Luther and gestured him to pull his chair closer to the table. Luther sat up straight, cleared his throat and took a quick gulp from a glass of water.

'Good evening ladies and gentlemen, brothers and sisters,' he began.

Blink. Blink. Blink.

II

mere anarchy

Suffering will beget suffering.
Sacrifice will beget sacrifice.
                    Billy Franks

eleven

When Larry woke up that morning he found that the bedroom TV was still on, he and Sophie having fallen asleep watching it the night before. It was tuned to HBO. Bill Murray was reaching across a double bed to find that Andie MacDowell was no longer there, Sonny, Cher and two DJs telling him once again that it was Groundhog Day. Larry was doing the same as Bill, Sophie unusually having gotten up before him. It was one of Larry's favourite movies, and each time he watched it he could never help but wonder how he'd cope with living the same day over and over again. Pretty good, he figured, long as it wasn't the day his son died.

He didn't know it yet, but the next twenty-four hours weren't likely to get his nomination either.

Larry looked at the clock. It was six thirty. The alarm hadn't gone off yet, so it must have been the noise of the TV that woke him. Sophie didn't normally rise for another hour, but she wasn't beside him, and the sheets were too cool for her just to have got up to pee.

Christ, he hoped she wasn't sick. He thought of last night's take-out shrimp tempura, of which he had eaten heartily too. Sophie always brought bad food up the next morning, but Larry's system was less alert. If she was in there chucking her guts up, that meant he'd be running to the can all day until his ass felt like it had been in a Tabasco bidet.

He got up and pulled some shorts on, enjoying the commingled ache and pleasure of a quick stretch, then walked out towards the stairs, where he saw that the bathroom door was open. He was about to go downstairs and look for Sophie in the kitchen when he heard the sniff.

'Ah, shit,' he said softly to himself.

He opened the door to David's room slowly and gently, cushioning his barefoot steps as he entered. Sophie was sitting on the rug in her nightdress, her knees up against her chest, her arms around her thighs and shins, her head slouched against one leg, eyes wide with dried tears and tiredness. She'd have been there for hours, he knew. She was rocking slightly, staring into nothing, and hadn't looked up when he came through the door. He might have entered the room, but he wasn't *in* yet, not where she was.

Between both hands she clutched a doll, a plastic action figure in a green-and-white-hooped soccer kit, that had been David's favourite. Their friend Jack had sent it to David 'on the express understanding that he treats it extremely badly and with very little care for its condition'. Jack's note said the doll's name was Paranoid Tim. David had done his imaginative best to meet the conditions and to justify the moniker, but the doll had proven stubbornly indestructible.

Dolls don't get meningitis.

Sophie had done this a few times, but not for a couple of months now. She went in there in the dark and stayed until morning. Larry knelt down on the floor behind her and placed his hands softly on her shoulders. She kept rocking. He moved forward until the back of her head touched his chest, and pulled his arms around hers. She rocked against him some more, then gradually leaned back into him and let him hold her, her arms falling away from her knees.

Sophie wasn't selfish in her grief; Larry was grateful for that. He couldn't have handled it if she shut him out, like it was something he couldn't understand. He did understand. David was his son too. But reciprocally neither did Larry try to intervene or coax her out of it, like it was a habit that needed to be broken or an ailment that could be cured. Sophie wasn't the only one to be found in there in the darkness some nights, picking up toys and clothes and crying silently. She needed her grief, and so did he. Sad-smiling memories might come in time, but right then the pain of missing gave its own strange comfort, like it was the only emotion that rendered enough of David's presence to feel him again. Widow. Orphan. There wasn't even a word for this.

It had been the same every time. Larry didn't talk to her, just moved in behind her and touched her until he was in there with her and she knew he hadn't come to drag her out. He'd crouch there with her until she was ready to leave. Sometimes it would only be a few minutes. On a few occasions it had been nearer two hours.

This was the first time since he started back at work, at the new precinct. The routine of getting up and going out to meet other responsibilities had been a distraction, something else to occupy his mind, giving him a break from thinking about their pain and loss. However, finding Sophie in there once more made him realise the wounds hadn't healed much while he'd been looking the other way.

Holding her on the floor again, crying for their son again, it brought back the feeling that nothing else mattered, but he knew that that soothed and repaired little either. *Everything* else mattered. Otherwise they might as well end it all together right here on this rug with his service revolver.

Everything else mattered. He loved his wife and she loved him, and he wanted so much for there to be a future beyond that open bedroom door. They deserved a future.

'Sorry baby,' Sophie said quietly.

'Shhh,' he told her, stroking her hair. 'We're gonna make it. We're gonna make it.'

When he came out of the shower Sophie handed him a coffee, which he placed on the bedside table as he got dressed. She kissed him and patted his chest, then went into the bathroom herself. Larry swallowed down the espresso and pulled on a shirt and pants, strapping on his holster as he went out into the hallway where he could hear the splash of the shower through the bathroom's open door.

'Honey, I gotta run,' he said. 'Expectin' a prelim call from Forensics this morning bright and early, so I better be there. Gotta call Maria Arazon too. You be okay?'

'Sure, sure,' she called. 'I'll be all right. You have a good one, you hear? Maybe you'll catch a break and there won't be a bomb hoax at the Pacific Vista today.'

'Yeah, well, that would be nice.'

He grabbed his jacket from the rack at the front door and went out to his car.

She said she'd meet him on the roof, the enduringly unpopular elevated swimming-pool being both scenic and private. In fact, as Steff learned in conversation with one of the hotel staff, just about the only time people went up there was to do shoots, usually swimwear stuff for fashion mags. Most of the models drew the line at taking a dip, however, not without a new clause in the contract. Anyone who actually fancied a swim went to the Beachview pool downstairs.

Steff stood by the rail and looked out to sea, the bright morning sun rendering all the colours sharp and vivid. The Pacific looked calm and inviting, its surface sparkling in a melody of blues to bely the fact that you'd need asbestos boots to paddle in its toxic waters. He could see the vessel hired by Moonstar leaving its widening wake as it headed out to sea, full of chirping execs in designer shorts, all dressed down for their day off. The guests were welcomed aboard by two leggy blondes in vaguely maritime outfits, evidencing more of the navel than the naval, probably hired by Moonstar along with the boat. Before it left Steff had glanced at his watch and told himself he wasn't looking down at the hotel's pier for Madeleine Witherson, wasn't half expecting to see her climb that gangplank and be kissed hello by lots of shiny movie people.

The boat eventually moved off with a loud horn-blast and then the excruciatingly over-familiar opening chords of Prince's '1999'. Steff hadn't heard a song played so fucking much since every restaurant, supermarket, joinery, plumbing firm, tyre-fitter's, DIY store and travel agent boasted to the world that they were 'Simply The Best'. The Huns used it too, over the PA when the team took the field, further proof if it could ever be needed that individuality and original thought were largely incompatible with supporting Glasgow Rangers Football Club.

He turned his head once more to look towards the door to the stairwell that led down to the elevator's highest stop. His stomach was churning. His bloody stomach was churning. He hadn't felt like this since he was about fifteen, and the worst of it was that it was for all the same reasons as back then. Thinking about what she looked like, what she smelt like, her smile, the sound of her voice. Excited by the very thought of seeing her, worried by the thought that she wouldn't show, nervousness multiplied with every unfeasibly long minute that passed.

This was daft. It was only a shoot, for God's sake. Except that it wasn't. Or at least it might not be. He tried to replay yesterday's conversations, yesterday's moments, re-analysing, dissecting, deciphering, looking for whatever had been done or said to make him think there was something between them.

'I got a better offer,' she said, didn't she? But was she just being a good networker, knowing it was in her interests to get this shoot done, and going out of her way a little because she'd let him down last night? Or was there something really going on in those strange moments before Jo came back and knackered it?

He knew he had walked out of this place on air last night, so why did he feel sure of nothing this morning?

He looked at his watch again. The feeling of excited expectation had given way to nervousness, which in turn was stepping aside in deference to a hollow nausea riven with disappointment and an unmistakable sense of loss. Never mind just being a good networker – she wasn't even coming. He sighed, a long, slow exhale, staring back out to the shrinking shape of the Moonstar boat as it headed for the horizon.

Then he heard a door close, and there she was.

She was dressed in beige deck shorts and a sleeveless top, her dark hair tucked under a skip-cap, bangles a-jingle as she walked towards him carrying a duffel bag over her shoulder. She seemed smaller than yesterday. Steff looked at her delicate shape, her skinny legs, waist, chest, shoulders and neat wee head, and it seemed incredible that everything he remembered about this person, everything he'd thought about her could be contained within this tiny frame. An exquisite noseful of perfume/bodyspray/whatever reached him half a second before her outstretched hand. Steff wanted to drop to his knees and worship before her.

They went through the ritual of she apologising for being late and he pretending he hadn't noticed.

'Other clothes,' she said, putting the bag down. 'For later on.'

'Where are you going later on?'

'Taking you to lunch, if you're free.'

Steff tried too hard to think of the right reply and ended up saying nothing.

'I thought I'd make up for running out on you so you don't print the ugly shots. You a vegetarian?'

189

'Eh, no,' he said, before he could think about the diplomatic consequences.

'Good thing. Place we're going is so carnivorous, they *eat* the vegetarians. You up for that?'

'Eh, ay,' he managed.

Oh gaun yourself Steff, he thought. Bowl her over with charm, confidence and erudition. Sam Shepard would be shiting himself.

A phone was ringing as he entered the station house, Rankin telling him 'Yeah that's yours, Larry' as he walked by, the younger cop looking once again like he'd had yet another fight with the wife and sacked out on the station floor. A lot of mornings when he came through the doors and heard a phone, Larry'd be hoping it didn't turn out to be the one on his desk. On this morning, however, knowing it *was* the one on his desk, his hopes were pinned on the smell assaulting his nostrils not coming from too near the same place.

As he approached his open office door he knew it was forlorn. Zabriski was sitting opposite, eating the stinkiest sandwich this side of a turd melt.

'What the *fuck* is that?' Larry asked, eyes almost watering. Zabriski grinned, chewing faster so that he could empty his mouth and explain. Larry held a hand up. 'Forget it. I don't think I want to know.'

He swallowed as Larry threw his jacket into a corner. 'Hot tuna melt from across the street at Tino's, but I added my own runny gorgonzola to pep it up.' He held up a plastic tub with a tightly sealed lid. 'I brought some in here. You want a free sample?' He gripped the lid and began to pull it open. Larry drew his gun. Zabriski dropped the tub.

'Ah, fuckin' Philistine,' he muttered.

Larry picked up the phone.

'Yeah, Freeman here.'

'Hiya Larry, it's Carol Adebo, Forensics.'

'Morning, Carol. So what'd you catch on your boat trip?'

'Well, the lab won't be through until probably this evening, but if you just want the headlines, we found a shell.'

'Congratulations. A shell on a boat. Who woulda thunk it? What, is the oyster a witness?'

'A shell, Larry, as in powder casing for ballistic projectile, expelled from ejection port of firing device, known colloquially as a gun.'

Larry dropped the attitude. In fact he did well not to drop the phone too. Everything was different now. Multiple homicide different.

'Shit. Sorry, Carol. Wrong train of thought. Wait a minute, though. You found a shell yesterday, why are you only telling me this now?'

'We didn't *know* we'd found it yesterday. We flushed out the deck drainage sluices and collected all the gunk that came out for the lab to sift through. They found the shell among all the yuk pretty late last night. I've been trying your line for half an hour this morning.'

'Sorry again. So, you typed it yet?'

'It's with Ballistics now and I haven't heard back from them, but it was a high-calibre slug, I can tell you that much. We're looking at a rifle, not a handgun, probably an automatic assault weapon. Ballistics are gonna run the shell through the system and see if they got any of its brothers and sisters in custody. But I'd say the bottom line is that you're not looking at a boating accident any more.'

'You got that right. Jesus. You find anything else?'

'Not so far. But we're pretty sure the aft deck's been hosed down. There's lots of watermarks on the foredeck, just what you'd expect from spray and from these guys walking around in wetsuits, but the aft is way too spick and span.'

'Are we talking mopping up blood here?'

'I doubt it. It's a wooden deck and blood would leave a stain. Maybe not real dark, but you'd definitely get shading. More than you could wash out with just a hose-down.'

'So what *were* they washing out?'

'Can't even guess yet, Larry. But if you want my gut instinct, I'd say – among other things – more shells, and lots of them. We'd have to be real lucky if there was only one shot fired and the shell rolled right into that sluice for us to find. But if there were lots of shells scattered around that deck and someone was hosing them out into the sea, there's a chance they might not notice one of them going down a grille instead of all the way over the edge. And if it was dark, they might not have noticed the sluice grilles at all.'

'Christ.'

191

He put down the phone and sighed. Zabriski had finished the sandwich and left the room, but what the hell, it hadn't smelt half as bad as what the *Gazes Also* was starting to reek of. It was discoveries like this that pointed up the dichotomy between being a detective and being a cop: mind and body, theory and practice. The detective in him had never been satisfied by the hypothesis that four missing persons could merely have met with an unfortunate accident and sunk to the bottom of the pond; maybe because the cop in him knew it was too much to hope that the explanation would be so simple. The discovery of the shell was the kind of thing the detective wanted to hear because it pointed towards a more familiar and tangible explanation, even though it posed a shitload more difficult questions. But for the cop it was confirmation that he now had a thousand times more trouble on his hands than when he woke up this morning. The detective gets to play questions and answers; it's the cop who gets to play with the bodies and the baddies.

Carol Adebo was right. They definitely weren't looking at a maritime misadventure here no more, and gunpoint abduction didn't have enough cred to be anything more than an implausible but as-yet-uneliminated possibility. Why abduct four scientists in the middle of the goddamn ocean? To take them where? To use them for what? Hostages? He sure hadn't heard any ransom demands.

Uh-uh. This was a multiple murder. Someone – and most likely more than one person – had got on to that boat, probably while these guys were finishing their Sunday dinner, and taken them out. Maybe lined them up against one side and shot them so they fell back into the water. Or maybe fired off a few threat rounds and forced them to jump overboard, hundreds of miles from dry land. Then they hosed down the deck to dispose of the spent cases.

So he had a scenario, but what he didn't have was the first hint of a who or why. Or where the shooter or shooters came from, how they got aboard, why their vessel and its approach weren't noted by anyone on the *Gazes Also*. And what about the missing submarine? It certainly seemed to confirm that someone had forced Mitchell Kramer to record a dubious note about the sub in the ship's log, the captain secreting his coded SOS in the terse entry. Did the bad guys ditch it to provide an explanation for the disappearances? Possibly, but that left him scrabbling around for a motive for offing four scientists whose research carried no more threat than boring the ass off anyone who wasn't into rocks.

Or seismology.

He remembered with a shudder the brush-off he had given Arazon, when she'd suggested it might be more than a coincidence that this had happened only a few months after Sandra Biscane was murdered. Carol's words were still rattling around his head – 'probably an automatic assault weapon' – and the spectre of the Southland Militia was beginning to rise from the waters around that mysterious goddamn boat. The idea excited the detective in him and scared the pants off the cop. But neither of them could venture a stab at what the hell interest those assholes could have in oceanography. To his knowledge their philosophy was 'if you can't fire it, fuck it'.

However, there was one simple explanation, with an older, purer motive: theft. It could well have been the sub they were after. Janie Rodriguez had said it was valuable, state-of-the-art, but worth killing four people for? Dumb question. He'd dealt with guys who'd kill ten people to steal a fucking rowboat if they wanted it bad enough.

So who'd want a submarine?

As well as the Southland Militia, Steel had mentioned the possibility of the *Gazes Also* running into drug-smugglers or gun-runners. But what if it was the bad guys who had made a point of running into the *Gazes Also*, acting on information that it was trailing a piece of hardware like the *Stella Maris*? Drugs, guns, whatever, a submarine would be a lot less visible to the DEA or the Coast Guard than the usual launches – especially if no-one knew you possessed it, and no-one even knew it still existed.

He would call Ballistics, tell them to start checking that shell against the DEA and the Coast Guard's spent cartridge collections. He reached for the phone, but it rang as his hand gripped the receiver.

It was a weird shoot. Occasionally you got subjects who were edgy and uncomfortable, depending on how used they were to this sort of thing. It was less normal for the photographer to be self-conscious.

193

At the start there was a faint air of embarrassment about the proceedings. Steff's problem was that he had lost the protective barrier of just being the man with the camera, there to do a job. He wore a security laminate with his name on it, which had meant nothing to most of the people he'd snapped that week; to them he was still anonymous. But not to Maddy. She asked if she could call him Stephen rather than Steff, saying she liked the name. From a professional point of view, he wished she hadn't said that. The rest of him, however, shivered with pleasure every time the word fell from her lips.

Maddy, who of all people he thought should be used to the camera, was a bag of nerves too, enough even to seem oblivious to Steff's feeling like a shambling amateur.

'I'm sorry I'm so self-conscious today,' she said. 'I don't know what it is. You must be wondering how someone who's had my career can suddenly be camera-shy. I guess it's like you said, it's easier when you're playing a part. I'm trying to be me today, and it's making me feel a lot more naked than I did on any set.'

'That's okay. We can take a wee break.'

'No. I'll be fine. Wait, I know,' she said, and jumped backwards into the pool.

Steff was doubled up for a few seconds with surprise and laughter, recovering enough to start shooting as she swam to retrieve her cap and put it back on her soaking-wet head.

'Yeah, that's much better,' she shouted, giggling. 'I was nervous because I was worried about looking stupid. Now I don't have to worry.'

Steff clicked away as she trod water and smiled up from the pool, changing film as she climbed out. He shot her sitting on the far edge of the pool, arms around her knees, dripping with water, then standing up, her back to the ocean, arms out, looking skywards. He could make out every excruciatingly desirable curve and contour of her small breasts through the wet and flimsy material, and suddenly felt an unaccustomed desire to keep them out of the frame to spare her modesty. He realised this was as hypocritical as it was patronising (as well as probably being sexist in some hideously complicated ideological way), and made the best of the shot.

She jumped back into the water, this time giving him notice, and splashed down, laughing as she surfaced, shouting things at him, smiling and smiling and smiling.

And she was taking him to lunch.

Steff was smiling too, fearful of doing anything that might break whatever spell was making all this happen. He tried not to hope, tried just to enjoy what he was doing.

He tried not to think about the celebrities the press had linked her with, as confirmed when Jo asked her yesterday about who she'd been 'seeing'. Seth Kolbeck, lead guitarist with Death Head, currently off on a stadium tour of Europe. Mike MacAvoy, star of TV ratings sensation *There Goes the Neighborhood*, currently shooting *Close Action*, his first above-the-line-credit, big-budget thriller for Warner Bros. Apparently neither of these relationships had worked out, but Steff feared it was long odds that this was because what the lassie really needed in her life was a big skinnymalink from Lanarkshire.

However, if he wanted to indulge the daydream, it was worth remembering *why* the above hadn't worked out. Who knew whether she needed big skinnymalinks from Lanarkshire, but she definitely didn't need rock stars and adolescent sitcom actors.

'We "went out" inasmuch as we attended a few movie premières and launch parties together, but these were not dates,' she told Jo. 'I can barely remember having a conversation with either one of those guys. I was little more than a walking photo-opportunity. Mike MacAvoy invited me out to a couple of things because he wanted to be seen with me on his arm. He was in the frame for *Close Action*, but the director wasn't sold on him because of his boy-next-door image on TV. I was just part of his makeover. Instant notoriety: just add Maddy. Seth was merely *maintaining* his image. They wanted to be seen in the company of me the media phenomenon. Me the person wasn't invited. I think they also both reckoned that with me having been a porn star I'd be an easy lay. I'm not.'

She was taking him out to lunch. Him, not Seth Kolbeck or Mike MacAvoy. But then she did say that it was to make up for yesterday – the good little networker routine. And then again, Steff reminded himself, she didn't have to, and nobody he shot had ever done it before. He looked at her smile up at him again, giggling girlishly, a million miles from affectation or concerns about deportment. He thought of the way she'd responded when he said she looked prettiest in her civvies.

There had to be something going on.

It was a Catholic thing, this fear, this worry, this I-am-not-worthy pish. You could ditch the beliefs but you couldn't quite repair the damage. Years of supporting Motherwell FC had been contributory too: he always got nervous when everything seemed to be going right, because that was usually when the roof fell in.

Normally, this was just a figure of speech.

'Arguello here,' said a voice – firm, quiet, controlled, direct and totally out of character. 'Drink your coffee, Sarge, sit down and listen up.'

Pedro Arguello was on babysitting detail at the Pacific Vista for the second week of the market, replacing Tommy Andrews. Pedro had been monitoring the bomb-threat phone tap (thirteen hoaxes and counting) among other hand-holding duties, such as convincing a Legion of Decency delegation to abandon their lie-down blockade protest at the front of the horseshoe drive. He had gone for the practical and diplomatic tactic of pointing out how the glare meant that drivers might not even see the protesters and would just roll right over their fundamentalist asses. That was him all the way: a cool, cheerful, smooth operator. He'd even laughed when one of the protesters said, 'Never mind your badge, let's see your Green Card.'

He wasn't laughing now.

'S'up Pedro?'

'Take your all-time worst nightmare and multiply it by the biggest number you can think of. We got a situation here, I, eh . . . Look, power up your computer, man, I'm sending something over. You've probably already got it, except you don't know it yet, though that's another story, but I'm sendin' it anyway. We got . . .'

'Hey Pedro Pedro Pedro,' Larry said, switching on the PC that sat against the wall between his desk and Zabriski's. 'You ain't makin' sense. Take a deep breath and start from the beginning.'

There was a pause.

'Okay. From the top. Conchita Nunez got a phone call a

196

little while ago. No chance of a trace, voice just said, "There's a bomb on the Moonstar boat – check your computer now," then rang off. We recorded it, but he used a disguiser. Nunez looks at her screen, and there's a bomb icon on the desktop, little black ball with a fuse like in fucking Bugs Bunny or something. She clicks on the bomb and it opens a text file and like a video window. Text says there's a bomb on the *Ugly Duckling*. Turns out that's the boat one of the movie companies is having its booze'n'schmooze cruise on today. Eighty-eight people on board. Video window shows the bomb attached to some pipes in what looks like an engine room. That plays for ten seconds, then you get a ten-second loop of the upper decks from a vantage-point some place at the front, shots of people getting on board to prove it was recorded this morning.

'But in case that's not enough, beneath the video window it gives the frequencies these images were transmitted on: there's two goddamn cameras broadcasting live from that boat, and this *pendejo*'s looking at 'em. I'm tuned in right now – he ain't kidding. Text says we can have someone go to the engine room to verify that the bomb's for real, but if anyone tries to screw with it, he'll see, and he'll detonate. Same goes if anyone gets off the boat. Same goes if we jam the transmission. Same goes if the boat moves out of transmission range. Same goes if the cameras fail by themselves.'

'Jesus fuckin' Christ. Have you contacted the boat?'

'Yes sir. Captain verified the position of the device then barfed. This is not a drill, man.'

Larry felt his own guts turn over.

'So what does this asshole want? Money?'

Arguello sighed. 'I wish. The bomb's only half the nightmare. Oh man, this is so fucked up. I never seen shit as sick as this.'

'Jesus, Pedro, tell me about it.'

'He wants . . . he wants a human sacrifice.'

'*What?*'

'I ain't shittin' you, man. And worse than that, a suicide. He's a fucking space-case, man, fucking *loco*. Says everyone on the boat's a sinner who deserves to die, but they can be saved if one person repents and makes the ultimate . . . you know.'

'You gotta be fucking kidding.'

'No, man. And he don't mean any one person, neither. He's made a specific nomination.'

'Who?'

'Maddy Witherson. That senator's daughter who became a porno actress. Calls her the Whore of Babylon, lots of crazy shit, says she's got until dawn tomorrow to throw a seven or the boat goes bang. Wants her to do it with a knife, on the deck of the boat where his camera can see.'

Larry closed his eyes. 'Pedro, I'd give real money if you'd tell me this is a joke.'

'Oh sure, Sarge. You want the punch-line? The girl ain't *on* the fuckin' boat. I spoke to the captain over the telephone. She was supposed to be on the trip, she was on the invite list, but she was a no-show. Her and about a dozen other lucky folks who overslept or whatever.'

'So where is she?'

'I don't know, man, but we better find out real soon, and get to her before anyone else does. That thing appear on your screen yet?'

'No. It's taking its time decompressing the file.'

'Well, here's another joke. The text says those little bombs are already inside a ton more computers, but they're programmed not to show up on the screens until a little bit later.'

'Which computers? Oh shit,' Larry said, realising. The number he'd thought of to multiply the nightmare by wasn't nearly high enough.

'TV, radio, news agencies. The works, Larry. This guy wants the eyes of the world looking in, and he'll get 'em. Ever hear the expression "a crowd like for an execution"? We gotta find that girl soon, warn her, get her into protection, some damn thing. Forget the white Bronco chase, man. Every TV on the fucking planet's gonna be tuned to this. And we better think seriously about how we're gonna break it to the folks on the boat before the media do it for us. Okay, maybe they ain't watchin' TV out there but these are movie people, for Christ's sake. Every fucking one of them'll have a mobile phone, man. Plus their buddies back on-shore ain't just gonna hear the story, they're gonna see the action. The stations'll be able to pick up these camera signals from the boat same as us, and the air's gonna be thick with choppers about ten minutes after the news guys see this file.'

'Which is gonna be when?'

'He doesn't say.'

'I don't get it. He wants a circus, so why does the hotel – and therefore the cops – get the scoop? What's he waiting for?'

'Who knows, man? Maybe a response from us. Who cares? What the fuck are we gonna do?'

'All right, give me a second here.' Larry breathed out and tried to detach himself enough for his brain to offer something constructive. 'Okay. I want you to get on to Bannon – the response call is way over my head. I'll transfer you right now. And I also want Nunez to call me this second on Zabriski's line. She'll be the fastest chance we've got of locating the girl.'

'You got it, man.'

Larry transferred the call, carrying the phone to the door so he could see through the glass partition into Bannon's office. He waved to get the Captain's attention, gesticulating to him that it was urgent. There was a click as Bannon picked up.

'Got Arguello at the PV. There's a bomb on a boat. Eighty-eight people on board. This is for real.'

Larry put down the receiver to connect Bannon to Arguello, then dialled the code to pick up Zabriski's already ringing phone on his own line.

'Who can tell us where Maddy Witherson is, Conchita?'

'I've been calling her agent since we found out she wasn't on the boat,' she said. 'Line was busy until about thirty seconds ago. Don't worry, I didn't tell him anything. He said she was meeting a photographer for a shoot, some movie magazine. He wasn't totally sure, but he thinks they were hooking up right here at the hotel. You want me to put out a call?'

'No. Absolutely not. Have someone go look for her, get her into your office and I'll come pick her up, but don't do anything that's gonna attract attention to her or to the fact that she's there – *if* she's there. We don't know when this whole thing's gonna go public, but when it does, I don't want anyone knowing where she is.'

'Okay. I'll check the security monitors first. Then I'll . . . Wait a second. What the hell?'

'What is it? Talk to me, Conchita.'

'Something else just appeared on my screen. The end of the text file extended itself, like there was another part folded behind the page.'

'What's it say?'

'It says "MORAL DILEMMA" in capital letters. Then: "Before anyone would be prepared to sacrifice themselves to save the lives of others, that person would have to be completely convinced of the reality of the threat. I appreciate this, and would now like to remove the element of doubt."'

'Then what?'

'Then nothing. That's all it says.'

'So how is he planning— Oh shit shit shit. That's what he's waiting for. That's why he ain't told the media yet. Jesus, Conchita, get everybody out of the fuckin' building, right now!'

'I heard a loud bang.' That was always what some stupid fucker said on the news after the IRA had passed their latest damning comment on contemporary metropolitan architecture. Like the nation needed to be told bombs went bang.

However, this one didn't, not to Steff. Because bombs only go bang when you're a hundred yards away.

He remembered the pool cleaner coming through the door, carrying a bundle of tubes and brushes in both arms. She stopped to hold the door open because someone was coming up behind her. Maddy was holding on to the steel ladders at the corner of the pool, Steff kneeling down and getting ready for another shot. He looked up and saw a young woman walking urgently towards where he was crouched, a gold-metal staff badge on her blouse.

'Excuse me, I've a message for Miss Witherson,' she called out, halfway between him and the door from which she had emerged. He pulled the camera away from his face and gestured to the pool.

Steff felt like he was suddenly surrounded by loudness, a white noise, screaming, creaking, bending, tearing, crunching, cracking, all at once, and all amid a massive sense of force and movement. It was so total, so engulfing that he could not tell what parts he was hearing and what parts he was feeling, sounds in his ears and vibrations through his body indistinguishable. He was knocked on to his back by the jolt as the ground seemed to rear up at him, then the entire floor began to tip in the direction of the stairwell door. Except there was no stairwell door, and no stairwell either. That entire corner had disappeared, and with it gone, the rest of the rooftop terrace was now sloping into the gap. The pool cleaner, who had been assembling equipment in that area, was gone. Clouded by the dust Steff could just make out the messenger, prostrate and bloody, at the far end of the pool. Maddy had been knocked back into the middle of the water and was spluttering and wheezing as she struggled, having gone under and swallowed when the blast hit.

Then there was another shriek of surrendering metal and the floor felt like it had fallen away from beneath Steff. Another support had given at the north-east corner, and the terrace suddenly tipped sharply further towards it. The water in the pool rushed that way too, whipping Maddy along like she was on a rope, and spilling over the side in a voluminous wave. Maddy was flung hard against the wall but remained in the pool as the water cascaded towards the crevice, where it hit the messenger like a bulldozer, scattering her over the edge along with the sunbeds and trestle tables.

Steff lay on his back, digging his heels into the plastic turf to stop himself rolling. Shock, disbelief, terror, pain, all the things that were supposed to occupy his mind failed to register. Or rather, he was aware of them, but it was as though they were going through the mind of someone else, like a TV show on a different channel in the room through the wall. He knew the show was being videotaped, and he'd be forced to view it later, at least once a night for the rest of his life, but right now he couldn't afford to watch.

Maddy was still floating, languidly flapping an arm. The water had levelled out at an absurd angle across the pool, lapping against the bottom of the shallow end like it was a glass shore. She wasn't going to be able to climb out of there herself.

Steff climbed up on to his knees and began to manoeuvre carefully around towards where the water was spilling over the edge, as that would be the easiest place to pull her out. There was another slight jolt, but this time the force seemed to be pushing straight downwards rather than towards the corner again. Then he heard another breaking sound.

'Aw, in the name of fuck, this is not happening.'

There was a crack visible in the glass under the water, snaking across all the way from one side to the other and even up the walls. The entire pool was ready to split in half, and when it did, the end Steff was moving towards was going to collapse into the crevice. The contents, of course, were going to fall out like the inside of a neatly cracked egg.

Steff scrambled back around the edge of the pool and unhooked from around his waist the bum-bag he kept his used films in, pressing a button on the buckle and playing out the strap's slack as far as it would go. He descended the metal ladder at the shallow end into where the water should have been, then edged down the slope. Through the glass he could see that water was pouring out of the crack on the left-hand side, spraying down into the lobby. He caught a glimpse of the scene below and closed his eyes, then looked straight ahead when he reopened them. He couldn't afford to look down there, couldn't afford to let what he had seen register.

He inched nearer the edge of the water then let his feet slip out from under him. He landed with a thump and slid into the first few inches of the chlorinated liquid.

'Maddy,' he shouted. 'Grab this.'

Steff got to his feet again, waded further in and threw the bag out towards her, keeping tight hold of the strap. He was glad to have bought a bum-bag with a Pavarotti setting, but it still seemed an agonising distance Maddy needed to cover to reach it, striking out as she did in a dazed and feeble splashing. She got hold of the bag with one hand and pulled herself near enough to grip it with both. Then Steff began to back up, dragging her to where she could put a foot down and get enough of her body out of the water for her own weight and her wet clothes not to drag her back in. He got his hands under her armpits and pulled her backwards up the incline towards the ladder. Her eyes were half closed, unfocused, her mouth trying to form words but just dribbling pool water and emitting moans and coughs. He helped her to her feet and she grabbed the silver tubes of the ladder with either hand. Steff lifted her so that she could get a foot on the lowest rung, then got his shoulder under her bottom and nudged her upwards until she spilled her torso over the side. He lifted her legs level with the sloping floor, then she crawled clear of the edge and rolled on to her back.

Steff had just taken hold of the ladder himself when the egg cracked. There was a high-pitched, prolonged shattering sound, then the water was sucked down and out as the far side of the pool and what was left of the terrace swung backwards and away like a trapdoor. The resultant shudder swung Steff around on the ladder and twisted his wrists out of their grip. He spilled to the tilted and slippery floor, at the end of which there was now only a jagged edge and a sheer drop into the carnage of the lobby. He dug his heels against the slick tiles, Doc Marten Airware his only ally in a fight to the death with gravity. In the underpant-saving moment of relief when he became sure that he was no longer sliding nearer to the precipice, he noticed that what was left of the glass bottom was starting to dislocate from the remains of the pool's walls.

Steff lifted one heel closer to his body and dug down with it, pushing himself back up the slope and repeating the move with the other as quickly and steadily as his panicking mind could manage, given the screeching aural accompaniment of cracking glass. Turning on to his front, he slung the bum-bag over the first rung of the ladder and grabbed it, pouch in left hand, strap in right, one frantic breath before the bottom of the pool fell away from the two side walls as if hinged at the near end. He felt the weight go from his feet and transfer to his hands in a sickening drop, his shoulders wrenched painfully by the sudden jerk. Steff's body was swung inwards against the torn seam where the pool's floor had detached from the walls, a glass wedge finding its way easily into his right arm and breaking off.

The giant glass slab, formerly the bottom of the swimming pool, had swung slowly backwards until it was almost plumb with the only wall it remained attached to. Then it dropped off completely. There was a reverberating crash from below as it hit the concourse. Short of another bomb, it was about the only sound loud enough to drown the screaming.

Steff could handle the agony in his upper arm as long as he didn't look at it, but he could feel his grip weakening, and stoicism wouldn't be able to compensate for that. He braced himself for the pain then took hold of both ends of his lifeline with his right hand for the moment required to stretch upwards and sling his left arm over the plastic rung. He gripped his left wrist with his right hand until he was steady, then freed up his right hand again to loop the bum-bag over the next rung and fasten it like a harness.

Suspended there, catching his breath, he could finally see the extent of the damage. In those first confused moments, given his location his initial thoughts had been of an earthquake, but if he needed any confirmation of what had really happened, it was horrifyingly apparent. The hotel's landmark canopy was crippled around the north-east corner, its vast panes disintegrated and its steel spokes buckled and broken. The remains of the other part of the swimming pool and terrace still dangled on the far side of the hole, folded over like the lid of a cardboard box pushed in on itself.

While below . . .

Blood ran off Steff's elbow and splashed on to his shoes as they hung in the air above the carnage. Drops in the ocean. He was a hundred feet above but he could still make out the red. Not even the deluge from the shattered pool could wash away that much blood.

Explosives, glass and gravity. A crowded concourse.

'There is a God,' he muttered, some deeply sick synaptic sub-station in his brain throwing in some sarcasm, like the situation wasn't quite bad enough. Or maybe it was trying to cheer him up.

There is a God. Fucking stupid expression. People always said it when their wishes were granted, when all went well, an egotistical notion that their overseeing deity had recognised their desires and smiled specifically upon them. Funny, nobody ever said it when something went wrong, nobody ever took the corresponding view that their overseeing deity had recognised what a prick they were and reached, smiling, for the thunderbolts. Nobody ever looked at the cinders of their razed house, or stood over the grave of their dead relative, and said: 'There is a God. I've been a selfish wanker recently, and I thoroughly deserved that.'

Nobody ever dangled precariously by one hand, fuck knew how high, over a blood-drenched scene of carnage and destruction, racked with pain, fear and shock, and said: 'There is a

God.' Not until today, anyway, and that didn't count because the bloke concerned didn't mean it.

He twisted the strap in his right hand and tried to tug his body upwards, but the limb just wasn't up to it, and he succeeded only in spinning himself around 180 degrees. He could see Maddy again now, and this time she had an unfocused eye open. She coughed and wiped some blood-matted hair from her face, then seemed to remember where she was and who he was.

'Stephen,' she mouthed hoarsely, then began crawling towards the edge. Time for her to return the compliment.

Steff felt the earliest stirrings of relief. It left a tiny space in his furiously cluttered mind for thoughts unrelated to gravity and the vast distance between his feet and the floor. The first was of her face, and the now shortened odds that he was on for at least a wee snog once they were through this. The next was that it would have to wait until he had found and thoroughly leathered whoever was responsible for the bomb.

Larry recoiled from the earpiece as a sound like a massively amplified static crackle pierced the right half of his skull. A couple of seconds later there was a bang from outside that passed through his internal organs like a shockwave.

He put out the emergency call himself, telling every ambulance and paramedic in the area to get down to the Pacific Vista stat, appending a warning to the news crews who would be monitoring the police bands that 'if anyone sees one of your vans in front or in the way of an ambulance, you'll be goin' home in one'.

Bannon strode confidently into the centre of the station, silencing the hubbub, dispensing orders. Cops only panic when they've got time to panic, he'd once told Larry. Keep 'em busy and you'll keep 'em calm.

'Freeman,' he said, 'your job is to locate the girl and bring her in before the media get wise to what the real story is here. Zabriski, you get down there and organise the cordons. I want the streets blocked off to traffic between the Vista and St Mark's to the north, SM Mercy to the East. I want clear corridors for those ambulances and I don't care who gets pissed off in the process. Baker, I want you to liaise with the bomb squad, get them in there looking for whatever's left of the device, I don't care if the building's still on fire . . .'

By that point Larry was walking swiftly out of the main doors.

Maddy took hold of the strap and helped Steff climb out on to the terrace, then they made their way to where the slope levelled out near the opposite corner. They sat down shakily, side by side on a sun lounger.

Steff said nothing, just stared into space. He could feel now how buggered up his system was. He didn't know whether he was about to shit, puke, faint or spontaneously combust. The screaming below had given way to shouting and sirens, and it was all starting to sound further and further away. He could see the yawning gash in the roof, the jagged bite taken out of the building, the twisted and broken girders jutting accusingly at the sky.

The motion stilled, the dust blown away on the breeze, the roof was starting to look like it had always been that way, as though the pair of them might have climbed up here to see this radical piece of architectural sculpture. That was when he knew it was over; whatever it had been, it was over.

Steff looked at his watch but didn't know why. He didn't need to know the time; maybe he needed to know that time was still passing. That it was still the same day, that the world was still turning, that two blocks away there were people in an office who heard a distant bang, looked up from their computers for two seconds, then got back to work.

'The pool cleaner? That woman?' Maddy said croakily.

Steff shook his head.

'Jesus.'

'You all right?' he enquired.

'Yeah. Got a bit groggy for a while after I hit the side of the pool. I think I'm okay. I'm gonna have nightmares for the whole rest of my life, but other than that I'm cool.'

Maddy got up and walked to a low table nearby, next to which her bag still sat where she had left it. One of Steff's cameras lay on the ground a few feet away. She retrieved that too and handed it to him as she sat back down. The object looked irrelevant in his hand for a few moments. Then he remembered what it was for – what he was for – and pointed it at the damage, but the film had run out. It had auto-repeated until the roll was finished. He rewound it and popped it into his pocket for safekeeping. It was either going to win him a mantelpiece full of awards or there'd be twenty-odd shots of a blurred floor-tile. Probably the latter.

Steff placed the camera on the floor at his feet as Maddy bent over and opened her bag. She pulled out a light summery dress, a blue one, laying it on the sunbed, then also produced a white T-shirt from inside the holdall.

She moved around to the other side of Steff, the T-shirt in her hand.

'Let me take a look at this.'

She tore the sleeve away from Steff's arm around the protruding piece of glass, wiping blood off gently.

'Looks subcutaneous,' she said. 'Messy and sore, but no biggie. If it had hit anything major, you'd be spraying all over the carpet here.'

Steff looked at her quizzically.

'First-aid training. Did it at college. Thanks for saving my life, by the way.'

'Don't mention it. I think you saved mine back. We're quits.'

'Hardly. We're a long way off quits. You don't get rid of me that easily. This is gonna hurt.'

'What? Owww!'

She yanked out the shard of glass in one smooth motion and held it up for him to see. It was about a quarter of the size it felt, and like the iceberg principle in reverse, what showed on the surface was far greater than what had penetrated underneath.

Maddy ripped the white T-shirt into a long strip and wrapped it tightly around the wound, then placed Steff's hand on the makeshift bandage.

'Just hold it there. Keep pressure on it.'

She stood up and pulled off her sleeveless top, dropping it to the ground in a damp thud, then reached for the dress, which she slipped quickly over her head. She removed her wet shoes, shorts and underwear, pulling on a fresh pair of knickers under the frock. Next she pulled from the bag a pair of dressy blue shoes with a substantial heel.

'Maybe not,' she decided, and settled for the wet canvas ones again.

'You think anyone knows we're up here?' she asked, sitting back down.

'Maybe. But the rescue services'll have their hands full downstairs.'

'Well, there's an emergency staircase runs down the outside of the canopy on this side, just there. You fit to walk?'

'I'll fuckin' well walk oota this place.'

Larry Freeman had seen a lot of things he'd rather have passed on working for the LAPD. Images that as soon as they met your eyes you knew you'd be seeing them until your mind failed in some drooling-years, casket-fitting waiting room. Sights that too graphically illustrated the fragility of the human body when it met with misadventure or with man's own tirelessly inventive cruelty. He had seen every kind of mutilation human technology could effect, every viciousness anger could blindly inspire, every death a man could die.

But he had never, ever seen so much blood.

Whether they were walking out or being carried out, everyone leaving that building was covered in it.

'Bomb turned the place into a giant fucking blender, man,' Arguello said when Larry found him on the steps, helping ferry the unconscious and the merely dazed into the hands of the still-arriving ambulances. Pedro's once-white shirt was sticky with red, none of which, he was able to assure Larry, was his. 'I was okay, bein' up in the office suite, but Christ, the lobby . . .'

Pedro's face screwed up and he shook his head. He looked close both to tears and to collapse. Larry pulled him away from the shattered doors and sat him down at the side of the steps. He held on to Larry's arms like if he let go he'd be sucked back into the horror inside.

'It was the glass, man,' he said, as if trying to explain it to himself. 'All that glass, like a million fucking razor blades flying through that place. Cut everybody to ribbons. And the roof . . . Bits kept falling. We were trying to pull everybody clear. Anybody who could stand, anybody who could see, we were all dragging people clear, out to the sides. But there were folks trapped . . . all those stalls and shit just folded up and collapsed into each other with the blast. I was trying to get one guy free when I heard a noise from above, like a crack, and water started pouring in.'

Pedro started shaking his head. 'It was the swimming-pool, man. It started to come apart, slowly at first, then it broke like a fucking *piñata*. I couldn't get back to the guy, man. The water came down and pushed me away, flushed me like a fucking turd, and I couldn't get back to him. Then this slab of glass . . . Oh man . . .'

Pedro finally broke down.

Larry put an arm round his shoulders. 'Take it easy, Ped, you did your stuff. Nothin' else you could do.'

'I'll be okay,' he announced, wiping his eyes. 'I'll be okay. I better get back to work.' He stood up, sniffing and taking a breath. 'They still ain't got everybody out of there.'

'No,' Larry said. 'You ain't goin' back inside. Fire crews are here now, they're trained for this shit. I need you cleaned up and thinkin' straight – downtown. This ain't over, remember. This was just the warning shot.'

'Shit man, I forgot. The boat. Jesus.'

'Don't sweat it. I'd understand if it slipped your mind in the last half-hour. You know where Nunez is? She okay?'

'Yeah, man, she's with the paramedics. She was takin' names from anyone who walked out, and tryin' to ID the unconscious ones, so we got some idea who's still missing.'

Larry looked across at the horseshoe drive, at the strobo-scope of flashing lights, the white shapes of the ambulances, the green-clad crews, the red-streaked figures of the wounded. He saw Nunez talking to a guy from the Fire Department, gesticulating back towards the lobby, and made his way towards her. She spotted him coming and nodded towards the grass area at the side of the drive, off the path between the exit and the impromptu field-hospital that was taking shape.

'You okay?' he asked.

'Not a scratch,' she said. 'My lucky day, huh?'

'Yeah, real lucky. You find—'

'She was on the roof,' Nunez said. Larry's eyes widened with concern. 'Don't worry, she made it. The girl I sent up there to find her didn't, though. She was nineteen.'

'Christ. Where's Witherson?'

'I don't know, I didn't see her myself. I talked to that guy there, the paramedic with the clipboard – he had her name. She and the photographer guy climbed down the emergency ladder on the other side, so they must be okay, comparatively. They're being treated on the spot. Go ask him to point them out. I gotta get back inside. Fire crew need the building plans.'

Steff sat on a kerbstone on the horseshoe drive while a nurse knelt on the grass verge beside him and put stitches in his arm.

Maddy was standing behind him holding a cup of water, wearing a blanket around her shoulders. There were ambulances everywhere, paramedics and nurses treating the walking wounded, presumably because the local ERs would be bursting at the seams with the more seriously injured. There were police cars behind the ambulances, providing a protective barrier against the next wave of vehicles, which was made up of TV vans. Maddy had been checked out by a triage nurse who declared her okay but nonetheless offered to arrange transport to a hospital for a closer look. She settled for a few sticking plasters and something to drink.

Steff noticed a paramedic pointing in their vicinity, and saw that the guy being directed was holding up some sort of ID. As he walked nearer, Steff recognised him as the big, bald, black guy who had been standing near him during St John's speech the other day. That was all the confirmation he needed about who had done this.

'Miss Witherson?' the guy enquired, displaying the ID again. 'I'm Larry Freeman, LAPD. Are you okay?'

'I've had better mornings, but I'm still here.'

'Miss Witherson, I'd like you to come with me right now. It's extremely important.'

'Where?'

'Just somewhere, away from here. We need to talk.'

'What's it about?'

'Not here.'

'Okay. Soon as the nurse is through with Stephen, we're all yours.'

The cop looked down briefly at Steff, giving him a do-I-know-you? stare. Steff waved with his free hand. 'Saw you across the road the other day,' he clarified. 'One of those mental God-squad wankers did this, didn't they?'

210

'I'm afraid I can't comment, sir.'

'That's a yes. You'd have said you didn't know otherwise.'

'Excuse me,' the cop said, 'you are?'

'Steff Kennedy. Photographer. Motherwell supporter. Bomb victim.'

'He saved my life up there,' Maddy added, perhaps to compensate for his attitude. She'd have her work cut out if she planned to keep it up.

The cop nodded. 'Well, Mr Kennedy, as Miss Witherson has indicated her desire to have you accompany her, and providing you assent to that, I will be explaining to both of you just as much as I know myself once we are out of sight and earshot.'

'Do you mind coming along?' Maddy asked.

'Not at all. I was brought up to consider it bad manners to refuse any woman who pulls you oot a wrecked swimmin'-pool a hundred feet above a major disaster area.'

Freeman led them to his unmarked police car, parked around the side of the building furthest from the devastation.

'A car?' asked Maddy. 'Where are we going? I thought you just wanted to talk.'

'Mr Kennedy, I'd like you to ride up-front beside me. Miss Witherson, I'd recommend you get into the back and keep your head down on the seat until I say otherwise. I apologise for the inconvenience, but it would be very much conducive to your safety.'

'My safety?' Maddy seethed. 'What is this cloak-and-dagger bullshit? What the hell are you talking about? Are you telling me we walked out of that nightmare and I'm *still* in some kind of danger?'

Freeman opened the passenger-side rear door and sighed.

'Miss Witherson, I appreciate what you've been through this morning, I really do, but believe me, the nightmare's just warming up. And once I've filled you in on the bigger picture, you'll understand why I had to say the following: get in the fucking car *now* and keep your goddamn head down.'

twelve

Larry felt a sickening sensation in his guts as he watched the two of them sit and stare at the printout. He'd always thought nothing could match the hollow feeling of that first time you informed someone their loved one was dead; something that never became easy, but was never again quite so wounding. He remembered that woman's face still, the name of her murdered son, his street name, the address, the screen door, the beat-up Hyundai in the drive.

This came pretty close.

What made it worse was his guilt at opting to let them read the file instead of telling them straight out. But how the hell did you break something as weird and fucked-up as this? And to two people in the shape they were in?

Neither of them had said much since Larry got them into his car. They seemed dazed, slightly disconnected, like they were taking a time-out from whatever screwed-up game was being played here. The reality of what had happened today would be hitting them only in instalments. As the images and details returned to their consciousness they'd find it hard to believe these were things they were actually remembering rather than imagining; then they'd feel the truth of it, cold and hard as a mortuary slab.

The girl had done what she was told and lain down in the back, the guy sitting up-front and just staring, like one of those plastic dolls women put in the passenger seat when they're driving downtown at night. She was wearing a light cotton sundress and her hair was wet. Looked like she'd just stepped out of the bath on a hot summer's day – until you saw what was in her eyes.

Larry hadn't paid a shitload of attention to the stories about her in the papers or on TV, having little interest in either Senator Witherson or pornography. He didn't know what he thought a porno actress was supposed to look like, but he was pretty sure this wasn't it. Mind you, nobody looks much like themselves when they've been scared out of their minds.

The guy had this pissed-off look on his face, but not an especially pissed-off look. It was like this was merely the latest in a long line of inconveniences.

'Whaaat a friend we have in Jeee-suuus,' he'd sung, glancing out of the rolled-down window.

'You okay there, man?' Larry asked him, worried the guy might be in shock.

'Ay,' he said. 'Sorry, that's "yes" to you.'

'I know what "ay" means, Mr Kennedy.'

'Oh right. I'm fine. I just couldn't help singing after my spiritual experience this morning. Tell me, Sergeant, have you found God yet?'

Larry looked around at him warily. 'Yeah, but he had an alibi,' he said.

'Well, if I was you I'd take him doon the cells for a good kicking anyway.'

The guy's jeans were damp and his T-shirt wet and bloody. When they reached the precinct-house Larry got him an LAPD sweatshirt and some running pants from his own locker, figuring they'd be the only spare clothes that would fit him. He escorted them swiftly through the station's mêlée to a free interview room, where he had Torres fix them some coffee while he fetched the clothes and had a brief word with Bannon. Bannon told him, as expected, that the town was now swarming with FBI agents. Less expected, there was one in Bannon's office who had asked specifically for Larry Freeman.

Larry told Bannon he'd talk to no one until the girl had been brought up to speed, and headed back to the interview room where he locked the door and handed them the printout.

SINNER'S REPENT, FOR THE KINGDOM OF THE LORD
IS AT HAND.

TOO LONG HAVE THE FILTH-PEDDLER'S IGNORED
GOD'S WORD. THEY HAVE SPREAD THEIR EVIL ACROSS
AMERICA AND THE WORLD BEYOND, PREACHING A
BLACK GOSPEL OF FREE FORNACATION, SODAMY,
PORNOGRAPHY AND SIN. IN THEIR HEART'S THEY KNOW

213

WHAT THEY DO IS WRONG, AND YET THEY REFUSE TO
ADMIT THIS AND CHANGE THEIR WAYS.

THEY REFUSE TO REPENT.

THIS ARROGANCE MUST BE HUMBLED.

TODAY A HUNDRED SINNER'S OF THE UNAMERICAN
FESTERING FILTH MARKET SET SAIL ON THE UGLY
DUCKLING, CHARTERED BY MOONSTAR, INTENDING TO
ENJOY THE HOSPITALITY AFFORDED BY THE PROFIT'S OF
THEIR FILTH. HAD THEY READ THE SCRIPTURES THEY
WOULD SURELY HAVE KNOWN THAT FILTH DOES NOT
PAY IN CHAMPAGNE AND LOBSTER – THE WAGES OF SIN
IS DEATH.

AS YOU CAN SEE FROM THE RECORDING ABOVE, THERE
IS A BOMB IN THE BOAT'S ENGINE-ROOM, AND I HAVE
A CAMERA TRANSMITTING FROM THERE CONSTANTLY.
YOU MAY SEND SOMEONE TO VERIFY THAT THE SCENE
SHOWN IS REALLY WHAT IT APPEARS. HOWEVER, IF YOU
MAKE ANY ATTEMPT TO INTERFERE WITH THE BOMB, I
WILL SEE IT AND I WILL BLOW THE BOAT UP. YOU WILL
NOTE ALSO THAT I HAVE A CAMERA TRAINED ON THE
UPPER DECK. THE FOLLOWING WILL ALSO RESULT IN
DETONATION:

IF I SEE ANYONE GET OFF THE BOAT.

IF I SEE ANYONE GET ON THE BOAT.

IF THE TRANSMISSION'S FROM MY CAMERA'S ARE
INTERFERED WITH.

IF THE BOAT ATTEMPTS TO SAIL OUT OF TRANSMISSION
RANGE.

IF MY CAMERA'S MALFUNCTION, EVEN IF IT IS BY
THEMSELVES.

ALL OF THE SINNER'S ON BOARD DESERVE TO DIE
AND FACE GOD'S JUDGMENT. THE WORLD WOULD
BE A CLEANER PLACE IF IT WAS RID OF SO MANY
FILTH-PEDDLER'S.

HOWEVER, I AM WILLING TO SPARE THEIR LIVES AND
ALLOW THEM THE CHANCE TO MAKE AMMENDS, BUT
ONLY IF THEY HAVE LEARNT THE TRUE MEANING OF
REPENTANCE.

THE WHORE OF BABYLON IS AMONG THEM. THE
QUEEN OF SLUT'S, WHO HAS FLAUNTED HER PERVERSE
FORNACATION BEFORE THE WORLD AND BLASPHEMED

IN DEFIANCE OF ALL DECENCY, DESERVES MORE THAN
ANY OTHER TO BURN IN HELL FOREVER FOR HER EVIL.
BUT SHE CAN SAVE HER SOUL AND SAVE THE LIVES OF
EVERYONE ON BOARD THE BOAT IF SHE FIRST REPENTS
ALL HER SINS AND THEN PROVES HER PENITENCE
THROUGH SACRAFICE.

THE WHORE OF BABYLON MUST TAKE HER OWN LIFE
BEFORE THE EYES OF THE WORLD – BY THE DAWN'S
EARLY LIGHT. THIS SHE MUST DO BY CUTTING HER OWN
THROAT, THAT THE OTHER SINNER'S ON THE BOAT MAY
BE CLEANSED BY HER BLOOD.

ONE LIFE IN EXCHANGE FOR SO MANY MORE, THE
ULTIMATE SACRAFICE, AND A REMINDER TO THE
WORLD OF THE TRUE MEANING OF CHRISTIAN VALUES.
IF MADELEINE WITHERSON CAN PROVE THAT SHE HAS
SOME DECENCY IN HER, THEN SHE WILL ACHIEVE WHAT
"LOT" COULD NOT.

NB: THIS COMMUNICATION HAS BEEN TRANSMITTED
TO ALL MAJOR NEWS AGENCY'S AND TV NETWORK'S
– IDENTICAL BOMB ICONS WILL APPEAR ON THEIR
COMPUTER SCREENS TO ALERT THEM TO IT IN A
SHORT TIME. HOWEVER, ONLY THIS FILE CONTAIN'S
THE FOLLOWING CODEWORD FOR VERIFYING FURTHER
MESSAGES.

CODEWORD: MATTHEW 21:12-16

– – – – – – – – – – – – – – – –

MORAL DILEMMA: BEFORE ANYONE WOULD BE
PREPARED TO SACRAFICE THEMSELVES TO SAVE THE
LIVES OF OTHER'S, THAT PERSON WOULD HAVE TO
BE COMPLETELY CONVINCED OF THE REALITY OF THE
THREAT. I APPRECIATE THIS, AND WOULD NOW LIKE TO
REMOVE THE ELEMENT OF DOUBT.

So it was, as Steff had suspected, all for God. One more
needless atrocity in a long history of needless atrocities per-
petrated in the name of something that didn't even exist. Well
halle-fucking-lujah.

215

Steff wouldn't say he *knew* there wasn't a God, for the simple quantum reason that he couldn't prove it; equally he wouldn't say he *knew* there weren't invisible pink flying armadilloes buzzing around the ionosphere, undetectable by human instrumentation, for exactly the same reason. But if you asked him to take a side, he'd fall the same way on both issues. No, Steff didn't *know* there wasn't a God, he was merely one hundred per cent fucking certain.

Neither was he going to be eating much humble pie if he got to the other side and found out he was wrong. Never mind getting prostrate and making good with the big apology: if there turned out to be an omnipotent beardy in charge, Steff Kennedy would be demanding a few straight answers. And it wouldn't be about how He could tolerate starving kids in Africa or torture and mutilation in Saudi Arabia, or England winning the fucking World Cup in '66, or any other of the usual 'if a tree fell in a forest' philosophical chestnuts. Steff would be ready to go fifteen rounds arguing why he had still been right – on the basis of all available evidence – *not* to believe. But first he'd want a quiet word with this God cunt about His fuckwit followers blowing a big hole in the roof he had been standing on, and filling Him in at length about the overall discomfort and inconvenience of being at the sharp end of Christian fundamentalism.

'Well fuck me up the arse with an epileptic hedgehog,' he announced. 'There's me getting all upset about what happened this morning, and it actually turns out it's all for a good cause. We're saving the world, here. Thank fuck for that.'

'I have no idea what to say to this,' Maddy mumbled. Her face registered fear and anger, but mainly a more profound disgust than Steff had ever seen before. He guessed this was because neither had he encountered such a profound insult before. It wasn't like the guy had just called her "smelly" or something.

'No, don't be like that,' he told her. 'Get into the spirit of it. Don't think of it as death – see it more as a kind of sponsored suicide. It's all for God, remember.'

'This is not fucking funny,' she told him. 'I think I'm gonna puke.'

The cop, Freeman, looked at Maddy and gestured towards the door.

216

'The restrooms are down . . .'

She waved her hand. 'Figure of speech, Sergeant, but I appreciate the concern. I appreciate the coffee, the privacy, and the soft tones too. But I guess you have to be real sweet to me, don't you, before you try and convince me to do the right thing? That's why you were in such a rush to bring me in, isn't it?'

Freeman shook his head. 'Miss Witherson, I was in a rush to get you out of reach of the cameras before the media got their little messages this morning. I'm sure there's a few issues they'd be real keen to ask your opinion on right now. My principal concern is for your safety. That's what I get paid for. That's my professional position. If you want my personal position, I'll give you that too, which is that I'd rather cut my own goddamn throat than see this motherfucker get what he wants.'

'That's very generous,' she said, her voice bearing an uneasy sarcasm, 'but no offence, I don't think you'd cut it as my body double. Right now it's me or . . . what? Close to a hundred people on that boat. At least twenty of whom I know; some of them I even like.'

'Jo Mooney's on it,' Steff added. 'Supposed to be, anyway.'

'Oh terrific. Let's up the ante. Why don't you both tell me your mothers are on it too? Jesus. Whoever planted that bomb must hate me off the scale. Either I die a horrible death or become the most loathed person on Earth. Forget the bomber – the fucking public will, anyway. He's just a nutcase, but *she*—'

'We're gonna do whatever it takes to make sure it never comes to that,' Freeman interrupted. 'Either outcome. We've got about eighteen hours. We can find this guy, Miss Witherson.'

'But you're hanging on to me as a last resort in case you can't, or in case whatever stunts you pull don't come off.'

'Believe me, we won't have a last resort. If we try anything that doesn't come off, that's it. Eighty-eight more funerals. This guy killed eight people this morning – and counting – just to let us know he ain't bluffing. If he thinks we're fucking him around, he'll blow the boat. So yes, we do need you to be here, and we need him to know that, to keep his finger off the goddamn button until the clock runs out at dawn.'

'You've told him I'm in police custody?' She sounded livid.

217

'We got the captain of the *Ugly Duckling* to write it on a card and hold it up to one of the cameras. We were afraid he'd detonate when he found out you weren't on board where he was expecting you, especially if he found out second-hand through the media. We had to pre-empt that.'

'So what are you planning to do?'

'There'll be a co-ordinated operation: LAPD, the FBI—'

'Oh, I feel better already. The Feds arrested any security guards yet? Anyone talked to Richard Jewell? Jesus Christ.'

Freeman couldn't conceal a smile. Steff didn't get the joke, but he could at least work out that the cop shared Maddy's low opinion.

'All right, I ain't gonna pretend I'm any more confident about this than you,' he said, 'but we're stuck with it. And I can't do anything to improve the situation if I'm sitting here arguing with you. So why don't you and your boyfriend sit tight while us cops go "pull some stunts"?'

'Oh no,' she said, standing up. 'I'm not sitting in here like I'm waiting for the doc to come out and tell me whether it's terminal. Whatever you and your buddies are planning, I want to hear about it. I think I'm entitled to that much.'

Freeman seemed to think about this for a moment, then nodded. 'Can't hurt. Follow me.'

He opened the door and gestured for Maddy to exit. She walked towards it then stopped and turned around, shooting Steff an insistent glance which he interpreted to mean 'Come on, then'. He didn't know why he felt surprised that she kept asking him to tail along. They might not have known each other for very long, but after what they'd just come through together, even the ex-Catholic and nervous 'Well fan inside him couldn't discount a certain element of bonding.

'I'm not her boyfriend, by the way,' he said to Freeman, going through the door. 'I'm just this bloke she met hangin' around.'

Maddy gave as close to a smile as she was likely to manage that day.

Larry escorted them into Bannon's office, another niche of comparative calm cordoned off from the cacophony of the precinct-house's open area. Bannon was standing by the window, in conversation with two besuited men sitting by his desk, a silenced TV showing helicopter shots of the devastated Pacific Vista. They all turned around at the intrusion.

'Captain, gentlemen, this is Madeleine Witherson and her . . . companion, Steff Kennedy. Miss Witherson has requested that she be brought up to speed on the current situation, and I'd kind of like to know the latest myself.'

'Sure, sure,' Bannon said, walking over to them. 'There's more chairs in the corner there. I'm Captain Pat Bannon. This is Special Agent Tom Brisko and this is Agent Peter Steel of the FBI.'

The agents stood up, offering handshakes and assistance with chairs.

'Peter Steel,' Larry said. 'You didn't just *happen* to be one of the guys they sent down here, did you? You figure this—'

'It's not a coincidence,' Steel confirmed. He was a slight but athletic white man with blond hair and a boyish face, probably late thirties, who gave the impression of wearing his suit under protest. Larry pictured him with a surfboard under his arm and a long-neck in the other hand. Must have filled in the wrong order code in the vocations catalogue.

'But it doesn't mean we *know* anything either,' added Brisko, a black forty-something with grey hair and so many worry-lines his face looked like you were seeing it through a bath-room window. He was nervous now, which Larry found paradoxically reassuring. A lot of Feds gave off an impression of impervious confidence, and it was usually because they didn't give a fuck: they were playing good guys and bad guys while the civilians were just points on the scoreboard.

'So what do we know?' Larry asked.

Bannon moved around and leaned against the wall behind his desk. He was a guy who never seemed comfortable sitting down. Larry hadn't known him long enough to ask whether it was because he missed the streets or just suffered from piles.

'Well, first thing to tell you: regards the media, the pin's been pulled. They know.' He indicated the TV on his desk, where a photograph of Madeleine Witherson was now occupying the right-hand corner of the screen above the on-the-spot report-er's head. Fortunately, the spot remained the Pacific Vista, as opposed to the station, so they didn't know where she was yet at least.

'Oh terrific,' Witherson said.

'The captain of the boat, Micky Baird, and the Moonstar CEO, Linus Veltman, are doing their best to keep everybody from freaking out, but that's about as much control as they can reasonably exercise. Suffice it to say, it's lucky for Miss Witherson that she wasn't on board or she might be involved in some real high-pressure negotiations right now. We've got police launches alongside the *Ugly Duckling*, but apart from shouting through megaphones, there's not a hell of a lot they can do, as we're not allowed to put anybody on the boat. Not that the megaphones'll be much good once the fucking news choppers start circling.

'We have to accept that news management is not an option,' Bannon continued. 'It's an information free-for-all. We know there are TVs on the boat, radios too, and we have to assume that with all those mobile telephones, the passengers are in two-way contact with the mainland. Plus we have to bear in mind the close relations between many of the passengers and media personnel. There's gonna be very few secrets today, folks. We can't play bluff because everybody's hands are gonna be on the table at all times. The bomber wanted the eyes of the world – he's got 'em.'

'Miss Witherson,' said Brisko, leaning across the desk and talking as softly as if he was asking her to pass the salt while the head of the table was speaking. 'The FBI informed your father of the situation before the media broke it.'

The girl's tired eyes burst into angry life. 'My *father*? What the hell did you talk to him for? Did you tell him where I am?'

'No, we didn't. But we had to ask him whether anyone had been in contact with him regarding the bombing or the demands. It was possible someone was trying to get to him through this thing.'

'Kind of a roundabout way to lean on someone, don't you think?' she snapped. 'Blow up a building and hold eighty-eight people hostage on a floating bomb to the ransom of a suicide sacrifice? You think someone would do that just to intimidate a political mediocrity with his head up his ass?'

'He's a United States Senator, Miss Witherson. We had to investigate. He'd heard nothing. He wanted to talk to you, though, make sure you're okay, see if there was anything he could do. This is his mobile number.'

He handed her a sheet of paper. She ripped it in two and dropped the pieces on the floor.

'He wants a quote for the fucking TV cameras when they arrive, that's what he wants. So he can tell them all how his unruly daughter turned to him for a comforting word in her time of need. Well, I'll give him a quote. Tell him if I have to kill myself I'll be consoled by the thought that I'll never see his fucking face again.'

'Miss Witherson,' Brisko appealed, 'your father—'

'Has nothing to do with this. This isn't about him, okay? And it's not even about me. This is about a religious lunatic with a big bomb and a remote-control. Let's talk about *that* guy for a minute, huh?'

'Okay,' Brisko said, sitting back to concede ground to her. Larry could see the guy hadn't meant any harm, he just – like everyone else – had no idea how poisoned the waters must be between the girl and her old man. 'Let's talk about him, as you say. Agent Steel?'

'Well, first of all, we are merely assuming this is one guy, and we are talking about "he" or one guy for purposes of convenience. We don't know whether anyone else is involved. The computer message doesn't identify any group or faction, but as in this case the motive is to further the greater glory of God rather than of an organisation, that may not mean anything.'

'You must figure the Southland Militia are involved, otherwise you wouldn't be here,' Larry opined. 'Am I right?'

'The Southland Militia?' Witherson asked Steel. 'Those *Rambo* needle-dicks? You think they did this?'

'I was sent here *in case* evidence pointed to militia involvement, not because we yet have tangible reason to suspect it. And I'm not going to be disappointed if the facts point the other way. Believe me, I would much prefer this to be the work of a lone nutcase.'

'Yeah, me too,' Larry agreed, thinking of the shell found on the *Gazes Also*. 'So what do we know about *whoever* did this?'

Steel sighed. 'So far, not much. We've got agents at the marina where the *Ugly Duckling* was moored, interviewing

221

the security guards there, but our best hope is the hotel. Unlike the marina, the Vista's got security cameras. Our agents are going through the tapes, but they only started a short while ago. We may get lucky, though. A face would sure speed things up. Obviously we couldn't release it for a public appeal because he'd blow the bomb, but we could run it through the computers. We could have a name and possibly an address in a matter of hours.'

'Well that would be nice, Agent Steel,' said Witherson, 'but right now let's stick to what we do have, which I believe at the last count was jack-shit, am I right?'

'We're trying to construct a profile of the guy,' said Brisko. Witherson rolled her eyes, which he ignored. 'We know he's a Christian fundamentalist. We start with that, feed it into the system and cross-check it against whatever else comes up.'

'And what if he isn't on your system?' she demanded.

'I'll admit that remains a very real possibility, but on the other hand, this is pretty large-scale for a first offence. This isn't bombing one-oh-one, this is something you graduate to. From the look of the bomb on the boat, the guy's no expert, but he's no beginner either. His bomb isn't super-sophisticated, but it'll do the job. And he knows both those facts too – that's why he put a camera on the device and issued orders not to screw with it. It probably wouldn't take much defusing, but it would still take longer than for him to notice and press the button on the detonator.'

'Okay,' she said, her expression still challenging but her voice slightly less combative. 'So what can you cross-check against? What else do—'

'He's a computer nerd.'

Everyone looked round in surprise. It was Kennedy who had interrupted.

'Yes, well, he seems versed in computers,' Brisko agreed, 'but these days, who—'

'He's a computer nerd, believe me,' Kennedy continued. The Scottish guy's voice was a low, easy drawl that sounded effortlessly sardonic. Kind of tone that could wish you good morning and part of you would suspect he was somehow taking the piss. 'And he *is* one guy, working on his own. He's Nigel No-Friends, sitting at home every night with his PC, his *X-Files* posters and his Believers albums. This is obviously a social group the FBI don't have a typing profile for, which if you ask me is negligent, because there's fuckin' thousands of them.'

'How can you possibly—' began Steel, but Kennedy was in flow.

'Listen. There's a difference between being computer-literate or even a computer expert and being a computer nerd. The difference is that the former use computers to achieve something, and the latter think use of computers is a worthy achievement in itself. The former might take pride in their work, but the latter is proud simply of having done their work on a computer, whatever that work might be.

'Take these messages, for a start. He didnae need to tell umpteen TV and radio stations and news agencies in order to get the result he was looking for. He only needed to tell the one. And he didnae need to tell them all at the same time, either, with some smart-arse programme that keeps the bomb icon cloaked until an appointed moment. He was showing off. Showing off to himself and showing off to you guys. He's also running the signal from his TV cameras into his computer instead of into a telly, or *as well as* into a telly, so he could show off by putting those video playback windows into his wee electronic press release. If he only wanted to prove he had surveillance running, he could have quoted the frequencies and let you check it out for yourselves.

'But if you want conclusive evidence, you just need to take a look at the text. His English is fuckin' appalling. Dead giveaway.'

'What?' Steel asked. He seemed happy to go along with the previous theorising, but this had lost him.

'Have you ever seen any of these news-group things on the Internet? It's like syntax meets chaos theory. Problem with computer nerds is they were always happiest in maths and science lessons at school. This guy knows how to use state-of-the-art digital electronics, but he doesn't know how to use a fuckin' apostrophe.'

'He's right,' Bannon observed. 'From the message, it looks like this guy took English at Dan Quayle Junior High. But wait. If he sent these messages to so many computers, isn't there a way of tracing the source?'

Steel shook his head. 'I asked our own computer nerd the

same question already. He told me a guy like this wouldn't be dumb enough to send anything direct; he'd do it all through the Net, and probably through a firewall, which would totally cover his tracks. The most we could hope for – and even this would be a long shot – would be to identify which service provider the files emanated from, on the off-chance that he hasn't bounced the stuff all round the globe *en route*. But even then, these servers have thousands of people hooked up at the same time. He said it would be like trying to unravel a ball of string the size of Jupiter. It can be done, but only if you've got a spare thousand years. Forget it.'

'All right, Peter, have 'em cross-refer Christian fundamentalists and computer, er, enthusiasts,' Brisko instructed.

'Sure thing. I can get our analysts to sift through fundamentalist news groups and websites. It's long odds they'll deliver something against such a tight clock, but there's no harm trying.'

'Cross-refer Communion of the Saved too,' Witherson interjected.

'What'd you say?'

'You think he's a fundamentalist Christian. I think we can get more specific than that,' she explained. 'He's one of Luther St John's little devotees. He refers to me as the Whore of Babylon – that's copyright the Rev nineteen ninety-eight. And St John's been mouthing off about the AFFM for months, long before his Legion of Decency rally at Little Nuremberg across from the Vista. I'd say Luther wasn't the only one planning a public event to coincide with the film market.'

'And what is this Community of whatchamacallit?' Brisko enquired.

'Communion of the Saved. That's the people who fully subscribe – and I mean that financially as well as ideologically – to the hard line of the Rev's thinking. What you might accurately call the fully paid-up members of the St John hardcore, people whose commitment goes a bit deeper than just paying to get CFC on their cable system. Fanatics. People who find regular Christian fundamentalism a little too warm and fuzzy.'

'Well there's no question marks over this guy's commitment,' Kennedy observed, dabbing delicately at his injured arm with some tissue paper. 'Just a shame somebody sold him a Bible with all the tolerance and forgiveness passages missing. He should sue the Gideons.'

'You don't know the half of it,' Witherson said, her voice lowering ominously. 'There's a lot of those Bibles around. These people think everyone outside their "Communion" is a sinner, damned before God's eyes. They think they're the only folks with any chance of missing out on the big fire, because contrary to what that wishy-washy pinko Jesus asshole said, *their* God isn't all that forgiving. If you aren't toeing the line as closely as they are, you're Satan's Pop-tarts. Toast. Trouble is, there's a fine line between imagining someone's eternal soul is condemned and thinking their earthly life is worthless. Safe to say this guy crossed it way back.'

'So would there be a list of these people at St John's organisation?' Larry asked.

'Bound to be,' she said. 'St John's mob computerise everything on a database. They got records of all cable subscribers, obviously, but I'm told they got records of how much individuals donated and when: times of year, intervals, regularity. So that they know exactly how much they can squeeze people for and when's the best time to call, from the well-off businessman to the widow in the trailer-park.'

'How do you know all this shit?'

'When someone identifies you as an omen of the Apocalypse, Sergeant, you're kind of forced to take an interest. My money says the bomber's name is on St John's computer. Cross-check *that*.'

'We can't,' Brisko said flatly. 'Whether someone belonged to this Communion thing is not a detail that would have been recorded if they were ever arrested, questioned or even just listed on our files. No more than whether they belonged to the Raiders' fan club. It's not like if they were a member of the Klan or some other extremist group.'

'No, not much.'

'It's easy with hindsight, Miss Witherson. Until now, membership of this organisation has never been associated with any kind of crime or even any kind of threat.'

'Yeah, but you can get a list from St John anyway,' she argued.

'We don't have the power to demand that. It's subject to data protection and confidentiality regulations.'

'Oh yeah, like that normally stops you. Why don't you hack it? If it was some fundamentalist Islamic set-up you'd—'

'Why don't you just *ask* St John for it?' Kennedy suggested. It was difficult with that voice to guess whether he was being serious. Witherson, who had had longer to get used to the guy's flippancy, nonetheless shot him a look that warned him she was still a long way from enjoying it.

'I don't mean phone up and say please,' he explained. 'Although you'd have to do that in the first instance. But I mean lean on St John. Put a spin on it. He's been standing across the road telling everyone how movies influence people to do violent and terrible things, but you can point out – or threaten to point out – that it was listening to him and watching his shitey TV station that influenced this bampot.'

'You're right,' Steel said, nodding. 'You're damn right. We can *use* the media on this one. St John whipped up the hysteria, he pointed the finger at the AFFM and he's been attacking Miss Witherson for months. He can argue that no one should be held responsible for the actions of a madman, but he's gonna look extremely unChristian if he doesn't make some kind of reparation, especially if he obstructs our investigation. St John knows what crucifixion-by-media feels like. He's not gonna want a second spell on the cross.'

'Okay Peter,' Brisko said, pulling out his portable phone, 'I'll get McCluskey on to St John's people. He'll paint a picture of the anticipated coverage that Francis Bacon would puke at. You talk to the silicon section. Then we'll play Snap.'

The two Feds commenced their respective phone calls, Brisko engaging deferential tones as he talked to someone a lot further up the chain of command with a progress report. Or, more accurately, an ideas report. Progress would be if any of these lines attracted a bite and they got some feedback.

Bannon, with a daughter about Witherson's age, was fussing solicitously over the poor girl and probably getting on her nerves, offering yet another cup of coffee to the person in the world least in need of caffeine stimulation to stay sharp and alert. She remained polite, but Larry suspected she would accept sympathy and support from only one source: the guy sitting on the other side of her. He could only imagine what the two of them had gone through together on that roof, and whether it was that alone that had made the connection, but neither looked a good bet to survive long without the other right then, and Larry sure knew all about that.

'Thanks for sticking around,' he heard her tell Kennedy. She spoke as if everyone else had left the room. Guess there were times when you cared less about privacy; Madeleine Witherson was probably the most public figure in the world at that moment, so comparatively a room with just two Feds and two cops in it was splendid isolation.

'Any time,' Kennedy told her. 'Besides, I've nowhere else to go. I was here to cover the AFFM. Now there isn't one. This tit blew up the market and now he's threatening to murder my writer.'

'God bless America, huh?'

'Oh ay. Wonder if the bomber knows what it feels like to have an apple pie shoved up his arse while it's still in the hot oven dish. 'Cause he will if I get my fuckin' hands on him.'

There was a rap on the glass partition before Arguello stuck his head round the door. 'Hey Captain, we got another message on the computer. It just popped up on every screen in the building. It's for real, it's got the codeword. You better check it out.'

They turned to the computer screen on the castor-wheeled workstation next to Bannon's desk, it having been rolled against the wall to make room for the assembly. Larry noticed that the screen-saver – a little guy in LAPD uniform chasing a crook with the full striped jumper, mask and swag-bag regalia round the black square – had been cleared, presumably by the appearance of the new icon.

'Charming,' Witherson observed. The icon was an elaborately crafted knife, unmistakably a sacrificial dagger, or 'sacraficial' in the mind of the sub-literate bomber.

Bannon double-clicked on it.

CODEWORD: MATTHEW 21:12-16

PACIFIC VISTA BEACHSIDE SWIMMING POOL.
DAWN.
NO LATER, NO EARLIER.
NO RESTRICTION'S ON NEWS CAMERA ACCESS.
WHEN A QUALIFIED DOCTOR HAS PRONOUNCED THE
WHORE DEAD, YOU MAY EVACUATE THE BOAT.

NB: WHEN NIGHT FALL'S, LIGHT'S ON THE DECK AND
IN THE ENGINE ROOM MUST REMAIN ON. IF I AM
LEFT IN THE DARK, I WILL HAVE NO CHOICE BUT TO
ALLUMINATE THE SITUATION.

THIS MESSAGE WILL SHORTLY BE RELEASED TO THE
MEDIA, MINUS THE CODEWORD. YOU <u>WILL</u> CONFIRM
THAT IT IS GENUINE.

'Motherfucker,' Bannon muttered.

'Oh, I don't doubt it for a minute,' said Witherson. 'Beggars can't be choosers.'

'I guess we misunderstood the original message,' Bannon said. 'When he said "by the dawn's early light", we assumed he was giving us *until* dawn. But he specifically wants it to happen then. Why?'

'He wants to give us all time to talk about it,' the girl said. 'He wants the whole watching world to sit up all night saying "will she or won't she?" and yabbering on about the moral issues raised by this situation. Won't be long before they've all forgotten about the morality of what the bomber's done because they'll be busy discussing the morality of what *I've* done, and what the movie business has done to precipitate this. By midnight this asshole's not going to be the bad guy any more, he's going to be "a symptom of America's spiritual decline" – just like the pornography, promiscuity and godlessness he's striking out against. Trust me, there will be more bullshit spoken between now and dawn than on any single night in the history of this planet. You're gonna need waders to watch TV this evening.'

'She's right,' agreed Steel. 'Guy wants a lot more than the standard fifteen minutes. Shit, he isn't just going to be the lead item on the news, he's going to be the whole schedule on every network.'

'He and me,' Witherson observed bitterly. 'Good excuse to trawl through last year's scandal and sensation one more time, remind everybody on the moral Right of all that I've done to bring this upon myself. God works in mysterious ways, those self-righteous fucks'll be saying to themselves.'

'Now calm down, Miss Witherson,' Brisko implored, lowering his tones to what he probably thought was soothing. Larry winced. No matter how human G-men got, they still forgot how much easier it was from the grandstand.

'Calm down?' she asked, incredulously. Her voice didn't rise, but the pH in it took a sharp dip. 'I'd say I'm pretty calm, under the circumstances. I was blown up this morning, Agent Brisko, don't know whether you caught that. I saw someone vaporised in front of me by the blast. I fell into a swimming-pool with one hell of a wave machine, and I'd either have drowned or been flushed straight down into Bloodworld theme park if Stephen here hadn't intervened. I escaped from *that* only to be driven over here and told my own death is the sole bargaining chip against the lives of eighty-eight more people. And in response to all of this, I have remained, in my opinion, admirably composed. So please indulge me if I want to let off steam at the fact that all over America right now there are people who think I deserve all this because I fucked a few guys in front of a video camera.'

Whatever attempt Brisko might have made at reparation was lost as his mobile phone rang. His voice remained steady as he answered it but Larry could tell he was praying for good news, so that he wouldn't have to turn around and face the scared, angry girl with the admission that he couldn't help her.

It didn't sound much like his prayers were being answered. Lots of 'Ah, shit' and 'You gotta be kidding,' and 'Yeah, yeah,' and 'But what about—'

He finished his call and sighed, facing a silent, expectant room.

'That was Ginsler at the Vista,' he said resignedly. 'They got the guy planting the bomb on videotape, but they don't have a face. The tape came from a camera on a stairwell leading to the roof from the lift – timecode says yesterday afternoon, about two forty. Guy's got his back to camera going upstairs, wearing a hooded sweatshirt, carrying a metal case. There's an access panel in the wall, underneath the stairs, for regulating the pool's water supply, chlorination, all that stuff. The panel's barely in the edge of the shot, but Ginsler says he's pretty sure they can make out the guy crouching down and screwing around with it. Guy comes back, hood up and head down. It's useless. Wouldn't even be much good as evidence that he did it, never mind for finding the guy.'

Witherson rolled her eyes and tried to concentrate on just looking pissed off, but Larry could tell she was fighting back tears. Her companion swallowed and grimaced, but he didn't say anything – no dumb cracks, no vacuous reassurances, no useless platitudes; even his smartass remarks had so far all been relevant. He might have a pretty weird sense of humour, but Kennedy didn't seem to talk unless he had something to contribute. Larry thought he should be giving lessons.

'And the security staff didn't react to this at the time?' Steel asked, nominating himself as a first pupil.

'Ginsler says it was nothing to look twice at,' Brisko stated evenly, a man calling on everything he had to hold it together. 'Hotel security are mainly about monitoring what's going on in the lobby or in the corridors, checking nobody's trying to bust into one of the rooms. They see a guy go upstairs towards the swimming pool, that's nothing to worry about, they'd look at the next screen. Besides, they're mainly on the lookout for theft, not terrorism. This is a hotel on Santa Monica beach, for God's sake, not the Israeli embassy. Nobody was ready for this.'

'Except him,' Larry said. 'He was very ready. I mean, mad bombers aside, security was pretty tight for this AFFM deal. They've got a bead on everybody coming through the door, and you don't get in unless you got a cute plastic laminate with your picture on it. The only people who get through the doors without are couriers, and they get escorted all the way: make their delivery, get a signature then straight back out – do not pass Go, do not collect two hundred dollars.'

'So what are you saying?' Brisko asked.

'I'm saying he had ID. He didn't just need to get in, he needed to move freely, come and go, check the place out. He knew in advance there was a security camera close to where he wanted to plant his bomb. This guy didn't just *happen* to be wearing his jogging outfit yesterday.'

'So how do you get one of these IDs?' Brisko asked.

Larry looked to Witherson and Kennedy.

'You have to be accredited by AFFMA,' Witherson said. 'The companies pay a participation fee and supply a list of attendees. My accreditation was done through Line Arts. Stephen's was presumably through *Scope*.'

He nodded. 'That was only because they were paying. If I'd

wanted to do it strictly off my own bat I could apply as a freelance and pay the fee myself. It's not that much, because the AFFM want the coverage, but they still have to charge to deter time-wasters. But basically the guy would only need to supply a name and the money and he's in.'

'A guy like this could also have just hacked himself into the accreditation lists,' Larry suggested. 'But either way, he'd still need to give them an address to send the laminate out to, which would be on AFFMA's files.'

'He's bound to have used a false name,' Brisko said. 'And no doubt a box number for the address, or some empty place he rents.'

'Plus,' added Steel gloomily, 'if he could hack his name on to the list, he could sure hack it off again after he received the ID.'

'He couldn't use a false photograph, though,' said Kennedy. 'What?'

'You have to supply two passport-size shots. One's for going on the laminate, the other one goes on file somewhere. He could hack his name off a computer, ay, but he couldnae disappear the second pic, and the name and details he supplied will be attached to it in a filing cabinet somewhere.'

'I'll get on to Paul Silver at AFFMA, if he didn't get blown up this morning,' Larry said, getting to his feet. 'Got his mobile number in my Rolodex.'

'You can't,' Witherson told him. 'He's on the boat. At least, he was meant to be. I spoke to him yesterday before my press conference. Call AFFMA HQ in Century City. That's where the files'll be.'

'Okay, but I also need someone in the know to go through them and eliminate everyone they know to be legit.'

'There'll be people at AFFMA who can do that,' Witherson assured him.

The senior FBI bloke, Brisko, was running a hand through his thinning hair, holding a notebook in the other. He was recapping the various investigative lines the police and the Feds were pursuing, trying to make it sound likely that a couple of them would soon intersect at the location they needed. He wasn't glib or removed, Steff had to give him that; he wasn't offering complacent reassurance, though he was definitely trying to encourage a wee bit of hope. But basically this was the 'we're doing everything we can, fingers crossed, time will tell, all bases covered' routine. Any second now he was going to say 'smoke 'em if you got 'em'.

Except, not all the bases were covered. There was something no one had covered, something nobody was talking about, and the longer nobody talked about it, the louder not talking about it got. Steff wanted to say something, but didn't know whether he should pre-empt Maddy. It wasn't likely it had slipped her mind. She looked across at him from her chair, less than three feet away, like he was the only friend she had in the world. Why couldn't wonderful women ever look at him that way when they *weren't* in fear of death?

Then she reached a hand over and took gentle hold of his T-shirt sleeve, just pinching at the material, a light pressure on his arm. He realised he had just become a human security blanket. It had never been a vocation of his, but for her he'd make a career of it.

She spoke, holding on to him for support, comfort, reassurance or whatever. 'I appreciate that you're all being very polite and sensitive right now, and will continue to be very polite and sensitive until the last possible moment,' she said, 'but there is something kind of important that we have to discuss.'

'What's that, Miss Witherson?' Brisko asked in his sincerest 'I'm listening' voice, probably wanting to jump out the window because, like everybody else in the room, he already knew the answer.

'Well, I realise that you're doing all you can, and that you've got all this manpower and technology and expertise at your disposal, but what you don't have is a lead, and what else you don't have is time. Now I know you don't want to think about this but believe me, I *have* to think about this.' She swallowed. 'What happens fifteen, sixteen hours from now if you've still got nothing? Because let's not pretend we don't know the eventualities here, Agent Brisko. And let's not pretend that you – or your boss on the end of that phone – don't have a timetable for how you're going to play this thing, with a specified point of no return at which you are authorised or required to address the zero option. When is that, exactly? When are you *officially* required to start talking about trading my life for eighty-eight others? One hour before dawn? Two?'

'Miss Witherson,' Steel said, trying to help out his boss, an obvious admission that she had hit the spot, 'it is *not* going to come to that.'

'Oh bullshit. Yeah, sure, you guys might pull the goddamn rabbit out of the hat, but I don't think I'd like to hear the odds, and neither would the people on that boat. Even if you do find him, how are you planning to stop him? You think you can talk him out of it? Because let's face the truth here, this guy will press the button. If he doesn't get what he's asking for, or if he thinks you're trying to screw him, he will press the goddamn button. Might even be rigged up so that if you kill him the bomb goes off anyway.'

'If we find him – and we will find him,' Steel said, convincing no one, 'we can stop the clock. We've got trained negotiators standing by for whenever we can establish a dialogue.'

'He's taken steps to *avoid* establishing a dialogue,' she countered. 'He's set up a codeword so that if he has to say more, you'll know it's him, but it's still one way. He doesn't want to negotiate. He knows negotiators are just there to buy time and psych out how far you can push him, estimate whether he's got the balls to execute his threat. Well he's got the balls, and this guy isn't looking for money, or the release of comrades-in-arms, or any of the other shit you're used to dealing with.

'Look at the codeword: Matthew chapter twenty-one, verses twelve to sixteen. It's Christ throwing the money-changers out of the temple. It's the bit where Jesus kicks ass, where he loses patience with the sinners and resorts to violence and rage. This guy wants to teach the world a lesson: he wants an ultimate act of repentance from what he sees as the ultimate sinner. Otherwise the whole class gets punished. So you guys can go play detective if you want, but before the night's through, it's me who's gonna have to come up with an answer.'

She stood up, lifting her bag from the floor in front of her.

'Where are you going?' Bannon enquired.

The G-men didn't look like they could meet her eyes, far less ask her anything. Only the big cop, Freeman, had given

233

the impression of genuinely appreciating what she was going through.

'I don't know,' she said. 'But this is gonna be a shitty enough day without me spending it in a police station. I was supposed to be taking Stephen here to lunch. Maybe I'll do that. And don't worry, I'll stay in touch.'

She slapped a card down on Bannon's desk with her mobile phone number on it, then walked to the door and gripped the handle.

'You coming?' she asked.

Steff was no longer quite sure what planet he was on today. The only place that felt remotely familiar was a close gravitational orbit around Maddy, and he feared if he was removed from her company for too long he'd just fall to pieces. Thousands of miles from home, blown up, alienated and pissed off, she was the only anchor he had to the reality of what was going on – whatever the fuck was going on.

'Excuse me gentlemen,' he told them, and followed her out the door.

'I'll check it out,' Larry said, in response to the six eyes that had fixed themselves rather helplessly upon him.

He found the pair of them standing near the exit leading through the corridor to the front desk, or (Hostile) Reception as the precinct smartasses called it. Their progress was being obstructed by Arguello, looking almost as beat as they did, the diminutive Pedro standing up admirably in the face of Witherson's distressed determination and Kennedy's distressing height. All three of them looked plaintively at Larry as he approached, each believing his intercession would assist them.

'More good news, huh?' Larry asked. 'What is it now?'

'Reporters,' Arguello explained. 'Dozens of them. They know she's . . . They know Miss Witherson's here. At least they think she's here. Gleason's out bullshitting them at the front desk, but they ain't buying it. There's more vans pulling up every minute, man. They must have sussed that the cops had Miss Witherson when the new message went out. Look.'

Arguello pointed to a nearby TV screen, on which Larry could see the outside of the building, but it wasn't closed circuit – it was network news. A patrolio came through the

234

swing doors in front of him and for the moment they were open Larry could hear the babble of voices echoing down the hallway.

Full-on media siege. He'd always known this would be among today's trials, but that didn't make it any easier when it happened. Larry felt sure the Bible would have been a role-model short had Job been faced with suffering an infestation of *these* assholes:

And verily Job didst freak, and didst smite his tormentor most terribly, yea, threatening even to lodge his microphone in his fundament.

Witherson's eyes were red. She was a brave lady, but she was fast running out of juice.

'She cannae stay here, Sergeant,' Kennedy said. It was his first presumption to speak on her behalf, which Larry figured was significant, like he'd switched on the siren. 'Her head's nippin'. She needs some space.'

'Where can you go?' Larry asked. 'Miss Witherson's place will have even more of these lice crawling around it.'

'His place,' Witherson said tiredly. 'He's at the Armada in West Hollywood. Nobody knows who he is and nobody knows he's with me.'

'They'll follow you out of here, man,' Arguello warned. 'They got choppers and everything.'

'Christ.' She put her hand to her forehead, her eyes filling up.

Another two patrolios came through the doors, Carver and Chase, bemoaning the chaos they'd found on their doorstep. Larry watched them turn and walk towards the locker rooms.

'The Armada, yeah?' Larry asked. Witherson looked up, nodding. 'Okay, follow me.'

'Where we going?'

'Bilbo Baggins's place. Gonna ask for a loan of his ring.'

Lisa Chase's uniform was maybe just a little big for Witherson, which prompted Carver to chide his partner about cutting down on the Twinkies, but what the hell, she wasn't looking to pass parade inspection.

'Don't listen to him,' Witherson told Chase gratefully, slipping on shades and pulling the peak of the hat down. 'If I actually had tits it'd be a perfect fit.'

Kennedy was more of a problem. They did eventually find a uniform close to his elongated dimensions, but no amount of pins could restrain his conspicuously non-regulation mane of hair under the hat. He didn't walk right either. It was hard to pinpoint just what exactly he was doing wrong, but as soon as he took two steps it was obvious from any distance that he was not a cop but a guy badly disguised in a cop's uniform.

There was only one way around it. Larry made him put his own clothes back on and slapped some cuffs on his wrists. Then Witherson and Carver led their 'prisoner' out back to a patrol car and drove up the station-house ramp through the gauntlet of cameras and microphones, all of which turned away when they saw who was – or more importantly who wasn't – in the back seat.

Larry watched the car head off towards Santa Monica Boulevard, glancing at a TV screen for reassurance that the girl's escape had gone undetected, then sat down at his desk and swallowed back two headache tablets with a lukewarm styrofoam cup of coffee.

He looked at his watch and realised that its objective sense of time was thoroughly out of synch with his own. It seemed like days had passed since he woke up this morning, yet it was barely two in the afternoon.

Christ knew how Madeleine Witherson felt.

The sun wasn't due to set for several hours, but her longest, darkest night had already begun.

thirteen

Paul Silver liked to think he was not normally neurotic. He *was* normally Jewish, however, which was probably why he so much hated getting all hyper and paranoid. The business he worked in traded prosperously in stereotypes, which had always made him agitatedly self-conscious about behaving like one. Even when he was feeling neurotic, he tried his best to keep it below the surface, concentrate on his breathing, think carefully about whatever he was going to say, and not burble on like a speed-freak reading James Joyce. This was because everyone else was allowed the occasional bout of public fluster: people just thought, Golly, he's got enough on his plate today. But if you were Jewish and you lost it one time, they all thought, Typical neurotic Jew.

In a way, Woody Allen had pissed in the water tank they all had to drink from. Paul often wished the little jerk had sent off to the Charles Atlas ad in his *Superman* comics as a kid. If he had a time machine he'd go back and bribe every girl in Woody's neighbourhood to blow him carnivorously throughout his teen years. All right, the world probably wouldn't get *Sleeper* later on, but you had to balance these things out.

Unfortunately, it was the Woody the world did get that formed Paul's self-image any time he felt under pressure. And not just any incarnation either: it was the damned *animated* version from *Annie Hall* that he saw, exaggeratedly diminutive and helpless-looking. Why couldn't Lenny Bruce have lived longer and become an acclaimed auteur? That's what Paul wanted to know. Cool, streetwise, in control, turning the accusatory neurosis outwards at the world instead of inwards at himself.

Most of the time, Paul was a real calm guy. That was what had got him where he was. He could put people at ease, he could deal with logistics, he could negotiate, he could juggle responsibilities. You couldn't survive in the independent sector otherwise. Working for small production and sales outfits like Line Arts, ImageTech and KinoKraft, you had to do a dozen jobs at once to bring in a movie under its already minuscule budget. He knew that if you were paying close attention to *Killer Instincts III* you could spot the film's producer (one P Silver) in four different cannon-fodder villain roles, getting repeatedly killed by the hero, Nuke Powers, in a variety of bad wigs. But then if you were paying close attention to *Killer Instincts III*, you probably weren't the type to notice these things.

When he got the post with AFFMA, it was on the strength of his reputation for, quite simply, *handling* it. He was younger than the previous incumbents, and had a lot less experience within AFFMA's organisation, in terms of how they liked to run things, but everybody was confident because Paul Silver 'could handle it'. And handle it he had, right throughout all the preparation, organisation, administration and build-up. Compared to some of the logistical miracles he'd had to pull off in the past, his first eight months at AFFMA was a breeze. The event itself was a far huger affair than any production he had ever co-ordinated, but it was still a much smoother ride, and he didn't once have to fall screaming into a vat of slime wearing a blood-spattered space-lizard costume.

However, the nearer it had drawn to the commencement of the market, the more he began to fear that Woody would be running the office. It was as though he had been concentrating so hard on scaling the cliff that he'd failed to notice how high it was until he reached the summit, and instead of experiencing a feeling of achievement, he was suffering a woozy vertigo.

And there was something else too. It was irrational to the point of embarrassment, but he had what he could only describe, in the hackneyed words of the shitty scripts he was used to working with, as 'a bad feeling about this'. Maybe it was just what they were calling 1999 Syndrome, seeping silently and undetected into the subconscious, but whatever it was, it sure wasn't comfortable.

He was pretty good at hiding it when he moved in familiar circles. Talking to AFFMA's CEO, Brad Getzen, or to execs from the attending companies, he slipped so easily into leisurely confidence that he could almost convince himself he had nothing to fret about. But people on the outside could see Woody three blocks away. That cop twigged how anxious he was straight off; so did Nunez, although she seemed to find it funny, which worked as reassurance through mild humiliation.

Sergeant Freeman seemed to relish the threat of chaos presented by the Jesus-freaks across the street, with their protests and hoax bomb warnings. It was like the big cop was telling him to enjoy the ride, trying to make him fast-forward to the bar-room where he'd look back and laugh about what a crazy time the '99 market was. And though something inside was resisting it manfully, it was starting to work: Paul was beginning to tell himself that if Freeman and Nunez weren't worried, it wasn't because he was the only one smart enough to anticipate trouble, nor that he was the only one who'd be firing off resumés in a month's time.

Nonetheless, something *was* resisting it. Woody would not pack up and go home to New York, and the twisted feeling in his gut warned him that he feared the little jerk would yet get to say 'I told you so'.

So on his mid-market day off, his time to relax and have a few drinks aboard Moonstar's hospitality charter, when the captain and a hollow-faced Linus Veltman asked everyone to sit down and remain calm then announced there was a bomb on the boat, Paul's curious first reaction was a feeling of eye-rolling vindication. It was like finally being told the answer to a stupid but exasperating riddle – Ah! So *that's* what it was. There was almost an element of relief about it. After so long desperately trying to hold it together, he could now comfortably go nuts along with everybody else.

Stephen was right about her being safe at the Armada. Okay, cop outfit or not she'd felt conspicuously female on the way up to the room, but in the bigger picture absolutely nobody was going to think of looking for her in the place anyway. It was perfect – the only drawback was that she couldn't hide there past dawn. One way or the other.

Stephen held open the door for her but without any hint of ostentatious chivalry. He wasn't trying to be her saviour or her guardian or even her advocate, all of which she was grateful for because she had enough on her plate without attempting to salve someone else's conscience by making them feel useful. Nonetheless, there was still a part of her that could have used just a little bit more of an idea where she stood with this guy. He'd saved her life, so it was safe to assume he held her in higher regard than some in this town, but beyond that it was difficult to discern. Ironically, saving someone's life isn't necessarily personal.

He had a detached manner and a weird kind of humour that combined to suggest he found everything around him faintly ridiculous – but not ridiculous enough to be amusing. Between that and his physical imposition, she'd have been scared even to talk to him, had circumstances not introduced them. He was here with her now, but that was because they had been thrown together; and because she had asked him; and because he was a decent and considerate guy. He looked like he'd have some tall blonde waiting for him back in England, someone elegant and artistic who understood what the hell he was talking about. There'd be framed shots he'd taken of her all round their apartment.

That's why she'd been so nervous at the beginning of the shoot. He'd seemed all interested and complimentary yesterday, and she'd felt like killing Tony for lining up that meeting that had forced her to run out on him. But by the time morning came she'd been far less certain of what their previous conversation had meant – wasn't making you feel comfortable, confident and attractive part of a good photographer's technique? Wasn't he just being professional? And why would a guy like that be interested in her, more than for just the shoot and the story?

She'd spent ages waiting on that stairwell, composing herself, getting into character, ready to walk out on to that roof all Hollywood confidence and goddammit just *tell* him she was taking him out for lunch. It was when he said nothing in response that the façade crumbled and she turned back into a quivering amateur.

But this was all back when shit like that mattered. Guys, dates, photo-shoots, careers. Back in the ancient history of five hours ago.

She walked into the hotel room and sat on the edge of the bed, her elbows on her knees, chin in hands. The sound of the door closing brought out a lung-crumpling sigh, like she hadn't breathed out since the bomb went off. It should have been the moment of blessed relief, when she looked back at what had happened from the disbelieving perspective that comfort and security afford. It should have been the moment that her mind had been focusing on when she was in that swimming pool, and later as she took Stephen's wrist in her hand, trying not to look at what lay beyond his dangling legs. Instead it sounded like the closing of the condemned prisoner's deathwatch cell. There was a release, yeah, but only because the time of uncertainty was over. Now came the calmer time, the slower time, to contemplate her fate.

'Hell of a date,' she sighed, speaking because she wanted to hear his voice and she knew he wouldn't say anything first.

'Well I'm sure it could have gone a wee bit smoother,' he said, his tones soothingly reverberant. 'But on the plus side, from my point of view, I did manage to get you back to my bedroom.' His voice was drily languorous; he wasn't trying to cheer her up, just laughing with her in the dark.

'Yeah, well, that's only a qualified success,' she replied, her throat swollen from gulping back tears and chlorinated water, not to mention shitty coffee. 'A porn star, Whore of Babylon, fornicating slut like me gotta be a sure thing, even on a first date.'

He smiled. He was leaning against the dressing table, his straggled blond hair hanging down across the left half of his face like a half-drawn curtain. It was the look Evan Dando had been aiming at for years for his album covers: variously evocative of humour, pity, pain, fear, affection, fatigue, knowingness, innocence, infatuation and unknowable depth. She was sure Stephen could organise the photo-shoot, but was less sure that Ev could handle the being-blown-up part.

'I should really offer you a cup of tea,' he said.

'Oh, no more caffeine, please.'

'No, not for refreshment purposes. It's just traditional where I come from to offer a brew to the hopelessly afflicted. You know, "The doctor says it's the big C, I've got three months to live" – "Never mind, have a cuppa tea". This would be my chance to set a new international record. There can't be anyone on the planet a cup of tea would make less difference to right now.'

'You got that right.'

'You're hangin' on by your fingernails, aren't you?' he said softly, his tone bereft of its previous wry levity. It wasn't an offer of help; it felt like an entreaty to her to grant herself some sympathy, telling her it was all right to feel that way. She had been fighting it so hard, and part of her hated him for so deftly puncturing her efforts, but maybe she needed to let go. She nodded, feeling her eyes fill up again but determined not to break down. It felt like an easeful temptation, an abandon to luxuriate in, the comforting release of giving herself to crying, from the eyes, the mouth, the shudder of her body like a distant shadow of orgasm. But she feared that if she let go now she'd never recover.

'I know it's not gaunny solve anything,' he said, 'but would a bath do you any good?'

She rubbed at her puffy cheeks with the over-long sleeve of the police uniform and ran a hand through her tangled hair. 'More than you could possibly imagine.'

Jo Mooney didn't have the energy to join in the wide-spread histrionics, the practisedly supercool movie people metamorphosising into headless chickens around her as they finally encountered a problem they couldn't get their lawyers to sort out for them. She wasn't frozen with fear or exhaustedly resigned to her fate either: it was more like she'd been punched in the gut and was taking time to reconstitute herself before considering her next move.

She sat and listened to the details, the shouting, the questions, the panic, the disbelief, absorbing it all as though it would inform her response. But she knew there could be no response. There was no next move.

That was what everyone on board was finding so hard to accept. There was no-one they could call, no 'people' to put this on to, no deal to be done. They had heard the rules and knew they had no option but to obey, blindly and unquestioningly. Veltman and the captain, Baird, hadn't said what the bomber wanted. Jo guessed they knew more than they were letting on, but knew also that it made no difference. All they needed to know was that there was a bomb on their boat and they weren't allowed to get off it.

Reaction gradually changed from fear and anger to a mixture of rationalisation and comradely bravado, like they were conspiring to convince each other that somehow it wasn't for real, or at least that the worst wouldn't come to the worst. These guys never actually detonated their bombs, they told each other. That wasn't what they were about. They were about publicity, first and foremost, and negotiation after that. Or they were after money, like Dennis Hopper in *Speed*. But no matter, the bomb was merely the bargaining chip with which they acquired those things. Terrorists – guys who really wanted to blow people up – just blew people up. No rules, no warnings, no games. If that was what this bomber was interested in, they'd all be dead already.

Jo overheard a group of execs discussing a co-production deal for a movie based on the day's events. They reasoned they should pool resources rather than everyone make their own dramatisation. After all, nobody would have exclusive rights. Pretty soon they were arguing over casting and producer credits. Jo just hoped there'd be a happy ending.

'Paul Sorvino as me? Get the fuck outta here. I'll sue your Jewish butt off, you suggest that again. How about Kathy Najimi as your wife?'

A couple of guys mooned the camera on the mast that was monitoring the deck, raising a few cheers.

Then the news began filtering through about an explosion at the Pacific Vista. Jo didn't know where the reports started – whether somebody got a call on their mobile or someone with a Walkman was tuned to a news station – but it spread through the boat like a blaze. Veltman confirmed it, admitting that he and Baird had heard about the explosion minutes before, but had been advised by the cops not to pass it on, at least until the cops themselves knew exactly what had happened.

Exactly what had happened began to emerge over radios, phones and the boat's TV – and it changed everything. You could see it on every face: the comfort of doubt and specu-lation had been withdrawn. This was not about bargaining, negotiations or publicity.

This was about atrocity.

Nobody spoke. They sat silently, blank-faced, the only voices audible those of the radio and TV reporters describing the scenes at the Pacific Vista, and of the captain, Micky Baird, in quiet communication with the authorities on land.

People were dead, people they probably knew. Hundreds were injured. The hotel that was so familiar to them, the lobby they had walked and met and schmoozed in yesterday was now the site of unimaginable destruction and horror. A merciless, massive violence was abroad, and its gaze was fixed upon them now.

Veltman took the boat's microphone and asked for attention. He didn't have much in the way of competition. He held a sheet of paper in front of him and read from its hand-scrawled notes, relaying to them the full text of the message that the bomber had sent out to the world.

Aside from the standard levels of guilt that were attendant upon every non-Republican in late twentieth-century America, Jo didn't feel much like a sinner. Then again, Jeffrey Dahmer probably hadn't felt much like a sinner either, but that aside, she was pretty sure that on the list of people whose deaths would 'cleanse the world', there were a lot of names ahead of her own and everyone else on the *Ugly Duckling*. (Anyone on daytime chat shows for a start, and the cast of *Friends* would do to be getting on with.)

But then that was what this lunatic wanted them to think about, wasn't it? That was what he wanted the whole world to think about. Not generally who would most deserve to die for their perceived sins 'against God and America', but whether Madeleine Witherson deserved to die more than the people on the boat.

Morality as a mathematical equation, the cold logic that would occupy the minds of the vultures back home, watching the pictures relayed by the 'copters sweeping back and forth over their floating limbo.

The people on the boat may have been accused of polluting minds with their movies but, really, do we know exactly which movies these particular people were responsible for? Or quite what effects they had on their viewers? Because basically, they were just making a living, really, weren't they?, and a few transgressions of taste aside, they surely didn't *set out* to pollute or corrupt or any of these things. But Maddy Witherson, well, that was a different story. No room for interpretation there. She was a sinner. She was, by definition, a whore. She had sex for a living. And worse, she had sex before the cameras so that her behaviour could disseminate its influence far and wide.

Those people on the boat had families. Children, wives, husbands. Witherson didn't have a husband, or kids either, and her father had all but disowned her. So who would miss her?

Fortunately, so far the only mention anyone on the boat had made of Maddy Witherson was when Tom Wilcox stood up and held out his portable phone. 'That bastard Tony Pia's line is still fuckin' busy,' he said to anyone in earshot. 'Mark my words, he's behind this. He's Witherson's agent. The son-of-a-bitch hired a stalker to trail Tanya Lee two years back. This stunt's got his name written all over it.'

A few made an effort to laugh, Jo among them.

There were people using their mobiles to call the mainland. She heard one guy on the phone to his wife, his voice cracking as he failed to choke back the tears. She heard another on the line to his lawyer, dictating changes to his will. On top of that there were at least four passengers giving live 'from-the-scene' interviews to radio and TV stations, and she heard another negotiating a per-minute fee before commencing, telling the guy at the other end to up the price because 'it might be all my kids have to live on after dawn tomorrow'.

Jo sat and stared at her own portable, sitting uselessly in her hand, unsure whether to use it. Her daughter, Alice, would be in kindergarten all day. Playing games and drawing pictures, eating cookies and drinking soda. She didn't know whether to call the place, talk to Mrs Crenshaw, ask to speak to Alice. Would it be fair? Would it make a difference? She began dialling the number then felt the tears well up in her throat, threatening to choke her voice. She pressed Cancel. She'd give herself five minutes then call her sister, make sure Alice got picked up when class was out.

The police launches had pulled up either side, not too close for fear of making the bomber nervous about a possible evacuation attempt. Further back there were boats bearing news crews, medical teams, Coast Guard, you name it. There were boats front, back, left and right, helicopters overhead. It seemed like the busiest stretch of water in the Pacific right then, but the Moonstar charter might as well have been the only vessel on the ocean.

245

The *Ugly Duckling* was the centre of the world's attention, but it was also the most isolated place on the planet.

Dusk started to fall.

It was going to be a very long night.

Madeleine bent her knees, pulled her thighs against her calves, and sank lower into the caressingly warm water, drawing her head under and closing her eyes. She wished she didn't have to breathe, wished she could stay there. She felt her head lifted from the bottom, her hair lifted from her scalp, heard the succussion of the water against the sides, all sound muted and distant, a world away. She imagined the percussive syncopation of a heartbeat; it was all that was missing. But no-one gets to stay in the womb.

She surfaced and sat up, eyes still closed, enjoying the sensation of the water running off her face and body. She reached for the soap and began running it along her legs. That was when she first noticed the bruising and abrasions. There were marks across her thighs, discoloration down her side, cuts and scratches on her upper arms. She realised that she had been feeling their aches and stings for hours but been unable to pay them any heed. Sorrow welled up in her once more, the constriction in her throat that heralded crying, as the revelation of what bad shape she was in took her by surprise. It was like she was fleeing for her life and she'd just noticed the red light blinking on the fuel gauge.

Now the sobbing took her, or maybe she gave herself to it, its cathartic flow, its soothing solitude, its intimate retreat. She sat up, her arms clasped between her thighs and calves, her face pressed against the wet flesh of her legs, crying quietly. Her body shook a little with each wave, but she made no sound in her throat, so that her weeping was like coughing; private, whispered, minute. It was a comfort no other's arms could offer. Some lonelinesses can't be cured by company.

'What do you get if you cross Mommy and Daddy? – Maddy!'

Ha ha ha.

That was their little joke, about as risqué as Robert Witherson thought humour should get, and the only hint throughout much of her childhood that there was more to know about

246

her origins than cartoon storks with two ends of a diaper in their beaks.

Well, maybe it was churlish to suggest that her formal sex education was so limited when her father had provided such a hands-on guide to these matters. When she was very young she had learned from him that little girls come from God; and when she was a bit older she'd learned from him that big men come from manual or oral stimulation of the penis.

She started to remember it all when she was sixteen. She'd never really forgotten, though, only suppressed the thoughts, the feelings, the images. It was as if she knew where they were inside her head, so she knew where not to look; but she was still aware that she was not looking, and of what she was not looking at. The kind of duality that makes you sound nuts, when in fact it's the only thing keeping you sane. Maybe she thought she could run away from it, leave it behind – that one day the awareness would start to fade, and after that the memories.

There was no single spark or trigger, no sudden in-rushing of her banished past. It came in like a slow tide, over time, in small waves, but nonetheless ever deeper and irreversible. She knew in retrospect that it was tangled up in the belated stirrings of her teenage sexuality, as she sought out secret places within herself, places that should have been new and known only to her, and found them already discovered and defiled.

If other people enjoyed a sexual 'awakening', Madeleine had opened her eyes to find a monster sharing the bed.

There were all these moments of wonder that turned to disgust: a tingling between her legs late at night when she thought of a boy in her class, her hand descending in curious exploration; that second of surprised pleasure at the sensation when her fingers brushed her clitoris, then the paralysing coldness of a recognition.

I've been here before. I was *taken* here before. And now I know why. Or if I always knew why, now I can no longer deny it.

She was eleven when Mommy got sick. Well, she had been sick for a long time, but when she got really sick, when she was in her bed more than out of it. That was when it started, Daddy coming into her room last thing at night, lying beside her, giving her special hugs. And they just got more and more special as time went on.

'You remember that movie you saw,' he said to her, 'where there was the little family and the farm? And remember the mommy got sick, and everybody had to do a little extra to keep things going, do all the work Mommy used to do? Well you and I are going to have to help out a little more, just like that, help Mommy, and help each other. And just like in the movie, we have to try and do it in ways so Mommy doesn't know, because she'll get sad if she thinks she can't be a proper mommy any more.'

There were things they had to keep secret for Mommy's sake. And with Mommy sick, it was only natural that Maddy would become even more special to Daddy, but again, they couldn't let Mommy know because she might get upset.

The hugs got longer and longer. Then came touching, touching that was okay because he was her daddy and he loved her very much, but that she must never tell anyone about in case Mommy found out and became jealous, which would be so hard for her to take because she was very, very ill. Then came her touching him. It was called helping. Doing things Mommy would if she could, only she was too sick. Maddy was helping her mommy in secret, like the little girl in the movie. She was a good little girl, and God could see how much she must love her mommy by doing all this for her. But God would become angry if she ever told anyone how she was helping: it said in the scriptures that in acts of charity the right hand must not know what the left hand is doing. It didn't mention anything about the mouth, but she got the point.

During the two years it went on she tried to banish thoughts of it from her mind. She was confused by it, didn't understand it. It didn't hurt but she felt it was wrong; she knew it made her feel uncomfortable, ashamed, but didn't know why. She also knew she couldn't stop it, knew she had to do it, knew it would go on. Mostly she thought about it in bed, lying awake and wondering whether he'd come in tonight; or afterwards, unable to sleep, asking herself why, if she was being such a good girl for her mommy and daddy, she felt guilty, like she had done something terrible. When it popped into her mind by day she smothered it, like holding her ears and

248

shouting when she didn't want to hear what someone was telling her.

It stopped after Mommy died.

Not a while after, not soon after, but right then. He never came back to her room, in fact became very distant from her, reluctant to hug her or show any physical affection. She wasn't sure why it had stopped, but she did know she was glad; that was as much as she wanted to think about it.

She knew now, though, why it had stopped when it did, and why it had started too. Reasons never soothed, but they did make the torment quieter by silencing the screams of all the other possible explanations why something had happened to you.

Finding answers hadn't been easy. She couldn't talk to her father about it, because he wouldn't acknowledge that anything had ever happened. He had married again and his political career was skyrocketing. Louisa had been ordered from the Sears Catalogue GOP Candidates' Wives section: early forties, blonde, tall, big tits, big shoulders, big hair, glamorous without being overtly sexy, supportive rather than strong, and well spoken but with just a measure of Southern accent and down-hominess to offset any offputting impression of intellectualism. The right-wing Christian bandwagon was progressing at a rollicking tilt, and he had a seat up-front and a hand on the reins. It was hardly surprising that he would deny any knowledge of what she was 'supposedly' remembering. He sounded so convinced of himself she figured he could probably pass a polygraph test.

The closest he came to conceding their past was even in itself a warning to her to back off.

'Mathilde's illness was a very difficult, very painful time for all of us, Madeleine,' he'd said, a grave but defensive tone in his voice, vulnerable but ominous, dangerous when cornered. 'A very difficult time. That disease struck this whole family, not just your mother. In times like those you do what it takes to get through. And you don't look back, because you'll only find more pain.'

He talked about her mother's trials, her tortures and indignities. The implication was simple: the Witherson family had been blighted by a tragic ailment, of which they all endured different symptoms; Maddy should be glad she wasn't the one who had died in agony, and neither should she forget her other fellow sufferer.

It wasn't something he had done to her, or even that they had done together. It was something that had *happened* to them. All of them. And now it was over.

Yeah right.

Her subsequent behaviour and his dynastic wealth brought her into contact with a number of shrinks, but they could only dissect the rubble of the aftermath. And anyway, they had been employed mainly for her father's benefit, seeking a palatable diagnosis to present to those who had heard the stories about Bob Witherson's daughter. Like the time she had her stomach pumped empty of two bottles of vodka and three dozen aspirins; or the time she slashed her forearms with a steak knife under the table at a reception dinner then sat up with her elbows on the wood and her chin on her palms, bleeding messily over the clean white plate in front of her while talking politely to the State Governor's wife.

'She took her mother's death very badly – she's in therapy, you know,' the onlookers were told, but their sympathy was reserved for the poor widower who had to put up with this basket-case daughter on top of the dreadful tragedy he'd suffered. He was so strong, so dignified and stoical throughout these things – but then he had his faith to help him, hadn't he?

Madeleine had more than the usual complements of self-doubt and self-accusation, but she was still strong enough to know that the explanations for what had happened to her were not to be found within herself. Unfortunately, of the two people who could have shed some light, one was in the ground and the other was not about to get on the couch. However, that didn't mean she couldn't get inside his head and have a look around.

She tried to immerse herself in the kind of crap he read and construct a model of the Bob Witherson world-picture. It wasn't hard. He had shelves and shelves of 'Christian literature', rows of books with nauseatingly pious titles like *Faith Is the Way*, *Led By His Light*, *Know Thyself Through Him* and *Living the Word*.

She had only to flick through a few pages of these things

to understand how little any of them had to say. They all took vague and undefined concepts, such as 'Faith' or 'God's Word', then yabbered on for pages and pages in this weighty-sounding but utterly vacuous religio-babble. 'God's Word is to be found wherever you look, on the printed page and in His signature upon the world of nature. Each tree and bird you see, each blade of grass and summer sky is a chapter in the endless tale of His wonder.' Your brain could melt reading such drivel. It was the philosophical equivalent of a placebo. But this was just the airy-fairy, 'don't we all live in a wonderful white-bread Christian world' stuff. The hard-core material was, appropriately, on the higher shelves.

The Constitution said everyone should have the freedom to believe what they liked. Madeleine didn't have a problem with that. Anyone who wanted to buy into all that 'God's Holy Path Through the Forest of Fluffy Bunnies' shit had her blessing, long as she never had to sit next to them on a long trip. But it didn't stop there, and that was the tricky part. For these guys, it wasn't enough to believe what you believed and to live your own life accordingly – because part of your belief was that a whole lot of what other people did, said or believed was wrong, sinful, disgusting, depraved and, of course, forbidden. So it was your duty to God – and to them, poor misguided souls – to put them right. Out of Love, of course, but sometimes you had to be cruel to be kind.

Hate the sin and love the sinner, the Bible said. They were often a little short on love for the sinner, but they sure made up for it on the hating-the-sin side.

At first she thought the Fluffy Christianity books were a sort of cynical window-dressing for her father's true beliefs, but she gradually came to understand that there was a genuine symbiosis: this wonderful holy world was what he saw in himself when he looked in the mirror; the unforgiving, harsh morality was the backing that caused the glass so to reflect.

We may all be sinners, he believed, but there was a hierarchy of sins, and some were more damnable than others.

It was in a book about child abuse that she finally found corroboration for her theories, and in it the seeds of an explanation. The book talked about the Child Sexual Abuse Treatment Program in Santa Clara, CA, and quoted the organisation's founder, Dr Henry Giaretto. When she read the sentence concerned she wanted to put a blow-up of it on a billboard on Sunset, right next to one of those 'The family that prays together, stays together' posters.

'In contrast to common belief,' it read, 'a great number of men who turn to their children for sexual purposes are highly religious or morally rigid individuals who feel that this is "less of a sin" than masturbation or seeking sexual liaisons in an outside affair.'

Especially when your poor wife is seriously ill and it would break her heart if you cheated on her.

Madeleine felt safe in her own embrace, clutching herself in that hotel-room tub, but the cooling of the water told her how long she'd been in it and reminded her that she couldn't stay. She turned the hot tap on to refresh the bath then stood up, leaning out to the three-legged table that sat between the tub and the wash-basin. There was a small wicker basket on it, holding mini soap bars, bottles of shampoo, bubble bath, all the usual stuff. There was also a neat paper parcel enclosing two razor blades, and it was this that she was after.

She sat back down and removed one of the metal slivers, then gripped it tightly between her thumb and forefinger and drew it across the darkening patch on the front of her left thigh, bleeding the bruise. She watched the blood run out of the slit and trickle down off the skin, dispersing cloudily in the clear liquid below. Then she repeated the operation on the other thigh before submerging both, suppressing thoughts of how blotchy legs were the last thing she had to worry about right then. The bruise-blood drifted in cotton-candy wisps, gradually and faintly pigmenting the water. She looked at the razor in her right hand, then at her wrists and their scars. Another bath, another blade, another bleeding.

Irony seldom came crueller.

And it wouldn't be lost on the watching world if it got out. From their side of the line there was a logic to it, kind of like rape shouldn't matter so much if the victim was promiscuous.

It was during her first and only year at college, here in LA.

They said people who opened their wrists didn't really mean to kill themselves. They wanted attention, it was a cry

252

for help, all that stuff. Parasuicide, they called it. Opening the wrists was messy and dramatic, and it took a hell of a long time, making it more likely that the person would be 'found', and maximising the impact when they were. Another aspect of the longevity was that even if they thought they meant to kill themselves at the start, suicides had so much time to think about it that they often changed their minds midway through.

Madeleine hadn't changed her mind. She hadn't intended to be found either, or at least she believed so. She still asked herself what clues she might have given, what she might subconsciously have said or done so that her room-mate came back to check on her that night instead of going out to that party with her friends.

There were easier ways to kill yourself, people said, but it hadn't seemed that way to her. A warm bath and a sharp blade seemed simple enough. There was no barrier to cross about penetrating her own flesh, either. The reception dinner hadn't been the first time Madeleine had cut herself, just the first time she'd meant anyone to see it. So by the time she'd lain in that tub with the knife in her hand the feeling of steel breaking her skin was too familiar for it to hold any fears.

There had always been a sense of release in the pain, a strange fulfilment. That night she had intended to find total release, ultimate fulfilment.

At least, she thought she had, at the time. Those days and weeks remained an enigma to her now. She could never be sure of her true intentions, or her true motives, or quite what caused that pursuant sense of cumulation. She could only look back at discrete fragments. If she tried to put several of them together it was like opening the door to an asylum scene from a Terry Gilliam movie, a cacophony of hysteria and a kaleidoscope of frantic chaos.

She did know that it was related to losing what was technically left of her virginity – there had been a sense of hopelessness after that, maybe from the pain of finally understanding the extent of the damage her father had done. Her hymen had remained chastely inviolate, but her sexuality had been rent to pieces.

She'd thought, stupidly, that sex – intercourse – would be different, would make things different. That all she had done

253

before, all she had known before, might come to seem like just a naughty little game. Real sex would be something *adult*: she would be initiated into this mystical rite they made so much goddamn fuss about, and what she and her father had done together would seem an infantile insignificance, something she had moved on from.

But it was no different. Lying on Ben Myers's bed with him inside her, she felt the same as she had making out with him and all his predecessors, on couches, in cars and on messy coat-room carpets. It started out fine. Kissing was fine. Tongues were fine. Having her breasts touched was nice. But when it went further, something inside her turned to ice. She was no longer an adolescent indulging with her boyfriend in the grope-a-Sutra sexual phoney war known as heavy petting; she was an eleven-year-old girl 'doing things' with her father, *for* her father. But she didn't call a halt and throw them off; she wasn't frigid. She was something worse than that: she was *compliant*. She did what she was told, like a good little girl, all the time feeling dirty, used and wrong.

And nobody could help her. She couldn't talk to anyone about it, or rather she didn't want to, because anyone she confided in always said the same thing: 'Why don't you tell people? Why don't you go public with it?' They never realised they'd answered their own question: all they could think of was her father, the senator, and this wasn't about him. This was about her. Her pain, her injury, her distress, not his fame, his stature, his crime.

Even the shrinks were guilty of it when she told them, though they masked their reactions in a shrewd professionalism. 'You have a great deal of anger towards your father. Do you think it might make you feel better if you exposed his hypocrisy?' On the couch, as soon as she dropped her bombshell she was no longer the Patient, she was Bob Witherson's daughter. The smug sons-of-bitches: they were winning every way up. They couldn't disclose anything she'd told them if she did make an accusation, but their own private outrage nudged her in that direction, and all the while their bills were being paid by the man they wanted to see punished.

Madeleine wasn't looking for punishment, she was looking for healing. Bringing her father down, having the world know what he had done, wasn't going to help her. Because it didn't matter that he was a senator, or rich, or a moral crusader. It didn't matter who he was, who the perpetrator was. It only mattered what she had suffered, what had happened to her. Did it help the rape victim that the world knew her assailant's name?

Yes, she did want him punished, exposed before the world, forced to contemplate the enormity of his guilty secret. As one shrink got her to admit to herself, what else could have been behind her bloody stunt at that reception dinner but wanting to accuse her father in public? And yes, seeing her father up there, pontificating, putting plenty of Right into righteous, unburdened by his crime, that did make her angry. It added insult to injury. But it wasn't the insult she was worried about.

Another reason she didn't want to go public was that it would never work. She knew this because she had seen someone else try. Juliette Miller was the eldest daughter of Harland Miller, CEO of one of the major auto companies. She went to the media with accusations that he had abused her from the age of eight. Nobody believed her.

He was just such a stand-up guy. A good Christian, a family man, not a whiff of scandal or extra-marital impropriety about him, whereas she was a nut. History of mental problems, drug abuse, alcoholism, overdoses, suicide attempts. She had done so many things to hurt him when he had obviously given everything he could to help her and keep her together. This latest outrage was a real desperate throw of the dice. Anyone could see her stories were a bunch of preposterous lies. Who's gonna believe a screw-up like that against a pillar of the American establishment? Your heart went out to the poor guy, having to contend with such accusations on top of everything else he'd put up with from that girl.

Madeleine saw the equation the right way round. Saw that all the reasons presented to society why it shouldn't believe Juliette were actually the reasons why it should. But nobody else did – or at least, nobody who was prepared to stand up and be counted on pain of multi-million-dollar libel suit.

Juliette Miller sought salvation in telling the world what her father had done to her. What she found was new depths of suffering. Every aspect of her disastrous personal life was trawled through the media as the establishment endeavoured to protect its own by destroying her. It was an all-American crucifixion. Her medical, social and sexual histories were made public property. Former 'lovers' told all. Photographs of her after overdoses and suicide attempts found their way into the mainstream press; more 'intimate' ones were 'happened upon' by the 'adult' publications. She was a photo-composite hate figure for just about every demographic: a slut junkie alcoholic rich-kid slacker. And on top of that, she had tried to drag her poor father – a good man, a decent man – into the slime alongside her.

America wouldn't have pissed in her mouth if her teeth were on fire.

She bought a snub-nose and blew her brains out. A week later Madeleine opened her wrists in the bath.

Juliette's suicide definitely spawned its own banshee wailing inside the vortex of Gilliam's Kaleidoscope. This ultimate act of surrender by someone whose experience offered so many parallels, warnings and premonitions served to intensify her own spiralling despair. But looking at it now, the difference in method seemed significant. At least, Madeleine hoped it was.

Juliette Miller had cut her wrists also. Twice, in fact, on top of several less immediately life-threatening acts of self-harm. But when she actually committed suicide she used a gun. The wrist-slashings, the parasuicides, were not attempts to kill herself. They were attempts to draw attention to herself, and more specifically to the fact that there was something wrong with her and she needed help. When all of that failed, when she decided she actually wanted to end her life, she shot herself through the head. Quick, comparatively painless, and utterly decisive. No chance of rescue, no opportunity to change your mind.

Madeleine knew *she* hadn't changed her mind that night, because she lost consciousness (though that could have been alcohol intake as much as blood loss). But she *was* rescued, and the question remained: subconsciously, had she known she would be? She couldn't see anything inside the Kaleidoscope that would tell her either way. She couldn't remember what she had said to her roomie Carole-Ann in the hours and days before. She couldn't even remember whether she locked the bathroom door. She desperately wanted to think that there was something she had said, something she had done to ensure she would be found in time.

It scared her now to consider what depths her mind had visited, but it terrified her more to think how close to death she might have come. How near she had been to losing all she might ever be; how the things that had wrecked her past had almost stolen her future too.

Madeleine didn't experience any Capra-esque awakening to the value and joy of life. Coming round in a hospital room, realising where she was and why, was not a euphoric moment. Considering how low your self-esteem has to get before you consider offing yourself, it's not comforting to think of the new levels of shame and embarrassment you've just descended to as a failed suicide and bona-fide basket case. However, with the knowledge that she hadn't hit the bottom came the understanding that she was no longer sinking, and if you're no longer sinking, there's only one way to go.

She moved out of the shared house and got an apartment on her own, using the latest instalment of guilt money from her father. She didn't have any pride obstacles to negotiate in taking his cash; if it meant he could tell himself he was helping her, or that she needed him, then that was just a couple more bubbles in the hot-tub of self-deception the prick already luxuriated in.

She went back to college the next semester. She didn't feel as self-conscious as she had feared around people who knew – or were likely to know – about her suicide attempt. Maybe it was the thought that she'd nothing to hide, certainly nothing to gain from pretending to be anything she was not. However, she was self-conscious about the scars. Their visceral ugliness appalled her, as if they were the face of the person she was when she inflicted them, a face she didn't want anybody else to see. She also didn't like the story they told about her to anyone with the eyes to notice, and took to wearing long sleeves at all times. The paralysis in two fingers of her left hand could not be covered up so easily, but chances were the type of people who knew what that signified would also have knowledge enough not to be judgemental.

It was through her psychology class that she had her first encounter with pornography. She was working extra hours to catch up with what she had missed through her convalescence and the rather unproductive weeks that had preceded it, and as she was staying late around campus most nights anyway, she volunteered to be part of an experimentation group. Sexual psychology was starting to hold an ever-keener interest for her, as she searched for the Holy Grail that would help her diagnose quite what was wrong with her own.

The study was into what Professor Farraday called 'Desensitisation', monitoring the effects upon attitudes of a group exposed to explicitly sexual material. He was seeking to test the hypotheses that exposure to pornography made men callous in their sexual attitudes to women (leading to a greater disposition to rape and a lack of sympathy towards victims of sexual violence et cetera et cetera, see Dworkin, McKinnon *et al*); and that it made women feel degraded, objectified, dehumanised and all the other pathetic things they were supposed to turn into any time a skin flick met a VCR. He gave all the members of the group a number of videotapes and a viewing schedule, plus a rota for passing each other's tapes around. Watching the material alone in the privacy of your own home, he observed, was conducive to a more accurate reading of reactions, as most pornography users tended not to view it in seminar rooms alongside a dozen people they hardly knew.

As she had quickly come to learn, there is no such thing as an 'experiment' in academic psychology, because that would suggest the prof was in some doubt as to what the results would be. He knew all along that sustained exposure to this material would make the depicted behaviour seem more natural, commonplace and perfectly ordinary; the effect was 'demystification' rather than desensitisation. So a blow-job neither elevated the recipient male to a position of dominance and supremacy any more than it made the woman a debased slattern deserving of all contempt: it was just a blow-job. A pussy wasn't any kind of mystic portal to the sexual dimension: it was a pussy. The men were neither perverts nor superstuds for doing what they were doing; the women neither whores nor goddesses. They were all just people fucking. And it was no big deal.

Madeleine knew the prof had no doubt what impact the porn would have on her sexual attitudes; he could have less easily predicted the impact it had on her sexuality. In short, it turned her on. It was deeply ironic that this should seem so surprising, as that *was* the material's intended purpose, but then in the current climate, the list of expected effects placed dehumanisation, depravation and damnation a long way ahead of titillation.

It excited her. It made her feel the way she imagined sex was supposed to but in her unfortunate experience never had. She watched tapes and tapes of the stuff with a compelled mixture of fascination and arousal. However, it wasn't the men that turned her on, it was the women; what they were doing, how they were doing it. They weren't 'passive' as she had heard one Dwork opine; and by God they weren't 'compliant'. They were freely, energetically, uninhibitedly indulging their desires, in a fantasy world where it appeared they had every right to do so; a world without shame and guilt, a world where sex wasn't dirty and dark, but natural, healthy and joyful.

Watching these women was the erotic revelation of Madeleine's life: the only thing that had ever made her feel, damn it, *sexy* about being female, about having this body, this mind. And this was not because of any latent lesbian tendencies, however attractive she found many of the women. It was not because she desired them.

It was because she wanted to *be* them.

Pretty soon she found herself asking why she couldn't, and truth was she didn't find a long list of reasons. Unlike the prescription beauties of the mainstream media, the women in these videos came in all shapes, sizes, proportions, colours, ages and races. It seemed pornography was the one visual medium that still believed beauty was in the eye of the beholder: whatever turns you on, literally.

She started buying the *LA X-Press*, looking up the want-ads offering work in the 'adult business', as it was referred to. That was where the reality brakes applied themselves, as she asked herself what she might be getting into here. Through door number one: a new career as an adult movie star. Through door number two: white slavery. Choose carefully now.

But one of the ads quoted a name she recognised from some of the tapes she had rented after the prof recalled his own 'research materials'.

259

'New adult models required. Hard or soft – however far YOU want to take it. Contact Marco Pia . . .'

She became aware through the *X-Press* that Marco Pia was a comparatively big name among porn directors, but the videos she knew him from were a different matter. He did a series called *First Timers*, which she guessed was really a compilation of the auditions – or screen-tests or whatever you'd call them – of women with no experience in front of the camera, who were either trying to get into the business or just wanted to experiment. She had initially picked one of these up after watching a tape in which she felt the actresses were 'performing' too much, as if trying to fit a rather immature male fantasy of how a woman should behave in bed. The *First Timers* tape promised a less polished product, and delivered a more honest depiction of sexual behaviour than she had seen so far. For one thing, the progress of the encounters – from athletic feats of sexual gymnastics down to just stripping for the camera – was dictated by the women rather than by Marco Pia or whichever other male he brought along. That was how she knew the ad was for new First Timers – 'however far you want to take it' was the phrase that kept cropping up during the often lengthy on-camera discussions between Pia and the women.

She rented a few more of these tapes as the idea of getting involved herself took hold. It seemed there wasn't going to be a better way of getting in or simply of finding out whether this stuff was really for her after all.

Marco Pia was taller than he seemed on her TV screen, but then it occurred to her that she'd probably never seen him standing up. He seemed like a bit of an old hippie in the videos: early forties, grey streaks in hair that shouldn't be allowed to grow that length past thirty-five, and looked like he would smell of joss-sticks and pot. In the flesh he appeared slimmer, more lithe, and smelt only of shower-gel and body spray. His house smelt so fragrantly of fresh coffee that she wondered if he was trying to sell the place.

He had asked her to come around at eight in the morning. His place was in Burbank, so having risen at six to be there in time she was glad of the coffee, both in aroma and liquid form. The drive over was weird, a mixture of trepidation and anticipation, worry and excitement, plus the freeways were quiet, which was always a little freaky. They traded small-talk while she drank from the mug and he set up the camera and lights in front of a fold-down couch in his expansive lounge. She found his décor slightly amusing. If tacky could be conservative, this was it. It wasn't garish or gaudy: everything looked new or immaculately maintained, but all of it seemed about twenty years out in a precise and pristine sort of way.

'All right, first of all I'm gonna sit you down on the couch and ask you questions, and I'm gonna be behind the lights here,' he said. 'It's to get you used to the camera. I'm gonna introduce you, but rule number one is you never use your own name.'

'I know,' she told him, sitting where he pointed. 'I'll be Katy. Katy Kox, with a K.'

'I think there's already a Kelly Kox, but that's fine. Long as you're in front of this camera, you're Katy Kox. Maybe with two xs, huh? Now, just try and relax, and don't worry if you don't feel relaxed, because you'll get there eventually.'

'I'm relaxed,' she lied.

'That's good, that's good. But before we start, let me just state rule number two, which is: you're in charge. You do what you want to do, and remember that you can leave at any time.'

'I know. However far I want to take it.'

'That's right.'

He began asking her questions, the familiar Q&A she'd seen on the videos. She imagined most people cued through those parts of the tapes to get to the action, but Madeleine had watched every second of those interviews, wanting to find out a little about who these women actually were. Mostly it was sexual stuff, like what kind of thing turned them on, their previous sexual experiences, and why they had come along – did they want into the business or was it just curiosity? Sometimes they talked about what their day-jobs were, whether they were in a relationship right now. They told – in keeping with the spirit of the thing – as much or as little about themselves as they felt comfortable with.

Madeleine didn't feel comfortable telling much. One of the first things he asked when the small-talk faded was how many partners she'd had. He always asked that, and she'd often been surprised at how low the figures were in reply. The notion that you had to be a prolific sleeparound before you'd consider doing porn turned out to be a total myth; it was also reassuring, given her own limited history. However, she didn't want to admit that technically speaking there had been only one, and she certainly didn't want to widen the definition to include certain other experiences.

'Not many,' she settled for. To head off any further pursuit by Marco she added: 'Let's say we're talking less than the fingers of one hand, even if this hand was on a yakuza.'

He smiled. He liked that.

She was a long way from relaxed when he asked her to take her clothes off. She stripped down to her underwear, not feeling anything remotely erotic about what she was doing, concentrating mainly on preventing the fit of giggling that this whole scenario was threatening to brew up. She felt a need to disguise her discomfort, fearing Pia's disapproval if he could sense it, like he'd pull the plug on the whole thing if he thought she wasn't up to it. It wasn't that she was afraid he'd get mad at her: he was a very laid-back kind of guy. It was that she felt she wanted to please him.

That was when she realised what was going wrong. She was complying. She was trying to be a good little girl for Daddy, and that wasn't why she was here. Marco Pia wasn't Daddy, and she sure as hell wasn't a good little girl.

She was Katy Koxx.

She stopped, put her hands on her hips, and looked at Pia. 'This isn't really doing much for me,' she said.

'That's fine, that's okay. You wanna quit?'

'No. I want you to get over here.'

'Is there some kind of release I have to sign?' she asked. They were in his kitchen, drinking Pepsi from bottles, her hair still wet from the shower. It was Katy Koxx who had climbed in and turned on the faucets, but although it was Madeleine who emerged, it wasn't the same Madeleine.

'There is, yeah, but you should cool off first.'

'Cool off?'

'Yeah. Come back over here tomorrow. I'll let you watch the tape. Then, once you've seen what it looks like up there on the TV screen, you can decide whether you want to sign the release.'

'I want to sign it now,' she said. 'I want to commit myself before I change my mind.'

'And that's why I'm telling you to cool off. Right now you're still getting off on what you just did. It's all a big buzz, right? But once you sign that release, for the rest of your days, wherever you go, that tape's gonna follow. So you should take a fresh look at it in the cold light of day, so to speak, before you "commit" yourself to anything.'

'But . . .'

He put down his Pepsi on the table. 'I'll be honest with you, Madeleine. I think you're pretty hot. I think you could go places in this business if that's what you want to do. I could use you, definitely, and I would really like to use you. But I don't *need* you. I make maybe twenty *First Timers* tapes a year. I cast and direct the same number of professional adult features too. And I can fill *all* of them with people who *want* to be there. I don't need to dupe, deceive or harass anyone to be in one of my pictures.

'Now, I don't care what people think about adult movies – I've got a clear conscience about what I do. So if you come back tomorrow, watch the tape and you're cool to continue, great. I've got a feature shooting in a fortnight I can put you in if you want the start. But if you've changed your mind, then it's no loss – we both had a good time and that's the end of it. Okay?'

'Okay.'

'Hey, don't look so freaked out. I'm sure you came along here today with the idea that everybody in this business is a sleazeball. Everybody in this business *is* a sleazeball. But some of them are okay sleazeballs and some of them are asshole sleazeballs. You're gonna be vulnerable if you don't know the difference.'

In a way it was an extreme form of role-playing therapy, stepping outside of herself to become this voraciously sexual person, confident, in control, getting what she wanted. She now fully understood what people meant by the term 'abandon'. When she was being Katy Koxx she was abandoning everything about Madeleine Witherson, existing without the

263

constraints of fear and worry for a while. And when she returned to being Madeleine Witherson she brought a little more of Katy Koxx back with her each time.

The sex itself was far from great. For one thing, the sense of adventure about what she was doing was always going to wear off, and there was little chance of orgasm when at any second the director was likely to interrupt and call a halt for the dozenth time.

But that didn't mean the whole thing wasn't one enormous turn-on. It was like having a secret lover: she had this other life, this other self that nobody knew about, and the thought of it was a constant thrill. While she was in familiar company, she got off on thinking how surprised they would be if they knew. The paradox was that the longer she was a porn actress, the more the public Madeleine changed into someone they'd be less surprised to learn that about.

She didn't think much about the future. She had done half a dozen features, and was moving up the credits as her face got known, but she didn't have any great sense of ambition about it. She was just rolling with it, and that was probably because she always knew it wouldn't last. Although she had taken precautions to protect her anonymity, she'd always known it was inevitable that her identity – or rather, who she was related to – would be discovered in the end (and that it *would be* the end). That hadn't been part of her motive for doing it, certainly not consciously, but deep down she'd always known it was going to limit her stay; and maybe that had made it easier to get involved in the first place.

It hadn't been a career move; it hadn't been a springboard; it hadn't been a protest; it hadn't been a cry for help. It had just been something she had done, something she had *had* to do. And something that had made her feel better. Just a pity it was also something that was considered punishable by death in certain quarters.

She pulled out the plug to drain away the water, standing up and turning on the shower as she did so. A bath was soothing, but you ended up sitting around in what you had just washed off, which was bad enough when you hadn't been bleeding off bruises with a razor blade. The first blast from the shower-head was cold, discharging what had been lying in the pipes. It brought her skin out in goosebumps and sharpened her up after such a long meditation.

She thought of the last shower she'd had. It had been that morning, a few hours and a lifetime ago, when the biggest thing on her mind was making the right impression – and on the photographer rather than the photographs. She'd stood there under the spray, nervous and still glowing from their meeting yesterday. The way he'd looked at her, the way he'd talked to her. No games, no postures, no bullshit. Refreshingly, it seemed here was someone who really couldn't give a shit about her having been a porn star. There'd been so many who didn't want to know her because of it, and plenty who only wanted to know her because of it. Even those who claimed not to have a problem with it still saw it as a vastly disproportionate part of who she was. This guy Kennedy wasn't interested in a porn star, ex porn star, to-be movie star, senator's daughter or whatever the hell else. He was interested in Madeleine Witherson, and it had been a while since anyone else was.

He'd said she was pretty. It didn't matter why he had said that; it only mattered that he had.

Madeleine hadn't thought she would get to be 'pretty' ever again. Little girls were pretty, and sometimes they grew up into pretty young women as long as that little girl remained somewhere inside. Maddy hadn't been a little girl since she was eleven years old and her mommy got sick. In the business, the aspired compliment was 'sexy', which she'd been called plenty of times. But sexy was as much about behaviour and attitude as appearance, and a thoroughly affected appearance at that; sexy was something you became, something you played. Pretty was something you *were*, something natural, something pure. Pretty was a quintessence of yourself, of a person you had always been.

Stephen telling her she was pretty made Madeleine feel that the little girl she'd once been was still a part of her; it made her feel there were places inside her that her father hadn't spoiled.

It made her feel she had survived.

Madeleine turned off the water and reached for a towel, shaking her head. Survived, she thought bitterly. Yeah. Survived child abuse, drink, drugs, insanity, self-loathing and

265

suicide attempts, so she could be here now – healthy, 'pretty' and straightened out – in great shape for a human sacrifice.

'I see you got *Babylon Blue* on the in-house movies,' she observed, walking back into the bedroom. Her blue dress was sticking to her skin a little, the heat of the shower having rendered the bathroom as humid as a rainforest. 'D'you check it out?'

'Purely for research purposes,' he answered, going for brazen rather than bashful. If he'd said no she wasn't sure whether she'd have been disappointed or simply not believed him.

'Well, I guess you didn't see a whole lot if it was on SpanVision. Adult movies the whole family can enjoy.'

'I think you're being a wee bit harsh,' he countered. 'The edits were all extremely sensitive and unobtrusive. The story was still very clearly conveyed. Made me ask myself if there was any need for all those prurient interludes in the first place.'

'Yeah, great dialogue like that will always stand up on its own.'

Madeleine sighed. Wasn't smartass banter just the easiest thing in life? You could slip in and engage no matter what the occasion. Even with your own death (or eighty-eight others) hanging precariously over your head.

'So, the room's got a movie channel. Don't suppose it's got a minibar too?'

''Fraid not. This any good to you?'

He held up a bottle of whisky, which she assumed must be Scotch. Cragganmore, the label read, but she was only interested in the part that said '40% vol'.

'Cool. Just hope you got another one there for yourself.'

There was a knock at the door, and she felt her heart leap. A few moments of bullshit small-talk had taken her mind off quite how scared she was, just long enough for it to knock her sideways when it rushed back in.

'It's okay,' Stephen said. 'Room service. Get back in the bathroom.'

She re-emerged once the visitor had gone, to find a tray on the double bed bearing two towering club sandwiches and some cans of Coke.

'You're a very, very nice man,' she told him.

It was only when she started eating that she realised how hungry she was. She tore into the sandwich ravenously, the feeling of food in her mouth like a long-forgotten pleasure. A crack about the condemned woman's last meal flitted into her mind, but she felt that pre-sob constriction in her throat when she even thought about forming the words.

She took a long swallow from her can, then poured a very large whisky into a glass on the dressing table and topped it up with the sweet black fizzy liquid.

'Now that's *my* idea of heresy,' Stephen said, smiling.

'My apologies.' She gulped back half the glass, feeling a warmth run through her insides as it went down.

'Never bother. I'm not a fundamentalist. I like a straight dram myself, but each to his own.'

The word 'dram' rolled over his lips in a low growling burr. It was like someone stroking the inside of her ears.

She didn't want to die.

'I take it you're not religious,' she said, trying to hide from her thoughts in a conversation.

'Not unless football and whisky count. I was once, I think it's fair to say.' He wore a look she recognised, a combination of anger, sadness and vulnerability, as though he was unsure what he was giving away, what doors he was opening. 'I was at a Catholic seminary.'

This was way out of left-field.

'You mean like priest-school? I take it you dropped out.'

He gave her a strained look, with a glint in his eye like he was only half reluctantly owning up to something.

'Or did they throw you out?'

'Bit of both. There was an aspect of the training I objected to.'

'What was that?'

'Getting shagged up the arse by fat, middle-aged Irishmen.'

'*What?*'

'Long story.' He didn't sound like he wanted to elaborate.

'Bit of a change of track then, vocationally,' Madeleine said, co-operatively changing the subject. 'Would-be priest to photographer. What got you into that?'

'There was a fire-sale at the careers office. Photographer was the only thing left by the time I got there. I actually wanted to be in a guitar band, but in Lanarkshire you have to be from Bellshill to do that. Motherwell doesnae qualify.'

'Bellshill? Is that like Seattle or something?'

'I suppose – it's on a smaller scale but with even more rain.'

'And that's where all the bands play?'

'No, it's just where they all seem to be from. The Soup Dragons, Balaam and the Angel, Teenage Fanclub . . . even Sheena Easton.'

'She was from there? I've heard of her. Not the others, though.'

'Further proof, I believe, that there is no God. Any being that was truly divine would want to spread the music of the Fannies far and wide across the Earth.'

'The fan . . . Oh, Teenage Fanclub? So they're pretty good?'

'Ay. I'll send you a tape when . . . if . . . I mean . . .' He put down his sandwich. The light seemed to go from his face. 'Sorry.'

Madeleine shook her head. 'Forget about it.'

Stephen stood up. He was starting to look as beat as she was. He might still be finding life faintly ridiculous, but his eyes suggested they were tiring of the relentless absurdity.

'I could use a shower,' he said, and retreated.

She was left alone on the bed, watching him disappear through the doorway out of which steam was still drifting. She picked up her drink and glanced at the blank black screen of the room's TV, from which her face darkly reflected. She knew that if she switched it on she'd probably see the same thing. She had to be one of the few people in the country not watching it right then, but as all good sports fans knew, the tube's no substitute for being there.

The electronic chime of her mobile phone sounded from inside her bag, and she leaped to pull it out with all haste, like the device had fallen into a fire. Desperation sure sharpened the reflexes.

'Hello?'

'Miss Witherson, it's Larry Freeman here.' His voice was neutral. Damn. Anything south of euphoria was bad. 'How you holdin' up?'

'You don't actually want me to answer that, Sergeant, do you?'

'No, not really. Look, I'm just callin' to tell you where things are at with the investigations. You probably already guessed there ain't nothing that's gonna make you jump for joy, but I knew you'd want to hear it straight.'

'Correct. If I want bullshit and speculation, there's a TV right here.'

'Ain't that the truth. Okay. First of all, bad news on the market-pass thing. We had someone from AFFMA check the list of names that they hold accreditation forms and photos for. She was able to eliminate all the names of company personnel against their files, which left a couple of dozen outstanding, but they all checked out. Photographers, reporters, agents, whatever, they're all legit. In every case, we've found someone to vouch that the person was supposed to be there. The only other option is actually to go through the photos and check against the names supplied, but this lady said even the head of AFFMA wouldn't be able to ID half these faces, so that's useless too.'

'What about the Communion of the Saved?'

'Well, your friend Mr Kennedy called it right. The Reverend St John's having to make with some fancy footwork to keep his balance up there on the moral high ground, so he coughed us up a list pretty quick. Unfortunately, the only names that cross-matched FBI records were a couple of guys under investigation for corporate financial shenanigans. Seems they spent so much money trying to buy their ticket to heaven that they didn't have much change left for the IRS.

'However, we did get something on a cross-check of Christian fundamentalists against computer nuts. It was a few years ago now, but there was a group of anti-abortion activists here in California who used to hack into clinics' computers so they could harass the women scheduled to have terminations. The group called itself Life Guard, something like that. Problem is, the only names we have are of the people who were caught when one of their stunts got ambushed by the LAPD. We're checking them out, obviously, but because it was all an Internet deal we don't know who else might have been involved with the group. But it *is* something, believe me. Put it this way, if we had a week I'd call it a great lead. As it is . . .'

269

'What would you call it, Sergeant? A lottery ticket?'

'I'd call it a chance.'

She disconnected the call and put the phone down on the tray, next to the crusts and crumbs and empty cans.

A chance. The words 'snowball' and 'hell' kept leaping to mind. Even in the unlikely event that one of these pro-Life nuts was the bomber, or told them who the bomber was, what were the authorities going to be able to do anyway? The minute he saw a badge this guy was liable to press the button, and the cops knew that. He'd nothing to lose, no line still to cross: he'd already killed several people today. If he got caught, they could only fry him once.

She'd known from the start that there was only one way to save the hostages on that boat, and neither the FBI nor the LAPD could do anything to change that.

Stephen came out of the bathroom, a towel wrapped tightly around his waist. She stood up and went towards him before he could speak, feeling herself conveyed there rather than consciously moving. She felt so alone, so scared and alone.

'I need to hold you,' she said. 'I need someone to hold me.'

She put her arms around his chest and felt his close around her shoulders. She shut her eyes, enveloped by his fresh smell and the warmth and softness of his touch. Madeleine had heard a thousand dumb song lyrics about wanting to hold someone for ever – she might have been the first person they'd ever accurately applied to. Every second there in his arms was a second of preciousness that she didn't want to end. She felt his lips descend and gently kiss the hair on the top of her head. It sent a wave through her body that began as rapture but turned to anguish in the same moment.

Don't kiss me. Don't hold me. Don't make me love you.

Not now.

'Freeman called,' she managed to say, gulping back air, her words half muffled against his chest. She had no tears left now. 'It isn't happening. They aren't going to find him. Stephen, I don't see any way out of this. I don't want to die, I really don't want to die. But if I let all those people die, I don't think I'll want to live.' She squeezed him, gripping him tightly as though she'd fall off the planet if she lost her hold. 'I don't know what to do. I don't know what to do.'

He kissed the top of her head again and began talking, softly, a half-whisper around her left ear. 'Well Madeleine, I was thinking about it in the shower, funnily enough,' he said. 'And to be honest it seems pretty clear-cut to me.'

She pulled away slightly and looked up at him.

He looked back down at her and shrugged. 'With eighty-eight lives at risk, I don't think you've got any choice but to give the bomber what he wants.'

She stared at his face in shock, unable to believe he could have suddenly delivered these pitiless words. Madeleine would admit that she was way short of getting her head round this guy, and not least of understanding his fucked-up sense of humour.

But she was still sure he shouldn't be grinning like that.

fourteen

'Reverend, will you hear my confession?'

Many voices, many faces, rising and falling from before his eyes like the visions conjured by the witches in *Macbeth*. But the one that kept recurring was not rising from the electronic cauldron, nor could it be dismissed with the magic wand of his remote control.

'. . . toll is currently standing at nine, but that is expected to rise, with reports of eleven people listed by doctors as "seriously injured", three of them described as "critical". Hospitals in the Southland are requesting that blood donors come forward as soon as possible, and although they aren't saying as much right now, the medical authorities are clearly preparing themselves for the possibility of many more casualties tomorrow if the bomber carries out his threat of . . .'

Click.

'. . . believed to still be in protective custody at a Santa Monica police station. There has been as yet no response from Miss Witherson as to her intentions, but what has emerged is that the senator's daughter attempted to commit suicide in nineteen ninety-seven . . .'

'. . . drawing parallels with the hit movie *Speed* from the summer of ninety-four, in which Dennis Hopper played an embittered ex-cop who put a bomb on a Santa Monica bus and demanded a cash ransom from the city of Los Angeles. The question some people are beginning to ask themselves today is whether, after years of criticism over violence in movies and the effects of that violence on society, Hollywood is now reaping what it has sown.'

Click.

'. . . am not condoning vigilantism, and would never condone vigilantism, Suzie. But what I *am* saying is that perhaps something like this was inevitable. There's a lot of Christian people out there who've been offended by what's been coming out of Hollywood for a long, long time, and their protests have always been ignored. Every once in a while there's a ground swell, like with Michael Medved's book a few years back, but the movie-makers just pay lip-service to the idea of cleaning up their act, then once the fuss has died down they're back bad as ever. If you ignore people when they're talking politely, Suzie, sooner or later they're gonna start shouting a little louder, and I think that's what has happened today . . .'

Click.

'. . . were singled out for extremely harsh criticism by the Reverend St John in a speech made at last week's Festival of Light event – *across the street* from the Pacific Vista hotel – reiterating statements made on his Christian Family Channel over recent months. The bomber echoes St John's words in calling Madeleine Witherson the Whore of Babylon and referring to the AFFM as the UnAmerican Festering Filth Market. There has been no word yet from the Reverend St John himself, but a spokesman for his organisation said the Reverend was "extremely disturbed" by today's events. The spokesman acknowledged the parallels and told reporters that Luther St John would not issue any statement on the matter without very careful consideration and possibly consultation with the authorities, as the effect of his words on the bomber could be highly unpredictable. It is not known whether . . .'

Click.

'. . . producer Charles Geisler, who earlier spoke to us from the *Ugly Duckling* on his mobile phone.

'"We're all doing our best to hold it together here. Everybody's trying to be strong, trying to be here for each other, but it's real hard, you know? Everybody's on their phones, talking to their kids, talking to their wives and husbands. Because they're in this too. They might not be here on the boat, but they're going through this too."'

Click.

'. . . appalling tragedy that has claimed nine lives and could claim as many as eighty-eight more, but isn't it too often the case that something dreadful has to happen before we are motivated to do anything about a situation? You have to reflect that maybe it was going to take a disaster like this to give America a moral wake-up call, forcing us all to look again at certain things we had come to accept but which we never *should* have accepted. There are people in this country who have been hiding behind the First Amendment because it saved them from justifying their conduct and their motives in any kind of open debate. But that debate's sure going to start now, because people are going to be asking questions about what's in our movies and on our TV screens that they should have been asking long ago. And it's a sad indictment of our society that it has required . . .'

Click.

'. . . our telephone poll, which found sixty-eight per cent of callers thought Madeleine Witherson should make the ultimate sacrifice to save the people on the *Ugly Duckling*, so let's get a sample of the mood among our studio audience. Martina, do you agree with the poll?

'"Yeah, I think she should do it. I mean, the folks on the boat, a lot of them got kids, you know? She ain't got no kids. It's tough on her, I guess, but she's the one in the position to save all those lives."

'And what about you? Lady in the red sweatshirt.

'"I think she's got very little choice. I mean, if she does nothing and the bomb goes off, she ain't gonna have much of a life that way either. This is her chance of, I dunno, some kinda redemption, you know? She's someone who has broken God's laws in front of anyone perverted enough to be watching these porno tapes. What kind of example has she given society? That's actually the second part of the Fifth Commandment: avoid scandal and bad example. If she did this it would set a more Christian example: selflessness and repentance."

'"Yeah, that's right. She's right. Nobody makes the news for doin' somethin' Christian-like, not normally. You make the news for doin' the opposite. *She* made the news for doin' the opposite. This could be one time somebody does somethin' Christian-like and the world pays attention. Besides, if she's suicidal anyway . . ."'

Click.

It had been the same all day. People weren't talking about terrorism, they were talking about morality. They weren't discussing the violence at the Pacific Vista, they were discussing violence in the movies. And instead of scrutinising the morality of the anonymous bomber, they were scrutinising the morality of Madeleine Witherson. Sure, there had been the occasional liberal popping up and trying to reroute the agenda, but it was like trying to stop a freight train with a bicycle. That woman in the red sweatshirt had summed it up, talking about the second part of the Fifth Commandment. The first part seemed to have been bypassed way back.

He couldn't have hoped for such a boon: it was his agenda, Luther St John's agenda, all over the networks. Neither could he have hoped for such a primer to illustrate how what he was planning was likely to work, how people were quickly going to cast off their modish accoutrements and turn back to God for warmth, shelter and security.

The only worrying aspect about it was that it had absolutely nothing to do with him. He had no more been expecting it than the poor suckers who'd got blown up that morning.

For it to have proven so fortuitously efficacious should have assured him that it was a gift from God, a vote of confidence in what he was about to do. He should have been thanking the Lord for it with a grateful and happy heart. And he should have been asking why he hadn't thought of it himself.

But what was disturbing him was that he had.

'Reverend, will you hear my confession?'

A conversation, a crucial, pivotal conversation. The development of logic and ideas through discourse, like a kind of fertilisation, helping him reach junctures and conclusions within himself that he might never have reached alone, in even the most reflective solitude. A conversation wherein the embryo of his great plan was formed.

Only now he realised it had a dizygotic twin.

'Reverend, will you hear my confession?'

'I'm not a Catholic priest, son, but if it would do you good to unburden yourself, go right ahead and shoot.'

If there were two foundation stones on which Luther St John had built his career, they were, firstly, the will and ability to be all things to all faiths, and secondly, a reverent respect for communications media. The second was why Daniel Corby was there. The first was why Luther was listening.

There were just so many denominations of Christianity, you had to widen your definitions or you were restricting your market. There was only so far you could go if you were too vividly identified as a Baptist preacher, or a Methodist preacher, or even more broadly as a Protestant preacher. You had to let all good Christians know that your message was relevant to them, and that you were on their side. Because in the end, it was all the one God, all the same Jesus. The hardest market to break into, obviously, was the Catholics, as they had been brought up to be suspicious of anything not endorsed by their own organisation. However, shows of solidarity with them on the right issues worked well to assure them that whatever theological small-print you might disagree on, you were both coming from the same place, and both heading for the same goals.

The tricky balancing act was in courting the Catholics to tune in – whether it be radio in the early days or TV later on – without alienating the Protestants who might fear your message was getting too Papist. Many members of the various Protestant factions were happy to overlook that you weren't one of their particular number long as they knew you weren't a Catholic.

Again, the secret was in sticking to the right issues: there were plenty of things that *everybody* agreed on. Course, it had sure helped having JP II in the Vatican all that time, giving a good, conservative, fundamentalist hard line to his multitudinous flock. Otherwise they might not quite have seen eye to eye with Luther on a lot of things, and he'd have missed out on a whole host of subscribers. It scared him to think what might have happened had the first guy lived longer, having read about some of the stuff he was planning to do. Luther had heard plenty of debate over whether JP I was murdered, but as far as he could see there was no argument: nothing as convenient as that ever happens by accident.

He'd always admired JP II. Like himself, the man had appreciated that we were living in the Communications Age, where it wasn't about letters and missives that would filter down gradually through your dioceses, but about words and images that could go global in an instant. Instead of letters that would be read out before somnolent and dwindling church congregations, the Pope issued press releases that would go on every front page in the world. And unlike his predecessors, boy, did JP II know how to exploit the World Religious Leader franchise. What a showman! All those outdoor deals, hundreds of thousands of people going nuts as he got driven around in his Popemobile, and pictures of it relaying across the planet. Forget mass, this was mass adoration, and the man didn't just know how to get it – he knew how to package it, label it and sell it to the media.

But to stay ahead of the game, you didn't just have to know how to work the communications media, you had to keep pace with its own evolution. When something new developed, you had to be able to recognise its potential without waiting for it to be demonstrated by someone else's success. Luther had been in radio since the early sixties, from the licensed local station that had grown out of his Sunday-night broadcasts, through syndication of hour-long slots across the major cities, to the development of nationwide affiliates and the establishment of the Christian Radio Network. But when cable TV came along in the seventies, all that had gone before became a warm-up exercise for an opportunity of breathtaking magnitude. Within two years the Christian Family Channel's annual revenues – subscriptions, donations, advertising – were more than all the CRN affiliates were accruing cumulatively.

In the eighties, CFC embraced satellite, which gave the channel another means of delivery as well as access to more remote, non-cabled areas. Then in the nineties came the Internet.

Luther St John was never going to be described as a technophobe, but neither did he have any illusions about the extent to which he could understand the workings of the electronic beasts his organisation harnessed. Television worked on simple principles. You pointed the camera at something. You recorded the image. You edited it. You broadcast it. You knew exactly what you were putting into people's living rooms, and you knew how they were going to perceive you through it. As long as you had control of the camera, the editing suite, the transmission, you didn't have to worry about how it all worked.

Computers were a different deal, because in Luther's experience you were never sure whether you were in control, or even quite what you were in control of. And the whole subculture surrounding them had always been ridden with a juvenile sense of mischief, like these guys couldn't resist making a monkey out of anyone unwary enough to play into their digital-electronic hands. So when he launched plans for the CFC Superhighway to Heaven, he resolved to personally vet whoever was going to be in charge of setting the thing up. There had been a CFC website for a couple of years, but so what – his local hardware store probably had a website too. If you wanted to get noticed you had to up the ante. For the Superhighway to Heaven, Luther envisaged something a lot more elaborate, an interactive deal that incorporated music, video clips, animation, credit-card subscription facilities: something that pretty much jumped through every hoop a modern computer could hold up. But he knew that the more complicated it got, the more chance there was of people hooking up to the CFC homepage one day and finding Luther's face superimposed on the body of some guy with his manhood up a black hooker's ass. He needed someone he could trust, someone committed to the Christian cause.

And the winner was: Daniel Corby.

Corby was a scary-looking character, with half his face so disfigured it looked like he used a waffle iron for a pillow and always slept on the same side. Luther was used to meeting the mutilated. There was just no end of people who had lost a body part but found God.

'It was after the accident with the threshin' machine, Reverend, I started lookin' at my whole life again in a different light. After I lost my arm I felt so incomplete, but watchin' CFC made me realise that God could put me back together again, at least spiritually.'

People got a lot less arrogant about their place in the Divine Plan – and about whether there *was* a Divine Plan – when God knocked them off their high horse. 'I thought I had no one to turn to after I lost my Marsha in the automobile crash. But you can always turn to Jesus. I only wish I'd been less blind to that before.'

But Corby didn't turn out to be one of those cases. Sure, God had helped him through the trauma and pain of getting caught up in that fire in the chemical plant where he'd worked, but he'd always had his faith. And if Luther was in any doubt over how long 'always' was, the accounts department was able to assure him that Daniel Corby had been subscribing and contributing for a good few years. He was in the Communion.

Luther reckoned his periodic flesh-pressings with members of the flock must be a lot like what rock musicians and movie stars experienced when they encountered the general public. He had to smile, pass on good wishes, look pleased to be so adored, then move on. It was part of the job, but it was also very boring. And what the rock and movie guys didn't have to contend with (except for the occasional competition winner) was having people presented to you who you couldn't walk away from after shaking hands and signing a book. Luther had an endless string of Good Christians on his daily show, who were there to tell the viewing public how God had changed or assisted their lives. Luther was the host, prompting and probing for the emotional highlights of their stories, and generally putting them at their ease in his famously genial company. The problem was that these bovine crackers didn't realise his interest in them lasted only until the recording ended, so backstage or on-set once the cameras were off, they insisted on sharing their views on the Lord with him. He didn't know what made them think they had the right. If they met Jack Nicklaus, would they start telling him about *their* short play?

He'd smile, laugh and volley off a standard gift-set of platitudes in response to their banal musings about God, Jesus, Love, Heaven, etc, all the while thinking there was something impolite about their imposition on him. They were effectively regurgitating the product he had sold them. If they did that in McDonald's they'd soon be shown the door; *he* had to grin and let them barf away until the next guest was ready.

So the first time he got talking to Daniel Corby it was like coming up for air. Any time a conversation with a tech-guy strayed from the matter at hand it was the usual familiar 'Golly Reverend, I'd just like to say what an honour' stuff, followed by the regurgitation routine. It was reassuring to know that employees gave that measure of commitment, far more than you bought with just their pay-cheque, but it was hardly inspirational. Corby was different. He didn't talk about the Bible or about any touchy-feely crap. He talked about what was wrong with America, and not in the usual hand-wringing way: he talked about it like a plumber talks about what's wrong with your pipes. He talked about

279

it like it could be fixed with the will, the know-how and the right tools.

Corby did all this Internet stuff freelance, setting up websites and homepages for companies and organisations. His involvement was never long-term with anyone: it was, in his own analogy, like he set up the billboard then left you to put up whatever posters you wanted. Luther spoke in-depth with him about just what kind of billboard this was going to be, then Corby went home and got to work. They were both busy men, so they didn't get to talk much in the mean time, but they still communicated via e-mail, and not just about the job either.

The day Corby delivered the finished package, Luther flew him out to Arizona to make his presentation to the people at CFC, and when the beer and Twiglets were done, they found themselves alone in Luther's executive suite.

'My face,' he confessed. 'My injuries. I was never in any chemical fire, Reverend.'

And so Corby began to tell him the truth about his past. About how Life Guard California had come about, what they had done and how the group met its demise. He told Luther about how angry he had become then and how the events following the arrest of his comrades had begun to test his faith: not in God, but in America. This was the country he loved, this was God's country, but it was being taken over by forces of evil, to the extent that people were being persecuted for trying to protect unborn innocent lives. Watching his Life Guard buddies be arraigned and humiliated was painful enough; watching them surrender and give up the fight was crushing. It had left him feeling so impotent and so angry that he felt he had no option but to fight back, not just to show the anti-Lifers his defiance, but to show God's people that *they* could get tough too.

Corby was the only one hurt when his car-bomb went off in Pocoima, brought into the nearest hospital as a John Doe because his wallet and all its identifying contents had fried and melted like a Doritos packet under a grill.

With nothing to connect him to the car or even to the disbanded Life Guard, he was the Innocent Bystander. He was scarred and maimed, but he was still alive, and he wasn't under suspicion. God had both spared him and punished him.

'You're the only person I've ever told, Reverend,' he said. 'I've been carrying this around with me on my own, and it has been a heavy burden. A heavy, heavy burden. I'm not telling you to lay it on you, though. I was just hoping you could help me make some sense of it. You see, I know God was angry because He smote me, like in the Old Testament. But He didn't kill me, and He didn't deliver me into the hands of the authorities for them to take away my freedom.'

The man's story set Luther's mind racing with excitement and fascination. Interpreting God's intentions was the gasoline his evangelism ran on, but this stuff was untreated crude: raw, unrefined, with its truths suspended in a dark and murky solution.

'This really must have been a burden, son,' Luther told him. 'Because there seems so little doubt that God *did* have a message for you, and it must weigh heavily when you don't know what the message means. God sends little messages to people all the time, but it's usually real clear: do this, don't do that. Like candies and spankings to a kid.'

'That's it,' Corby replied. 'That's the burden, not knowing what God was trying to tell me. For a while I thought it was simply remorse because I tried to take the lives of the people who were in the clinic that day, and God said Thou Shalt Not Kill. In time I learned it was more complicated than that. The remorse wore off, but the burden stayed.'

'Indeed, indeed. Because you were attempting to *save* lives primarily, weren't you? The lives of poor defenceless children in the womb. Now, God struck you down, of that there can be no doubt, but as you say, he also saved you from discovery. God punished you for trying to break one of His laws, but He didn't let the authorities of this country punish you for breaking theirs.'

'So you think maybe God was trying to remind me whose law was the more important?'

'Very possibly, Daniel. This is one of the greatest questions that we face in these difficult times, when the laws of the land seem ever more at odds with the laws of the Lord. We all want to be good citizens as well as good Christians, but is it one day going to come down to a choice between one or the other?'

'Well if it does, I know which side of the line I'll be standing.'

'I hear you, son. And God hears you too. Because it must break God's heart that America is becoming His enemy, and it is up to us, as Americans, to turn that around.'

'Yeah, but how can we do that, Reverend? What can we do that we aren't doing already? See, that's how I felt when I decided to bomb the abortion clinic. I wanted the women who were considering going into one of those slaughterhouses to think: what if it gets blown up like that place in Pocoima? Maybe they'd start thinking a bit harder about their other options, you know? I wasn't setting out to kill people; that was just a necessary evil. I was setting out to make a statement, and unfortunately, these days, folks don't listen until somebody gets hurt.'

'No, they don't.'

'Folks don't listen unless there's consequences, you know? They don't listen unless they're scared of something.'

'That's true,' Luther agreed. 'People who've long ignored Him turn to God when they're scared, but nobody feels they should be scared of having ignored God. People aren't afraid of God any more, and that's why they won't listen to His Word.'

'Damn straight, Reverend. And they ain't scared of Christians, either, which is why they think they can piss all over us, if you'll excuse the language.'

'Strong thoughts sometimes need strong words, son.'

'I mean, look at these Islamic guys. Everybody's been peeing their pants at the thought of offending them since they passed their death sentence on that Rushdie guy. Nobody's ever worried about offending Christians. Their faith is getting more respect than ours, and it's because folks are scared of them. You diss *their* God and you better be ready for a fight.'

'Yes, yes. And think how scared the Muslims are themselves of their Allah,' Luther said, the thought a revelation. 'Church and state are practically one in a lot of Middle East places. No abortions, no tolerance of homosexuality or blasphemy or obscenity. That's the law, and they're afraid of the law because it's the law of God. People in America are respectful of the law, but they aren't afraid of it, and that's because it's just the law of men, not the law of God.'

'If folks were scared of God, if folks were scared of upsetting

282

Christians,' Corby continued, 'it wouldn't be so hard for God's message to get through to people, and there'd be so much less sin, so many more souls saved. God must know that, Reverend, don't you think? He must know how hard it is for us to make His word heard.

'God could have killed me or disabled me that day if He wanted to stop me, but He only hurt me on one side, my left, and I'm right-handed. Now, if I'd succeeded in blowing up the clinic, I'd have achieved nothing. There'd be a new clinic there soon enough, and the babies that were scheduled to be murdered in Pocoima would be taken to a death-clinic someplace else. Lives would have been lost but not saved. So this is the real burden, Reverend. This is what keeps me awake at night: what if God was trying to tell me I was going down the wrong road, but that my journey itself was right?'

Corby shook his head, a look of real anguish etched on the lines of his ravaged face. And then he said it:

'We know God sacrificed His only son to redeem us from sin. Wouldn't He tolerate the loss of a few more lives if it would save millions of souls?'

Luther gasped.

It was, as he conceded to Corby, one heck of a question.

'That's why I had to talk to *you*, Reverend. See, I've struggled with it so long but I knew I could never understand God's will like you do, and as you can appreciate, it's not the sort of question you can take a chance on getting wrong.'

'No, it sure isn't,' Luther stated sternly. 'Not when there's God's wrath to reckon with. I can't answer it for you, Daniel, not right now, not without a lot of careful thought and prayer. It seems on the surface the simple answer would be that Thou Shalt Not Kill, end of story, but that's a little too easy, isn't it? That's not answering the question, that's running away from it. That's the answer most people would come to, and I'm sure that's okay with God, because not all His children are strong enough to wrestle with such a beast. But you and I are strong, and He'd expect us not to run away. God tells us Thou Shalt Not Kill, and yet we go to war in His name. God loves peace, and yet sometimes we have to kill to bring peace: we had to nuke Hiroshima and Nagasaki to end the greater carnage that was WW2.

'So if it was in our powers to make America see the light –

283

to save America's soul – but at the expense of some American lives, would it be right just to walk away? Would we be honouring the Fifth Commandment, or hiding behind it?'

To lose earthly lives for the sake of immortal souls. One heck of a question indeed.

He said he couldn't answer it for Corby, but he had answered it for himself as soon as it left Corby's lips. Truth was, his late, lamented uncle had answered it many years ago: 'Sometimes there's more at stake than the life that would be taken,' he'd said.

It wasn't a question, it was a doorway, and all of God's creation looked a whole lot different from the other side of it.

He knew God wanted him to be President. There was no vehicle upon this earth that could convey so many souls to the light, no greater device to spread God's Word and impose His will. God had been grooming and preparing him for it all his life.

Before '92 he thought the preparation had begun with his second start in life in the hands of his dear uncle, but he later came to understand that the trials of Bobby Baker had been part of God's training for him too. They had taught him what courage it required to stand alone, to be different, to uphold your belief in Him in the face of doubt and ridicule. They had also taught him that he had the strength to recover from pain, humiliation and defeat, plus the knowledge that God rewards faith with second chances.

He could see now why it hadn't worked out in '92, and it wasn't to do with the mistakes in his campaign or being outflanked by his opponents or any of that crap; those were merely the details. The truth was, he hadn't won because God hadn't wanted him to, and every aspect of his failure had a part to play in preparing him for succeeding when God did. God didn't want him to be President in 1992 because that simply wasn't the right time – Luther should have seen that. And God had knocked him down too low to recover in time for '96, so He didn't want him to be President then either. He wanted him to be President in the year 2000, the first new President of the new millennium, so that he could lead America out of the dark, sinful days of the Twentieth Century to a new dawn of true Christianity.

America simply wasn't afraid of God any more – that was the essence of the problem. Not everyone, obviously: America had the greatest population of practising Christians on the planet. But there had been a polarisation between the faithful and the godless, and it seemed the word of the godless held sway when it came to making laws, shaping attitudes and defining what was acceptable in society. God's will didn't come into it. The Lord didn't have a powerful enough lobby.

The sinners didn't accept that they were sinning because they feared no retribution: not from the law, and certainly not from the Lord. Even AIDS had taught them nothing. They didn't see that it was a God-given, illustrative lesson in the wages of sin: cause and effect, action and consequence. Instead they just treated it as an obstacle to be gotten around with 'safe sex', then went milking sympathy for this 'tragic affliction'. Even more insulting, they used it as an excuse to bury the country in an avalanche of condoms; something that used to be hidden under the pharmacist's shelf was now lesson one in science class.

There were people who *called* themselves atheists, but Luther knew there was no one who really – deep down – didn't believe, didn't know the truth. These atheists could kid themselves if it made them feel all hip and intellectual, but that was because they weren't scared of God's anger at denying Him. There wasn't much talk of atheists in the Bible, because that was an age when God's work was closer at hand. Even the sinners didn't deny God's existence back then because they could see His might: in works of wonder, in miracles, and most importantly, in acts of wrath.

Luther knew that despite its sins, despite losing its way, America was savable. In fact, it was crying out to be saved. Deep down, people wanted to believe, wanted to know that there were answers and greater mysteries beyond the mundanity of this life. And as the century drew to an end, they were trying to find those answers, those mysteries, in any ridiculous thing except God. They were prepared to believe in aliens, in flying saucers, the Bermuda triangle, Roswell. They were gobbling up the most outrageous conspiracy theories about everything from Kennedy to Princess Diana, and convincing themselves that Elvis goddamn Presley was still walking the earth someplace. They *wanted* to believe. They wanted to know that there was something more; they had merely forgotten what that something more really was, distracted by a hint of the unearthly in all kinds of dubious phenomena.

What they needed was an act of God.

He knew that it was not for God to prove Himself to man; it was for man to have faith in God. God would not act, would not *perform* before man in order to get his attention. But that was why He was calling upon Luther, His servant.

God did not need to act. Man only needed to believe that He had.

An act of God, and not some kind of wondrous work either, but a long-provoked act of rage: punishment for the guilty and a warning to those who were spared.

Luther had been in a hotel suite in New Orleans after giving the keynote speech at a True Love Waits fundraising gala. He found himself awake in the small hours, unable to get back to sleep, and inevitably started channel-surfing. It must have been the Discovery Channel or something like that. A documentary about 'the greatest – and least famous – natural disaster of all time'.

Some time around 1470 BC there had been a volcanic eruption in the Mediterranean, on the island of Thera, estimated to have been four times as powerful as Krakatoa. And just like on that occasion, for all its fire and fury, it wasn't the volcano that had done the real damage. The seismic waves that followed the eruption in Krakatoa killed 37,000 people. 'What followed in Thera,' the presenter said, 'was almost beyond imagination.'

It was an incredible story. The waves caused by this eruption struck every coastline for a radius of about three hundred miles, all around the eastern Mediterranean, the Levant, North Africa, and were responsible for many of the great flood legends of pre-history. 'Given the lack of communication between most of these places and the variations in each culture's chronology, different flood legends and myths developed independently of one another, but all in fact depicted the local experience of the same event. For instance, the flood of

286

Deucalion in Greek legend was that caused by the destruction of Thera, but perhaps the most famous legend to have roots in this disaster is the story of Atlantis. The Minoan civilisation on Crete . . .'

Luther watched, fascinated. The show went into all kinds of detail about the extent of the catastrophe, but the phrase that stuck in his mind, the phrase that came hurtling out at him with a force as if borne on one of those waves, was that 'the devastating physical impact of this incident must have been paralleled by its impact on religious beliefs'.

No kidding. Talk about wrath of the gods; it was a safe bet there weren't many atheists swimming around the debris the day after *that*.

And so it came to pass that a plan was born.

A flood, Luther thought: what could be more Biblical? There was the niggling problem that, according to scripture, God told Noah He would send no more floods, but on the other hand, the human race hadn't done much to honour Noah's side of the deal either.

So what was the difference between an act of God and a natural disaster? Quite simply: intention.

Throughout history there had been floods, earthquakes, volcanoes, famines and droughts, and always a retrospective claim of the events having been divine retribution. But it impressed no-one to identify the hand of God after the fact. That was why AIDS had changed nothing. The sodomites were afraid of the big stick, but still refused to see that it was God who was wielding it.

However, if you predicted *what* God was about to do, *who to* and *why* – and then God delivered . . .

How had he put it? A long-provoked act of rage: punishment for the guilty and a warning to those who were spared. *What* would be a terrible flood, water to cleanse the earth of impurity. *Who* would be the godless, amoral, sin-ridden damned of Los Angeles, source of the filth-tide that was polluting America. *Why* needed no elaboration.

What did need elaboration was how one created a massive seismic wave off the coast of southern California, but there was an old adage that stated where there was a will, there was a way. So if it was God's will, then by God there would be a way.

287

A night in the desert. A clandestine rendezvous. A proposal. A deal.

Liskey laid down what he wanted Luther to deliver once he was President, Luther what Liskey would need to deliver to make that happen. The alloy of their bond was forged in the flames of mutually assured destruction: once the plan was set in motion, neither could betray the other without undoing himself. Liskey told him that if Luther could front the money, he could acquire the hardware. He had the knowledge and the contacts, and since the collapse of Communism, there were places in the former Soviet bloc where it was easier to get hold of nuclear warheads than it was to get hold of a decent car. If Luther had the will, Liskey had the way.

And by sweet Jesus Luther had the will.

He knew well that there would be much death, much suffering, and could but imagine how heavily it would ever after weigh upon him. Many would die in the flood as that was the role God had chosen for them; if they were innocent then surely they would receive their reward. Had He chosen such a role for Luther, he would have happily accepted it, for Luther knew that what stood to be won was far greater than what would have to be lost, as God Himself reasoned when He gave up His only son. However, God had chosen a special role for him; he had to be strong and accept the burden. He could not ask God to let this chalice pass his lips.

When the flood waters abated, America would be listening hard to God's word once again, and listening especially carefully to the man who was speaking it, the man who knew God's will. The next Presidential election campaign would be a very different story. He wouldn't have to play the politicians at their own game: they'd have to play him at his, and they wouldn't stand a chance. Truth would be the highest suit once again, not fashionable opinion or political correctness. The words of the scripture would be his ace, not a joker. And there sure as hell wouldn't be any smartassed wise-cracking from the galleries: we'd soon see how many TV pundits still thought Christianity was a laughing matter after their atheist predecessors got swept away.

The clamour of filth would be silenced. The movie business would be paralysed, production brought to a standstill, and no one would be under any doubt about its role in provoking the catastrophe. No matter what could be salvaged of its material remains, Hollywood would not be allowed to rebuild itself, and neither would film-making in the rest of the US be spared.

The days of film as a courier of disease and decay would be gone, and the people responsible would not be allowed behind a camera again, no matter what penitence they laid claim to. The movies and TV shows of the next century would be vehicles for exemplifying the pure morality of a new Christian age. And a very great deal of them would be made at Luther's own Bleachfield studios.

It was not going to be a simple matter of detonating a nuclear bomb under the ocean. As France's South Pacific undersea tests had demonstrated, doing that only got you a big splash and a whole load of radioactive fish. At both Thera and Krakatoa, the opening of vast caldera sucked in billions of gallons of water, the sea sweeping in to fill the holes where landmasses had previously been. This surge created its own imbalance as the waters overfilled the depressions, and the countersurge back outwards was the force behind the waves.

The principal cause of seismic waves was crustal plate movement, the resultant earthquake forcing part of the seabed up or down. Undersea landslides – or turbidity currents – were another cause. Put simply, it wasn't about moving water, but moving ground. Luther therefore needed to know two things: first, what level of sub-aquatic disturbance would be required to trigger a wave of the magnitude he had in mind; and second, where that disturbance might most effectively be wreaked. It was around then that he became a generous (if admittedly disingenuous) patron of ocean-geological research, and found the scientists he funded to be most helpful.

Sandra Biscane's 3D-modelling programs demonstrated precisely what kind of sub-oceanic site Luther should be looking to plant his explosives in; then Mitchell Kramer went about finding one that met all the relevant criteria. The CalORI project was also beneficial to the credibility of his prediction, so that he could claim to have seen God's preparatory handiwork writ large in the information the research vessel *Gazes Also* was bringing to light.

None of the scientists had any idea what they were really doing for him, but this was not a time for playing the percentages, so unfortunately they had to be added to the weight on his conscience necessary for the success of his divine mission. Biscane was neutralised as soon as Luther had what he needed. The CalORI team was allowed to continue its work for a while after it delivered, in case a better site was located and because Liskey had pointed out the advantages of a disappearance at sea rather than several conspicuously coincidental deaths back on land.

In the mean time a deal was set up in the Ukraine to purchase three ex-Soviet CHIB-class nuclear warheads, removed from vehicle-mounted tactical missiles, yielding a combined payload of 180 kilotons. Luther knew he could trust Liskey as long as their fates were bound together, but he wasn't about to put any unnecessary temptation in the man's way. Having shelled out the required millions for the bombs and organised their transport back to US waters, he wasn't going to risk the Militia assassinating him and running off to have their own fun, especially as the intended means of planting the nukes – the *Stella Maris* – could just as easily be employed to bring them ashore on to US soil. Therefore, Liskey took possession of the warheads and supervised their transport aboard Luther's private yacht, the *Light of the World*, but only after the Ukrainians received the *second* half of the agreed cash-transfer. The first half resulted in delivery – direct to Luther's Kiev hotel room – of an encoded detonation device without which the warheads would not go off.

As well as detonators, Luther was also – and more ostensibly – in town to purchase religious artefacts: three statues that were relics of the region's early Christian history, thought lost but once again discovered in the aftermath of Communism's collapse. The Father, the Son and the Holy Spirit had been featured on a recent CFC documentary on the great Christian statuary of the world. The show ultimately lamented how little of it, despite the ebb and flow of time's tides, had ended up in America, which was now the world's most overtly Christian country. Luther St John was, as CFC viewers knew, in the Ukraine on a mission to begin redressing the balance.

Archaeologists and religious historians would have found

less significance in the three statues than was suggested by the documentary's gravitous content, as they had in fact been made in Arizona. The footage of them after their 'discovery' in a disused Kiev churchyard was shot in one of Luther's own Bleachfield back lots where his Christian Family Entertainment division produced dramas for CFC. After that they were taken aboard Luther's yacht, bound for the Ukraine, and transported to their point of 'purchase', which was filmed for later CFC transmission using locally hired actors.

The Father, the Son and the Holy Spirit, although worthless, were not without points of interest as works of sculpture. For one thing, not many statues tended to be made of lead. It wasn't the lightest material when it came to transportation logistics, but then that would explain why he opted to send his own yacht around the world to collect them. Neither was lead very pleasing to the eye, but it did have radiation-insulating properties; not much of a consideration aesthetically, but extremely handy when you wanted to conceal a CHIB warhead inside.

Luther switched off the TV, like that would make it all go away.

The *Light of the World* was now off the coast of California. The timing of its voyage had been calculated for it to arrive during the AFFM and after the Festival of Light, at which Luther was able loudly to denounce the enemy one more time, as well as launch the protest movement that would be given irresistible force by the events to follow. He had been pouring particular condemnation on the filth-peddlers for months now – for as long, in fact, as he had been predicting the flood – but he needed that final, high-profile platform to underline God's agenda for America before the action started.

Now the talking was over. Liskey's men were ready to rendezvous with the *Light* as soon as it was at the correct co-ordinates. One phone call – maybe only a few hours from now – and it would be time to transmit the detonation codes, whereupon the last, short, digitised stage of the months-long countdown would begin. The moment of destiny was almost upon him, and its anticipation should have been consuming him.

But Luther could think of only one thing: Daniel Corby.

Long they had talked into that portentous night: debating,

advocating, hypothesising. Luther's eyes had been opened to the vision that would finally save this tormented country, the Lord poetically revealing Himself through one troubled patriot. Corby could not understand God's message, of course, because he was never meant to. Corby was merely its vessel, the parchment God's Word was inscribed upon. Luther was the sole intended recipient.

Unfortunately, it appeared Corby had not grasped that.

If Luther needed any confirmation of his fears, it came when he accessed the Communion files requested by the FBI. He had gone in to wipe Corby's name before he submitted them, but it was already gone. In fact, all traces of the man had been excised from the entire CFC computer system – Corby had anticipated that the authorities would look for a connection, given the content of his communiqué. He was protecting himself, but he was trying to protect Luther too, bless his heart, because in Corby's warped mind they were co-conspirators.

Luther saw now how divergent the two sides of an apparently harmonious conversation had really been. While he had been talking about fear of Allah, Corby was talking about fear of Muslims. While he was talking about the wrath of God, Corby was talking about the wrath of Christians. God had granted Luther a shining vision of how he could redeem America. Corby had seen only the shadows cast by that vision's light, but it had been revelation enough to inspire a man like him.

Luther's last words to him came clanking back like the chains of Marley's ghost: 'You can't answer this question yourself, Daniel, and I'd caution you once more against the risks of trying. Maybe I won't be able to answer it either. But if I do answer it, you'll know – you alone – and you'll be strong.'

He was simply telling the guy to keep his mouth shut about their conversation, and not to pull any stunts without Luther's blessing – which he had no intention of ever giving.

Once Corby's job at CFC was done Luther had all but forgotten the man, so thoroughly immersed was he in realising the vision God had granted him. Seeds soon became dwarfed by what they grew into, oak over acorn. It was therefore easy to forget that Corby was out there, let alone consider that he'd be combing Luther's every broadcast word for what *he* thought was a signal.

And looking at it now, Luther's calculated declamations of the movie business, the sharp-tongued Madeleine Witherson and in particular the AFFM must all have seemed pretty unambiguous to Corby. Whether he had meant to or not, he had given him the green light.

Corby had sure learned a heck of a lot about bomb-making (and other things) since that abortion clinic in Pocoima. But then, he had been exposed to far better information than the amateurish crap he'd downloaded from the Internet back in those days: on Luther's recommendation, Liskey had contracted him to set up the Southland Militia's websites.

So Corby certainly knew what he was doing this time, and so far he was getting what he wanted, too. But none of that guaranteed he would never be caught.

It was not comfortable to think of him a few years hence, chatting in his death-row cell to some FBI agent about how he and President St John had once discussed whether fatalities were acceptable in restoring the fear of God to America. Even the Feds might notice a certain parallel.

'Hey, come to think of it, that tidal wave didn't hurt St John's career any, did it?'

Luther reached for the telephone. His conscience was about to get twelve stones heavier.

Cody sipped back the last of her beer and watched Mitch pouring Armagnac into three plastic tumblers and a china mug. They didn't have glasses, and the fourth matching vessel had fallen casualty last Sunday when Coop, in a gregarious gesture of flamboyance and flammability, set fire to his brandy and melted the tumbler.

Cody's legs were pleasantly sore, arms too. They ached with a hard-earned languid weight that felt so good; a satisfying heaviness to her arm as it raised the cold brown bottle to her salt-bitten lips, a pleasant, hanging lifelessness to her calf muscles. She had been in the water much of the day, working on the outside of the *Sado Masochist*, cleaning, adjusting, checking, preparing. Most of the morning had been spent underneath, a time-haze of concentration as she worked to eradicate the jamming problem that had been recurring with the umbilical socket on the belly of the sub. The umbilical linked the *SM* to *Slave*, their remote-controlled 'drone' submersible. Rock and shell fragments were getting trapped between the rubber insulating layers inside the socket, and these were being ground against the sides by the pull and twist of the cable. The rubber was being worn down – salt water didn't help – and although there was no danger of water leakage (with so much insulation on the other side of the sub's wall), the couplings linking lengths of the umbilical were catching on the exposed metal in the socket's snout. This was preventing the slack cable from paying out, and occasionally causing *Slave* to writhe and squirm at the other end like a dog tied outside a grocery store.

'OK, what we drinkin' to?' Mitch asked, holding out his cup across the table.

'Luthah Saaaint John,' barked Taylor, fake Southern accent, standing up and holding his brandy against Mitch's.

'Amen, brother,' said Coop, joining them with the mug.

'Amen,' Cody concurred, raising her glass to the others, grinning.

Mitch said nothing. He gave a weak smile, avoiding, she noticed, Cody's eyes. The others seemed too preoccupied (or maybe just too drunk) to acknowledge his discomfort.

'Gaawd bless his soul,' continued Taylor. 'And when we're

all of us dead, may he look down upon us from Heaven, us suff'rin' damnèd souls below in Hell, and give us a goddamn vulcanology grant!'

'Praise the Lord!'

This time Mitch laughed, but there was sadness in it, if you knew what to look for. It was difficult to hide much from anyone who had been down there in the blackness with you. Down there in the abyss.

There was a unique intimacy of shared awe and shared quiet fear as you descended together in the sub, your words trading only navigational and technical observations, but your voices exchanging frank confessions of fragile humanity. The darkness and the silence, the vastnesses, the feeling of being so alien: it stripped down all the levels you ever built around yourself, the people you presented to the world, the people you thought you were, the civilisation you thought your species had achieved. It stripped you beyond naked. Beyond the flesh. Beyond the rational. Beyond the soul. You didn't get to be female or male, black or white. You were barely a consciousness. All you were was *there*.

And whoever said that all the darkness in the universe couldn't snuff the light of one candle had never seen the way that endless nothingness swallowed the blazing fires of the *SM*'s floods until they seemed like dying embers on a moonless forest floor.

Down there, you were grateful that there was someone beside you just because they reminded you of what a human being was. Reminding yourself that you were one too was usually the next step. You saw each other differently in the *SM*, while two avatars guided the sub, took the readings, the photographs, the samples, spoke to topside. It wasn't like stepping outside of yourself: it was like the skin shed *you*. The avatar got on with the job, wore the clothes of the geologist or the seismologist, the colleague, the fellow professional. You became passengers, or maybe kids in the back seat. And the people you saw beside you . . . you didn't fear them or feel threatened by them, like you would up above. Maybe it was because, down there, you were truly equal.

Equally insignificant.

Taylor was soon pouring second shots. 'What I still don't understand,' he said, measuring out the last of the bottle, 'is why he would spring for the *SM* if he was gonna shut the project down in a few weeks.'

'Who knows, man?' Cody offered. 'Maybe he found himself a new hobby to spend his allowance on. Just got bored playing with his oceanography toys. We should look on the bright side. CalORI still got itself a state-of-the-art sub out of it, and more than just a paint job for the *Gazes*.'

'I heard that,' agreed Coop. 'Course, he might ask for the *Stella Maris* back if he ever finds out what we've been calling it.'

'He could be planning to take it back anyway,' Taylor said. ''Cause if his prophecy comes true he's gonna need it to get around town.'

Everyone laughed, but when the laughter stopped, they all found themselves involuntarily looking at Mitch. There was a moment's silence.

'I'll fix us some coffee,' he said, getting up from the table. He chucked Cody lightly on the shoulder with his huge knuckles as he moved around behind her, a gesture of reassurance or apology, or something.

'Shit, we out of UHT?' Mitch asked, kneeling down in front of the fridge.

Coop put his hands up.

'Sorry, sorry,' he said. 'My fault. We're not out, I just left the carton through in the Brain.'

'Well go git it, boy,' commanded Mitch, with an exaggerated pointing gesture.

'Yes cap'n, right away Cap'n.'

Mitch poured the coffee into four mugs and carried them over to the table. Taylor up-ended the rest of his brandy into his mug with a shameless grin.

'You're an utter goddamn Philistine,' Cody told him.

'"Remnant of Kaftor,"' he quoted, holding up his mug as if to toast himself, then taking an obviously savoured gulp.

'Hey, now knock it off,' Cody warned. 'We wanted to hear all that shit again, we'd have brought Maria 'stead of you.'

A tributary offshoot of Maria's archaeological preoccupations meant they had all been *very* frequently corrected on the maligned Philistines' cultural superiority to the Israelites. Taylor and Coop were always pulling her chain about it.

'Hey guys, I think you should come see this,' Coop called,

his voice partly muffled by the wood around the tight stairwell.

'Forget it, Coop,' Taylor replied. 'Right now I have just enough energy to crawl to bed, and maybe enough to digest all this shit once I get there. Any extra expenditure would seriously jeopardise all that.'

'Just bring the milk, Coop,' added Mitch.

'I really fuckin' think you should take a look at this,' Coop persisted, his voice now devoid of any mischief or humour.

Mitch sighed and put down his mug, then got up and headed for the Brain. Cody looked at Taylor, who shrugged with a 'search me' widening of his eyes, before getting up too.

'Jesus, I hope he hasn't found something real gross floating in the milk again,' Cody muttered, walking down the stairs. 'I'm like one mouthful off barfing as it is. That second helping of – oh shit . . .'

'Smartass theory, anyone? Coop asked, his face bathed in the blue light of the sonar screen.

The *Gazes Also* was represented by a transparent scale overlay on the centre of the image, the *SM* showing up as a blurred lozenge right alongside. North of them both was a bullet-shaped object, moving nearer to the centre by the second.

'I'd put it at twelve, fifteen feet,' said Coop.

'Shark?' Taylor offered.

'Could just be the image, but it looks too wide to be a fish. Moving pretty slow, too. But whatever it is, it's definitely comin' our way.'

'How deep?' Mitch asked.

Coop adjusted the calibrations on an adjoining computer screen. 'Less than ten feet,' he said. 'It's just below the surface.'

'Whale?' Cody suggested.

'It's possible,' Coop agreed. 'Why don't someone get up top, check out if you can see anything? And if this thing doesn't go deeper or change course, we better get ready for impact.'

'I'll go,' said Cody.

'Me too,' Mitch grunted, bending down to the bulkhead and lifting a flashlight. Cody cut off the CD player as they made their way back through the galley and out on to the aft deck.

Mitch swept a beam of light across the surface of the water. 'See anything?' he asked. Cody shook her head. 'Me neither.'

'Wait,' Cody said. 'Back there.'

'What?' Mitch trained the beam where Cody had pointed, maybe twenty yards away from the boat.

'Bubbles, I think. Gone now. Shit.'

'You see anything?' Coop enquired.

'Nothing, Coop,' Mitch shouted back. 'Some bubbles, is all.'

Mitch swept the flashlight across the glinting blackness again, the pair of them straining at the rail, trying to penetrate the opaque shield with their feeble vision.

'Jesus, guys, tell me you see something,' Coop yelled, a heightened concern in his voice.

'What's wrong, Coop? We near to impact?'

'Please, God, tell me you see something.'

'Talk to us, Coop, what you got down there?'

A few moments later Taylor appeared behind them on deck with another flashlight, furiously plunging its beam towards the water as if the light would cut the surface with a splash.

'Three more shapes just pulled away from it,' he said, urgency in his voice.

'So it's a school of dolphins, maybe?' Cody asked, hopefully.

Taylor shook his head. 'It didn't break up. It's still there, still moving. Three shapes plus *it*.'

'Jesus fucking Christ,' Mitch breathed. 'Talk to us up here, Coop, ' he shouted. 'Tell us what you see.'

'It's slowing down,' Coop replied, 'but the other things ain't. Two of them are headed straight for the boat, and the other one's broken off and veering to one side. Looks like it's makin' for the *SM*. Impact in about three fuckin' seconds.'

Reflexively, all three of them ran to the side, Mitch and Taylor aiming their flashlights at the *SM* where it bobbed gently a few yards from the *Gazes Also*.

'Two seconds.'

'There!' Taylor barked, pointing at a fizz of bubbles bursting on the water between their boat and the sub.

'One second.'

'Jesus, I still don't see jack shit,' Mitch hissed in furious frustration.

'Where are they, Coop? Time's up,' called Cody.

'I don't know. I don't goddamn know. I think they're under the boat. The other one's almost to the *SM*, and the big one's approaching the stern, still about six feet down.'

'This is givin' me a fuckin' heart attack,' Mitch spat. 'What the fuck's goin' on?'

'Jesus, look,' Taylor said.

A black shape began to emerge from the water behind the *SM*, on the far side from the boat. It was a cylindrical metallic object, with a rounded end like a torpedo. It rose into the air, at which point Mitch's flashbeam picked out the rubber-clad arm that was lifting it on to the top of the sub.

'Goddamn propulsion tube. That's a fucking diver,' Mitch growled. 'Hey, what the hell do you think you're doin'?' he shouted.

There was a dull clanging noise from behind. The three of them turned in time to see two more divers clamber over the rail on the other side of the deck.

'What the . . .'

Cody didn't finish her sentence, silenced by the sight of the assault weapons, cocked and levelled, held steady in the dripping hands of the two faceless figures before her.

Then one of them spoke. 'This is your basic nobody-move-nobody-get-hurt deal, okay?' he stated. 'Just do as we say and this'll all go smooth as silk.'

His companion lowered his weapon and slung it around to his side by the strap, then unfastened first his own then the other diver's air tanks. He walked to the aft rail and flashed a torch into the water three times, while the diver who had spoken remained statuesque, gun trained on the three crew, finger around the trigger-guard. The water below the stern of the *Gazes Also* began to erupt in a cauldron of foam and bubbles, from which a fourth diver emerged, gripping the handlebars of an open submersible vehicle, the bullet-shaped object that had shown up on the 'scope. He cast a rope up to the diver at the aft rail, who tied the vessel securely to the *Gazes*. Then he retrieved something from the rear of the submersible and climbed aboard, throwing the object to his companion as he did so. Whatever it was, it appeared to be wrapped in plastic sheeting. The diver let it drop to the deck and nudged it to one side with his foot.

'Where's the other guy?' he said to the diver guarding the three of them.

'Don't know.'

'Go find him then.'

'Yes sir.'

He removed his air tanks as the third diver raised his weapon and resumed guard duties.

Mitch took a deep breath then spoke. 'You gentlemen gonna tell us what it is you want?' he challenged.

The boss, as he appeared to be, took a step closer. 'Are you the captain of this vessel?' he asked.

'Yes I am.'

'Then in that case, Captain, the first thing we want is you.'

Coop, Taylor and Cody had their hands tied behind their backs down in the galley, while the bossman took Mitch down to the Brain, where he wanted something with the ship's log. Cody looked at their captors, the two men in wetsuits, faces obscured, automatic rifles constantly trained. She wanted to wonder where they had come from – they hadn't seen another boat in days – or even what they wanted, but the only thought her mind could process was the desperate hope that they kept their masks on.

Once the prisoners were secured, one of the divers headed back out to the aft deck. 'Everybody stay cool,' he instructed.

Mitch re-emerged from the stairwell, the bossman at his back. Mitch's hands were bound tightly with the same kind of stiff plastic seal as was already gouging welts in his colleagues' wrists.

The diver returned from the aft deck, sticking his head around the door.

'Let's go,' he said.

The bossman and the other diver jabbed at Mitch and Coop with the noses of their guns, indicating all of them to follow the figure at the door. They climbed the steps to the deck, where the front man had halted. He stayed by the doorway and gestured to them to continue walking.

'All right, stop there,' he said. 'Now spread out, slowly,

facing us. And don't anybody try anything stupid. You've all been models of co-operation so far, let's not spoil it.'

They stood in a line: Cody, Taylor, Mitch, Coop.

Then Cody looked down and noticed what they were standing on. Plastic sheeting, covering the deck from port to starboard.

Oh Christ.

That was when you were supposed to look to God, to seek salvation, consolation or just explanation, searching for a comforting glimpse of His reason, whatever it might tell you. But instead, that was the moment Cody saw the real secrets of the universe.

The helpless desolation of solitude.

The conspired illusion of order.

The dance we called morality.

No meaning, only incident; and sometimes record, for those few who might read it. Like the changes in the rocks, but far briefer, far smaller.

Incident.

Explosion. A first explosion, and from it the elements. Gases, solids, liquids. The shaping of the bodies. The cooling of the continents. The forming of the waters. The accident of life.

The change and process we groped clumsily to grasp, fashioning our own crude picture of its shadow like the wretches in Plato's cave. The picture we called Chemistry.

Energy, endlessly metamorphosising, the act of each manifestation in itself precipitating the next transformation.

Explosion. A last explosion. Chemical energy becoming light, sound, kinesis. Propelling metal, hurtling, spinning.

Through skin.

Through flesh.

Through bone.

Through brain.

III

the blood-dimmed tide

I'm fed up with all these Weary Willies saying
'Thou shalt not. Thou shalt not.'
Yes, we fuckin' *shall*!

Billy Connolly

fifteen

'That is my information, Suzie, yes. There have been news helicopters circling overhead for about an hour as dawn approaches, but none of them got any footage of Madeleine Witherson and her police escort's arrival. It is possible that she may have already been in the hotel before the announcement was made. The likelihood is that she is in the south wing of the building, most of which was left undamaged by yesterday's bomb blast. The beachside terrace is, as you may have seen from our skycam footage, strewn with wreckage – a lot of the debris from the hotel lobby has been dragged out there – but police and hotel staff have cleared a space near the edge of the swimming pool, and a camera crew has been allowed to start setting up in that area. That crew is from a different network but I've been assured that their pictures will be simulcast on all stations.

'As you probably heard, the police have appealed to the public to stay away from the Pacific Vista, but that plea seems to have fallen on deaf ears. The hotel beach itself is cordoned off, but a small crowd started gathering either side of the barriers yesterday after the bomber transmitted his new appointed venue, and they've been there since, kind of reserving their ringside seats. There are reports that they even had a beach barbecue, and certainly there were fires burning down by the ocean throughout the night. But since this *morning*'s announcement, as you can imagine, Joe Public has been rolling up in droves. I'm told the centre of Santa Monica is gridlocked with cars bringing people to the beachfront area, and there's even been a few motor launches dropping anchor out there.'

'Bob, if I can interrupt for a second, we've had some callers back here asking about the legal implications of what – it now appears – is about to take place this morning. They've been pointing out that suicide is, technically, illegal, and yet the authorities are allowing and even assisting Madeleine Witherson, who has stated her intention to take her own life.'

'Well, Suzie, the same thought did strike me, and I talked to one police officer who said simply, "Who's gonna hold up a badge and say 'Stop' when there's eighty-eight other lives on the line? Not me."'

'It's a very good point, Bob, thanks. However, it seems pro-Life groups aren't so convinced by that rationale. Mary Jo Brennan from the Sacred Heart Trust has been on the phone to say that it is for God only to take life, and . . .'

'Christ, can't we turn that shit off?' asked a tired voice, but everybody knew they couldn't. Maybe change the channel for a different running-bullshit accompaniment, but not cut off the images coming from that hotel.

Jo yawned and shifted position on the floor, her back against a seat, her ass almost numb from reclining there so many endless hours. The boat had been told the news before anyone else, as they were the ones most in need of reassurance. Veltman had received a call and then relayed it to everyone on board, with the instruction that they weren't to go calling their families yet as the cops wanted strict control over when this information went public. It seemed a lot to ask, with people painfully aware of what their loved ones were going through back home, but then they were all learning a new perspective on the concept of sacrifice.

The reaction was far from euphoric. Everyone was feeling the same thing: a tentative, cautious relief, and equal shame at whatever comfort it gave them. Some of them couldn't bear to look each other in the eye, although that might have had as much to do with what had gone before as what was about to happen. Suffice it to say, dignity had been the first casualty when night fell and the fear really set in.

The illuminated decks became surrounded by a thick blackness, sparsely punctuated by the lights of the surrounding vessels, all of which seemed further away now that their lamps were all you could see. That was when tough talk made way for desperation, and that in turn for abject stupidity.

First, several of the execs decided that this was a problem their lawyers darn well *should* be able to sort out for them, and started punching away at their mobiles while the batteries still held out. The world and his dog were going to be sued, by the sound of it. Luther St John first, for making threatening speeches, which was 'incitement to something or other, I ain't sure what yet, but I want his ass in court'. Pretty soon they moved on to the cops and the FBI for not having caught the bad guy yet, which led inexorably to asking 'how shitty the security must have been for this asshole to have got on board and planted not just his holy hand-grenade of Antioch, but all his gadgets too'.

Phones were dispensed with as a grumbling group moved in on Veltman and Baird, the latter as representative of the charter firm, the former for having organised the whole thing and invited them on board his floating Pinto.

'What you got lined up for Cannes, Linus?' one shouted. 'A re-enactment of the *Challenger* disaster maybe?'

A potentially very ugly development was defused by the distraction of a fight breaking out on the aft sun-deck, where Nova Image's Jack Ritchie and EyeCandy's CEO Saul Fleder were rolling around on the floor. It was only when Jo noticed a surplus to the regular number of arms and legs that it became apparent they were not in fact duking it out, but teaming up to restrain the surgically sculpted action-Aryan Max Michaels. Michaels had committed himself to EyeCandy for three pictures in the 'fifteen-to-twenty-million-dollar budget range' (actually five-to-seven), but as this was before their CEO sat on his head, Jo hoped they had it all down on paper.

Michaels had evidently reasoned that there was little chance the bomber would notice one person slipping over the side and swimming across to the safety of the police launches. Fleder had spotted him taking off his shoes and socks and reasoned differently. 'We're not gonna be the stake for your bet, asshole,' Saul had explained, as Baird helped tie the muscleman's hands together to discourage any further excursions. Jo was faintly concerned that she had seen Michaels extricate himself from just such a knot in *Vendetta II*, but then in that movie he had also beaten the shit out of several guys a lot bigger than the five-foot Saul Fleder or the sixty-two-year-old Jack Ritchie.

But the worst hideousness of that longest, darkest night of the (ass) soul had to be Paul Silver's fevered and insistent orchestration of a Christian prayer ceremony. Jo thought Silver had flipped into catatonia earlier, having burned himself out in a relentless, turbo-boosted stream-of-consciousness. Any time she'd met him he'd struck her as a vessel of concentrated nervous energy, which made him real useful when there was a job to do, but the last person you wanted near you at a time like this. Truth was – and you could ask anyone – Paul Silver was regarded as a good man in a crisis, because he'd do whatever and as much as he could to alleviate it. But in a situation where there was nothing anyone could do, well, all that nervous energy had to find an outlet somewhere. The high-octane head-rant had merely been the overture; the period of catatonia time for the orchestra to rest and retune.

A small group of execs with predominantly Irish and Italian surnames had gathered in Silver's quiet vicinity to say a few prayers that everything was going to work out. Observing this Catholic pow-wow, he hit upon an idea that was less than inspired, and even further from divine. Silver figured it might stay the bomber's hand if they all made a show of reverent Christian prayer for his cameras; there was no sound link, so hopefully he would interpret it as an act of penitence or even just as evidence that they were all a whole lot more God-fearin' than he had assumed.

Convinced that this could be their salvation, Silver had embarked upon a frenetic campaign of evangelism to amass a devout host of head-bowed Christians on the main deck. What made it worse was that there were so many takers, many of whom were equally Jewish.

Jo refused any part of the dismal pantomime, and hoped fervently that the bomber wasn't watching too closely. It was unlikely enough he'd be buying any of this wholesale Damascene conversion bullshit, but the flapping attempts at a sign of the Cross proliferating around the deck were less a giveaway than an act of provocation.

'Dumb schmucks,' muttered a guy beside her, Lenny Weiskov, one of the few who had resisted Silver's entreaties. 'What do they think, the bomber's gonna believe this was some gentiles' day out? It's the movie business, for cryin' out loud. Jews pretending to be Christians – pah! Jews in the movie business shouldn't even pretend to be *religious*. It's incompatible from an early age – kids' matinée's always been on the same day as schule.'

* * *

It had been a long night for Daniel Corby too. Everything had gone off without a hitch, but none of it had made him feel quite the way he'd hoped or expected, and darkness had brought its demons. The sense of purpose, the feeling of control, had been surging through him throughout the scheming and preparation, and had grown in its intensity right up until he triggered the detonator at the Pacific Vista. Nothing seemed quite so certain after that moment as it had before; not even his own conviction.

Filth-peddlers and pornographers bled, he had learned, just like anyone else. Copiously, in fact, according to the collage of TV images. Their flesh yielded also to flame and steel and glass. And however damned their souls, their bodies were nonetheless a pitiful sight as they staggered or were carried from the hotel. Blood-spattered and tearful faces filled every lens. Stretchers with sheets covering faces. Dead people. Murdered people.

Murdered by him.

He hadn't meant it to be so big. He'd learned plenty more about bombs and explosives since Pocoima, but his judgement as regards quantity was still way out, especially as he knew so little about the fabrics and construction of such a weird edifice as the Pacific Vista's landmark canopy. It was supposed to be a firm, even shocking declaration of intent; he hadn't meant to total the place.

Daniel tried to re-summon up all his hatred, concentrating on his greater mission, and thought hard about Luther St John's powerful words. But while St John remained in the realm of words, Daniel had moved into the world of deeds, and the two were a long way apart. He had stuck to his schedule and continued with the plan, sending over a new venue for the sacrifice, but he feared this might have been because he didn't know what else to do. As events unfolded, he found himself praying that Witherson would go through with it – not for all the reasons he'd intended, but so that he could feel that something had been achieved, that it had all been worth it.

He hadn't been ready for those TV images. He'd thought only of his plan, of Witherson, of God, and planting his bombs had been like playing cards, a matter of strategy. It was almost as though he'd forgotten what those things actually did. The pictures reminded him of the World Trade Center and, inevitably, of Oklahoma City, which prompted an even more urgent concern, regarding electric chairs and lethal injections. Until then, he hadn't given a second's thought to the consequences for himself of getting caught, only of the consequences for the success of his mission.

He watched the famous faces on his TV screens, faces he saw every day, every night, faces who had always seemed a world away behind desks, under studio lights, surrounded by captions and logos and talking heads. Tonight they were all talking about what had happened today; what he had *done* today. And the more they talked, the more the enormity of what he had unleashed seemed to grow.

It took serious nerve not to panic. Crazy, desperate thoughts began flitting into his head, and sometimes not flitting out again too quickly. It would do no good to give himself up, he knew. Charged with killing eight (or did they say nine now?) people, it wasn't going to be much of a mitigation to point out that he had held off killing eighty-eight more. His thoughts turned to flight. Blow the house up behind him, obliterating all the evidence. But then maybe such an explosion would only lead them to discover that the place's occupant had been the bomber, and his name and picture would top America's Most Wanted within hours. Maybe he should just pack a bag, disengage the failsafe, get in the car and split, come back when they had busted some other guy for it all.

But weakened as it was, he still couldn't completely shake off the belief that had brought him to this juncture. Inside, he still knew that he had to make this happen, that America had to get that wake-up call through Witherson's death. He had to stay strong, resist the allures of ease and security, as the Lord had done in the desert. After all, if God didn't want this to happen, He could stop it, couldn't he? And yet it was all running smoothly. Maybe it was all going to be worth it, he pondered. Maybe he just needed to have faith.

That was when the phone rang. He feared the worst initially, but then it struck him that if he'd been fingered, they wouldn't just call him up.

It was Nate, the nearest thing the Southland Militia had to a tech-head, whom Daniel had dealt with when he was setting up their Internet sites. To his shock, Nate informed

Daniel that they knew he was the bomber, but this was eased by the qualification that it was St John who'd worked it out and told them, and eased further by the hearty assurance that they were all right behind him.

'The Reverend would like us to bring you in for a little chat when it's all over,' Nate added. 'So we can talk about where we all go from here. He's real impressed, let me tell you. Mind if I come over right now to catch the big finale?'

'Do I mind? Hey, bring a six-pack!'

When Daniel put down the phone it took admirable restraint not to physically jump for joy. This was surely God's way of telling him he had passed the test of temptation, and his faith was about to receive fitting reward.

If Jo was embarrassed by the antics of her fellow hostages, they seemed models of solemn propriety compared to the circus sideshow going on all around them. The TV news 'copters had often been compared to vultures, but seldom had the parallel been so close; they had deserted the *Ugly Duckling* and headed for the Pacific Vista when they learned that was where the fresh blood would be.

Jo felt the tight grip she'd kept on her outrage loosening as she saw what an infotainment spectacle this was all being turned into. She saw shots of the crowds gathering on the beach, the camera picking out the placards being held up. 'The wages of sin is death,' said one. 'Bleed for your sins Witherson,' said another, while a third opted simply for 'Burn baby burn'.

There seemed little doubt that the networks were going to broadcast the event itself, ostensibly for the eyes of the bomber, but Jo couldn't help choking on the irony. These were the same terrestrial channels on which you couldn't use the word 'fuck' or show some bare tits.

Like the guy who'd shouted, Jo wished they could turn it off. She wished she could take a walk around to part of the boat where there wasn't a TV screen. But she couldn't, no more than any of the eighty-seven others on the *Ugly Duckling*. Because whatever assurances they had been given, they knew they weren't getting off the bomb-rigged hulk until they saw Maddy Witherson actually do this.

*   *   *

'A Worldwide TV special in suicide-vision, courtesy of Daaahn-yeeeel Corbeee! Wooh!' Vern said, clapping his hands. 'Hey, c'mon man, you're missin' your own show,' he added. Nate glanced up and rolled his eyes. Vern was slapping Corby on the back and pointing to the TV screens, but Corby wasn't watching, having limited his activities to dangling limply from a rope tied over one of the basement's ceiling beams.

Liskey had commissioned Nate for the hit because Corby knew him. They figured he wasn't going to be in much of a mind to open the door to strangers, and that night he was unlikely even to answer the doorbell, so Nate had phoned ahead. Corby was happy for Nate to come round and enjoy the show; in fact happy wasn't even close. It must have been eating Corby alive that he had pulled all this shit off but couldn't tell anyone about it. Showing off his handiwork to sympathetic Militia members had probably made him come in his shorts. And if what they say is true, he'd have come in them again when Vern suddenly slung a noose around his neck and hauled him up.

'Shit, this is for real,' Vern said, staring at the identical images on the six TV screens set up around the desk. Add the three computer monitors and they were probably getting more radiation off this gig than Liskey would planting the nukes. 'The porno broad's really goin' through with it, look.'

'Well, I'm kinda busy right now, Vern, but I'm sure it's real exciting,' Nate told him, his fingers rattling impatiently across the keyboard. The guy's set-up was a nightmare of mutated technology: self-customised boards, chips and cards all wired up to each other like they had been built by the fucking Borg. It served as a worrying reminder that Corby had probably forgotten more about computers than Nate had ever learned – and much of what he had learned he had learned from Corby. Nate was supposed to be wiping anything that could connect the guy to the Militia or St John, but it was almost literally like walking through a minefield: Corby himself had told him the system was booby-trapped. If you tried screwing around with the detonator control programme, you'd set off the bomb on the *Ugly Duckling*. Same went if the computer detected a change in the signals coming from his TV cameras, so the cops couldn't loop in a fake shot while they evacuated the boat. Same went if you shut down the system or if you wiped the whole thing.

But the bomb on the boat wasn't Nate's problem. He was more concerned about whether the asshole might have a bomb concealed a little more locally, like right under where he was sitting, as a built-in revenge against the Feds if they got to him. A booby-trap intended for anyone who went snooping around the secrets of Corby's computers in his absence. It wasn't as paranoid a concern as it sounded: Nate had rigged up precisely such a trap on the Militia's own system. He'd never mentioned it to Corby, but Nate was unlikely to be the only guy in the world ever to have had the idea. Of course, if he was right then they could walk out the door and wait for some dumb field agent to wipe the evidence for them in one big bang, but if he was wrong then there might be all sorts of incriminating shit for the Feds to sift through. As Liskey pointed out, this guy could've been stockpiling stuff to offer up in a deal to avoid the chair if he got caught.

Christ, he thought, sweat forming on his forehead as he opened another file. Why couldn't the fucker have lived in Venice, someplace on the coast? That way him and his fucking system would just get washed away. But Glendale was probably only going to get its carpets wet, so here they were.

'Girl's gonna kill herself on national TV,' Vern muttered. 'Wonder what they're charging for spots. More than for the Superbowl, is my guess.'

Nate needed to be rational about this. Corby had obviously learned plenty about making bombs since the abortion clinic deal St John had told Liskey about; the big hole in the Pacific Vista illustrated that. But on another monitor he could see the bomb on the *Ugly Duckling*, and could see also why Corby had placed it under his own surveillance. It would sure do the job, explosion-wise, but it wouldn't take a bomb-squad technician five minutes to defuse it. He was still a long way short of being an expert, and he knew it.

Corby had blown himself up once and been lucky because the explosive wasn't powerful enough. What he was using these days was a different story. Would he – knowing his past record – really take a chance on rigging up something like that under his own ass?

'Fuck it, I'm just gonna wipe the whole thing,' Nate decided aloud.

'But won't that set off the bomb on the boat?'

'Sure, but who gives a shit? They're all gonna be dead in a coupla days anyway. We're planting nuclear fucking weapons off the coast of LA and you're worried about blowin' up eighty-eight people?'

'No, it ain't that. If you blow up the hostages, the girl won't need to do this. I wanna see if she really has the guts to off herself.'

'You're sick, Vern.'

'We're just talkin' a few more minutes, man. Come on. I got a hundred bucks says she goes through with it. If she chickens out, it's yours. You can go ahead and clear the system after that.'

Nate looked up at the TV screens, all but two of them showing Madeleine Witherson's face, pale, tearful and nervous, as she stood by the Pacific Vista's beachside swimming-pool. She looked like she might pass out from fear at any second. A hundred bucks. Jesus. A short time from now they'd be millionaires, and there'd be an annual hush bonus topping it up, too. He sighed and smiled.

'Shit. All right, you're on. It's just about dawn now – I'll give her five minutes to start slicin' for your hundred bucks. After all, that's how our late buddy here would have wanted it.'

A motor launch bearing a network camera crew pulled up to join the ring of police and coastguard vessels surrounding the *Ugly Duckling*, all engines idling.

There was unbroken hush across the boat as pictures of Witherson's emergence from the hotel came into focus on the TV screens. With all voices silenced, the sound of waves lapping gently against the hull could be heard above the noise of the television. There was something perversely idyllic about it, Jo thought, looking up momentarily at the blue skies of a crisp, silent dawn over the Pacific.

Witherson wore a white dress. Given the nature of what they were dealing with, it had obviously been decided there was no point skimping on the symbolism. The camera zoomed in on her face. She looked scared to death. There were no more aerial pictures now, just the shots from the crew that had been

314

given access to the terrace. Jo wondered distantly about how they had decided which broadcaster got the nod, and guessed the LAPD would be getting a shitty press from the others for the foreseeable future.

Witherson looked straight into the camera.

'I have something to say,' she announced, swallowing. She closed her eyes tightly as if fighting back tears.

'I want to apologise. I want to say sorry and beg the forgiveness of the Lord, and of the Lord's people whom my life has offended. I have been a sinner. I have sinned against God's Word and against God's law. I have denied the Lord. I have been a heathen and a fornicator. I have led a life of carnal lust and shameful example, and I accept now that these sins have polluted the world.'

She swallowed again, tears visible around her reddening eyes.

'I accept also that the wages of sin is death.' Now her voice broke up and the tears ran down her cheeks. 'Romans 6:23. But that verse also says the gift of God is eternal life in Jesus Christ our Lord. I do not deserve such a gift, but ask only that . . . that my death will spare those eighty-eight other sinners, so that they may yet have the chance to see the light in *this* life, accept God into their hearts – and change their ways for ever.

'May they find . . .' She sobbed, her face contorting with tears as she struggled to speak. Her last words were a broken whisper. 'May they find salvation through my death.'

Witherson knelt on the ground before the swimming-pool, in which blast debris could be seen floating. She was side-on to the camera, which pulled back to reveal a med team standing a few yards away: doctor, paramedics, nurses.

'God, looks like a fuckin' state execution,' muttered Lenny Weiskov.

'It is,' Jo replied.

Witherson produced a long knife, which she gripped tremblingly in both hands.

'Aw Jesus,' another voice gasped.

She brought it up to her neck, bowing over to meet it. Then she stopped and collapsed into sobbing. Nobody breathed. They were all thinking the same thing, heaven forgive them.

Witherson's back straightened once more and she lifted the

blade up to the side of her neck. She applied pressure and drew it across.

'Aw Jesus. Aw Jesus fucking Christ.'

The blood seemed to well over the blade at first, running down her neck and chest and on to the dress. Then there was a spurt from somewhere, arcing out of the wound like it was a busted garden hose, provoking further gasps from those who were still watching. Witherson's hands dropped to her lap, the blade clattering to the ground in front of her. Gradually, as if in slow motion, she slumped forward and lay down at the side of the pool, blood pumping out from her carotid artery and washing over the side into the water.

There was a sound of engines, startling all of them in their entranced silence. The police launches were moving in, getting ready for the evacuation. People started climbing to their feet, looking back and forth uncertainly at each other and at the image on the TV screen. Witherson's body lay still while the red fluid continued to trickle out into the swimming pool, clouding amid the dust and flotsam.

The launches stopped a few yards short of the *Ugly Duckling*. Shouts were exchanged. Jo picked up something about 'waiting for the doctor's declaration'. On the TV screen, sure enough, the doctor was standing over Witherson, motioning to the paramedics to stay back. He held one of her hands in both of his, presumably testing for a pulse. Then he knelt down beside her and took hold of her head, his back to the camera.

A short time later he stood up, ran a hand through his hair and nodded to one of his assistants. Jo was no lip-reader, but she could still make out 'She's dead,' from the doctor's mouth. One of the nurses could be seen crying in the corner of the shot. The doctor approached the camera, whereupon his name and hospital were flashed up at the bottom of the screen.

'I have checked for vital signs,' he said, anger barely concealed beneath the calm timbre of his voice, 'and it is my reluctant duty to confirm that Madeleine Witherson died a few moments ago. Now if you will excuse me, I wish to leave. I want no further part in this.'

The police boats began moving again, pulling right up alongside the *Ugly Duckling* and throwing ropes across to Baird and his crew members. Boarding planks were being lowered into place at the stern and on both sides of the deck, the cops motioning to the passengers to come forward.

'Wait a second,' said Paul Silver nervously, as the people around them started surging towards the gangways. 'I know the girl's been declared dead, but isn't there supposed to be any kind of green light from the bomber?'

'Oh for Christ's sake, come on,' Jo urged, pushing Silver forward impatiently. 'The guy's got what he wanted. To be blunt, if he's still planning to blow us up, it won't be because we're being presumptuous. He got Witherson – let's get off this thing before he starts asking for the President.'

'I'd stay on for the President,' growled Weiskov. 'Can we nominate?'

'Get off the fucking boat, Len.'

'Live snuff movies on daytime television. I ask you, Nate, what is the world coming to?'

'Isn't "live snuff" an oxymoron?'

'A what?'

'Never mind.'

'Pretty gross, though, huh? That bit when it squirted. Blech. Kitchens all across America man, bye-bye breakfast, I'm tellin' you. Like something out of that *ER* show.'

'Must have hit an artery. Big red mess.'

'Yep. Colour of money, Nate. One hundred dollars flowing right out of her neck and into my pocket – via *your* wallet. Come on, ain't you done yet? I've seen this erasing shit before. You just drag everything into the little trash basket and that's that.'

'Well it's just a little more complicated in this case, Vern, but thanks for offering me your considerable knowledge and expertise.'

'This is takin' too long. Why can't we just shoot the shit out of the thing?'

'Why didn't you just shoot the shit out of Corby?'

''Cause it had to look like a suicide.'

'Exactly, and this has to look like he wiped his own stuff, okay?'

'Yeah, okay. Just hurry it up – the world's gonna start peeling itself off the TV screen pretty soon.'

'Well you were the asshole wanted to watch *Good Morning Suicide*, otherwise we'd already be gone.'

'Yeah, okay, okay. Hey what does that mean?'

Active files could not be erased. Close and erase all applications? <u>Y</u>es/<u>N</u>o

'At last. It means we're one keystroke away from outtahere.'

'Cool.'

<u>Y</u>.

Boom.

Larry was sitting at the bureau in the Pacific Vista suite they were using as an *ad hoc* operations room, praying to the great gods Caffeine and Aspirin to give him the strength to get through this. He heard noises in the corridor outside. There was a TV on in the suite, and all stations were showing the action from down by the pool. Well, maybe not all stations. He hadn't checked Nickelodeon or the Home Shopping Network, but give it a month and the former would have an animated version and the latter would be selling commemorative kitchen knives.

From the window Larry had seen the paramedics lift Witherson's body on to a gurney before rolling her back into the building. Kennedy was first through the door of the suite, holding it open and gesturing to Larry to close the curtains.

'Show some fuckin' respect, Sergeant,' he commanded.

There was a blanket draped over the body, but the blood had soaked through it in dark patches around the chest. The paramedics stepped away from the gurney as Steel pulled up the rear and closed the door.

'She gave her life for our sins,' Kennedy pronounced solemnly, placing a hand over his heart and looking down at the gurney, which erupted in movement as an arm threw off the blanket.

'Yeah, but I ain't waiting three days to rise again – I need a shower right now.'

Witherson sat up and wiped a red-stained hand on her white dress. Kennedy took her arm and helped her off the

318

gurney. She reached up and planted a kiss on his right cheek, at which he smiled bashfully; the guy behind the camera seldom enjoys the limelight.

'So, everybody get off the boat yet?' she asked.

'Still waiting for confirmation,' Larry told her. 'I think one of the networks has pictures, though.' He reached for the remote and flicked through the stations until the parade of aghast reporters gave way to diminishing images of the *Ugly Duckling*. The camera crew's boat, like the others, was pulling back fast from the centre of attention.

'Yeah, looks like your canonisation papers'll be coming through, Miss Witherson.'

'So what happens now?' she asked.

There was a crackling sound from the TV, followed a few seconds later by a muffled bang from outside the window, just like Larry had heard at his desk yesterday morning. Everyone looked instantly at the TV.

'Jesus,' was the consensus. Witherson, having recently risen from the dead, sensitively resisted the temptation to say 'Yes?'

The *Ugly Duckling* was obscured by flames, smoke and heat-haze. A reporter's voice was burbling hysterically amid the pandemonium. He was taking an awful long time and using an awful lot of words just to say the boat had blown up.

The sound of a mobile phone broke the stunned silence a few moments later. Steel, over by the door, reached into his pocket and held the fragile-looking little black pad up to his face.

'They were all off,' he relayed to the room. 'Nobody was on board when it blew. No major injuries. Just a few cuts from flying splinters here and there, and probably a change of underwear all round.' Steel lowered his voice again and resumed talking to his ocean-bound associate.

'Do you think he made us?' Witherson asked.

'Doubt it,' Larry said. 'Maybe just the opposite. Got what he wanted, then suffered a serious dose of anti-climax. His fun's over, his fifteen minutes are up. So now we have to hope that he's suicidal. Otherwise he's soon gonna want another day in the sun, and we could be looking at Unabomber II.'

'Oh terrific. Think I'll stay dead.'

319

'That can be arranged.'

She smiled and headed for the larger of the suite's two bathrooms, picking up a bag of clothes retrieved from her apartment by Pedro Arguello as she went.

Kennedy got himself a bottle of still water from the minibar and sat down opposite Larry, throwing his head back against the sofa and sighing loudly. One of the 'paramedics', make-up effects artist Josie Orland, stepped over and patted the big photographer on the head, ruffling his hair.

'Best director I ever worked with, man,' she said.

Kennedy smiled and gulped back some water.

Larry gave a loud laugh, out of relief and probably a little nervous hysteria. Another day like this and he'd be turning into Herbert Lom in those Pink Panther movies.

On reflection it wasn't really so strange that it had taken Kennedy to come up with this: maybe everyone else was too used to living in this town to have that kind of perspective. Despite the bombs, the fear and the pervading air of insanity, Kennedy hadn't lost the first-time visitor's perception that this was La-la land: the world capital of faking it.

Brisko had been apprehensive, pointing out that there would be no opportunity for reshoots if this went wrong. Kennedy, in return, had pointed out that they weren't exactly tripping over alternatives, and suggested Brisko extend whatever co-operation he could: they were going to get ready for showtime at sun-up; if the cavalry got a result in the hours that remained, they'd be only too happy to cancel.

Witherson's agent, Tony Pia, armed only with a Psion and a mobile, assembled a production team at the Vista in less than an hour. Pia's brother Marco, a leading porn-movie director, was to be cameraman, with sound and lighting handled by his regular assistants. All of them seemed to be on kiss-hello terms with Witherson. That didn't always mean much in this town, but Larry figured it did today. It wasn't much of an occasion for affectation.

The Feds came up with a real doctor and some real paramedics to add authenticity to the 'confirmation of death' procedures. The doc had no ethical issues to wrestle with as regards complicity in this gross act of public deception. 'It's my job to keep people alive', he said simply. 'That's what we're doing.'

The star performer, however, was Orland, who turned up with two heavy boxes of tricks and a reassuringly tacky CV. *Fangoria* magazine had once called her 'Queen of the Carotid' in reverential appreciation of her work on dozens of slasher flicks, significantly VisionTek's *The Peeler* franchise. Significantly, because VisionTek's Alison Moore (producer of *Night of the Peeler*, two sequels and the forthcoming *Children of the Peeler*), as well as being Orland's long-term girlfriend, was on the *Ugly Duckling*.

Orland covered Witherson's neck with a latex layer that concealed a small reservoir of fake blood and a slim, transparent plastic syphon tube. The reservoir was to provide the first evidence of the blade cutting flesh, but the 'fatal' damage would be apparent from the spurting carotid. The tube led down to a number of bloodbags attached to Witherson's body, the jet driven by a pump attached to her navel. Orland had placed the largest two bags on Witherson's chest ('the only place a bulge won't be conspicuous – sorry honey, but you ain't stacked') and layered another latex strip over the top of her bust before covering it all with thick foundation.

Kennedy directed how he wanted the show to unfold, explaining the shot sequence carefully to Marco Pia so that Orland's handiwork wasn't subject to intense scrutiny: close-up on Madeleine's face for the penitential bullshit, showing nothing below the chin; then pull way back for the suicide.

Orland showed Madeleine how to handle the blade, doing a test run on her wrist with another latex-covered reservoir. Kennedy suggested she kneel side-on to the camera when she did the deed, and reminded her to fall forward when she collapsed 'so that nobody notices your boobs deflating'.

Of course, the above-the-line star of this picture was Witherson, who was a revelation. By the time she'd keeled over Larry thought she was so convincing he might now actually have to go and see *Angel's Claws*. Admittedly it was something of a method performance: eighty-eight lives were riding on her pulling it off, so if she looked authentically terrified then that was probably because she was. Still, he'd seen Oscars given for less. Much less, if you were talking about *Forrest Gump*.

It was the turn of Larry's mobile to disturb the exhaustedly quiet atmosphere. He instantly recognised the voice as Bannon's.

'Larry. Thought you should know this. We got reports coming in about a major explosion.'

'Yeah, I know, it's cool. Everybody got off in time. Splinters in the ass, I'll bet, but—'

'No, not the boat, Larry. A building. Domestic address in Glendale just went kaboom. Local dispatch got about ten calls in the last few minutes, all witnesses timing the explosion at roughly the same moment the *Ugly Duckling* went up. Hell of a coincidence, huh? I figured you might want to let your little FBI buddies know, if they don't know already.'

'Thanks boss.'

Hell of a coincidence. Sounded like they could cancel Unabomber II, and what a sweet, sweet sound that was. It was the sound of sheets being pulled back on the bed he was planning to weld himself to as soon as possible.

Steel's phone rang before Larry could get his attention, but all he needed to hear was 'Really? In Glendale?' to know he had been scooped.

'Sergeant,' Steel said, hanging up, 'I've just heard . . .'

'Yeah, me too. Puréed perpetrator, I'm figuring.'

'Well, either that or I'm about to drive across town through rush-hour to check out a gas explosion. What are your plans?'

'Plans? Right now? What are you, a speed-freak? My plan is to go straight home this minute and have me a miniature coma. Call me in a month, I might be out of it by then. And remember I said "might".'

Steff woke up to two surprises. The first was that he had been to sleep. The second was that Madeleine's body was tucked behind his, her knees pressing into the backs of his thighs, her left arm slung over his side, hand resting against his chest. It had been the kind of sleep that follows long-haul flights: short, heavy-limbed, disorientating, taken at an inappropriate hour of the day, and when you woke you felt (a) that you'd been out for three times as long as you really had; and (b) that it was still nowhere near enough.

Focus returned to his confused eyes, enough to tell him he was in a room far too grand and insufficiently pink for it to be his billet at the Armada, and to read from a matchbook in a

322

bedside ashtray that this was, in fact, the Pacific Vista. As the shampoo and perfume scents of Madeleine's hair and body wafted freshly into his nostrils, he enjoyed a brief, wonderful, bleary moment of wrongly piecing together what he was doing here. They had met for a photo-shoot on the Vista's roof. This was Madeleine's suite. They were on a big double bed together. Everything must have gone very smoothly indeed.

Then his eyes picked out the once-white, red-spattered dress lying crumpled on the floor, like a prop from the Madonna video *he'd* have made.

Aww, keech.

Bombs. Blood. Dead people. Mental Christians. Polis. FBI.

He closed his eyes again, but none of it was going to go away now; his oblivion prescription had run out. He saw the messenger being washed away again, Madeleine buffeted in the swimming-pool. He saw panic and chaos hundreds of feet below his dangling legs.

Funny. The cops, the FBI guys, Madeleine's agent, they had all bailed out to a room down the hall to give her some peace. No, to give *them* some peace. They were being treated like a married couple or something.

He wished.

Madeleine had lain down on one of the double beds to get some seriously overdue rest. Steff thought his head was buzzing far too much for him to get any sleep, but flopped down on the other bed anyway. Turned out there were more zeds in buzzing than he'd previously appreciated.

Steff got up delicately, sliding out from Madeleine's grip so as not to disturb her. He stood by the bed and looked at her a moment, lying peacefully there, and remembered the girl he had been standing waiting for yesterday. The girl who'd made him feel like a teenager again – that's who was lying there. Not the hurt, scared and haunted girl, but the one who'd filled his head with thoughts and words not normally acceptable in a big cynical bastard from Lanarkshire.

Thoughts and words which, he was comforted to discover, all still applied.

He walked quietly through to the bathroom and took a shower.

He'd been standing in the tub a long while, letting the water splash his face, enjoying the warmth, the comfort and the lack

323

of threat from high explosives, when he thought he heard footsteps. With the noise of the shower in his ears he couldn't be sure. Then he definitely heard the curtain being tugged back. He turned around. Madeleine was stepping naked into the bath beside him. They were kissing before she got her other foot over the side.

They both dropped to their knees with the spray cascading warmly about them, pulling themselves to each other and just holding that embrace, Madeleine's face buried in his neck, her arms gripping him as tightly as on that rooftop. He felt like he never wanted to let go, never wanted that moment to end.

Until she reached over the side to where she'd left a condom.

He could live with it ending after that.

Larry got bored staring at the ceiling after a valiant three hours of trying to get to sleep. The Land of Nod's borders remained closed, due to breaking off diplomatic relations with the neighbouring republic of La-la Land. He should have known better. There are times when you're so physically tired that you can't sleep, often because your brain is still processing shit left over from whatever exertion had you bushed in the first place. But that was only part of the story. Something else wouldn't let him rest, and it wasn't any cop's sixth-sense mumbo-jumbo – just the simple nagging in his head that this wasn't over, at least until he got confirmation of what they had scraped off the sidewalk in Glendale.

The Vista thing had all gone family-sized, with the Feds muscling in and the media beaming the whole show to a worldwide audience of ghouls, remotes in one hand, dicks in the other. But at the very core it was still homicide on *his* turf – a section of turf he was specifically looking after these two weeks – and he didn't have a perp.

He had come in the door as Sophie was going out. They had time for one hug in the hallway.

'Call in sick, baby,' he'd pleaded half-heartedly.

'I'm not going to the school just now, I'm going to the clinic.'

'Oh shit, I forgot. Hey, let me come with you.'

'Go to bed, Larry. I've seen *some* sicknotes in my job, and the day you just had definitely gets you out of this morning's classes.'

It told him how tired he was that he agreed. Accompanying Sophie to the doc's had become the closest thing in his life to religious observance, and like religious observance it had all the trappings of irrational superstition. He felt like if he didn't go with her, if he wasn't present, there would be bad news; if he couldn't be there to protect her, that would be the time she had to face something awful. Maybe he was just scared of hearing anything second-hand, like there was anything he could change if he was there when the news was broken.

A male thing, he knew. It was an ugly hangover from what had happened to David: the paralysing feeling of impotence, of uselessness, sitting on those plastic seats waiting for updates from exhausted-looking doctors. Having nothing to offer Sophie but arms to hold her and a pocketful of quarters for the coffee machine.

There had been nothing he could do for his own son. Knowing that was like being disembowelled. He hadn't failed David. Maybe it would have seemed different if he had; if he could see what rule he'd broken. But there was nothing he had done wrong, and nothing he could do to put it right, neither. It was as though he wasn't there at all.

That was when people were supposed to turn to God, wasn't it?

Larry had gone to church with his mom every Sunday morning until he was old enough to be allowed to go alone, to a different service if he liked. He chose the service two blocks away: there was an altar at each end, recognisable by a wooden board with a hoop in front of it. Since then, if someone had asked him he'd have said he believed in God, but the truth was he hadn't ever much thought about it.

He was damn well forced to think about it in that waiting room, and realised not only that he didn't believe, but also that he never really had. It wasn't a case of abandoning God because he felt God had abandoned him: that was no better than the rock singers and movie stars who were always thanking God and Jesus and babbling on about their 'faith'. Pretty easy to believe there's a Divine Plan when the Divine Plan has such a sweet role in it for you, and the flipside is denying the same DP just because it deals you a shitty hand. That isn't atheism, that's egotism. Plain old spite.

When Larry found himself helpless, impotent and alone, the option of begging divine intercession seemed no option at all, because, quite simply, he realised he had no faith. When it was playing-for-keeps time, when life was drawing a line in the sand, he suddenly knew which side he stood. It was cold, dark and scary that side of the line, and there was nobody there to help you, but once you're there you can't return. Once you've seen behind the backdrop, you can't walk out front again and believe that what's painted on it is real.

The world this side of the line is indeed a more foreboding place, but even though you have to tread with more caution, you walk with more dignity.

The telephone was ringing as Larry stepped into the kitchen, a towel round his waist, heading for the bubbling coffee pot. He wasn't quite dry and had left damp footmarks on the tiles, but his need for espresso superseded all concerns, including answering the phone until he had filled a cup and taken a mouthful. The answering machine kicked in after a few more rings. That always made him wince a little: you could hear David shouting something in the background on the outgoing message, but neither he nor Sophie had been able to bring themselves to wipe over it.

'Sergeant, this is Peter Steel here. I appreciate that the designated month isn't up yet, but I thought you should know—'

Larry reached over and picked up the handset. 'Hey, Agent Steel, you got me live in concert now. Couldn't sleep. I was thinking about going in to work, maybe you can talk me out of it. What's the deal?'

'Well, it wasn't any gas explosion in Glendale. I think we found our bomber.'

'Who is it?'

'House belonged to one Daniel Corby, sole occupier according to neighbours, so we're assuming he's one of three bodies – all male – pulled out of the rubble.'

'Three?'

'Oh yeah. The good news is Corby sounds like our man. The bad news is this is a long way from over.'

'Who are the other bods?'

'Ah-ah. All in good time,' he said drily. 'Let me tell you about Corby first, get you some perspective. He's some kind of computer nerd – the Kennedy guy called that right – does freelance work on the Internet, setting up other people's websites or something. But here's the juice: we ran his name through the system; he doesn't have form but he's in there, innocent bystander victim of a car-bomb at an abortion clinic in Pocoima in 'ninety-five. Lost some fingers, massive scarring down the left side of his face and body. Looking through the retrospectoscope it seems possible he was blown up by his own device that day and was better at covering his tracks than he was at bomb-making. But recently he's been pretty good at both.'

'How so?'

'I've seen the guy's picture: he had a face – or half a face – you wouldn't forget in a hurry. Sent a copy down to AFFMA and had somebody go through all those passport shots one by one, figuring a match wouldn't be hard to miss. He's in there after all, under a false name, ID mailed out to a box number in Glendale. But the sneaky son-of-a-bitch applied under the same name as an executive from one of these B-movie companies – better yet, an executive who wasn't attending the market. Must have hacked AFFMA for the list of participants then looked up *Variety* or something to see who else worked for each outfit. Picked a name that wouldn't stand out as unfamiliar on any list.'

'Including the list we asked AFFMA to check through yesterday.'

'That's right.'

'So you got a computer-nerd pro-Lifer, probably a Jesus-freak and definitely a stereotypical quiet loner – except he had company today. What gives?'

'Well, here's where it gets interesting. There's a Pontiac Grand Prix out front, not belonging to Mr Corby. Plates-check said the owner was one Terence Nately of Millyard, Orange County.'

'Who he?'

'Résumé as follows. Born San Francisco nineteen fifty-six. Joined US Marines nineteen seventy-four. Two tours of duty in Vietnam. Left the service 'seventy-nine, taking his skills freelance. Pops up hither and thither in various Central American hell-holes over the next few years, before returning to Uncle Sam's embrace and joining the Southland Militia.'

'Oh shit.'

'Oh shit is right. Now, we don't have a third name to go on yet and we don't know for sure which corpse is which, but the smart money says Corby's is the one with the noose.'

Larry almost choked on his coffee. This was getting more horrible by the second. 'Noose?' he spluttered.

'Yeah, when I say corpse, I mean, well, assembled . . . bits. We're not sure which limbs belong to . . . Anyway, one head and torso was found with a rope tight around the neck, other end attached to what's left of a wooden beam. Autopsy won't be through for a while yet, obviously, but I doubt he was wearing it as a fashion statement.'

'No, nooses were just *so* 'ninety-seven.'

'Quite. But my guess is the Militia were there to suicide Corby, and either he'd already arranged to suicide himself or they set off a booby-trap. Either way, whatever it was must have been linked to the detonator for the bomb on the boat, because it's looking a lot like they went off simultaneously.'

'So what do you figure? They were in this together somehow?'

'I haven't got a clue what to think, Sergeant, to tell you the truth. The Southland Militia do have Christian fundamentalist sympathies, but other than that I can't work out the connection. See, *he* did this. Corby's the one with the AFFM pass so that he can plant the bomb at the Vista. Corby's the man with the computer know-how to send off all those little messages, all that shit. This was all his show, including the twin firework extravaganzas at the end. Where Nately and his buddy fit in I don't see. The Militia wouldn't hire someone else to plant bombs for them, certainly not a guy like this, and it doesn't look like he hired them either. I mean, unless they were involved in planting the device on the *Duckling*, but why would he contract that one out and do the hotel one himself? The hotel was by far the trickier of the two.'

'So you don't know what put them together and you certainly don't know what made the Militia want to break it up again.'

'No. But *that* connection's just the supporting feature. You ain't heard what's top of the bill.'

Larry finished his cup. 'Do your worst,' he said.

'We opened the Pontiac's trunk. Found four Calico 9mms in there, preferred assault weapon of the Southland Militia, plus a canvas bag full of Archimedes-wheel coil-tube mags, a hundred rounds a time – snap right into the breach. Single-point laser sighting, Cutts compensator, muzzle break to keep her steady. Compact, deadly, state-of-the-art and, most importantly, an all-American gun. Wouldn't find these guys using Uzis any more than you'd catch them driving a Toyota.'

'So we got bad-ass guns for bad-ass guys. So what?'

'I've seen the Ballistics report on that shell from the science boat. It was CCed to me this morning, and there's a copy waiting on your desk. Guess what?'

'Shit.'

'Right again. The report says the shell was fired from an automatic assault weapon, quote, "most probably a Calico", unquote. Accepting the fact that the Southland Militia are not the only people on this planet who own or use Calicos, it's still hard to escape the conclusion that they were the ones who fired that shell – plus a shitload more – on the *Gazes Also*. Especially as these four lab-rats wouldn't have been the first oceanological scientists the Militia ever took a homicidal interest in – remember the late Professor Biscane. And if they were on board the *Gazes Also*, then it's a distinct possibility that they are now in possession of the missing submarine, a thought that's scaring the shit out of me.'

'Unless they stuck the bodies in it and sank it to cover the murders.'

'That's possible, yes, but I'd have to be in a far more optimistic frame of mind to believe it. If I was being slightly less optimistic, in light of our previous discussion, I'd ask myself whether they might be planning to do a little drug-running to help keep the wolf from the door.'

'But you ain't that optimistic either, I'm guessing,' Larry said.

'Not hardly. These guys have been building up to something for a while. We've tried to infiltrate them, but they're tight as an ass in a bucket of maggots. Ask too many questions and you're made, and if you're made . . . We've lost two undercover agents already. The foot-soldiers don't know dick, they just know what they're told – and they're being told to get ready. There's been contact with other militia groups, but again, nothing more elaborate than a nod to get geared up.

'So I started to ask myself what they might want with a submarine – a submarine nobody knows they have. What might they be planning to import that they can't buy, build or steal in the US?'

'You got me.'

'Well, let me give you a clue. I ran some names through Immigration's computers to check movement in and out of the US. Arthur Liskey, the Southland Militia's founder and commander-in-chief, has flown back into the country from Frankfurt six times in the last year, most recently less than a month ago.'

'What's in Frankfurt?'

'Nothing. That's just his point of entry and departure. It's where he might have been in between times that worries me, like Eastern Europe. Like the former Soviet states. Like Kazhakstan, for instance, or some other shithole where you can buy ex-Soviet nukes on the black market. I've contacted the German immigration authorities to see if they got records of where Liskey arrived *from* on his way back to the US. I should hear from them—'

'Wait a second,' Larry interrupted. 'These guys are crazy, but surely they ain't that crazy. I can understand them taking out a government building here and there, like in Oklahoma City, but a nuclear weapon? Radioactive fall-out snowing all over their beloved Uncle Sam's lawn? Why would they want to do that?'

'Because it's nineteen ninety-nine, Sergeant. Every crazy asshole in this country got ten times crazier on January first because the Judeo-Christian mileometer's about to click round to three zeroes again. It is not a good time to be ruling things out on the grounds of rationality, because there isn't much going around.'

'Yes, but what would these guys want—'

'What *wouldn't* these guys want with a nuclear weapon? At the very least they could hold the country to ransom. But if they really want to dance they could take out Quantico or Maryland or Capitol Hill, or the goddamn White House. Three or four of these things at once and they could cripple the entire infrastructure and stage a full-scale coup. Plus think about this: that sub's been missing for a week and a half – they could *already* have used it for whatever they're up to. What if that's what the Corby thing was about? Contracting him to pull off a stunt that keeps all eyes focused elsewhere while they bring a cargo of MIRV 6s or CHIB 4s on to the beach?'

'Sounds to me like you've picked up a mild strain of nineteen ninety-nine syndrome yourself, Agent Steel. I think you should get some sleep. Ask someone to wake you when the Germans come through on Liskey. Meantime, let's not start shitting our pants before we need to, huh?'

Steel had been on the Southland Militia's tail for who knew how long, poor bastard. He knew they were up to something, he knew how dangerous they were, knew what they were capable of, but *didn't* know what the hell they had in mind. It was inevitable that in such a vacuum he would start imagining all kinds of horrendous possibilities, especially if he suddenly had something tangible to latch on to, like this goddamn submarine.

One thing he wasn't imagining, however, was the Ballistics report. Larry had little doubt over Steel's conclusions regarding who had been on the *Gazes Also*, and what they'd done to its crew. A military-style night assault on an unarmed and unsuspecting science vessel. Wouldn't be too difficult to get everyone at gunpoint, march them on to one of the decks and execute them, then hose away the blood and shells. Maybe do the thing on a plastic sheet or tarpaulin – Christ, a sail would do the trick. Weigh the bodies down, drop them overboard (or stick them in the sub and let it go glug-glug), then split. *Voilà Mary Celeste*.

Steel was too hung up on the bad guys to be thinking about the victims, and Larry couldn't help but wonder whether that was really where the clues lay. What if, forgetting all the peripheral circumstantial crap for a second, this was principally a hit? The Militia took out Sandra Biscane, then a few months later they take out four other rock-bashers. Maria Arazon hadn't believed the two incidents were a coincidence even when the latter looked like an accident, and Larry had asked whether the two unfortunate parties could be connected through more than just a shared academic field. Well they could now: they had been murdered by exactly the same people. Question was, why?

'Ah, shit,' he muttered, remembering. Zabriski had left a message on his desk two days ago, asking him to return a call from Arazon. He'd been planning to phone her back yesterday morning, but it was fair to say he'd been a little busy.

He figured a trip to CalORI was long overdue.

sixteen

Madeleine was sitting on the sofa in a hotel bathrobe when Steff emerged from the shower, finally having left him to complete his intended ablutions. The TV was on, Madeleine pointing lazily at it with the remote, surfing the channels. Steff leaned over and kissed her, her hand reaching up and tugging his T-shirt from his jeans so that she could place her palm on his bare chest beneath. It was just about worth getting blown up for.

Steff felt a fleeting moment of disloyalty to an old cherished cause (and one over and above the international male solidarity of emotional imperviousness), but he had to admit it: the '91 Cup Final had been dislodged from his Greatest Moment In My Life pedestal. Tommy Boyd would, he was sure, understand, especially if he could have seen Madeleine Witherson's face and the look in her eyes in that bathroom. But it wasn't the sex. Not just the sex anyway; steam and soft-focus love-scenes notwithstanding, showers and bathtubs are not entirely conducive to comfortable, contortion-free shagging. It was in the way she looked at him, the way she touched him, the way she held him. It was in everything they'd been through, everything they'd been afraid of, everything they'd imagined, everything they'd hoped for. When she climbed into that tub and reached for him, it hadn't just felt like they were coming together – it felt like they'd finally found each other.

'Ah, shut up ya big poof,' he tried to tell himself, but he wasn't listening. This was for real. If he could handle explosions, mad bombers and hostage crises, surely he was growed-up enough to handle love.

'I thought I'd check out what everybody's got to say about the late Miss Witherson and her ultimate sacrifice,' Madeleine said, indicating the TV. 'Discover what a wonderful citizen I've suddenly become through the simple act of not being a citizen any more. I hope somebody's taping all this shit so I can quote it back to these assholes.'

'Fuck,' Steff muttered. 'Does that make me a necrophiliac?'

'No. Far as I remember it wasn't me who was the stiff one. Oh shit, here he is. The main man. This I *have* to hear.'

Steff looked at the TV. Luther St John was looking back at him, outdoors somewhere sunny, microphones around him like spines on a sea-urchin.

'. . . dark week for America,' he was saying. 'That unfortunate hotel in Santa Monica has been witness to two great tragedies in as many days, and we mustn't dwell on the irony of such horrors being visited upon a place where bloodshed has often been sold as a packaged product. Because the one thing we must remain focused upon is the fate – the life and death – of Madeleine Witherson.

'Madeleine Witherson lived a life of sin, let none of us forget that, as it makes it all the more remarkable that she died a death of grace. For the Lord is the shepherd who will go any distance to bring even the most stray sheep back to the fold. Despite her sins, despite turning her back on God for so long, the Light of Christ found its way into her heart in the end, and she was able to do this brave and selfless thing – with the Lord's help.'

'Hey, I'm not only a necrophiliac. I'm God as well.'

'Ssshhh!' Madeleine warned. 'Quiet and let the man dig.'

'But the most important thing is not Madeleine Witherson's death, but that she repented. She prostrated herself before God and asked His forgiveness for her sins, accepting the wrong in her past words and deeds. She lost her life, but through repentance she surely saved her soul.

'Now, I know some will say – and rightly – that this was something of a gunpoint confession. But I also know that anyone who looked into that little girl's eyes as she spoke those words this morning could see how genuine she was. Bombs or no bombs, Madeleine Witherson meant what she said, for how could she have sacrificed her life if she had not accepted the Lord? She repented, and that is what should shine out from Santa Monica today like a beacon, an example to sinners that redemption is always possible. You may turn your back on God, but He will never turn His back on you.

'One can only pray that the sinners Madeleine Witherson

saved – and all their friends in Hollywood – will repay what she did for them by repenting also, and mending their depraved ways. But I fear that may be a little too much to hope for.'

There was a clamour from behind the microphones, until one voice was allowed to carry. '. . . think this act of sacrifice will have an effect on whether God sends the flood you've been predicting?'

'I'm afraid – as the citizens of Sodom and Gomorrah found out – it takes more than the actions of one good citizen to change the mind of the Lord.'

'Motherfucker,' Madeleine spat, aiming the remote like it was a ray-gun and switching the set off. 'Only took the prick a few hours to *appropriate* my death and turn it into a theological soundbite. Well, let's see if he's still got that fucking pious look on his face when the corpse starts answering back.'

There was a knock at the door.

Steff opened it to find Special Agent Brisko standing in the hallway, and stepped back to let him in. Brisko stayed put.

'Miss Witherson, if it's convenient, there's something important we have to discuss,' he said, looking past Steff to Madeleine, who was leaning round from her position on the sofa.

'Sure,' she said. 'Come on in.'

Still he stayed where he was.

'Em . . . and there's someone here I'd like you to talk to.'

'Fine.'

'Senator,' Brisko said quietly to whoever was out of sight; deliberately too quiet for Madeleine to hear, Steff realised. He backed further into the room beside the sofa as Brisko and another man entered. It took one look at Maddy to confirm who he was.

Steff reckoned that if Newt Gingrich shagged Margaret Thatcher, then Michael Howard shagged Nancy Reagan, then their respective resultant progeny also got it together, what would ultimately be spawned would look something like Senator Bob Witherson. But that was just his first impression.

'What is *he* doing here?' Madeleine demanded quietly, clearly exercising difficult restraint.

'Miss Witherson,' Brisko appealed, 'if you'll just take it easy and let us all talk for a second, please.'

335

Brisko gestured the still tight-lipped senator to the other sofa and sat down beside him.

Steff thought he had seen Madeleine go through every emotion known in the human condition over the past day or so (granted, there was one she might have been faking about an hour back; he wasn't egotistical about such things). However, her reaction to her father was something new altogether. If five minutes ago Maddy had been a calm pool of fresh water, the senator's very presence lobbed a boulder-sized chunk of potassium into it. This was no daddy-daughter huff, no familial fall-out, no hatred-on-the-flipside-of-love deal. She didn't draw him daggers; instead her eyes widened and stared at nothing, panicked and livid. This was a loathing that was disarmingly impersonal, like the allergic to a bowl of peanuts.

She simply could not tolerate his presence. He was burning her skin from the inside.

Steff felt her grip his hand with both of hers and draw closer to him on the seat. He couldn't tell whether she was trying to hide behind him or hold on in case she flew at the man opposite in fury. He saw the whiteness in her face, the tension in her muscles, the fear, anger and uncertainty in her eyes. He looked at the scars on her wrists then looked across at the man beside Brisko.

He could guess, but maybe he owed it to Madeleine not to. Not yet, anyway.

Steff figured Brisko for a family man, maybe with kids around Madeleine's age. The middle-aged Fed probably sympathised with the senator in a fucked-up situation like this. Knew how it can get between family, but how it can be resolved too, especially in times of crisis. Had to bring the father in on the secret ASAP – maybe even in advance. Can't let a fellow daddy think his daughter is about to die . . .

So he could forgive the G-man's lapse of judgement. But what followed was a lapse of taste.

'Miss Witherson, earlier today there was an explosion at an address in Glendale,' Brisko said, 'and to cut to the chase, we believe the bomber was among three people killed in the incident.'

'Who was he?'

'We haven't officially confirmed his identity yet, but who

336

he is – *was* – is not so important right now. What is important is that we also have reason to believe that the two other victims of the blast were members of the Southland Militia, an organisation we regard as being potentially very dangerous indeed. Now, until we can find out a little more about the extent of the Militia's involvement and their possible motives for what has happened over the past two days, we think it might be wise for us to hold off revealing that you're still alive. We're understandably a little nervous as to how the other Militia members could react when it's revealed that they've been had, as it were.'

Madeleine nodded. 'I can appreciate that, Agent Brisko,' she said calmly, 'and I've made it known at all times that I would give your advice every consideration, regards the matter of when to rear my head. I thought that was clear. So why don't you cut to the chase and tell me what *he's* got to do with any of it?'

'Maddy,' the Senator said, leaning forward. 'I've been talking to Special Agent Brisko about what is best here, and there are some very important issues to consider, a very big decision to be made. Maybe not so much a decision as an opportunity. A unique opportunity.'

Madeleine's tone could have cooled the sun. 'Excuse me, *what* are you babbling about?'

'A new beginning, Maddy. A whole new chance at . . . *life*.'

'I'm sorry, am I missing something?' she asked.

Steff tutted, catching on. The wankers. The absolute fucking wankers.

'You want her to stay dead, don't you?' he stated. 'You want this to be real. Fuck's sake. Have you ever seen *Capricorn One*, Madeleine? I'd start making for the exit if I was you.'

'Now, there's no need to imply anything sinister, Mr Kennedy,' Brisko insisted. 'Miss Witherson's free to do whatever she chooses.'

'But you should think carefully about this, Maddy,' the Senator continued. 'About what's in front of you here. A chance that would evaporate if you just walked out of the door. A chance to wipe the slate clean. We can give you a new identity, a new start. You can be relocated, given a new name, money, whatever you need. You can put the past behind you once and for all, no shame, no . . . por— *videos* to follow you around. And what's more, the world would remember Madeleine Witherson as a *heroine*, a saint even, not a – a—'

'Hard-core fucking and sucking star?' Steff offered, wanting to make the bastard squirm. 'Whore of Babylon? Wouldn't hurt you either, politically, to have a holy martyr in the family instead of a porn actress. Would it, *Senator*?'

Madeleine said nothing, but for a woman with such a petite head, her bottom jaw was getting impressively close to the carpet as her father's idea was outlined.

'That's not what I'm concerned with,' he countered, getting slightly heated. 'I don't know who the heck you are, mister, but that girl there is my daughter, and it's her that I care about. Think about it, Madeleine. It's possible for the example you've set, the sacrifice you've made, to *remain*, to become *true*. Think what an impact that would have on this country of ours, spiritually, how it would change our values, our philosophies. What it would teach people about humility, selflessness and repentance, the true meaning of Christianity. By keeping them in the belief that this suffering and sacrifice was real, think what a gift you would give to the people of America. To the people of the whole *world*.'

'You mean like the Crucifixion?' she asked, seemingly interested.

'Yes,' he said, nodding enthusiastically.

'Well Daddy,' she sighed, 'far as I can see, the main thing the suffering and sacrifice of the Crucifixion ever gave to this world was its biggest and most enduring excuse for more suffering and sacrifice. Jesus suffered, so should you. Jesus sacrificed, so should you. That's pretty much been the logic. So if you think I'm going to help anyone give that vicious circle another spin, then you know where you can kiss.

'Lenny Bruce was right. Jackie Kennedy didn't dive across that back seat to protect her husband – she was trying to get away. Princess Di didn't cure cancer or bring world peace – she was just a pretty lady with a warm heart who died too young. And *I* didn't commit sacrificial suicide to make America repent its sins – I just pulled off a stunt so eighty-eight people didn't get blown to pieces. The last thing this world needs is more mythologised lives and fake ideals, so that hypocrites like you can blame people for not living up to them.'

She lifted her head, at last looking directly into her father's face. He didn't enjoy it.

'I don't *want* any new name or new identity, because apart from having a fuck like you for a father, I've nothing to be ashamed of. I don't want to leave my past behind, because that's who I am. *All of it* is who I am. You don't like the idea of being in porn movies? Fine – don't audition. But I don't have a problem with what I did. I'm *repenting* nothing. And I'm not letting you, or Luther fucking St John, or anyone else use what happened out there today to further your bullshit crusades, because that's what caused this thing in the first place. I have nothing to repent because I don't accept your idea of sin, and I certainly don't accept your fucking God.

'My conscience is clear, *Daddy*,' she told him, getting to her feet. 'How's yours?'

The Senator averted his eyes, suddenly finding the carpet the most fascinating thing in the room. It was way past time for Steff to guess.

'Come on, then,' she chided. 'It was your idea for Madeleine Witherson's life and death to become a shining example to America. Funny, I don't remember seeing a Norman Rockwell painting where the smiling fifties father's got his *dick* in the daughter's mouth. And I guess I missed the episode of *Little House on the Prairie* when Michael Landon got Melissa Gilbert to jerk him off.'

'What on God's earth are you talking about?' the Senator asked, his eyes squinting in puzzlement. It seemed a method performance to Steff. Brisko looked like a one-man hung jury, but you could see the cogs whirring and the pieces falling into place.

'Oh spare me another encore of your river-in-Egypt number. You'd be better saving it for the cameras – or better yet, the court.'

The Senator stood up, looking very shaken.

'Don't be absurd,' he blurted. 'There isn't a newspaper or TV station in this country that would risk its reputation or its finances on giving time to your – your *sick* allegations.'

'I wasn't talking about a libel court, *Daddy* – I'm going to get you *busted*,' she told him with smiling delight. 'I'm going to press charges of child abuse. The only reason I never did it before was I was too fucked up and didn't think I had the strength. Well, now that I've been blown up, ritually sacrificed and risen from the dead, I have to say I'm feeling a lot fucking stronger. And on top of that, I'm a national goddamn hero. I don't have to worry about nobody listening to me any more. After this morning, they're gonna be lining up around the block to hear *my* side of the story.'

She walked to the window and pulled the curtains back a little, looking down at the scene outside. 'Come on, Stephen,' she said, taking his hand. 'It's time to roll the stone away. I'm sorry, Agent Brisko, but I'll take my chances with the Militia men.' Steff stood up and they began walking towards the door.

'NO!' the Senator shouted, bounding to the doorway to block their path. 'You have to stop them,' he ordered, staring across impatiently at Brisko.

'Miss Witherson is free to do whatever she wants right now, Senator,' he explained, standing up with his hands behind his back. 'And she has my best wishes for whatever that might be.'

Madeleine smiled a thank-you. Brisko just lowered his head and gave a little nod, his eyes closed.

'I'd get oot the fuckin' way if I was you, Jim,' Steff advised the Senator. 'I've not had the best couple of days and I'm still lookin' for somebody to take it out on.'

'You lay *one* finger on me, mister, and I'll have you – ugh!'

He flew back into the corridor and hit the wall with a wallop, slumping down and holding his hands to a messily bleeding nose.

'You forgot to say anything about foreheads,' Steff told him as they walked past, heading for the stairs.

The camera crew looked like they were starting to pack up, having filed their last on-the-spot postscript report. All around the police cordons and beyond, there were other news crews and photographers also calling it a day, loading equipment into vans, litter blowing about their feet. The crowds having deserted when the show was over, the scene reminded Steff of the aftermath of a rock festival.

The reporter, a slim and predictably blonde woman in a blue jacket, was chatting to her cameraman as they approached, turning around when she noticed him do a double-take.

'Jesus Christ,' the reporter gasped.

'No, not quite,' said Madeleine, 'but we've got a lot in common. Look, if you can get me live in two minutes, you got the scoop of the century, otherwise I keep walking and let the next crew spot me.'

'James, get on to Brackley, make it happen, *now*,' the reporter ordered. She turned back to Madeleine. 'Can't we start recording just now and then—'

'I said live. And no seven-second delay, either.'

They got the go-ahead from one of the technicians in a little less than ninety seconds.

'Okay, we're on in twenty,' the reporter told Maddy. 'Incidentally, why does it need to be live?'

'Because I'm going to swear.'

The reporter got the signal from her producer, who counted her down from five. She got as far as 'Hi, this is Katie Law—' before Maddy snatched the mike and stepped in front of the camera.

'Let's dispense with the foreplay, shall we? Because time is short and people may actually be *drowning* in the self-righteous bullshit that's piling up around the country right now. So surprise, surprise, kids, I'm still here. That's the scoop. We faked it, all right? We faked it. I want everybody to know I'm alive and well, and that no act of ultimate sacrifice took place here today, so I guess you can start retracting all the nice things you've been saying about me and I can go back to being a slut or a whore or whatever else you thought I was yesterday.

'But the main thing I want everybody to hear is that what happened today was a necessary response to a terrorist threat, nothing more, so let's all put the Bibles down for a minute and listen up. It's the Piaf rap from now on, okay? My confession, my *repentance*, was as fake as my suicide.'

The other camera crews had been alerted as to who the woman in the bathrobe was, and began rushing across the grass, lugging equipment with them like prized possessions from a tenement fire. Cops began tearing after them, trying to form a makeshift human barrier so that no one got between Madeleine and the hotel.

'I want everybody to know that I meant none of that crap,' she resumed. 'The bomber asked for it, he got it. I'm not a sinner, the people who were hostage on that boat weren't sinners, and the people who died inside *that* building yesterday weren't sinners either. You want to talk about morality? Let's talk about the morality of the Reverend Luther *fucking* St John. Because whoever planted those bombs wasn't influenced by watching porno videos or action movies or anything else that came out of Hollywood. He was influenced by watching CFC, by the hatred and bigotry that's been pouring out of it towards me, towards the AFFM and in fact towards pretty much anything Luther takes a personal dislike to. You start telling people someone is the enemy of God and the enemy of America – that's not a sermon, that's a *fatwah*.

'Luther's been pretty happy to eulogise about me today, to turn me into some kind of latter-day parable for the consumption of his brain-dead flock. Well bad news, asshole, because I'm still here and your parable's gonna have a new punchline. You want to talk about the morality of my life, Reverend? You want to talk about the morality of what I've done and what I believe? Then you come ahead and talk to me about it, head to head, face to face, before the cameras. I'll meet you any place, any time. But until you do that, you keep your *fucking* mouth shut about Madeleine Witherson.'

She handed the mike back to Katie Law, who seemed temporarily to have forgotten what it was for. The reporters clustered around the ring of cops began shouting questions, but Maddy was already walking away back to the hotel.

'Golly,' Steff said.

She winked at him and smiled. 'How would you put it back home Stephen? Get *that* up you?'

'Close enough.'

Luther had expected there would be frights and scares right up until the waters hit the coast, but in truth he'd thought Corby's shenanigans must be the final shot out of left-field. Then Witherson's 'resurrection' had pitched its own late curve-ball and forced him back up on to his toes. He had been so riveted to the TV screen after this deception was revealed – sitting rapt through the reaction, comment and bleeped-out re-runs – that he lost track of time, and when he was through reeling from the impact he remembered himself with a start and looked down nervously at his watch for reassurance. Fortunately, he was still on time. It wouldn't have made a huge difference if he'd been a few minutes late, but he didn't want Liskey thinking he had experienced any degree of cold feet.

Luther felt nothing when he pressed the button, but nor had he expected to: no sense of moment, no surge of power. For his true hours of destiny were in the past and in the future, and such technical implementations were not gateways, but steps on the journey. If they entailed an option, then it was as emergency exits, points at which to bail out for those not strong enough to carry God's burden to the finish.

There was, in any case, no opportunity to dally over the action – for reasons either of relish or vacillation – as it had to be done at a precisely appointed time, and there was other vital work to follow. If his hand had wavered then it was only to double-check that his finger lay upon the correct button on the device, its keys and switches covered messily with black punch-tape to mask the original Cyrillic markings, the clumsy translations bearing their own sharp irony.

There were times when he could almost hear God chuckle along at His own little jokes. 'Termination,' it said below the red execute button. Across from it was a yellow one marked 'Abortion'. They had very different functions on the Ukrainian device, but were both terms for the same thing in Luther's country, and very soon they'd both be redundant in that particularly distasteful context. By pushing that keypad he was terminating all abortions, aborting all terminations.

With the button pressed there was no time for reflection, as his thoughts needed to turn immediately to how he should handle this new problem. He looked back at the television screen, turning up the volume with his remote control.

'You have to say, Jack, this young lady has really turned the tables on Luther St John and the entire puritanical lobby, laying a big chunk of the responsibility for what has happened at *their* door. She's effectively accused CFC of being a bad influence, pointing the finger at it the way St John has been pointing the finger at mainstream movies and TV channels.'

'Yes, Barbara, she's certainly thrown a gauntlet down, and

it's going to be very difficult for Luther St John to have any credibility on these subjects unless he picks it up. What's happened this afternoon has left a lot of people out on a limb they thought it was pretty safe to climb before Maddy Witherson reappeared, none more than the good Reverend. And now if he wants to talk about Hollywood, or pornography, or *any* of the issues arising from this, he's got to talk to her first or he's going to look chicken.'

'Thanks, Jack. And now, back to Don Arnold at the scene in Glendale. Don, have the police . . .'

His first instinct was to agree to a debate with her in a couple of days, even tomorrow night; this was one of the rare occasions in life when he could ignore something and it *would* go away. Same time tomorrow she'd probably be dead, especially if she was still in Santa Monica, and it would be a long while before anyone started talking about her again.

But it wouldn't be for ever, and that was the problem. Over the past twenty-four hours the eyes of America had been focused on that girl like they'd never been on a single person before, and her 'suicide' would be etched on people's minds as deeply as the JFK assassination. After tomorrow, whenever people thought of the tidal wave, they'd think also of the events and the words that preceded it. Dead or alive, Madeleine Witherson would hang over him like a cloud, casting a shadow of doubt on all he had to say.

Unless he took her on.

Faith turns every obstacle into an opportunity, the Lord had taught him. He shouldn't view it as a pitfall, but a platform: the perfect curtain-raiser ahead of the main event. Witherson was the one who had said 'any place, any time'. Then let her come here, to the CFC studios, where he could literally call the shots.

He would be statesmanlike, deferential and utterly magnanimous. Instead of snatching back his compliments, he would treat her with the reverence appropriate to his earlier words, as a brave, strong and ultimately *good* person. As though, despite her fury, he knew that deep in her heart she had seen the light. He would extend her every courtesy. He'd fly her to Arizona in his private Lear, treat her as a visiting dignitary, not an opponent. Under the studio lights,

344

he would discuss, not argue; posit, not pronounce. If still she raged, he'd depict her as someone with every reason to be angry, but whose energies were – equally understandably – misdirected.

He'd get to say his piece, she'd get to say hers. They would talk about Hollywood. They would talk about pornography. They would talk about morality.

He would dispense the Lear to fly her home again.

And then the Lord would pass His verdict on who was right.

Three red windows lit up without warning on the warhead's display panel, then two of them blinked off again. Liskey felt like his entire circulation system had been put on hold for a second, and he'd come uncomfortably close to crapping in his wetsuit. He hoped Rooke hadn't come any nearer himself; they'd be long enough in the decompression chamber without one of them smelling of shit.

'Jesus, I thought . . .'

'Yeah, me too,' Liskey said with a dry laugh. 'It's okay. Just St John's signal arming the bombs.'

'Too bad about Vern buyin' it,' Rooke observed. 'Fucker bet me a hundred that cometh the hour the preacherman wouldn't have the balls.'

'Too bad, yeah. Shit, I'd have taken some of that action myself. Look at this, he's bang on time – which makes *us* behind schedule. Let's finish this thing off A-sap.'

Liskey looked at his watch again and shook his head. Damn right he'd have fronted Vern a hundred on *that* one, poor bastard. He'd known Luther St John for a good few years now, and since this plan's inception he'd never doubted for a second that the man would go through with it. St John traded on his faith in God, but it was his faith in himself that was his engine. He was so cool, with the restraint of a man who doesn't have to strive because he knows he's in control. Like the way he handled the whole prediction thing, resisting the temptation to get too specific, even in recent days when they knew the precise timetable. Liskey had asked him why he didn't up the ante, tell America the catastrophe was at hand, name the goddamn day.

'People will feel awe if I give them the impression I know

God's mind,' he told him, 'but God must remain an unfathomable entity. If I give the impression I know God's *appointment* schedule, they'll just feel suspicious.'

Motherfucker never skipped a beat, no matter what came up. There was no point in even asking him whether Nately and Vernon's deaths changed anything. It hadn't been the ideal outcome, losing two men and possibly connecting Corby to the Militia, but the op's basic purposes were served: kill the bomber, wipe the computers, erase all links to St John.

Liskey wasn't worried about the Feds thinking the Militia had been in on the Pacific Vista thing. Apart from the stark fact that they *hadn't*, all evidence pointing either direction was about to be washed away for ever. And if some day, after everything that was about to happen, someone ever remembered about the two other bodies found at Corby's place, 'Well, officer, we had no idea these upstanding Militia members were consorting with such a dangerous individual, and it certainly wasn't in any capacity representative of our organisation. '

He looked through the window again at the warhead, gripped by the sub's mechanised arms in front of the vehicle, powerful twin floodlights peering into the depths before it. This was the last one to be positioned.

It was vital all the bombs went off at once. The customised CHIBs didn't have a clock system, just a timer: this provided a two-way guarantee to ensure that neither party could double-cross the other. For a simultaneous detonation, Liskey had to set the same countdown period locally on each warhead, then St John's signal would start them all ticking at the same time. Liskey's guarantee was that he had control of the timers, St John's that he held the trigger. From his place in the desert, St John could bounce the arming signal off a satellite to reach the warheads under the Pacific. Therefore, if the timers were set at zero for an instant result, there was nothing to stop St John hitting the button as soon as he knew the bombs were in position, silencing his co-conspirators and saving himself a big bill for services rendered. So they had agreed a countdown time-frame that accommodated both parties' needs.

Theoretically, the warheads were all supposed to be in place before St John armed them, but it didn't matter for the sake of a few minutes. Just as long as the nukes were all where they should be, the clock was running and there was plenty of time to get clear. The positioning schedule had always been intentionally tight – the intention being St John's, another aspect of his guarantee. After the *Light of the World* rendezvoused with the *Stella Maris* at a pre-ordained time above Wegener's Guyot, there was to be barely a spare second: St John wanted the bombs off the ship, in place and armed within the shortest possible margin, giving the Militia men no time to improvise. He didn't trust Liskey not to try hotwiring the warheads to bypass the remote detonator, so he could make off with them for his own purposes. But once they were armed that option was closed, and Liskey's only consideration was minimum safe distance. Soon as he could he'd be decompressing aboard the *Light*, way out in the ocean, hoping St John wasn't shitting him about seismic waves being only a few feet high on the open sea, otherwise the ship was going to be surfing into Honolulu.

Liskey tugged at the lever to partially release the mechanical arm's grip on the CHIB, testing whether the warhead would stay in place when he withdrew the sub. It rolled about forty degrees then settled, steady, the LED readout facing him as it blinked its count, like the kid who was 'it' playing hide-and-seek.

22:48:57
22:48:56
22:48:55

Five o'clock tomorrow evening, Wegener Guyot would be no more. Under the ocean, there'd be a crater where there used to be a mountain . . . and forty minutes later the rush-hour gridlock would clear in record time.

22:48:46
22:48:45
22:48:44

Ready or not, here I come.

seventeen

The atmosphere in the CalORI suites reminded Larry of a downtown station he'd been posted in around '89, when five officers went down in the line of duty one ugly July evening. It had looked like an opportune weapons bust when it was radioed in. Turned out to be an ambush, revenge by the Bloods for two of their members dying in a firefight with cops from the same precinct. In the days following it had to be business as usual, but there was an emptiness about the place, a pervading hush as though the precinct-house itself was the chapel of rest.

The receptionist was getting ready to lock up out front when Larry arrived. She let him in and offered to walk him through to where Arazon was working if he'd hang on until she shut down her computer, as the lab was on her way to the staff parking lot. He followed her slowly down the corridors, people wishing her goodnight as they passed, supportive little smiles being exchanged.

They came to an open-plan laboratory area, where Maria Arazon and a colleague were peering in turns into the same microscope. For some reason Larry had been expecting everybody to be in white coats – too much time around hospitals and pathology labs. Arazon looked up and noticed him, touching her companion on the shoulder as she walked away from the worktop.

'Sergeant Freeman, a phone call would have sufficed.' She sounded almost apologetic for his trouble.

'Yeah, I figured, but anything to keep me out of the station right now, you know?'

'I can imagine. Think I saw you on TV last night, outside the hotel. A bad business. Sick business. Still, at least the girl's all right. Were you in on that little hoax this morning?'

He smiled. 'That would be telling. So what were you calling for, Doctor?'

'Well, I didn't mean to put you to a lot of trouble. It's just . . . I think we've been burgled.'

'Burgled?'

'Yeah, or maybe just hacked. I know it's not the crime of the century, but given . . .'

'No, you were right to call. Go on.'

'See, there's nothing missing or damaged, nothing physical. It's the computers. The data's been wiped. Not on all of them, just the ones in Lab 2 over there – the ones Mitch Kramer's team were using.'

'When did this happen?'

'Well, that's the thing. I don't know. It could have been any time between, say, three days ago and, well, when the *Gazes Also* left on its last trip. Three days ago was the first time anybody turned those particular machines on since . . . you know. See, different projects have different teams here, and there's not always a lot of crossover. We had to start going through Mitch's team's work to see what the Institute could salvage. We were all putting it off for reasons you can understand, but eventually I was the first one who could bring myself to sift through it. Figured it was the long straw option. Some other sucker's gonna have to take down their posters and personal shit. Seeing all that stuff there makes you think they're all gonna walk through the door any minute. Anyway, I decided to begin with the computers for a project inventory, but there was nothing there.'

'Nothing pertaining to that project?'

'Nothing *at all*. The hard disks had been wiped completely. And there's more. After I called you I went down to the *Gazes* to check the two machines on board. They'd been wiped too. My late friend Sandra Biscane's disks were also wiped, if you remember. Do you see a recurring pattern here, Sergeant, or am I being irrational in my state of bereavement?'

'More rational than you know.'

'What does that mean?'

'I can't tell you right now.'

'It means you know they were murdered, right? You've found something. What is it?'

'Can we talk in private?'

349

'Sure.' She called to the young man by the microscope. 'Chico, can you take a walk for five?' Chico held up his hands and walked away.

Larry waited until he was out of sight. 'Okay,' he began, 'this is strictly confidential and if you tell anyone I'll deny it.'

'I'm not much for gossip, Sergeant.'

'Here's the deal, in short. The FBI are pretty sure your friend Professor Biscane was killed by the Southland Militia, always have been.'

Arazon rolled her eyes. 'Those slippery bastards.'

'What you gonna do. But now we got evidence that suggests it was also the Southland Militia who were on board your colleagues' boat – firing automatic weapons. So yes, it would be more than fair to say there is a pattern. Question is: what was it about? The Feds are hung up on thinking it was the sub the Militia were interested in, but to me it's looking more and more like a plain old hit. From what you just told me, in both cases there was something on the victims' computers that the militia didn't want public, so now we got a motive: silencing witnesses. But witnesses to what? How much do you know about what Kramer's team were working on?'

'I'm afraid it was nothing exactly juicy. Sub-oceanic topography, observing and recording, sampling, charting. Probably the least sensitive piece of research work this place has been contracted to carry out in a long time. Much of our work gets financed by mineral companies – you might have something to get your teeth into if some rich deposit had been found and somebody wanted it kept quiet. A thing like that happened to a contractor on the Gulf coast about twelve years back, to do with artificially undervaluing the exploitation rights, I think. But the only remarkable thing about what Mitch was working on was who was picking up the tab.'

'Who?'

'The Reverend Luther St Asshole.'

Larry paused a moment, fumbling in his mind for a connection that was just out of reach.

'Why would St John be sponso— *Tidal* waves,' he said, answering his own question.

'That's right,' Arazon confirmed, leaning back and resting her bottom against a worktop. 'At least sort of. At first we didn't know why he had any interest in oceanography, but we didn't much care either. When a billionaire comes along, expresses an enthusiasm and offers to fund your work, you cash the cheques and get started before he moves on to his next dilettante impulse. It was only when he went public with his prediction that we realised an ulterior agenda. Caused a few headaches around here, I can tell you.'

'Why?'

'He said on TV that he'd seen "evidence beneath the sea", something like that. Everybody was scared he'd cite CalORI's research, because then the team would've had to deny they'd found anything that supported his beliefs.'

'And he'd kill the funding.'

'Exactly. But it didn't happen. He told Mitch he never intended to cite the research, apparently. Said he needed CalORI to gather the data, but came out with some bullshit about science not being able to see what *he* could see in the team's findings. You know, there's a saying about gift horses and mouths. It rings even truer when it comes to mad billionaires dispensing funds. CalORI was getting a lot more out of the deal than St John. We were at least interested in the *reality* of what this research was uncovering. What it had to do with the Reverend and his fairy stories, I don't know.'

'And I guess we never will, now that it's all been erased.'

'Ah, but it hasn't,' Arazon said with a smile.

'What do you mean?'

'It was backed up. All of it.'

'Why didn't you—'

'I didn't know this when I called you, but us having back-ups doesn't change the fact that someone tried to eradicate the information.'

'No, it sure doesn't. So where were these back-ups that whoever wiped the machines didn't find them? Or was the stuff backed up to a file server someplace else?'

'In the ice-box.'

'Huh?'

'Chico, who I just chased out – he's our lab technician, computer manager and all-round technological trouble-shooter. When I told him the machines had been tampered with he went for the fridge. Said Mitch always backed data up to CDs and stuck them in the freezer compartment. Don't look at me like that – *I* thought he was joking too. Chico said Mitch's philosophy was that if this place got turned over, the insurance would replace the computers, but it couldn't replace what was on them. Wasn't enough just to back the stuff up, you had to put the disks or CDs where a thief wouldn't be looking anyway.'

'Tough break if the burglars decide they want a soda.'

'This fridge is in the basement store-room, surrounded by conspicuously unvaluable rock samples and drill-cores. Mitch knew what he was doing.'

'Sounds like it. So he was a cover-all-the-bases kind of guy?'

Arazon laughed a little. 'Mitch? He was a disaster area. You should see his office. I thought his idea of burglary insurance was making the place look like it had already been screwed. This wasn't his normal style at all.'

'Have you had time to look at what's on the CDs? . . . Dr Arazon?'

Arazon stared at the worktop beside her, seemingly oblivious.

'Sorry, Sergeant. I was just wondering whether Mitch might have got the back-up idea from the same person who taught him to use seismological modelling programs.'

Larry remembered hearing about this before: 3-D animation software, developed by . . .

'Professor Biscane,' he said.

Arazon nodded.

'Sandra was the kind of woman who'd back up her grocery list. Very obsessive. She had that SyQuest drive, but there were no cartridges, remember? Until now I'd assumed she backed up her work to the SyQuest and the killer had taken the carts. But what if she hid them someplace in her apartment?'

21:19:06

Larry drove Arazon to Biscane's sister's place to pick up the keys to the apartment. It had been on the market since a couple of months after the professor's death, but there had been no takers so far. The story that the previous occupant had been stabbed to death on the premises after disturbing a burglar had proven something of a sticking point. Another apartment

352

for sale in the same building was similarly suffering by association. Folks could get so antsy about security issues.

'I find places real spooky when they've been cleared out like this,' Larry observed, looking at the bare shelves and dust shadows where pictures had hung. 'Sometimes worse than the murder scene itself. It's more than they're empty – it's like they're bereft, you know what I mean? Divested of life.'

'You're obviously more of an empath than me, Sergeant. I just feel sick. The last time I was in here I was having coffee in the kitchen and Sandra was sitting across from me in a green T-shirt. Shit, I've lost five friends and I don't even know what the fuck this is about.'

'You okay to be here, Dr Arazon?'

She nodded, biting her lip. 'Sure. I'll be fine.'

'Good. So where was the prof's hidey-hole?'

'You try the fridge yet?' she said with a brave attempt at a smile. 'Just kidding. Beth would have cleared that out way back. In fact she'd have cleared out most things, so if the carts are here they'd need to be someplace not even Beth would have gone into, never mind a burglar.'

Larry thought of all the places he'd found drugs or weapons stashed, and even of a time he'd taped a handgun to the lid of a cistern in the house of a friend who was in a lot more danger than he appreciated. That option was out because moisture and SyQuest cartridges didn't go well together. He ruled out a few others on the grounds of inconvenience: backing up was a regular business, so you wouldn't put the carts anywhere that was a pain in the ass to access.

'How tall was she?'

'About five-one, five-two.'

Good. That ruled out a few more. Larry went to the front door and followed the line of the walls clockwise through the apartment, checking every spot Biscane could have reached.

He found two cartridges behind the hot-water reservoir in a cupboard in the utility room.

18:56:23

They pulled into the CalORI building's parking lot, where Arazon's Ford was the only vehicle left.

'You look pretty beat, Sergeant. You up all last night with the Witherson thing?'

'Yeah. Tried to sleep today but it wasn't happening.'

'Well, you get some quality shut-eye and I'll give you a call tomorrow afternoon some time when I've had a chance to see what's on these cartridges.'

That sounded good to Larry. Very good indeed. Sophie would be getting in from her school parents' night about now. Maybe phone out for some Thai, couple of beers and then that mattress moment. He scribbled his mobile number on the back of a card and handed it to Arazon, then pulled away.

He was two blocks from home when the phone rang. He felt tired enough to ignore it, but sometimes curiosity could be stronger than caffeine. Fate pivots on such impulses.

It was Arazon. After wondering so long why her friend was murdered, there'd been no way she could wait until morning to find out what was on those SyQuests, so she'd gone in and booted straight up

'Sergeant, I really think you should get back over here, and I mean right now. I just found out something else Biscane and Kramer had in common.'

'What?'

'Their sugar-daddy.'

18:14:47

'It was a time of earthquakes,' the scrolls had begun. *'The old ones called it that, in such a way as I could not; for they had known a time without. I grew up with earthquakes.'*

You and me both, *amigo*, Maria thought. You and me both. This was California, for Christ's sake.

California, like Kaftor, located in a region of fervent seismological activity.

California, like Kaftor, where the frequent tremors were no acts of God, just facts of life.

California, like Kaftor, where a terrible earthquake had once brought devastation to a great city, but after which men had learned *'to build towns and cities that could resist Poteidan's anger'*.

California, like Kaftor, where people were also, in certain eyes, *'vain fools, fussing over shining trivia'*.

'This country that was once so great, once held all God's promise, but now spurns Him. This country that God intended to be our land of milk and honey, but which has been turned instead into Sodom and Gomorrah . . .'

Decadent in our self-indulgence. Distracted by beauty and pleasure, wasting our potential. Giving no glory to Poteidan, who surely did not share our love of these shallow things.

'The law may allow you to fornicate like a mangy dog, it may allow you to sodomise, it may allow you to blaspheme, it may allow you to peddle pornography, and it may allow you to murder a child in the womb . . . but GOD DOES *NOT*! We have become so arrogant as to supersede God's laws with ones we've dreamed up for our own convenience . . .'

Poteidan is angry, Damanthys tells us, and by coincidence Poteidan is angry about the self-same things of which he disapproves. What, then, can save us? Surely only to live our lives as Damanthys would prescribe . . .

Same shit, different millennium.

From Damanthys to St John, through wandering charlatans and Wild West medicine-hawkers, the story had never changed. You could make it sound as grand as you liked, but in essence it was just a stick-up: Do as I say and you won't get hurt.

'I have seen His work beneath the ocean . . . He is preparing to strike, preparing a mighty wave to demonstrate His wrath, literally to wash away the sinners . . .'

Don't bet on it, *pendejo*.

Maria heard a car door slam outside and looked out to see Freeman walking towards the entrance. She ran down the stairs, praying that this time he wouldn't take so much convincing that her theory was right.

18:02:16

'Well, Sandra didn't back up her grocery list, but she backed up everything else, including all her e-mail correspondence,' Arazon said, leading him in from the back door to the lab where she had two computers running. One monitor displayed a page of text, the other a three-dimensional image above several columns of abbreviations and figures.

'What's this thing here?' Larry asked, indicating the latter.

Arazon arched her eyebrows. 'Sergeant, when I tell you what I think we've got here, I don't want you saying I'm loco, okay? You gotta hear me out.'

'Dr Arazon, I helped fake a ritual human sacrifice before a worldwide live TV audience this morning. My concept of crazy is pretty forgiving at the moment. You talk, I'll listen.'

'Okay, on this screen is e-mail to Sandra Biscane from Luther St John – plus there's more on-file. And on *this* screen is what he commissioned her to work on: it's the prototype for a new kind of modelling software. Now, here's why she wouldn't tell anybody about it.'

Arazon highlighted a section of text using the mouse. Larry leaned closer to the monitor.

'. . . I have to insist on the utmost discretion regarding this project and my involvement in it. As I'm sure you can appreciate, many of those who I consider my political allies would be most displeased to learn where my sympathies lie with regard to this particular issue. Some people might call me a hypocrite or a coward for not standing up to be counted, but if I had shown my hand before, I would not have been privy to the information that may now assist this cause.'

'So what the hell's he talking about?' Larry asked.

'Nuclear testing. He claims to be very opposed to it, which would indeed come as a shock to a lot of his GOP buddies. He tells Sandra he's learned from friends in high places that the US is planning to follow France's lead and carry out underwater weapons tests. Says he's concerned not just for the environment but about the possibility of deeper seismological consequences.'

'Tidal waves.'

'You got it. Says the government couldn't give a shit about the first but the threat of the second might carry some weight, so he commissioned Sandra to adapt her modelling software – thus.'

Arazon pointed him to the other monitor.

'You feed in the details of a specific location – supposedly the test site – and then the program simulates what would happen if you caused an explosion right there. What's on the screen just now is a default, Myora Atoll. These columns here are all the variables, and the program's calculations get more accurate the more blanks you can fill in: weapon's nominal yield, distance to nearest land mass, average water depth around test site, density of surrounding rock types, silt compaction density, sonar-tested silt stratification depths, et cetera et cetera et cetera. The idea isn't simply to demonstrate that you could cause a seismic wave by setting off a nuke in the wrong place – this thing could tell you exactly what kind of place the wrong place is.'

'However, the late professor was working on the assumption that causing a tidal wave was something you'd generally like to *avoid*,' Larry observed. 'So if, for instance, you had prophesied that LA was going to be flooded by an act of God, and you happened to be in possession of a nuclear weapon . . .'

Arazon nodded solemnly. 'This would tell you where to plant it for maximum effect. Of course, you'd then need someone to supply geological data about various sub-oceanic sites until you found one that suited your needs. Someone like the Californian Oceanographic Research Institute.'

'Jesus Christ. Are you really sure about this?'

'Have I been wrong so far, Sergeant?'

'Unfortunately not.'

'Only doubt I have is how Luther St John could procure an atomic bomb to play with.'

'Well, he commissioned this software and then after that he made his prediction. Sounds to me like he was pretty confident of getting hold of one. No, wait a minute, he *knows* someone who could get hold of one for him. The Southland Militia – that's who he's in this with. They whacked Biscane and hit the *Gazes Also*.

'The FBI are worried these assholes might have stolen the sub to smuggle nukes into the US. Agent Steel told me the Militia's Oberführer has been back and forth a lot from Frankfurt recently, possibly *en route* to somewhere in the former Soviet bloc. I thought Steel was getting carried away with himself, but . . .'

'The Ukraine,' Arazon said suddenly, eyes wide.

'What?'

'St John was in the Ukraine, Jesus, only about a month ago.

CalORI couldn't get hold of him because he was in Kiev. He was buying statues or something, religious relics.'

'Aw, Jesus Christ, tell me this ain't happening.' Larry reached for his mobile and the card bearing Steel's number. 'Tell me I fell asleep and I'm gonna wake up in time for *Oprah*. I'll even *watch* the piece of crap.'

He punched the number. Steel answered after two rings.

'Hey Peter, Larry Freeman. Please tell me you heard back from German Immigration and Liskey wasn't in the Ukraine.'

'He was in Kiev four times, plus Odessa last month. How the fuck d'you know that?'

'Shit. Peter, you better get down here to the Californian Oceanographic Research Institute, and it'd be a good idea if you didn't stop at any red lights on the way. I'll give you the address . . .'

16:31:26

Steel was talking quietly but frantically into his telephone, his back to Larry, while Arazon tapped at the keyboard, sifting through the data accumulated by the *Gazes Also* and refrigerated for safe-keeping. The thought was rolling round and round his mind to call Sophie and tell her to get the hell out of town, but Sophie wasn't the kind of woman who did anything without knowing precisely why; and if he told her, how could he ask her not to warn everyone else in the city?

No. That way worse things than madness lay.

Stay focused.

Steel snapped his mobile shut and turned around.

'Okay, I'm afraid this doesn't get any better,' he said. 'I made some calls. St John's private yacht, the *Light of the World*, was indeed dispatched to the Ukraine to transport religious artefacts back to the US. The artefacts in question were statues, and the bad news, if things can get any fucking worse, is that there were supposed to be three of them.'

'Where's the ship now?'

'Don't have a fix on it,' the Fed admitted. 'But even if we did, what could we do? Board it? I mean, *we* all think we know what we've got here, but they might not see it that way further up the chain. Getting authorisation to raid the private yacht

358

of a politically connected billionaire takes more than software and speculation. It also takes time, which we may not have. If St John did transport nuclear weapons from Odessa, they could already be off-loaded, and a pantload of good it would do us to raid an empty ship.

'Basically, if these bombs exist, we have to deduce their final destination, and we have to consider the possibility that they've already reached it. So if Dr Arazon can work out where the nukes are likely to be planted, then we seek, locate and defuse. If we're real lucky we might be early and run into the Militia when they turn up in their stolen sub. But I wouldn't count on it.'

16:11:44

'Shit, I'm wasting my time with this,' Arazon muttered angrily.

'Now just keep it together, stay calm,' Larry urged, pulling his chair closer.

'No, I mean I *am* wasting my time. What was I thinking about? Can you hand me that CD there?'

Larry passed the glinting disc into her hand. She popped it on to the awaiting tray and it slid inside the computer.

'I've been trying to feed data from the *Gazes Also* into Biscane's prototype – from scratch. I was forgetting: Mitch constructed 3D models of each location to present to St John – the models must be compatible for both programs because they were both developed by Sandra. That's how St John would have worked it: use Mitch's model as a base, then key in the extra data that the new system requires. Yeah, look, here we go.'

The screen came to life, displaying a rotatable frame diagram of a section of ocean floor.

'See? The model by itself is running fine. Just missing some stats on stuff the *old* program didn't need to know – mostly to do with how the environment would or wouldn't withstand an explosion.' She pointed to the columns under the diagram, where several bars were flashing on and off, denoting undefined variables. 'For instance, SCD – that's Silt Compaction Density. You gotta use the mouse to outline the area that the density figure you're keying in applies to. Same with the stratification depths. Let me call that stuff up on the other machine here.'

She rolled her chair a few feet to the next keyboard and stuck another disc into its CD-rom drive, quickly calling up some documents on to the screen.

'How many locations did Kramer's team study?' Steel asked, fidgeting, unable to keep his eyes from the clock.

'There were four expeditions, but we can discount the last one because they never got to report any findings for that. Hey, don't worry, this isn't gonna be a needle-in-a-haystack deal. I'll admit I don't know exactly what I'm looking for, but I *will* know it when I see it.'

Arazon worked the keyboard feverishly, tapping at the cursors to zoom in and out from the model. To Larry, watching the shapes and features scroll past, it was like looking at a model of the surface of another planet.

He noticed that parts of the land/seascape were shaded in different tones.

'Dark grey is pre-charted topography,' Arazon told him. 'Old news, in other words. Features or details discovered and charted by the *Gazes* are in the lighter shade. They were working along this margin just south of the Murray fracture zone. Anything further north or south would be no good because the brunt of your wave would hit Frisco or San-Dee. St John's targeting LA.

'Okay,' she announced, 'let's give this place a shot. Jasper Seamount. Sergeant, can you read out the stats from that screen as I ask for them?'

'Sure.'

Larry watched the model change colours as Arazon used the mouse to define areas of the digital reconstruction and carefully keyed in the corresponding figures. The flashing bars were stilled one by one until a single blank remained.

'Okay, Agent Steel, this last one *you're* gonna have to fill in,' she said.

'What's that?'

'How big is the bomb – in kilotons?'

'Shit, I don't know.'

'Just an educated guess is fine. Sandra's notes admit there's a big margin of error in the software's estimate of blast impact. It won't be pinpoint accurate in telling us how big a hole your nuke would make, so I only need a rough figure.'

'Then what good is it?'

'Because it *will* be pinpoint accurate in telling us what that hole would cause, whatever size the computer estimates it to be.'

'Okay,' he said, running a hand through his hair. 'Let's see, if it was a MIRV 6, say around thirty kilotons nominal payload – but there could be as many as three of them.'

'So that's ninety?'

'Depends. If they're tactically positioned, a cumulative simultaneous blast could . . . Ah, fuck it, call it a hundred. And if it's three CHIBs, call it two hundred.'

'We're dealing in worst-case scenarios,' Larry said. 'Go for the biggest figure.'

Arazon ran the simulation. The screen went blank, then the model reconstructed itself, with a large section of the seamount now missing. Arazon began pulling up sub-menus and banks of statistics. Larry was wondering whether the thing had worked; maybe he'd seen too many video games, but he'd been expecting a little more spectacle.

'What gives?' he asked.

'Not much. Nuke a seamount like this and the rock itself is soaking up a lot of the blast. Debris tumbles two miles down into the abyssal plain. The computer estimates nothing worse than a good day for hanging ten.'

'So you don't know what we're looking for?' Steel asked, exasperated.

'On the contrary, having seen this I think I do.'

Arazon zoomed back out and began scrolling along the model at speed, then got up and crossed the lab to a cupboard from which she produced an outsized book. She laid it on the worktop beside her machine and opened it, revealing a map of what looked like the surface of the moon.

'Sergeant,' she said, her eyes flitting back and forth from the book to the monitor, 'I'd like you to shut down the file you've got on screen and call up the data on Wegener's Guyot.'

361

'Oh dear.'

'What?' Steel demanded.

'This has to be it.'

'Why "oh dear"?'

'Because I didn't think worst-case scenarios got quite as bad as this.' She pointed at the map. 'This thing here, like an anthill, this is Wegener's Guyot, seventy-five miles out. It's comparatively small, not a real textbook guyot, not like these giant things out in the deep ocean basin. It's right on the edge of Patten Escarpment, on the continental slope, and it's where a prevailing undersea current runs out of steam, so it's like a giant silt-dumping ground all around here. There's deep, deep layers of stratified matter before you get to impervious crustal rock. Any kind of nuclear blast is going to leave a very big crater. Two hundred kilotons, even half that, less . . . Jesus.'

Larry and Steel looked at her, confused and impatient.

'See, it's all about the water's equilibrium,' she explained. 'You disturb it and it doesn't just compensate, it overreacts. The forces pulling billions of gallons of sea-water into a newly dug hole don't stop when it's full. The water at the back of the queue is still pushing to get in, you know? And then it all comes back out again, which is when you get a wave.

'The wave's only a few feet high on the open sea, but then it hits the continental shelf, and that's where the trouble starts. It meets shoal-water and the friction slows it down, like fifty per cent every two miles, so as that wave-front slows and the depth gets shallower and shallower, you get millions of tons of water piling up behind it. And incidentally, the continental shelf is particularly wide west of the LA conurbation.'

Arazon breathed out. Larry and Steel breathed in.

'A wave hit Hilo, Hawaii, in nineteen sixty. It drove entire buildings through one another, and I'm not talking about straw huts, here. These were steel-reinforced concrete office blocks, and they were smashed like matchwood. The wave was approximately thirty-five feet high. According to the computer, two hundred kilotons at Wegener's Guyot could give us a wave five times that size when it hits LA.'

'Fuck me,' Steel gasped.

'Even half or a quarter of that and the devastation would

still be incredible. Not just on the coast, either. LA's flat as a pool table – with such volume behind it, the sea would flood in for miles. The sewage system and water supplies would be crippled, so apart from the initial damage, you'd have drought and disease to contend with too . . . And if all that isn't scary enough, seismic waves don't travel alone. The water would pull back out, then forty minutes later surf's up again. There were three waves at Krakatoa; the maximum recorded is *nine*.'

14:02:02

The *Gazes Also* pulled slowly away from the CalORI pier, Arazon at the helm, striking out for the ocean in defiance of those who'd ended its last voyage. Steel had said he wouldn't blame her if she jumped in her Ford and headed literally for the hills, long as she kept her mouth shut, but she'd been adamant: it wasn't a matter of sailing to the right co-ordinates, sticking your head under the water and spotting a bomb – the FBI divers needed someone to direct the search from the surface. Not only could Arazon operate sonar to map out the submerged landscape, she was also the one best able to estimate where the nukes might be placed for maximum effect.

Larry knew nobody could have kept her off the boat anyway. There was nothing worse than feeling everything is out of your hands at a time like this, a sensation he was about to be harshly reacquainted with.

He stood beside Steel on the pier, the darkness lit by a three-quarter moon and a priol of floodlights. Arazon had been joined on the *GA* by another field agent, a young, bright-looking Oriental guy, and they were to rendezvous at the guyot with a team of divers travelling on a fast-picket Navy launch out of San Diego.

'You should go home, catch some shut-eye,' Steel said. 'It's gonna take them a few hours to get there, and a few more before we'll know anything . . . either way.'

It was Steel who looked like he could really use the sleep. Larry felt for him, in such a shitty Catch-22 position: he'd called the situation up to Brisko and beyond to get the nod for the assistance he needed, but at this stage it was still his show. If it was proved that there was indeed a nuclear threat

363

to a US city, then heaven and earth would be mobilised in response. But when all you got is a computer program and a bunch of theories, then you can only do the good lawman's job: pursue the line of enquiry to the best of your abilities and available resources. Steel confided that he was relieved even to get the dive-team and the Navy launch; despite what they said officially, the Feds were still reluctant to be seen going in like gangbusters since the Jewell fiasco in Atlanta in '96. And with undercover colleagues having been lost to the Southland Militia, questions had been asked of Steel about his judgement with regard to that organisation.

Larry remembered how crazy he'd thought Steel sounded less than twelve hours ago; then he thought of his own increasing fatigue and wondered whether he wasn't in the process of flipping out too.

13:19:25

Steff was awake again, standing in the half-light drinking water from a bottle as the clock mocked his disorientation. He looked down at Madeleine's coiled figure on the bed, naked beneath a single cotton sheet, undisturbed in her repose since they'd finally been sufficiently sated to leave each other's genitals alone long enough to nod off. An old Mutton Birds number played in his head, and he would have been content to sit and watch her sleep in some lyrical lovestruck daze, but for the hollow feeling in his stomach that kept telling him they were still a long way short of sailing off into any sunset together.

He pulled the curtains back a little and looked down at the swimming pool, where work was continuing through the night to clear the debris. Everyone else seemed to think the show was over – why couldn't he? He knew what it meant to Madeleine, but couldn't escape feeling there was something of entering the lions' den about their impending trip to Château Luther. Everything was going to be on the preacherman's terms, everything was going to be under his control, but Madeleine didn't seem to care – she just wanted her shot at the guy. Steff, having seen a few away fixtures at Ibrox, had a more vivid understanding of the phrase 'home advantage', and was far less confident that she wouldn't get hurt – one way or another.

364

She'd told him all about her childhood, or lack thereof. All about her father.

He'd taken her apart, there and then. Dismembered her and scattered the parts; hidden them, buried them. Her whole life since had been an attempt to find them all and put herself back together again. She explained how it was only now that she'd done that that she could take her father on and make him face what he had done before the eyes of the public. And she made Steff understand why she had to face St John also. But she seemed so consumed by finally exorcising these ghosts of her past that he was afraid she'd be oblivious to the threats of here and now.

Which was why while Madeleine had been phoning Tony Pia and talking terms with St John's representatives, Steff had gone back to find Brisko. The gentle G-man filled him in a little more honestly than when he'd been in Senator Witherson's company, admitting apologetically that pressure had been brought to bear on him to make going underground sound Madeleine's best option.

It turned out the bomber was some sad wee wank called Daniel Corby, and all evidence so far suggested he'd acted alone. As far as they knew, he wasn't a member of the Southland Militia, but with two of them barbecuing alongside him in Glendale, there was obviously some kind of connection. Brisko told him the FBI's biggest concern was that the whole carry-on could have been a diversion to distract attention from something else the Militia was up to, but wouldn't share his fears or suspicions of what that something else might be. He tried to reassure Steff that Madeleine Witherson was under no greater direct threat from the Southland Militia than any other individual, as these bampots probably had bigger fish to fry. However, Steff remained very concerned that if the Militia had *any* involvement in what had happened at the Vista, he and Madeleine had effectively given them all a very public two fingers that morning, something they might yet wish to reply to.

He finished his water and climbed back under the sheets beside her. Her smell was exquisite, the feel of her still electrifying. Maybe he was just going a wee bit crazy, and after the past few days, who could blame him? But suddenly, maybe even for the first time in his life, he had something he was very, very scared to lose. It wasn't just how he felt about her; it was also how she made him feel about himself.

He was terrified of someone or something taking that away, and he was prepared to do *anything* to protect it.

12:21:43

Larry still couldn't sleep. He'd climbed quietly into bed beside Sophie, who mumbled dopily, rolled over so that her head was on his chest, then flaked out again. He lay there in the semi-darkness, aware of the lightening against the curtains as morning approached. He stroked his wife's soft blonde hair, breathed in her smell, wondering whether it would be for the last time. He thought of the son they had lost, of the child growing in Sophie's womb, and of those who would steal its life away too.

The end of the world was nigh.

Yeah, right.

He thought of all the stupid fucks who were acting like they'd be disappointed if the Lord didn't wrap up the party nine months from now. All the dumb shits who'd already committed suicide over it. All the sad assholes who thought Judgement Day was scheduled for December 31st, when God would come down and vindicate *them* personally, and all their shitty little beliefs and opinions. When God would punish *their* enemies and show the world that *they* were right about everything they ever thought in their entire fucking lives, from religion through politics down to how the ref was wrong when he made that call against the Lakers in '93. When they'd get their eternal reward for going to church every Sunday and sending off cheques to some redneck televangelist's box number.

1999. 2000. Whatever. There was no cosmic significance about the year, the decade or the century. The world's clock was calibrated for aeons; millennia didn't even register, and certainly not the pitiful few we'd been creeping around for.

It was just a date on a calendar. The *West*'s calendar. Islam wouldn't be getting around to the year 2000 for a few centuries yet. In Tibet they'd moved into the third millennium back in the fucking seventies. Awareness that our perception is subjective is what lifts our consciousness above that of the

366

animals: from where you're sitting, your dick might look taller than that skyscraper out the window, but only from where you're sitting.

It don't make it *so*.

Larry knew that reaching the year 2000 didn't mean *nothing*, but it didn't mean *everything* either. It was a lap-mark, not a finish line. A milestone for Western Judeo-Christian civilisation to stop at and take a look around, at where we had come from and where the road ahead might lead. A time of evaluation and assessment – but also of boundless opportunity.

From the end of the twentieth century, the twenty-first looked like a Klondike, where there'd be an anxious rush to fight for a slice. But on the periphery of every Klondike there were always con-men, gamblers and charlatans, looking to cash in on the climate of uncertainty. Chancers, his friend Jack Parlabane would've called them.

And chancer-in-chief was the Reverend Luther St John.

Steel was right: they couldn't touch him. Even if they went blazing in there, what was he going to do, what was he going to say? 'Oh sure guys, I admit it – even though you got no proof. And better yet I'll call the whole thing off, just for you. No hard feelings, huh?' They couldn't even squeeze the guy: all he had to do was wait it out until his bombs went off, because they were the only real evidence. Then he'd have his tidal wave and they'd have nothing. Anyway, how do you threaten a man who holds the lives of millions in his grasp? He knows the last thing you can do is kill him.

Larry had heard him on the radio in the car home, ballsy as you like. Little shit had agreed to take on Madeleine Witherson in a TV debate, even though, as the newscaster put it, he'd been given a standing count after the pasting she dished out earlier. But then St John knew she could stick it to him again and he would still have the ultimate come-back.

06:13:33

Larry had sacked out eventually, waking to find an empty house and a note from Sophie, obliviously explaining that she had slipped out quietly to let him catch up on his rest. She'd see him around six, how about dinner out so he could unwind and tell her everything that had been going on these crazy few days?

How about it indeed? he thought. If we still got a city left to dine out in.

He pulled on his clothes and hot-tailed it to CalORI. If he was needed at the station, they had his mobile number, but he wasn't going to be worth shit to them until he found out what the hell was going on at sea.

Larry walked back into the now Fed-annexed building to find Steel sitting in the lab in front of a big radio set, Brisko and another agent standing nearby drinking coffee.

'Jesus, couldn't anybody relieve this guy? What, you got a shortage of agents?'

'We did offer. Peter ain't for leaving.'

'I crashed out on the floor for a few hours,' Steel said, rubbing horribly bloodshot eyes.

'So any news?'

'Nothing from the boat,' Brisko told him. 'The divers are under, but . . .' He shrugged. 'Just have to wait it out.'

'But do you wanna hear the late-breaking stories?' Steel asked.

'What's that?'

'We sent agents to question Arthur Liskey,' Brisko explained, taking up the exhausted Steel's cue. 'He's nowhere to be found. Neither is William Rooke or Richard Kelloran, who are also part of the Southland Militia's high command.'

'Terence Nately and Oswald Vernon weren't home either,' Steel added 'but that's because they're both in blister-packs at the Glendale morgue.'

'However,' Brisko continued, 'it may be significant to note that the three I mentioned are listed as living at rented accommodation – all having sold properties in LA in the past two months. Also active in the real-estate market is our friend the Reverend St John. He's been buying up land in both Arizona and Nevada, which is going to be worth a hell of a lot more if LA floods and the city has to expand eastwards.'

'So now we get to call him Lex Luthor St John,' Steel said drily.

There was a burst of static from the radio. Steel proved that his fatigue hadn't affected his reflexes, grabbing the handset and responding in less than a second. Agent Chai's impatient voice cut through the breathless hush throughout the lab.

'Peter, this is all for real now. We got a bomb. They just found it.'

'Give me McCabe,' Steel ordered. 'Patch me through on a relay.'

'You got it.'

There was a moment of silence. Larry swallowed. Brisko was already reaching for his mobile.

'Agent Steel, this is McCabe,' said a distorted voice, words difficult to discern among amplified breathing noises. 'We're in real trouble.'

'What are we looking at, Jim?'

'It's a warhead all right, CHIB-class, and it's already armed, on a countdown. We got six hours, three minutes and fourteen seconds, then surf's up.'

Brisko's phone clattered to the floor. Steel looked briefly at the men surrounding him. No one had anything dazzling to contribute.

'Can you defuse it?'

'Not for sure. Maybe. But there could be two more of these things and it's taken us four hours to find the first.'

'Jesus Christ. We better get ready to evacuate.'

'No, wait up,' McCabe said. He spoke firmly and slowly, the echoing sounds of breathing punctuating his words. 'Listen. Your CHIB is a vehicle-mounted, remote-launch nuke. That means you don't arm the warhead locally. It was a safeguard against it falling into non-Soviet hands. You had to transmit the launch codes before you could fire the missile. The codes initiate the launch, and simultaneously arm the warhead.'

'So what?' Steel asked.

'So there's a gizmo out there someplace with an "Abort" switch on it.'

06:00:44

'We gotta evacuate,' Brisko declared, reaching down for the black plastic mobile where it lay on the tiles. 'We gotta evacuate.'

Larry kicked the phone away from his reach. 'Hold on,' he said. 'You're not from LA, are you man? We tell this city to

369

evacuate and the panic'll cause half as much damage as the wave. Instead of getting drowned in their homes, they'll all get drowned in their cars, caught in gridlock on Wilshire Boulevard when five million vehicles try to drive east at the same time. We got six hours. I say let's go after the detonator.'

'Are you nuts, Sergeant? How do you know it still exists? How do you know they haven't destroyed it?'

'No chance,' Steel said. 'I don't care how crazy you are, if you're dealing with fifty-kiloton nuclear weapons, you don't put gum in the Off switch. Especially not a control-freak like St John.'

'I can't believe I'm hearing this. Time is running out, gentlemen, and you want to play hunt-the-thimble.'

'Agent Brisko, I got a wife teaching right now in a Santa Monica high school – I do not need to be apprised of the gravity of the situation. *My* money says that detonator is still intact, and if Luther St John doesn't have it on him personally, then he knows a man who does. So just give us a little time, and if we get nothing, start the evac.'

'What the hell are you planning to do?'

'We can have agents at Bleachfield in twenty minutes,' Steel said. 'We get inside and we tear the place apart until we find the thing.'

'And what if it ain't there?'

'We get someone to stand on St John's balls until he talks.'

'No,' Larry said. 'We evacuate. If it ain't there, we evacuate the city, that's it. St John won't talk, no matter what you do to him. He knows you can only stand on his balls for a few hours and then all your evidence goes up in mushroom-shaped smoke.'

Larry looked Brisko in the eye.

'Give us one hour playing hunt-the-gizmo, please. That still leaves as much time as would make no difference to the nightmare you're about to unleash.'

'I can't afford to gamble an hour on—'

'You're gambling one hour, yes,' Larry interrupted, 'but believe me, it's worth the stake.'

Brisko sighed.

'All right, you got an hour on the announcement. But I'm calling the Governor now.'

'Cool.'

'Time for me to make a call too,' Steel said.

'No,' Larry told him, placing a hand on the telephone. 'I mean, sure, get your agents ready to rock, but think about it. He hears you guys are in the house and St John's gonna know he's made. He's got guards, guns – he gives the order and it's Waco Two. And let me remind you once more, if he turns it into a stand-off, Koresh's record isn't under threat. St John only has to keep you guys out for six hours.'

'So what do you want us to do? Teleport our way in?'

'A little simpler. You just need somebody to keep St John immobilised while your men get inside.'

'And how do we get *that* guy inside in the first place?'

'Easy. He's already there.'

'Huh?'

eighteen

'Well, Jesus johnnybags,' Steff said, walking back in and closing the door behind him. 'Madeleine, hen, you better take a seat.'

'Whassup?' she asked, looking up from the makeup bag she was unpacking in front of the mirror.

'What's up? Eh, how should I put this . . .'

Freeman's call had come on Madeleine's mobile shortly after they'd been shown to the dressing room. The sergeant asked to speak to Steff and he had gone outside to take the call, the fire exit at the room's rear leading straight out into the desert sun. Arizona was beautiful, absolutely fucking stunning. Luther St John didn't deserve to live there – Harthill would have been much fairer.

It had taken some stubborn insistence before Freeman finally spilled out exactly why he needed Steff's help, but Steff could hardly blame the guy for saying it was on a need-to-know basis. This was not the kind of thing you'd be in a hurry to share with members of the public. Nonetheless, you equally couldn't ask a member of the public to do what Freeman was requesting without disclosing fully what he was getting himself into. This was a bit more elaborate than asking some bystander to call an ambulance.

It would be fair to say the news took him a second or two to digest. Steff had long ago run out of surprise at what magnitude of stupidity religion could engender, but even he had to admit he was impressed with this one. It certainly vindicated his concern that he and Madeleine weren't going to be left alone quite yet to live happily ever after.

He disconnected the call and looked out across the desert, taking a moment to collect himself ahead of what he was about to undertake. He might have been reeling from the sheer scale, madness and plain old-fashioned evil of what

St John was planning, but that was sweeties compared to just how fucking angry he was, and he needed to be cool, focused and rational.

Once he knew the truth he hadn't needed to be asked twice, whatever the danger. Not just because of the multitude of lives at stake; not just because he was hoping to spend some time in LA with his new girlfriend and it would be easier if it was still there.

For Steff, this wasn't a matter of bravery, selflessness or even self-preservation. This was therapy.

This was pay-back.

The fundamental problem with fundamentalists was that no matter how much touchy-feely love and peace their religions professed, in practice they always turned into pre-scriptions for moral contempt. Reasons to hate were given divine sanction. 'Hate the sin, love the sinner,' they said, a phrase Steff had always considered among the most dis-ingenuous moral cop-outs the human race ever devised, right up there alongside 'I was only obeying orders'. If you consider somebody's behaviour or beliefs an affront to your God for which they will suffer an eternity of pain and humiliation, it makes it kind of hard then to treat that person as an equal human being.

Holy war. Crusade. *Jihad*. *Fatwah*. And now a tidal wave. That was what 'hate the sin, love the sinner' had led to. Please, Steff thought, love us all less.

All us sinners.

Because we were all of us heretics, every day committing obscene thought-crimes and unforgivable transgressions of moral and theological orthodoxies. All of us. Every one. Most of the time we didn't mean it, but that in itself was often the nature of the infidelity; and when was ignorance of the law ever a mitigating excuse?

With so many belief systems having evolved around the world, it was impossible to adhere to all of them; indeed, adherence to one was often deeply heretical in the eyes of another. Therefore, even the most conscientious devotee, leading the most ascetic, self-denying, disciplined, austerely moral, dull, drab, joyless and utterly, utterly self-nullifying existence was unfortunately guilty of acts and thoughts that would be found decadent, licentious and downright evil

373

in the scrutinising eyes of another religion. Some wee old spinster in Coatbridge, in her hairy coat, plastic Rainmate and furry boots, nipping into the Co-op minimarket for a half-pound of cheap mince on the way home from the chapel, *Scottish Catholic Universe* under her arm, might tell herself she wasn't, spiritually speaking, doing any harm. But she'd be kidding herself. And acting the humble innocent wouldn't help. Hardline Islamics would have her on the dress-code, for a start. Vain, shameless slattern, flaunting herself like that in public, for all the world to see. Hindus wouldn't go a bundle on her planned ingestion of bloody flesh, or her wider complicity in the sacred animal's slaughter. Attendance at the 'temple of the Satanic anti-Christ of Rome' remains something of a no-no as far as the Scottish Free Presbyterians and Ian Paisley's mob are concerned. And as for a woman being able to read, well, ask the Taleban about that in Kabul. Then duck.

Cumulatively, the world's religions could provide a God-given justification to hate *anything* about *anybody*. Steff had decided some years ago to hate them all back.

He was what the devout would call a 'lapsed Catholic', a term he resented because it sounded like he was suffering from some kind of helpless affliction. It also carried the insulting and deeply smug implication that this was a temporary fault and ultimately he would be back.

Steff Kennedy would not be fucking back. Put the house on it.

He had been brought up a Catholic; a 'good Catholic', even, as the phrase went. He'd always striven to be good, a good boy for his mum and dad, good at school, good at home, good at church. Being a good boy meant being a good Catholic; being a good Catholic meant being a good boy.

It was only when he became old enough to start thinking about what any of it actually meant that his 'faith' ran into difficulties. Unfortunately, this development came *after* he had signed up for the seminary.

Again, he was just trying to be as good as his parents – or more importantly God – would like him to be. At school the Catholic teachers told you about 'vocations', about the calling, about how God chose people to become priests and nuns. At the same time they usually laid it on pretty thick about the abject shortage of both and how miffed God would get if you KB-ed His job offer. They gave the impression that if you ever found yourself wondering – even for a second – what it might be like to be a priest, then that was your card marked: God was calling you, and it was a Mortal Sin to ignore Him.

He was not priest material, anyone could have seen that. Neither was any of the six other boys from his year at St Matthew's Secondary in Motherwell who signed up at the same time – all, coincidentally, after seeing the Augustine's College video. The Church in Scotland was just so desperate that they were cramming all manner of unsuitable candidates into the seminary in the blind hope that a few of them would go the distance.

The video worked like one of those Army recruitment films, where they show you guys skiing down Alpine mountainsides and drinking beers in Belize, when the reality is a street corner in Belfast with angry young Irishmen lobbing bricks at your head. The Augustine's College 'Do You Hear the Calling?' video was all swimming pools, tennis courts and walks in the hills. The reality was a damp, prison-like building in Ayrshire, where the angry Irishmen were middle-aged, and it wasn't their bricks you had to worry about.

Lives were wrecked in that place. Young lives.

Steff heard boys cry in their beds every night, tormented by things they would not talk about. Secrets stalked the halls; whispered rumours and silent fears. But he only learned the truth when the whisky-reeking Father Meehan summoned him to 'private prayers' in his study, and locked the door behind them.

Unfortunately for the priest, his drunken misjudgement had led him to pick on someone, even at thirteen, more than his own size.

Steff remembered hearing the sirens as he sat upstairs in Father Cahill's office, and being surprised when he looked out the window to discover there was only an ambulance, no police cars. But then he'd had a lot to learn about what the Church's priorities were that night. The ambulancemen were told Father Meehan fell down the stairs (which probably seemed fairly plausible, given that he was drunk), but pressure must have been brought to bear so that nobody asked how many times he'd fallen down them to end up with a face like that. Steff, having terrified visions of graduating straight from seminary to borstal for GBH, thought it was him the priests were protecting.

They had both spent their last day at Augustine's College. Steff went back to Motherwell the next morning, but he didn't know where Father Meehan went until nine years later when he saw him on TV, charged with a string of sexual offences against boys in his charge at a seminary in Galway. Steff hadn't been very happy to discover that these offences were not coming to light after decades of silence – the Church had placed Meehan in the Galway seminary *after* his expulsion from Ayrshire. Still, what were a few anal rapes to protect the Church's holy name from scandal? Didn't these kids have any sense of loyalty?

He once heard a Scottish archbishop say he wouldn't turn an abusing priest over to the police (it was up to the victims to complain) but instead would try to help him change through much prayer and Church counselling. Steff had wished for five minutes in a locked study with that guy, too.

However, the Meehan incident hadn't been the catalyst for the crumbling of Steff's faith: the questions that would pull down the temple had been in his head before then. What it did achieve, though, was to make him extremely resolute in dealing with religious bampots.

Luther St John could therefore consider himself claimed.

05:42:36

Steff closed the door to Madeleine's dressing room, having been given a sweet good-luck kiss and a nervous but redundant request to 'be careful'. He looked down the corridor where two armed security guards were having a discussion about what they referred to as 'football'. He winced, realising that even he wasn't immune to being offended by blasphemy. One of them chucked the other on the shoulder and walked away, lighting up a cigarette. Shift change.

Steff went for a quick circuit around the dressing and makeup area of the studio complex, all of which seemed too large for what was actually being produced from the place. It was also very new, like a huge low-rise extension to the older CFC buildings, the dusty smell of Gyproc and fresh construction materials still hanging in the air. Luther was getting ready for a much-expanded programme output in the very near future. Either that or he was going to rent out sound-stages to the major studios after theirs developed chronic rising damp.

There was hardly anyone about. The studio audiences were made up of 'pilgrims' doing the full CFC tour, including the Luther St John Museum and, of course, souvenir shop. But they only got access to specified parts of the compound, whereas Madeleine and he had backstage passes.

They'd been given the full VIP treatment, Luther presumably trying to disarm Madeleine with his charm and hospitality so that she wouldn't wipe quite so much of the floor with him. Flight in on his private jet first thing that morning, Special Guest dressing room, bouquets of flowers and a personal greeting from the man himself before he went off to present *Good Morning, Christian America*. He'd been all smiles: 'What a terrible ordeal, how brave you were, Miss Witherson,' and 'Let's hope we can maybe learn something from each other today.' Bags of warmth, politeness and consideration. Then he'd put the jet on standby for when the show was over, so they could both fly back to LA in plenty of time to drown with the rest of the condemned.

The security guard was standing a few doors along from Madeleine's dressing room. Steff sidled up and said hello. 'Place looks like it's on the up and up.'

'Sure is,' the guard said, a moustachioed plump man in his forties. Steff could see the butt of his pistol sticking out from a shoulder-holster, handcuffs hooked to his belt. 'It's all gonna get a lot busier after the great flood, when it comes. A lot more folks are gonna start listening to what the Reverend St John's got to say.'

'So you're a true believer? You don't just work here?'

'The Reverend St John only hires true believers.'

'Well, could you help me out with a wee theological question?'

'I'll do my best. I'm no preacher, though.'

'I was thinking . . . I know that in your faith you believe

sexual activity is intended solely for procreation. Therefore obviously homosexuality is out, and so are masturbation, sodomy, fellatio and cunnilingus.' The guy seemed to reel from every word. 'But I was wondering, where do you stand on the Glasgow Kiss?'

'Glasgow Kiss? I ain't never heard of that.'

'I thought not.'

Steff dragged the unconscious guard quickly and quietly into the empty and as yet unfurbished room behind him. He removed his gun, handcuffs and keys, tied his wrists to the water pipes with electrical flex, and fashioned a gag from some thick polythene that had been covering a new worktop. Steff examined the gun, never having held one before, and looked for the safety catch, flipping it off and on to familiarise himself with the action. Then he locked the door and went back to the dressing room.

Madeleine was pale with worry when he came back in, over-dramatically putting a hand to her chest and closing her eyes once she had seen that he'd returned safely.

'Okay, we ready for this?' she asked, standing up.

'Yeah,' he said, composing himself, checking again that he had correctly programmed instant-dial for the number that would greenlight the FBI agents' incursion. 'Oh no wait. Just a second. There's something I meant to ask Freeman.'

The sergeant had talked Steff through the logistics, explaining for instance that it was vital they made St John believe their actions were a protest stunt or some crazed act of vengeance. If he knew his big secret was out and Steff was working for the Feds, he'd know also that Steff couldn't kill him, which would make the wee shite far less co-operative. However, there was one crucial aspect of the whole exercise that he feared had slipped the big cop's mind.

He went back outside and pressed the recall button on the mobile.

'Hi, it's me,' he said. 'Phase one is complete, I've got the gun. But before phase two, well, something's been bothering me.'

'What is it, man?'

378

'This wee black box your guys are looking for. Will it just have a big shiny button on it that says "Abort"? It won't have, like, a keypad for entering a code that only St John knows, perhaps?'

There was a very, very, very long pause before Freeman said: 'Ah, shit.'

'That's what I thought.'

'Look, we still go ahead. Maybe once we got him . . .'

'Hey, it's okay, I can get the codes out of him,' Steff interrupted.

'No, man, I told you, he'll know we can't threaten him.'

'I'm not gaunny threaten him. But he'll cough, believe me.'

'How?'

'I'll require some assistance, but in the main I'm relying on my faith.'

'Faith? Faith in what?'

'Faith in St John being full of shit.'

'Well I'm heart and soul on that one, brother. What do you need?'

05:28:31

The makeup-room door opened inwards and the holy man emerged to fill the gap, looking up warmly at Steff. He was evidently still in charming magnanimity mode, which was what Steff had been relying on. St John had a beatific smile plastered across his smug coupon, like he *wasn't* in the process of murdering legions of innocent people. It was an enormous temptation just to banjo the wee bastard then and there, but apart from being catastrophically self-defeating, violence would be nothing compared to what Steff had in mind for later on. For crimes of this magnitude, there was no way he was getting off with mere physical harm.

His body would be left unscathed. It was his soul that was in for a kicking.

'Mr Kennedy. How can I help you, son?'

'I'm sorry to trouble you, Reverend, but it's Madeleine. She's got a wee touch of stagefright, I think. She's suddenly come over all nervous about the debate. Would you mind

379

coming round and having a quick word with her, just to reassure her about a few things?'

'That's no problem, son. I'll be right along.'

There was a knock at the dressing-room door a few minutes later. Steff pulled it open and held it there, beckoning St John inside.

'Thank you for coming to see me, Reverend,' Madeleine said.

'Oh don't worry, I'm only too happy,' he told her.

He was less happy when Steff closed the door behind him and stuck a gun in his face. 'You keep your fuckin' mouth shut and do exactly as you're told,' he commanded, 'or I become the first Kennedy to carry *out* an assassination.'

Before St John could respond, Madeleine pulled a gag over his mouth and secured it tightly. First things first: if he couldn't ask them any questions, he couldn't suss what they were really up to. Then she blindfolded him with masking tape and slapped the guard's cuffs over his wrists behind his back.

They led him outside through the fire-exit and marched him swiftly around the back of the shiny new studio complex to the landing strip, where they added hijacking to their police-approved rap-sheet.

04:27:58

The Lear jet touched down with a thump, the pilot's nervousness taking its toll on his landing skills. Through the windows Steff could see the police cars, Larry Freeman's figure unmistakable even from two hundred yards away. Maddy lowered the stairway and Steff nudged the still-blindfolded St John towards the door.

Agent Steel was first to the plane once it had taxied to a standstill, climbing the stairs to take hold of the baffled prisoner and lead him to a waiting car. Freeman strode up purposefully behind him.

'All right, Kennedy, it's all set up, let's get moving,' he said. 'The agents back in Bleachfield found the gizmo, so Brisko's given us an extra hour before they evacuate. But not a minute more, so this better work.'

'I told you,' Steff said. 'Have faith.'

Steel stood by with his phone to his ear, in contact with Bleachfield. Freeman tied St John's wrists to the wooden crossbeam, Steff binding his feet to the support-stock while Maddy removed the gag and the blindfold. Then together they raised him up and secured the life-size crucifix in place, fixed to the railings at the end of Santa Monica pier.

'Okay, Luther,' Steff said, looking up at him. 'Do you know what the big blue thing you're looking at is? It's called the Pacific Ocean. Here's the scenario. You're at the seaside, on an all-American pier complete with funfare and saltwater taffy, whatever the fuck that is. Your cunning plan has been rumbled, I'm afraid, so I believe your next line should be something about "pesky kids", but we'll settle for the warhead abort code.'

'Give us the code, Mr St John,' Freeman reiterated sternly. 'Your party's over.'

'Code? I don't know what you're talking about. You're a cop? Well, not for long. I'm gonna have your badge. Don't you know who I am?'

'You can play dumb all you want, sir,' Freeman replied, 'but you're stayin' on that cross for the next five hours, whatever happens. We're gonna start evacuating the city real soon, but believe me, you're the one guy who ain't goin' nowhere. So I was you, I'd give us the code.'

St John's face darkened in growing, genuine anger, replacing the mock outrage he'd been trying to sell them. He looked to the heavens for inspiration.

'Okay,' he said, swallowing back his fury, calming himself. 'I'm not stupid and clearly neither are you. You obviously know what's going on, so let's talk turkey. I'll pay all of you a *lot* of money, and you know I've got it. Just let me go and we can all fly out of here together on my plane, right now. I'll make every one of you rich people in a new America. A better America.'

'Give us the goddamn code.'

'For goodness' sake, you idiots, look at the bigger picture,' he yelled. 'This country's falling apart without God. America's only hope for salvation is if it can renew its faith in the Lord, and with this wave I can make that happen.

381

Can't you see that? I can make people believe again. I can make people *decent* again. I can *save* this country. There's so much more at stake here than just the lives that'll be lost. It's nineteen ninety-nine, the end of the millennium, and God's running out of patience. This could be our last chance – don't throw it away!'

'Well, that's entirely up to you, Reverend, actually,' Steff said. 'See, we're not exactly up to our arses in evidence here. Once the bombs go off, the only proof of what really caused the tidal wave will be a wee black box in Arizona, and we're not going to get far saying: "Honest, folks, this was used to detonate a nuclear weapon." So America will therefore still get its act of God as prophesied by yourself – and if that act of God is going to save America, then America will indeed be saved.

'You, however, won't. But as you said, there's more at stake here than just the lives that'll be lost. You'll still achieve what you wanted. You'll save the souls of those millions who will repent and change their sinful ways. All right, it's going to kill you, but your reward in the next world should be pretty substantial, even by eternal-bliss standards. You'll be remembered for ever, as well – the first American saint, the man who prophesied the wave and begged everyone to heed God's warnings. Plus,' Steff added, slapping the wood, 'we've even set you up in the classic martyr-messiah stance for your meeting with the big man. So, like I said, it's *your* call.'

He stepped away and stood next to Madeleine, who took his hand and gripped it tightly. Steel – phone still held to face – and Freeman flanked them on either side. In front of them, Los Angeles was going about its business. Classrooms, construction sites, hospitals, offices. Studios, sound stages, back lots. Cars and freeways.

People.

Steff stared up at the man on the cross, a man of professed deep faith – deep even as the ocean – in God and in the life that would follow this one. The man in turn was looking out upon the dark, dark blue of the endless Pacific, its waters poised to rise in divine rage against the oblivious city . . . but only if his professed faith was real.

382

The Fed, the cop and the actress looked understandably anxious.

The photographer wasn't.

It was the year of Our Lord Nineteen Hundred and Ninety-Nine.

The second millennium AD was well into injury time and the referee was looking at his watch. It was too late for the scoreline to change, and Steff Kennedy knew that the star player had utterly failed to live up to the hype.

Jesus Christ had changed nothing.

Sorry.

Two millennia after he 'gave his life to save the world', the world was no nearer to being saved – if indeed saving was what it needed – than before.

For the two thousand years since his death, and for many thousands more before his birth, people the world over had been loving their neighbour as themselves, turning the other cheek, and forgiving not seven times but seventy times seven. They had also been hating their neighbour, striking out in violence, and avenging every wrong done them. BC or AD, armies rampaged, men murdered, raped, stole, hated; BC or AD, people cared for one another, were selfless, loved, forgave.

Jesus Christ changed nothing.

Using his gift for oratory and communication he had sought to spread humanitarian principles, but he did not devise them. And those principles had survived until now not because of the churches that bore Christ's name; nor even in spite of them. They had survived simply because they were part of man's nature.

It was part of man's nature to love and to care, just as it was part of man's nature to hate and destroy. If the good side was ever to overcome the bad, then it would not be through fear of God, nor even through love of God. It would be because man had evolved.

Christ's teachings were irrelevant to the growth and self-sustainment of the Holy Roman Empire and all the sects it spawned. The legacy that was the Church, the legacy that was Christianity, was not the legacy of Christ, his words or his deeds. It was the legacy of men and their ambition. It was the legacy of power, of wealth, of dominion. And however much men like St John talked about the Kingdom of God, the kingdom they were really interested in was right here, on this earth.

'What does it profit a man if he gains the whole world but loses his soul?' Jesus asked. But Steff knew there was a very important flipside to that question. As they said back home, it's no use being the richest man in the cemetery.

St John's eyes closed slowly and his head slumped forward. Then the tears began to leak, seeping gently from the tightly shut lids and running over his contorted face, before heavy sobs started shaking his chest.

For all the souls it would save, the new America it would forge, the greater glory it would bring, upon his God and upon himself, the man on the cross did not want to die.

He mumbled, his croaking words barely audible.

'Sorry, what was that? Something about "See you in heaven?"'

St John sniffed and swallowed, then spoke again. 'One, six, five, eight, seven,' he said in a broken whisper.

'One-six-five-eight-seven,' Steel relayed immediately into the phone. 'Repeat, one-six-five-eight-seven.'

'You still ain't goin' nowhere until six o'clock, Reverend,' Freeman added. 'So if that code was bullshit, I'd own up now.'

St John hung his head and shook it gravely.

'Well hallelujah,' Steff shouted. 'Halle-fuckin'-lujah. You've justified my faith in you, Luther. I knew there was an atheist inside you somewhere – you just had to listen to his voice to see the light. And now you're one of us – a true non-believer.'

Steel held up a hand for quiet, then slowly clenched the fingers into a fist and punched the air. 'McCabe says we're clear,' he announced. 'Show's over, folks. Thanks for coming. It's been very.'

Freeman gave the longest sigh Steff had ever heard and slumped down on to a nearby wooden bench, like he had deflated. He held up a hand and Steel slapped it heartily, before the G-man also flaked out.

St John began weeping again, crushed moans rising from

his throat as his upper body trembled from the convulsions of his grief.

'Hey, c'mon, cheer up Rev,' Madeleine said, putting an arm around Steff's waist. 'It's not the end of the world.'

Madeleine Stephanie Freeman was born in a Santa Monica maternity hospital at 06:20 on August 13th 1999.

On December 31st the same year, at 23:59, she was shitting in her pants.

She wasn't the only one.

A minute later, the world failed to end.

Again.

A new century got under way, and despite the efforts of certain parties, it continued to witness unchecked the sins of godlessness, blasphemy, fornication, homosexuality, miscegenation, pornography and cheesy B-movies.

Amen to that.

From: Jerry Blake
Date: 9 March 1999 14:47
To: marazon@calori.com
Cc:
Subject: Uh-oh

Maria,
Just when the rest of us had decided to stab the pair of them, Bruno
Calvi and Helen Schwarz finally coughed up the fabled last frag.
I think it might cause some trouble.
Hold tight.
Jerry
blakej@past.participle.com

Extract: (site KS / sole fragment)

*In the desert, once, I met a man, a messenger. He was thirsty
and tired, journeying back to his people with tidings from the
south. We gave him water and received him into our tent for
the night, speaking in our shared tongue of the Egyptians.*

*He asked what had cast me so far from my homeland to be
wandering the earth, and I told him of my flight with Karu,
who sat at my side, my wife. In turn he told me of his own
people's escape from slavery in the land of Goshen, under the
yoke of the Egyptians. He told me of the plagues his god,
Jaweh, visited upon their oppressors, and I understood he
was one of the Israelites of whom Ankham had spoken when
last I ever saw him.*

*But he also told me of the strange events that had fol-
lowed.*

*His people journeyed eastwards, as many as six hundred
families. In time the Pharaoh mustered a force to pursue and
retrieve them. The Israelites learned of this army's approach,
and knew that, so many in number, they could not outrun it.
Greater despair fell upon them when they reached the place
called Baal Zephon, where the sea to the north breaks through
to mingle with the waters of a broad lagoon extending to the
south. Men had been lost in attempting to cross it, for though
it was not deep it was dangerous with quicksand. With the
Pharaoh's army drawing ever closer, they feared their freedom
was at an end.*

But then the waters withdrew from before them, retreating until the ground beneath them was dry. Their god, Jaweh, had moved back the waves that they could pass to the other side.

Once they had crossed, they looked back to see the Pharaoh's chariots in pursuit, but Jaweh sent the waters forth again, rushing in to wash the Egyptians' army away, that not a single man survived.

I asked the messenger how many years he was then, how many years he was now, and in which season this miracle took place. His answers confirmed to me that he spoke of the very time when Tira met its brutal end.

I was left to wonder.

If the god Jaweh caused these events to save his chosen people, why would he also visit so much destruction upon lands far, far away, bringing death to a thousand times the numbers of the Israelites?

If the god Poteidan caused these events to punish proud Kaftor, why would he at the same time grant such a boon to a people who gave him no glory?

Or could it be that there are no gods?

QUITE UGLY ONE MORNING

Christopher Brookmyre

Winner of the 1996 Critics' First Blood Award

Yeah, yeah, the usual. A crime. A corpse. A killer. Heard it. Except this stiff happens to be a Ponsonby, scion of a venerable Edinburgh medical clan, and the manner of his death speaks of unspeakable things. Why is the body displayed like a slice of beef? How come his hands are digitally challenged? And if it's not the corpse, what is that awful smell?

A post-Thatcherite nightmare of frightening plausibility, *Quite Ugly One Morning* is a wickedly entertaining and vivacious thriller, full of acerbic wit, cracking dialogue and villains both reputed and shell-suited.

'The dialogue is a joy throughout and the plot crackles along with confident gusto and intelligence . . . an assured debut by a talented writer' *The Times*

'Very violent, very funny. A comedy with political edge, which you take gleefully in one gulp' *Literary Review*

'A wicked satire . . . excellent plotting and a goodly amount of acidic one-liners' *The Scotsman*

'A sharp, funny novel, with strong characters and some smart dialogue' *TLS*

Abacus Fiction
ISBN 978 0 349 10885 8

COUNTRY OF THE BLIND

Christopher Brookmyre

HANG THESE BASTARDS NOW!

The headline of one now-ownerless Tory tabloid – the bastards in question being the four men who allegedly committed four murders in the course of a burglary. Along with his wife and two bodyguards, Roland Voss, the tabloid owner and millionaire media mogul, has had a country weekend in Perthshire cut short by a cut throat.

Investigative journalist Jack Parlabane wasn't too upset by the news – he had first-hand experience of his muscular methods. But suggestions that Voss might have been whacked on purpose pique Parlabane's nose for a conspiracy. And he's not the only one who thinks the accused might be innocent . . .

Fiendishly constructed, with dialogue as sharp as the plotting, *Country of the Blind* brilliantly reveals a world of danger and deceit, murder and betrayal, where defence is not a legal game but a fight for your life. A world that Jack Parlabane knows well.

'The defining quality of Brookmyre's writing is that it is perpetually in-your-face: sassy, irreverent, stylish.'
The Times

'The next star of the genre seems set to be Christopher Brookmyre (who) rejects the English tradition of James and Rendell in favour of the sassy, nasty, fast style of the American Elmore Leonard and Carl Hiaasen'
The Guardian

Abacus Fiction
ISBN 978 0 349 10930 5

Now you can order superb titles directly from Abacus

☐ Quite Ugly One Morning	Christopher Brookmyre	£7.99
☐ Country of the Blind	Christopher Brookmyre	£7.99
☐ One Fine Day in the Middle of the Night	Christopher Brookmyre	£7.99
☐ Boiling a Frog	Christopher Brookmyre	£7.99
☐ A Big Boy Did it and Ran Away	Christopher Brookmyre	£7.99
☐ The Sacred Art of Stealing	Christopher Brookmyre	£7.99
☐ Be My Enemy	Christopher Brookmyre	£7.99
☐ All Fun and Games Until Somebody Loses an Eye	Christopher Brookmyre	£7.99
☐ A Tale Etched in Blood and Hard Black Pencil	Christopher Brookmyre	£7.99

The prices shown above are correct at time of going to press. However, the publishers reserve the right to increase prices on covers from those previously advertised, without further notice.

─────────────── ⟨ABACUS⟩ ───────────────

Please allow for postage and packing: **Free UK Delivery**
Europe; add 25% of retail price; Rest of World; 45% of retail price.

To order any of the above or any other Abacus titles, please call our credit card orderline or fill in this coupon and send/fax it to:

Abacus, PO Box 121, Kettering, Northants NN14 4ZQ
Fax: 01832 733076   Tel: 01832 737527
Email: aspenhouse@FSBDial.co.uk

☐ I enclose a UK bank cheque made payable to Abacus for £.......

☐ Please charge £....... to my Visa/Mastercard/Eurocard/Maestro

☐☐☐☐☐☐☐☐☐☐☐☐☐☐☐☐☐☐

Expiry Date ☐☐☐☐   Maestro Issue No. ☐☐

NAME (BLOCK LETTERS please) . . . .

ADDRESS . . . .

. . . .

. . . .

Postcode . . . . Telephone . . . .

Signature . . . .

Please allow 28 days for delivery within the UK. Offer subject to price and availability.
Please do not send any further mailings from companies carefully selected by Abacus ☐